THE ROSE GIRLS

ALSO BY VICTORIA CONNELLY

Molly's Millions

Flights of Angels

Escape to Mulberry Cottage

A Year at Mulberry Cottage

A Dog Called Hope

Secret Pyramid

Irresistible You

The Runaway Actress

Wish You Were Here

A Summer to Remember

Three Graces

The Secret of You

Christmas at the Cove

SHORT STORY COLLECTIONS

One Perfect Week and Other Stories

The Retreat and Other Stories

Postcard from Venice and Other Stories

IN THE AUSTEN ADDICTS SERIES

A Weekend with Mr Darcy

The Perfect Hero

Mr Darcy Forever

Christmas with Mr Darcy

Happy Birthday, Mr Darcy

At Home with Mr Darcy

THE ROSE GIRLS

Victoria Connelly

LAKE UNION
PUBLISHING

Published by Lake Union Publishing, Seattle

www.apub.com

Amazon, the Amazon logo, and Lake Union Publishing are trademarks of Amazon. com, Inc., or its affiliates.

ISBN-13: 978-1477829325
ISBN-10: 1477829326

Cover design by bürosüd° München, www.buerosued.de

Library of Congress Control Number: 2014920271

Printed in the United States of America

To Roy with love.

'Some people are always grumbling because roses have thorns;
I am thankful that thorns have roses.'

—*Alphonse Karr*

1.

Some people mark the beginning of summer by the call of the first cuckoo or the arrival of the first swallow but, for Celeste Hamilton, summer began with the opening of the first rose. It wasn't surprising, really, because she had grown up in a family of rosarians and had been growing roses all her life. Her first word had been 'rose' and the family joke was that they all had roses in the blood. But, when Celeste had left home and married Liam O'Grady, she'd swapped roses for a reclamation yard and had thrown herself into her husband's business with the joy of somebody who had been given a reprieve. Roses were her past, she'd thought. Only the past had a funny way of catching up with you, didn't it?

And now I'm coming home, she thought to herself as the old Morris Minor van wended its way through the overgrown lanes of the Stour Valley. She wouldn't have ever believed she'd return home but, with the death of her mother and the small matter of her marriage being over, Celeste really had no choice. She sighed as she thought of the weeks that lay ahead of her and only hoped that she could sort everything out before those weeks turned into months because she certainly wasn't going to stay any longer; that wasn't part of her plan at all.

'In and out,' she told herself as she thought about her childhood home, her mind crowded with memories she'd sooner forget. 'In and *out*.' There was no need to get emotional about things. This was business pure and simple.

She wound her window down and the rich notes of a blackbird filled the car. The hedgerows were full of white campion and stripy-petalled mallow, and she spied a forest of foxgloves in the shade of a wood.

Entering the village of Eleigh Tye, she saw the familiar cottage gardens stuffed with sweet peas, honeysuckle and lupins but, despite the scent and the show they put on, Celeste knew that these flowers were only an overture to the brilliant symphony of summer and she soon saw what she was looking for.

Slowing the car at a corner, Celeste smiled as Mrs Keating's garden came into view and she spied the brilliant yellow of the rose Maigold which climbed up the front of the thatched cottage like a hundred little sunshines, almost completely obscuring one of the tiny downstairs windows. For Celeste, Mrs Keating's Maigold heralded the beginning of the rose season and she looked out for it every year.

Her mother, Penelope Hamilton, had told her three daughters that the rose was the 'queen of summer'. Indeed, one of her most famous roses had been given that very name and had provided them with a very good living for many years, but the business hadn't been doing so well lately. Her mother's poor health over the last few months had meant a slide in sales and the old manor house which had been the family home for three generations was rapidly falling apart. Sales had also been hit over the last few years by the recession, with people cutting down on the little luxuries in life. It had also been increasingly difficult to compete with the number of new garden centres popping up all over the place selling roses that weren't nearly as beautiful or rich in fragrance and colour as the Hamiltons' roses but which were much more affordable.

Celeste took a deep breath as she thought of the challenges that lay ahead. Was it really wise to go back? She'd thought she'd left Little Eleigh behind her forever, but what kind of big sister would she be to Gertie and Evie if she didn't help them now?

'What are we going to do?' she said, addressing the question to her rear view mirror and the reflection of the little wire fox terrier on the back seat. He'd been awake and alert for the whole journey. She'd left her rented house on the north Norfolk coast a little after midday and had managed to squeeze the boxes of books and bags of clothes that made up the sum total of her possessions into the tiny car, leaving just enough room for the dog on the back seat. There'd been a big squashy armchair which she'd bought with Liam but she wouldn't have been able to fit it into the Morris even if she'd wanted it so she'd left it behind. It seemed crazy to have to pack all her things and bring them back to her family home when she was planning on moving them out again in a few short weeks, but she hadn't been able to justify paying rent on a place when she wasn't using it and, if Gertie was to be believed, they needed every penny each of them could scrape together if they were to sort the mess out at the manor.

'We'll soon be there, Frinton,' Celeste told him, watching as he stuck his nose out of the window as far as his doggy seat belt would allow him. Frinton had been a birthday gift from Liam two years ago and she loved him dearly. Named after the seaside resort where Liam had proposed and where Celeste should have run a mile, he was a little bundle of energy and joy and never failed to put a smile on Celeste's face even when her days had reached their darkest.

'You're the best thing to have come out of my marriage, you know that?' she told the little dog, and how grateful she had been to have his warm company at the bottom of her bed on the nights following the breakdown of her marriage a year ago. But she wasn't going to think of that now, she told herself. She had more urgent things to think about.

They drove by the long, leaning wall of the church and then the road dipped down into the valley, the brilliant green fields of early summer stretching out before her. She passed the track to a farm and smiled as she remembered how she and her sisters would cycle there during summer holidays to pet the piglets and eat freshly baked scones and buns straight out of Mrs Blythe's Aga. It was always a real treat to eat home-made goodies. Their mother had never baked and had rarely cooked anything from scratch. Her head had been too full of roses to think about food.

As she passed by a stile where she'd had her first kiss at the age of thirteen, the road curved round to the right, the hedgerows now heading skywards at an alarming speed after the recent rain. Everything was so lush. She slowed the car down and, a moment later, turned left down a private road that was lined with horse chestnuts which provided shade in the summer and shadows in the winter, and littered the road with shiny fat conkers during the autumn.

There was an old slate signpost that read 'Little Eleigh Manor' and, next to it, a horrible handmade wooden sign which Evie had made years ago that read 'Hamilton Roses'. There was a painting of a faded *Rosa Mundi* on it and the letters were faint and cracked. Celeste made a mental note to get it replaced at once.

The wrought iron gates had been left open for her and she drove over the moat and around the rose bed at the front of the house which would soon be vibrant with Bourbons and Portlands in a dozen shades of pink. Her mother had planted it with some of her favourite species like the voluptuous *La Reine Victoria* and the gracious *Comte de Chambord*. Celeste could see some of the buds were about to open any day now and, despite her misgivings about being back, she couldn't help but look forward to sticking her nose into the soft petals and inhaling deeply. There was nothing quite like an old rose for scent.

Parking the Morris next to an old Volvo shared by her sisters, which was more rust than paintwork these days, she sat for a moment, looking up at the great house. Little Eleigh Manor dated back to the fourteenth century, although it had been added to down the decades with a Tudor wing here and a Jacobean one there. Mostly made of red brick which had mellowed and softened over the years, it also had great stretches of half-timbered construction that leaned precariously over the moat. Dozens of windows of all shapes and sizes winked in the early summer sunshine and the great studded wooden door made the place looked like a fortress.

The gatehouse was probably its most impressive feature with its two four-storey turrets shooting up into the Suffolk sky. Visitors were always impressed by the courtyard that greeted them when they walked though, marvelling at the medieval grandeur. Well, it would have been medieval grandeur once upon a time before everything started to fall apart.

Celeste's grandparents, Arthur and Esme Hamilton, had bought the property in the 1960s and it had been in a dreadful state. They had done their best to restore it and make it habitable for their family but, despite the success of their rose business, there was never enough money to spend on the house and whole sections of it were still in danger.

Celeste's mother, Penelope, had just turned a blind eye to it.

'It's been standing here for six hundred years. I doubt if it's going to collapse during *my* lifetime,' had been her philosophy. So, doors had been shut and whole wings abandoned. There might be a whole army of ghosts living in part of the old house and they'd never even know about it.

Before Celeste could sink further into depression at the state of the manor, a young blonde-haired woman walked across the driveway. Frinton spotted her instantly and broke into a volley of barks.

'You're here!' she cried, hugging Celeste as soon as she got out of the car. 'You're *really* here! And Frinton too!'

'Evie! You've gone blonde,' Celeste said, touching the golden halo of her little sister's hair. '*Very* blonde!'

'I got fed up with being a brunette,' Evie said. 'It was so *boring.*' Her brown eyes suddenly widened. 'I mean, it's not boring on you, of course. *You* suit being a brunette.'

Celeste gave a wry grin. She would be the first to admit that she'd never been terribly adventurous when it came to her looks, preferring to keep things neat and simple. In fact, when she came to think about it, she'd worn her hair in the same straight shoulder-length style since she'd been a teenager.

Evie opened the passenger door and released Frinton from his seatbelt. He leapt out of the car and ran half a dozen circles around Evie before jumping halfway up her legs in a bid for attention.

Just as Evie was giving in and scooping the mad terrier up in her arms, Gertrude emerged from the gatehouse, her long dark hair scraped back in a ponytail and a pair of secateurs dangling from a belt around her waist. Gertie was the middle sister and, when she wasn't pruning roses, could usually be found with her with her nose in a book in a quiet corner of the house, sitting Jane Eyre–style on a windowsill, wishing that her life was more like a Tennyson poem or that she was living in a villa in the sun-drenched hills of Tuscany instead of in a damp Suffolk manor house. She was the same height and had the same slender build as Celeste but her features were softer and finer and her expression was more wistful. Perhaps because she still had all her romantic notions of the world intact and hadn't had them knocked out of her like Celeste.

Celeste watched as Gertie approached her, shoulders slightly hunched, tense and awkward.

'Hi,' Gertie said.

'Hi,' Celeste echoed. 'You okay?'

Gertie nodded. 'This is weird, isn't it?'

'Yes,' she said.

'I'm afraid everything is a *complete* mess,' Gertie went on. 'I've not had a chance to tidy around because the boiler's broken again and we've had to move some of the books in the library because that damp patch is now the size of Sudbury.'

Celeste sighed. 'Well, at least give me a hug before you give me the list of chores to do,' she said, embracing Gertie and noticing that there was a hen's feather in her hair.

'I'm so glad you're home,' Gertie added. 'We've missed you. And it's been so awful getting used to the place without Mum.' Her face was pale and sombre and Celeste realised that her two sisters were still very much mourning their mother. It had, after all, only been a few weeks since she'd died.

'I've missed you too,' Celeste said, wishing that she could feel something, *any*thing that approached normality when it came to their mother.

'Can we help you with your stuff?' Evie asked and Celeste nodded.

'Do you want it in your old room?' Gertie said.

'Where else?' Celeste asked.

'Well, we thought you might like Mum's old room. It's got a much nicer view than yours and you'll have more space too,' Gertie said. 'Evie and I have been discussing it, haven't we?'

Evie nodded. 'We think it's too sad to leave it empty.'

'I *don't* want Mum's room,' Celeste snapped.

Gertie and Evie stared at her and Celeste bit her lip.

'I'll be happier in mine,' she explained in a gentler tone.

'Are you sure?' Gertie asked.

'I'm sure.'

'Okay then,' Gertie said.

They each took a box of books and walked across the driveway and through the gatehouse into the courtyard. Celeste swallowed hard at the sight of it, her heart racing unnaturally fast as if it were about to launch her into some kind of panic attack. It didn't seem a minute since she'd left it all behind her and yet three whole years had passed since she'd said her goodbyes and left to marry Liam. Things felt so different now. She didn't feel as if she'd grown up, exactly, but she had definitely grown away from her old home; she couldn't help feeling that she had slipped into reverse by coming home and that her life was tumbling dangerously backwards.

It won't be the same this time, she told herself, trying to keep a check on her emotions. Her mother was gone now. She was no longer there to criticise or belittle her. She was dead.

Celeste only hoped that Penelope Hamilton wasn't the sort of person to come back and haunt the living.

2.

Frinton tore up the stairs ahead of the three women, skidding on the bare floorboards at the top before taking off at lightning speed. He'd never visited the manor before and Celeste knew that he was going to have great fun exploring every nook and cranny that it was possible to stick a cold, wet nose into.

'You'll have to keep him away from my hens,' Gertie said as she watched the terrier's antics.

'I know,' Celeste said.

'I mean it. Terriers are the worst kind of dogs around chickens.'

'I'll keep an eye on him. Don't worry,' Celeste told her, feeling like a stranger in the place she'd once known as home.

They walked the length of a long corridor lined with old oil paintings and sepia family photographs and reached a room at the end. Gertie pushed the door open with her foot and the three of them entered, placing their boxes of books on the floor.

'I opened the window first thing this morning but it's still a bit musty, I'm afraid,' Gertie said.

'This old house is always musty,' Evie said. 'I bought some incense sticks and lit them around the place but Mum went bananas.'

'Oh, those things were *awful*, Evie,' Gertie said. 'You made the place smell like a hippie commune.'

'Well, one of us will have to create a really wonderful rose room scent,' Evie said. 'You know – like an air freshener.'

'There's nothing wrong with a musty smell,' Celeste said. 'It's the smell of centuries gone by, of woodwork and plaster and old books. I like it.'

Gertie and Evie stared at her as if she was quite mad.

'Actually, I think it's just the damp you can smell,' Evie said, wrinkling her nose.

Two more trips to the car and back and they were done. Celeste sat on the end of her old bed, her hands stroking the pink and green patchwork bedspread. Frinton was lying on the rug in the centre of the room, licking his front paws. It was, she thought, the first time she'd just sat still for months and she let her mind drift. Her eyes scanned the room as if she was seeing it for the first time.

It was a beautiful room. The wood panelling that enclosed her on every side was exquisite but it did make everything so dark. Other parts of the house were like that too. Tiny windows and linen-fold panelling might have historians in raptures, but it cost an absolute fortune in electricity because lamps often had to be put on during the day just so you could see what you were doing.

Celeste was touched to see that Gertie had placed a small vase of flowers on the bedside table and the latest copy of *Your Rose* magazine. She could tell that they'd been left there by Gertie and not Evie because Evie would have been sure to have spilt some of the water from the vase – probably onto the magazine. She smiled as she thought about how different her two sisters were and how relatively little seemed to have changed since she'd left.

Since throwing herself into her new life away from the manor, Celeste hadn't seen much of her sisters. She'd kept in touch with brief phone calls, and Gertie and Evie had visited her new home out on the Norfolk coast just after she and Liam had moved in, but other than that and the funeral in May, she hadn't seen them, and she now realised just how much she'd missed them. Gertie was still running around like mad, worrying about everything and Evie was still obsessed with what colour her hair should be.

And Celeste? What was her place there now? The last time she'd seen this room, she'd bid it a silent goodbye and had hoped that she would never see it again. She'd never thought that she would be back, least of all in her old role of big sister taking care of everything. She wasn't sure she was ready to resume that particular role; she wasn't at all sure that she could. She closed her eyes and then wished she hadn't because that was when a voice from the past invaded her mind.

Why can't you do anything right? You just assume that I'll pick up the pieces after you, don't you? You're meant to be helping me. Why are you so useless?

Celeste opened her eyes and got off the bed, banishing the voice from her mind. No matter how beautiful it was, she thought, this place was bad for her and the sooner she sorted things out and left, the better.

She walked to the tiny latticed window that looked out over the moat towards the walled garden that was Gertie's pride and joy. She was, out of the three of them, the most green-fingered. Everything she planted seemed to take, and the walled garden was filled with heritage apple trees, espaliered pears, plums, figs, quinces, gigantic artichokes and leafy greens and herbs. Of course, there were a few rose bushes in there too, to help attract the pollinators, but Gertie had put her foot down when Celeste had suggested turning the garden completely over to roses. It would have been perfect with its sheltered, sunny location.

'There's more to a garden than roses,' Gertie had said. 'We have to eat too, and this will save us money in the long run. We can even sell our produce. There are acres and acres of land we can use for the roses, so please don't take my walled garden.'

Celeste had backed down and roses were grown in earnest everywhere else except there.

Leaving her bedroom, Celeste walked the length of the hallway, pausing outside her mother's bedroom. The door was slightly ajar and, even though she knew there was nobody inside, she was reluctant to push the door open.

She swallowed hard. Too many memories lived behind that door and she wasn't sure that she was ready to face them yet.

᠊ᢙᢩ᠊

The old longcase clock in the hallway had a chipped face and a dented case, but it still chimed every hour on the hour. It was very much the heartbeat of the manor as well as its voice, and life rotated gently around it, with eyes glancing at it several times a day but, perhaps, not always seeing its stately beauty.

It had just chimed seven o'clock that evening – the time for which Gertie had arranged dinner.

'In the dining room,' she had told a baffled Celeste and Evie.

It felt funny eating in the dining room, but Gertie had made an effort to lay the table and Celeste had to admit that everything looked beautiful. Usually, they made do with eating at the large table in the old kitchen downstairs. The room was permanently warm with an Aga pumping out a comforting heat. By contrast, the dining room was formal and cold, and the great portrait of Grandpa Arthur above the fireplace always made Celeste feel as if she was in a headmaster's office about to be scolded. Grandpa Arthur had been one of the most jovial chaps in the county but the portrait was austere and shared nothing of his warmth and sense of humour. Any stranger entering the room might think he was a tyrant, and his presence always added a sense of gloom to meals.

The table was a long oak one laid with a white linen table-cloth. It could seat up to twelve people but, tonight, it was just the three sisters sitting neatly together at the end by the window. Celeste sat at the head flanked by Evie to her left and Gertie to her right.

'You settled in okay?' Gertie asked.

Celeste nodded. 'As much as I can be.'

'Where are you going to put all your books?' she asked.

Celeste looked confused for a moment. 'I won't be unpacking them,' she said.

'What do you mean?' Gertie asked.

'Well, I'm not staying, am I?'

'Aren't you?'

'Well, certainly no longer than I have to,' she said. 'I thought I'd made that clear.'

'No,' Gertie said. 'You didn't.'

'We thought you were coming back for good,' Evie said.

'I mean, it's not like you've got anywhere else to go, have you?' Gertie said.

Celeste frowned. 'But that doesn't mean I want to come back here,' she said, gauging the responses of her two sisters and realising that they were not happy. 'Look, I really want to help out but I didn't ever imagine staying here longer than it takes to get the job done.'

'And what job is that?' Gertie asked. 'Sorting out our mess? The mess you'd conveniently walked away from?'

'Gertie!' Evie said, a warning tone in her voice.

'Well, it's true, isn't it? You said so yourself,' Gertie said.

'What did you say?' Celeste asked, turning to Evie.

'I didn't say *any*thing,' Evie said, sending a glare towards Gertie.

'Yes you did,' Gertie said. 'You said that Celeste's always been good at running away from things.'

A dreadful silence hung over the dinner table as the three sisters looked at one another.

'You really said that, Evie?' Celeste said at last.

'I didn't mean –' Evie started awkwardly but stopped. 'I meant that we could have used your help more when Mum was ill.'

'I couldn't be here then,' Celeste said. 'You know I couldn't.'

'No, I *don't* know that,' Evie said, with a sudden burst of emotion. 'Tell me exactly *why* you couldn't be here when we needed you the most? When *she* needed you the most?'

The two of them stared at one another, dark eyes locked.

Celeste swallowed hard. 'Don't ask me that,' she said, her voice subdued.

'Why? *Why* shouldn't I ask why my sister couldn't be around when Mum was dying? You should have visited, Celeste. You should have come to see her. What is *wrong* with you?'

'Evie!' Gertie said. 'Don't!'

Evie's eyes were full of tears and Gertie's face was pale and drawn.

'You know how things were between us,' Celeste said slowly. 'She wouldn't have wanted me here anyway.'

Evie was about to say something but Gertie sent her a warning look.

Celeste sighed. 'Surely the important thing is that I'm here now, okay?'

'Of course it is,' Gertie said.

'But I haven't come back to fight with you both,' she said. 'We need to get things in order, I know that, and I know I should have been here sooner but we're not going to get anything done if we start like this.'

Evie was staring down at her plate and Celeste realised how young she still was and how much she'd been through.

'Evie?' she said gently. 'I'm sorry if you think I've not pulled my weight around here, I really am. I never meant to put so much of the burden on you but I'm here now, okay?' She reached her hand across the table and squeezed her sister's. 'Okay?' she repeated.

Evie nodded and looked up, her eyes still bright with tears. 'Okay,' she said.

'So shall we eat now?' Gertie said, and the three sisters smiled at each other.

'You won't have heard all the village gossip yet,' Evie said, clearly making an effort to move the conversation on to more neutral ground as she passed the silver salt cellar across the table to Celeste. Gertie had made lasagne and Celeste was looking forward to it very much even though it was probably stone cold now after their quarrel. She'd forgotten the last time she'd done any home cooking. The tiny kitchen in her rented house had not been conducive to making meals from scratch and, more often than not, Celeste had found herself chucking something into the microwave.

'I've been blissfully unaware of gossip for some time now, I'm very glad to say,' Celeste said. She was relieved that Evie had dropped the subject of their mother because she knew that she would find it impossible to defend herself without things getting very ugly, and she really wasn't ready for that.

'Don't be a misery, because I'm going to fill you in whether you want me to or not,' Evie went on.

'I'm sure you will,' Celeste said with a little smile.

'Jodie and Ken Hammond are getting divorced. She's had enough of his cheating. They went on holiday at Christmas to try and patch things up but rumour has it that she hit him on the head with his guitar and told him he was a lying son of a –'

'How on earth do you know all that?' Celeste interrupted.

'It's all over the village,' Evie said, unfazed by her sister's suspicion.

'Yes, and I bet each person who talks about it adds a new insult or a new item with which poor Ken gets hit over the head,' Celeste said, exchanging a grin with Gertie.

'Well, if you don't believe that then you *have* to believe this one because I saw it with my own eyes,' Evie said.

'Go on, then,' Celeste said.

'I was taking a shortcut through the churchyard this Sunday. The service had just finished and everyone was coming out and I heard this *terrible* shouting. Honestly, you've never heard such noise in your life. I felt sure somebody had been murdered!' Evie paused dramatically.

'Well, tell us what happened!' Gertie said.

'Yes, who was it?' Celeste asked.

Evie gave a satisfied little smile and then continued. 'It was James Stanton and he sounded absolutely furious. Well, I had to find out more so I hid behind that big angel grave and I waited for him to come out and he was shouting and cursing and – well I'm not religious or anything but it just isn't right in a church, is it?'

'So who was he shouting at?' Celeste asked.

'His wife, of course! He'd pushed her wheelchair out of the porch and she was quite red in the face.'

'Poor Samantha. I feel really sorry for her, stuck in a chair,' Celeste said.

'It's her own fault if she goes galloping half-wild horses across the county without breaking them in properly first,' Gertie said and was rewarded by a glare from Celeste.

'So what happened then?' Celeste asked

'He shouted at her some more. He said something about her being the cruellest woman he had ever met and that he'd happily push her chair off the end of Clacton Pier!'

'Oh, my God!' Celeste said. 'Poor Samantha!'

'Just because she's in a wheelchair, it doesn't mean she's a saint,' Gertie said.

'I never said she was,' Celeste said. 'But you have to admit that's pretty embarrassing.'

'You can't assume to know what goes on in another person's marriage,' Gertie continued. 'There are two sides to every story and it's not right and I wish you'd stop gossiping, Evie.'

'I'm not gossiping. I'm just saying what I saw and heard.'

'And what about Jodie and Ken?' Gertie asked.

'Oh, the whole village is talking about them,' Evie said, shaking her head in annoyance.

'That's no excuse for you to join in,' Gertie told her. 'You didn't see that.'

'But I haven't even told you the really juicy stuff yet,' Evie said.

'We don't want to hear it,' Gertie said.

Celeste bit her lip. 'Actually, *I* do,' she said and Gertie gave her a look to say that Evie should *not* be encouraged. Celeste shrugged her shoulders. 'I need to know what's been going on whilst I've been away.'

Evie took a deep breath and held both her sisters' gazes for a moment before beginning, enjoying the sense of power that a piece of unreleased gossip holds.

'Well,' she said, 'rumour has it that James Stanton is having an affair.'

Celeste's dark eyes widened and Gertie's knife clattered down onto her plate.

'Who's he having an affair with?' Celeste asked.

'That's just it – nobody knows!' Evie said.

'Then how do you know he's having one?' Gertie asked.

'Because *everybody's* talking about it,' Evie said, exasperation filling her voice at Gertie's lack of common sense.

'That's ridiculous,' Gertie said.

'No it isn't,' Evie said. 'Most things start as a rumour. Somebody sees something or hears something and passes the message around –'

'Like Chinese Whispers – getting it all wrong!' Gertie said.

'Well, he looks like the sort to have an affair,' Evie said.

'And how do you come to that conclusion?' Gertie asked.

Evie shrugged. 'He just does.'

'I adore your logic,' Gertie said with a roll of her eyes.

'So,' Celeste said, sensing the need to move the conversation on once again, 'what do you think we need to tackle first?'

'I didn't think you'd want to talk about business,' Gertie said. 'Not tonight at least.'

'It would be nice not to,' Celeste said, 'but I don't think we've got the luxury of time, judging by the state of the study.'

'Ah,' Gertie said, 'so you've seen?'

Celeste nodded. 'I poked my head around the door before coming in to dinner. I haven't taken a close look yet and I'm not looking forward to it, I have to say.'

Gertie's face seemed to be growing longer as the seconds passed. 'That's not the only problem,' she said.

'What do you mean?' Celeste asked. 'What else should I know about?'

'I think it's best if we just show you,' Gertie said and, bracing herself for the very worst, Celeste got up from the table and followed her sisters out of the dining room.

3.

They crossed the hallway, their feet echoing on the grey stone floor. 'We really didn't want to do this to you on your first night back,' Gertie said, 'but it's been preying on our minds for months and we think we should put you in the picture.'

'Where are we going?' Celeste asked. It was the kind of house that warranted such a question because it was so large.

'The north wing,' Evie said. 'Hiking boots and oxygen masks are essential.'

Celeste sighed. The dreaded north wing was nothing but trouble. It was the side of the house that got the least amount of sunlight, and damp had been a constant problem there. The roof, too, had never been quite right, and a whole army of buckets lived in the rooms in an attempt to catch rain water.

They walked down a long corridor lined with sixteenth-century oak linenfold panels. They'd once been told by a visiting architect that the old manor had some of the very finest linenfold panels in the country; they were exceptionally beautiful, there was no denying that, but they made this part of the house so dark that it was rather like walking through a tunnel.

Gertie, who was leading the way, suddenly came to a stop outside the room that was generally referred to as The Room of Doom. Celeste had guessed that that was their destination.

'Brace yourself,' Evie said, using one of their grandpa's favourite expressions.

'*Brace yourself – the west wall has tumbled into the moat,*' he would announce, or, '*Brace yourself – the boiler's packed in again.*'

Their old home seemed to be a permanently bracing experience.

Gertie opened the great wooden door and it made the most satisfying of squeaks. The three of them entered and allowed their eyes to adjust. The room was bare of furniture and there was an old damp smell rather like that of an empty church. The floorboards were dusty and there were cobwebs across the windows. It was a sad, unloved room that had been sorely forgotten and left to slowly die.

'Well, there it is,' Gertie said and Celeste turned her eyes from the window and stared in horror at the patch of wall that Gertie was pointing to.

'What *is* that?' Celeste asked. 'It's like a big black hole.' Her eyes widened as she tried to take it in.

'It's some kind of mould,' Evie said. 'It's disgusting, isn't it? I try not to think about it.'

'Well, that's not going to help,' Celeste said as she gazed in horror at the mass of black before her. 'Isn't that exactly what Mum did too? Her idea about just shutting doors on rooms wasn't a great one. It doesn't make a problem go away.' She took a few tentative steps closer to the black wall as if she were afraid that it might swallow her whole at any moment.

'We got a quote for the work to be done,' Gertie said.

'How much was it for?' Celeste dared to ask.

'Six figures,' Gertie said. 'I don't remember exactly. It's on the desk somewhere.'

Celeste took a deep breath and then remembered where she was and hoped she hadn't ingested any mould spores.

'We could just build another wall in front of it or hang a tapestry over it or something,' Evie suggested.

21

'We can't keep turning our back on things like this,' Celeste said. 'We've got to make the house safe or the whole thing will crumble into the moat.'

'The whole house needs attention – not just this room,' Gertie said. 'There are all sorts of horrors if you stop and look long enough, only we haven't had time to do that and we certainly haven't got any money to deal with the problems even if we do have time to spot them.'

'I don't know why Grandma and Grandpa bought such a monstrous house,' Celeste said.

'But it's a *beautiful* house,' Gertie said.

'And you're a hopeless romantic just like them,' Celeste said.

'There's nothing wrong with that,' Gertie said.

'There is if you don't have the bank balance to go with it,' Celeste told her.

'We've got to save it,' Evie said.

'I don't think that's going to be enough,' Celeste said. 'We've saved all we can save already and it's just a drop in the ocean. The money's got to come from somewhere else. From what you've both told me, the rose business is only just holding its own. There's nothing left at the end of the month and we've already got three overdrafts as well as the mortgage, haven't we?'

Gertie nodded. 'So, what do you suggest?'

'Well, to begin with, I think we're going to have to sell something,' Celeste said.

Evie swallowed hard. 'You mean the painting, don't you?'

Celeste nodded. 'I'm sure you hardly ever look at it anyway, do you?'

'Isn't there something else? *Anything* else?' Evie asked.

'To sell?' Celeste said. 'Well, unless we start ripping out fireplaces and selling off bits of furniture –'

Gertie sighed. 'I think Celeste's right. We've got to sell the painting. Mum said as much just before she died.'

'What *exactly* did she say?' Celeste said.

'She said, "Sell the Fantin-Latour".'

'Okay, well, that's unambiguous enough,' Celeste said.

Gertie walked towards the wall and tentatively pressed a finger against it.

'Oh, don't touch it!' Evie cried. 'You'll catch something horrible and die a slow and painful death.'

'It's just as it looks – cold and damp,' Gertie said.

Evie had backed out of the room and Gertie and Celeste followed her.

'There's a card somewhere on Mum's desk,' Gertie said. 'It's for an auction house in London that specialises in fine art.'

'I really don't want to sell the painting,' Celeste said, 'but I don't think we've got a choice. Grandpa bought it for Grandma as an anniversary present one year. Do you remember the story?'

The sisters shook their heads.

'There was a country house in north Norfolk that was selling up. Everything had to go. It was really sad. The auction took place over three days and people came from all over the world to try get a little bit of English history,' Celeste told them.

'And that's where Grandpa bought the Fantin-Latour?' Evie said.

Celeste nodded. 'It went for some ridiculously low amount.'

'Is that where he got the other paintings from too?' Gertie asked.

'No, I think they came later. Mum once told me that whenever a new Hamilton rose sold well, Grandpa would buy a painting. A rose painting. It was his way of commemorating the moment. Of capturing a beautiful rose forever,' Celeste said.

'Now who's sounding romantic?' Evie said with a smile.

'I'm not being romantic. I'm just saying what he used to do,' Celeste said. 'But perhaps we should have *all* the paintings valued, then. The new ones and the old ones. We might be sitting on a small fortune.'

They'd reached the hallway again and stood beside the longcase clock. By the enormous front door, a barometer hung on the wall. It had been there as long as Celeste could remember and its beautifully old-fashioned face always gave the same reading: *Change*. No matter what the weather – no matter if it was dawn-to-dusk sunshine or blowing a blizzard, the little hand would be pointing to the word *Change*. Which was probably about right for the English climate.

'I really do think we should get them all valued,' Celeste said again, looking at Evie. 'What is it?'

'I just can't imagine our house without those paintings,' Evie said. 'They've been here forever. Practically.'

Gertie nodded. 'I feel the same. They're so much a part of this place.'

'I know,' Celeste said and then she frowned.

'What is it?' Gertie asked.

'I've been wondering if there's actually a painting missing.'

'Which one?' Evie asked.

'That's it – I just can't remember,' Celeste said. 'But I could have sworn there was another somewhere.' She tutted. 'I'm probably imagining it. My head's so muddled at the moment.'

'Well, can't we *think* about all this selling business for a while?' Gertie asked.

Celeste sighed. 'Okay, then, but don't think about it for too long or this whole place will fall down around us.'

୧୦

Celeste knew that she should allow herself to enjoy her first evening back home – to take some random book down from the library shelves and find a comfortable old chair to curl up in or take a walk around the gardens and enjoy the sublime warmth of the evening, but it wasn't in her nature to sit and relax, especially when she knew that there was so much to do – including persuading her sisters to sell the manor. She was just beginning to realise how attached they were to the old place and how difficult it was going to be to make them see things rationally. She felt like she'd been put in an impossible situation: Gertie and Evie had asked for her help and advice, but did they truly want it? Were they really going to listen to her ideas or was she on her own in this?

Are you even sure that you can sell this place even if they agree to? a little voice asked, and she had to admit that she didn't know the answer to that. She loved the manor as much as they did – she was quite sure of that – but, for her, it was an emotion tied to so many other complicated issues that enabled her to view things far more dispassionately than her sisters could.

She shook her head. She was driving herself crazy already and she'd only just got back. She didn't have to answer all these questions yet; she just had to take one day at a time, one job at a time. With that in mind, she made her way to the study.

The study was at the front of the house. It was always called the study and never the office because, to their mother, the word *office* had sounded so rigid and conventional, and she'd wanted her work place to be one of inspiration and pleasure. It wasn't a large room. Two mullioned windows draped with old damask curtains, which had long ago lost their colour and most of their thread, took up two of the four walls and the other two were given over to floor-to-ceiling bookshelves. The dusty old tomes were mostly books about flowers and the history of horticulture. Celeste gazed at them now, noticing the dust and the occasional cobweb that had been left to gather. She'd been told that their cleaner, Mrs Cartwright, had had to be let go some months before and her absence showed in every room. It was a big house – far too big for just two or three people – and it was a full-time job keeping it all clean.

A large Victorian walnut partners' desk stood in the centre of the room and the two matching office chairs still sat facing each other like a pair of opposing generals. Celeste could still remember a time when she herself had occupied half of the so-called partners' desk but, almost imperceptibly, her mother had moved across the leather writing surface, her paperwork encroaching on Celeste's space like a determined army. She'd still been expected to do half of the work – more than half, if truth be told – but her mother didn't seem to think that she needed the same amount of space in order to do it in.

Celeste looked at the desk now. She'd known what she would find there: towers of paperwork and unpaid bills. Her sisters were two of the most hard-working people Celeste had ever known but they were both absolutely hopeless when it came to paperwork. Their talents lay in the garden and the greenhouse, and anything remotely related to paperwork was stacked up and forgotten – frustrating to somebody like Celeste who very much valued order and organisation.

She couldn't bring herself to sit down at the desk – that would be too formal. Instead, she kind of hovered next to it, scanning her eyes over the papers and envelopes, reaching out when she saw a single piece of paper with her mother's handwriting on it. Her fingers shook as she picked it up and read it. It was one of her infamous 'To Do' lists. It was the usual ordered itinerary of jobs to do around the house and garden, allocated between Gertie and Evie. Celeste's eyes scanned the page but came to an abrupt halt when she read the final item on the list.

Ring Celeste?

Celeste stared at the words before her. *Ring Celeste?* So, she thought, the idea had occurred to her mother but the all-telling question mark revealed so much and the phone call had never happened. Had the cancer taken her so swiftly that she hadn't had the chance to call? Celeste knew that the last couple of weeks of her mother's illness had been pretty rough; her sisters had told her that Penelope had spent them in her room. So when had she written the note?

'Was she ever really going to call?' Celeste asked the empty room. She couldn't help wondering what her mother would have said to her if she had called and couldn't help feeling an immense sadness that she would never know now.

She swallowed hard and let the piece of paper fall onto the desk, and that's when she saw the little cream card that Gertrude had promised her was there.

Julian Faraday – Auctioneer.

There was a London address in some square that sounded very grand, plus a telephone number and email address. So, this was the man who had the power to save them, was it? The man who would take a much-loved painting from a family home and sell it to the highest bidder whether that person was worthy of it or not.

Celeste silently cursed the faceless Julian Faraday and placed the business card next to the telephone on the desk. She knew in her heart of hearts what she had to do but she wasn't ready to make that call just yet.

4.

Gertie's strides were quick and long and took her across the moat and around the garden to a little track through a meadow. At this time of year, it was filled with bright buttercups and red campion. Gertie loved the wildflowers but she didn't have time to stop and admire them this evening because she was meeting somebody.

She followed the River Stour, which gently curved its way through the landscape, and it was just as she was approaching the fallen willow tree that she saw Mrs Forbes. Gertie sighed because, at this part of the footpath, there was no avoiding her.

Keep moving, keep moving, she chanted to herself as the inevitable happened and they virtually collided.

Mrs Forbes was a tall, straight-backed woman who ran an aerobics class in the village hall for the over-fifties. She herself was in her late fifties and had a voice like an army major. She would bellow so loudly at her students each Wednesday morning that you could hear her at the other end of the village.

'Good evening, Gertrude,' Mrs Forbes boomed. 'Going for a walk?' she asked, meaning, *Where are you going?*

'Yes,' Gertie said, not making the fatal mistake of stopping to talk. 'Good evening,' she said as she passed.

Mrs Forbes looked startled but she wasn't the sort to be easily offended, and Gertie kept on moving for fear of being followed.

She couldn't imagine Mrs Forbes was the following kind but, all the same, she kept looking back over her shoulder until her great bulk was nothing more than a dot in the distance.

She was surprised by how much her heart was racing at the unexpected encounter, and she kept telling herself that she was getting worried about nothing. Mrs Forbes was not a gossip and she probably didn't even care where Gertie was going. Nevertheless, she still couldn't quell her anxiety, and after a moment, she realised that it was all part and parcel of what she had got herself into.

Leaving the riverside, she climbed over a stile, careful to avoid snagging the dress she was wearing. She'd chosen a simple blue denim dress with little mother-of-pearl buttons down the front. It was the sort of dress that was pretty enough but wouldn't draw unnecessary attention to itself. If Evie or Celeste had seen her leaving the manor, it would not be obvious to them that she was heading anywhere in particular. The fact that she had washed and blow-dried her long hair and was wearing it loose, and that she was also wearing rather a lot of mascara as well as lip gloss, was beside the point. What was wrong with wanting to look nice for an evening walk?

It was as she was crossing the next field that a sleek black and white greyhound appeared. It was a beautiful animal but it had seen better days and now moved with a gait that was akin to that of an elderly gentleman. Gertie knew that it was the kind of dog that didn't need much exercise at all. In fact, it would have been quite content to stay at home all day long, curled up in its favourite chair, but its owner needed an excuse to get out of the house and the dog was as good an alibi as any.

'Hey, Clyde,' Gertie said as the old dog approached her, shoving his wet nose into the palm of her hand. 'Where's your master, then?' she asked but she already knew the answer.

There was an old ruined chapel just through the trees and leaning up against one of the knobbly flint walls was a tall man with dark blond hair. He didn't hear Gertie approach and she had the chance to watch him unobserved for a moment. He was wearing a pair of blue jeans and a brown-and-white-checked cotton shirt. His face looked drawn and his blue eyes looked tired, as if he hadn't slept for a week – which perhaps he hadn't.

'James?' she said as she approached.

'Gertie,' he said, giving her a little smile. 'I thought you weren't coming.'

'Of course I was coming. I've never missed one of our meetings, have I?'

He walked towards her, took her face in his large hands and kissed her gently on the mouth.

'You're wearing the perfume I bought you,' he said, stroking her neck lightly with his fingers.

Gertie nodded. It was Penhaligon's Gardenia which was deliciously light and sweet.

'I've got you something else,' he said, reaching into his jeans pocket and bringing out a small box.

'James – you mustn't keep buying me things!'

'But I want to,' he said. 'Now, stop protesting and open it.'

He handed her a little blue box and she opened it and gasped. It was a silver locket in the shape of a heart.

'I've *always* wanted a locket,' she said, her dark eyes bright with joy.

'I know,' he said. 'I didn't dare put a photograph in it, though. Well, not of me at least.'

Gertie looked up at him. 'There's something in here?'

'I think you'd better find out.'

Gertie gently opened the locket and smiled when she saw what was inside. 'It's Clyde!' she said with a laugh.

'I sized the photo down on my computer. Doesn't he look the business?'

'He looks very fine indeed,' Gertie said, just as Clyde approached to poke her with his nose as if he knew he was being admired. 'Thank you.'

James nodded and smiled. 'I just wish there was more I could do for you.'

Gertie shook her head. 'Don't.'

He took her hands in his and squeezed them. 'Do you know how much I want to be with you?'

'Don't, James!' she said.

'I just want us to be a normal couple. I want to take you out to some fancy restaurant –'

'You haven't got the money for a fancy restaurant!' Gertie teased.

'Okay – a nice pub,' he said, 'and get all cosy with you in a corner and tickle you under the table when nobody's looking.'

Gertie giggled as he tickled her now, but then she sighed. 'But you can't tickle me in public whether or not anyone sees us because you're a married man.'

James groaned and threw his head back to the sky. 'You don't need to keep telling me that! I live with the fact every day!'

'Well, I'm living with the fact too,' Gertie said. 'You've no idea what it's like for me, do you? Celeste's back home and Evie was going on and on about that incident at the church.'

'Ah,' he said with a sigh.

'It was horrible having to listen to her when she didn't know what was really going on. It's so unfair – Samantha gets all the sympathy and nobody stops to think about what you have to put up with.'

'Hey,' James said gently, 'don't upset yourself. You know the way things are.'

'Yes, I do,' Gertie said, 'and they're cruel and unfair.'

'I know,' he said.

They pressed their heads together in a gentle embrace.

'What happened when you got home?' Gertie asked.

'After the church?'

'Was she furious?'

'Of course she was,' James said. 'But she was enjoying every single minute too. There's nothing she loves more than being the victim and I had to spend the whole evening saying I was sorry when I wasn't sorry at all.'

'Did you really say you'd push her off Clacton Pier?'

James laughed. 'Did I say that?'

'Evie said you did.'

'Well, I guess I must have done.' He ran a hand through his hair and, once again, Gertie saw how tired he looked.

'Are you okay?'

He nodded. 'Just sleeping badly.'

'Have you swapped rooms yet?'

'No,' he said. 'Samantha won't let me. She makes this big scene every time I dare to mention it. She says she'll wake up in the night and have an accident but she never wakes up in the night. Once she's out, she's out. She doesn't need me there.'

'You've got to move – and not just bedrooms,' Gertie said. 'You've got to move out completely.'

'How can I when she's so helpless?'

'But she's got money – she'll just have to pay for a carer. You can't go on being her slave. Not with things the way they are between you.'

'What will people think of me if I do that?' he asked.

'Let them think what they like,' Gertie told him. 'They have no idea what you go through. Tell *them* to move in with her if they're so worried and then they'll see what she's like.'

James sighed. 'Why didn't we meet years ago?'

'Because I was still at school,' Gertie teased and James couldn't help but smile.

'I'm not *that* much older than you,' he said.

'You're thirty-eight. You're practically an old man!'

He looked suitably outraged by this comment. 'Well, if that's the way you feel about me, I'll go back to my wife right now!'

Gertie laughed and then they were silent for a moment.

'Evie said something else,' she told him at last.

'What?' James said.

'She said she thought you were having an affair.'

'Oh my God. Did she?'

'She doesn't have any proof, of course. She just said she'd heard a rumour.'

'Where from?' James said, concerned.

'I don't know!'

'We've been so careful,' he said. 'I don't tell anyone where I'm going and I never see a soul. Do you?'

'No,' Gertie said, shaking her head. 'I saw Mrs Forbes this evening but we didn't say more than hello and I don't think she's the sort to gossip, anyway, even if she did suspect something.'

'Are you sure about that? I don't trust anyone in this village. Just a whiff of a rumour and they're off.'

'What a thing to say!' Gertie said, her face full of outrage. 'Just because you're a Londoner where nobody talks to anyone and nobody cares what anybody gets up to.'

'That's not fair!' James said. 'I spoke to my neighbour at least twice in the five years I lived in my old flat.'

Gertie grinned and then her smile slowly faded. 'What are we going to do?'

James leaned forward and kissed her forehead. 'I don't know,' he said, 'but we've got to work something out. I want to be with you so much.'

'Then we have to start making plans,' she said seriously.

He continued to kiss her, working his way across the sensitive skin of her neck. 'Plans,' he said.

'Yes!' Gertie said. 'James?'

'What?'

'Are you listening to me?'

'Do we have to talk about this now?'

'Well, if not now, then when?'

'We've got so little time together,' he said. 'I don't want to waste it talking.'

Gertie tried not to flinch at his use of the word *waste* because she didn't want to spoil the moment, but she was becoming increasingly frustrated at not being able to make plans with him.

'Just tell me we'll be together soon,' she said.

'Of course we will,' he said. 'Very soon.' And he stopped any more questions she had for him with another kiss.

The crash in the night woke everyone, including Frinton, who immediately sprang up onto his mistress's bed from his place on the floor and started up a fearful growling. One minute, Celeste had been deep in a dream which had involved her trying to compost a mountain of paperwork . . .

'It'll feed the roses. It'll feed the roses,' she'd been chanting to Gertie and Evie, who'd been watching her in utter despair.

The next minute, she was sat up in bed, her heart racing like a wild animal's.

'Quiet, Frinton,' she told the dog as she tried to work out what was happening.

Gertie was in her room in an instant. 'What the hell was that?'

'I thought I'd dreamt it,' Celeste said, turning on her bedside lamp and pulling on a jumper.

'You didn't dream it. It came from downstairs. Or upstairs. I'm not entirely sure,' Gertie said.

'Gertie?' Evie's voice cried from down the hallway.

'I'm in Celeste's bedroom,' Gertie called back.

'Did you hear that?' Evie joined them, her pretty face pale in the lamp light.

'You couldn't exactly miss it,' Gertie said.

'What was it? It sounded like a whole room falling in on itself,' Evie said.

'Don't say that. *Please* don't say that!' Celeste said, shoving her feet into her slippers. But a room falling in on itself was not beyond the bounds of possibility in a place like the manor.

'What shall we do?' Evie said, turning to her big sister as if she would have the answer.

'Check all the rooms,' Celeste said.

A moment later, the three of them left her bedroom with Frinton in tow and started opening doors and turning on lights.

'Just be careful!' Celeste shouted. 'I don't want anyone falling through the floorboards or anything.'

'I don't think it came from upstairs at all,' Evie said a moment later.

'Just keep checking,' Celeste said. 'We've got to know for sure.'

A few minutes later, the three sisters met out on the landing.

'Nothing,' Gertie said.

'Not so much as a cobweb out of place,' Evie said.

'It must have been from downstairs, then,' Celeste said.

'Oh, must we go down there?' Evie said, pulling her dressing gown tighter at the neck. 'This house really gives me the creeps at night.'

'Don't worry,' Gertie said. 'Safety in numbers.'

'Right – so, if there's a mad axeman hiding in the shadows, it'll be okay because there are three screaming women in their night-dresses instead of just one,' Evie said.

'I'll go first,' Celeste said and she led her two sisters down the stairs. Frinton, who was absolutely delighted at this middle of the night adventure, charged on ahead and came to a skidding halt in the hallway a moment later, his front paws disappearing under an old threadbare rug.

'What's the time, anyway?' Evie asked.

The longcase clock chimed three at that precise moment as if in answer.

'Where shall we start?' Gertie asked.

'I'm not splitting up,' Evie said, 'so don't anyone dare suggest it!'

Celeste sighed. 'Well, let's start in the dining room,' she said, bravely opening the door into the room and turning on the main light. It was probably the least likely room to collapse in on itself and the suit of armour in the far corner was still upright. Anyway, if that had taken a tumble, it would have made quite a different sort of noise from the one that had woken them all up.

They moved on through the house, checking the study and then working their way around the rooms that were least used until they reached the long dark corridor.

'It's The Room of Doom, isn't it? Evie said.

'It's highly likely,' Celeste said. 'It's been falling down for years.'

'Can't we leave it until morning? Another few hours won't matter, surely?' Evie said.

But Celeste and Gertie were already marching down the hallway and, so as not to be left alone, Evie had no choice but to follow them. Luckily, Gertie had thought to bring a torch downstairs because, in this part of the house, the electrics were dodgy but, as they opened each and every door en route to the dreaded chamber and flashed the torch into every corner and crevice, they discovered that each was empty and untouched.

'Well, that only leaves one room,' Celeste said and, with hearts heavier than their footsteps, they ventured towards the Room of Doom.

As soon as the door was open, Frinton started barking, the noise echoing around the empty room.

'Frinton – *quiet!*' Celeste cried.

He looked up anxiously at his mistress as if to ask why she wanted to come to such a place when they could be tucked up in a nice warm bed together dreaming about rabbits.

Gertie flashed the torch around. 'What is *that?*' she said in horror as she saw the great big pile of rubble in the middle of the room.

'It's the ceiling. The ceiling's on the floor!' Evie said.

'Oh, my God!' Celeste said, closing her eyes, but the horror was still there when she opened them a second later and, as Gertie shone the light upwards, they saw that Evie was right. The ceiling was, indeed, on the floor.

They stood in absolute silence. Even Frinton was speechless.

Finally, Gertie spoke. 'You've got to call that man from the auction house,' she said.

Celeste, who was pale-faced and tight-lipped, nodded solemnly. 'I'll make the call in the morning.'

5.

Celeste was warming her hands around a mug of sweet tea when Gertie came into the kitchen. It was the morning after the incident with the ceiling on the floor and neither of the sisters had slept well after its discovery.

'You okay?' Gertie asked as she poured herself an apple juice and sat down opposite her sister at the enormous pine table.

'I'm fine,' Celeste lied.

'Well, you look awful, if you don't mind me saying,' Gertie said.

'Thanks. I'd forgotten how honest you can be first thing in the morning.'

Gertie gave a little smile. 'I didn't sleep very well – did you?'

Celeste shook her head. 'I couldn't stop thinking.'

'About what?'

'About everything,' Celeste said.

'Ah,' Gertie said, 'no wonder you couldn't sleep.'

Celeste took another sip of her tea and Gertie spoke again.

'Have you heard from Liam recently?'

Celeste shook her head. 'I don't expect to anymore, really.'

'I can't believe it's a year since you two broke up,' Gertie said.

'I know,' Celeste said. 'I still can't believe all that happened.'

'Does he know you're here?'

'He'll probably guess,' Celeste said. 'He knew I was only renting that place on the coast short-term and I let him know when Mum died.'

'I thought it was disgraceful that he didn't come to the funeral,' Gertie said.

'I asked him not to,' Celeste said. 'He never got on with Mum and she couldn't stand the sight of him.'

Gertie watched her sister for a moment before speaking again.

'I'm really sorry things worked out the way they did,' Gertie said at last.

'It was completely my fault,' Celeste said.

'Don't say that.'

'But it was,' Celeste said. 'If I hadn't been in such a rush to leave home and make a new life for myself, I might have got to know Liam better and I would never have made such a mistake and married him.'

'Was it really awful at the end?' Gertie asked, her eyes crinkling in sympathy.

'It was awful at the beginning,' Celeste said with the tiniest of smiles. 'No, that's not true, actually. We had some fun times. He was' – she paused – 'he was able to make me take my mind off things, you know?'

Gertie smiled. 'Tell me,' she said.

'Well,' she said, thinking back to the early days of her brief marriage, 'he was always doing silly things like taking me go-carting or wind-surfing or flying kites on the beach. We were always *doing* things – things I'd never done before.

'Sounds like fun.'

'It was,' Celeste said, 'but you can't have fun all the time and, once the activities stopped and real life kicked in, we realised we had absolutely nothing in common.' She shook her head as she remembered. 'We came home from work one day and were making dinner in the kitchen and there was this awful silence. It wasn't a nice comfortable silence like you might get between couples but a really awkward one as if we were total strangers. There wasn't a single thing we wanted to talk about.' She shrugged.

'Still, I'm sorry I didn't get to see your wedding,' Gertie said.

'I'm sorry I couldn't invite you,' Celeste said. 'It all happened so quickly.'

'Why were you in such a rush?' Gertie asked.

Celeste pondered for a moment. 'I think I was scared Mum would try and stop me.'

'Really?'

Celeste nodded. 'She always used to tell me that I'd never leave this place and that it was my responsibility to keep everything going.'

'She shouldn't have put that pressure on you,' Gertie said.

'I think that's why I made such a mistake with Liam. He gave me a chance to escape from here and that was really important at the time.'

Gertie nodded. 'I wish you'd told us how unhappy you were here. We had no idea – we really didn't. You should have said something to us – we could have helped.'

'There's nothing you could have done.'

'We could have *listened* to you,' Gertie said.

'I didn't want to cause trouble between you and Mum – your relationship was good and Evie always worshipped her. I couldn't spoil all that with my problems. I just couldn't.'

Gertie stretched her hands out across the table and Celeste took them and felt their comforting squeeze. 'So, you swapped one hopeless situation for another?'

'That about sums it up, I guess,' Celeste said, and the two sisters looked at one another.

'I'm glad you're home now, though,' Gertie said. 'I mean, I know that sounds selfish and I know you think we just wanted you to come back to handle all the paperwork, but we really missed you. This old house just wasn't the same after you left.'

'You don't have to flatter me,' Celeste said with a teasing smile.

'I'm not,' Gertie said. 'I'm telling you the truth. Something was missing when you left. Even Mum noticed it.'

'Yeah, right!'

'She *did*,' Gertie said. 'She might not have admitted it to anyone but I could see it in her. She looked –' Gertie paused.

'What?' Celeste said.

'Lost,' Gertie said at last and Celeste laughed. 'No, *really*.'

'Gertie, you're talking a lot of nonsense. Mum hated me.'

'Don't say that,' Gertie said, her face filled with anguish.

'But it's true. She couldn't stand me being in the same room as her, although she'd always moan if I wasn't there to help her. I could never please her. I could never make her happy.'

Gertie squeezed her sister's hands again and Celeste knew that Gertie was still torn between wanting to believe her and wanting to remember Penelope in a gentler light. 'But you made *us* happy,' she said, 'and we missed you.'

'Did you? Did you really?'

'Of *course* we did! We *all* did.'

'I missed you too,' Celeste said. 'God, I can't believe I'm thirty and divorced.'

Gertie couldn't help laughing. 'At least you've had a go and aren't an old spinster like me.'

'You're not old!' Celeste told her.

'I'm twenty-six and still on the shelf,' Gertie said with a melodramatic sigh.

'What happened with Tim?' Celeste asked, remembering the earnest salesman who'd arrived one day trying to sell them double-glazing.

'Oh, that finished ages ago.'

'And there's nobody else on the horizon?' Celeste asked.

Gertie looked at her sister, wondering if she should tell her, wondering if she would understand.

'There *is*, isn't there?' Celeste said, leaning forward a little as if getting closer to her sister's confession.

'Well –'

It was then that Evie breezed into the room, her platinum blonde hair piled up on top of her head with artless charm.

'Good morning!' she chimed. 'Sleep well?'

'No,' Celeste and Gertie said in unison.

'Oh, dear! I was out for the count after all that excitement with the ceiling on the floor business.'

'I couldn't sleep at all,' Celeste said, giving a yawn.

'And I was just falling asleep when my alarm went off,' Gertie said.

'Are we ringing that man again?' Evie asked as she opened a cupboard and reached in for a large mug covered in pink roses.

'What man?' Celeste said.

'The one we ring when something breaks or falls down and he arrives in a funny little van and then sends an outrageous estimate in the post and we never get back to him.'

'I think we should,' Gertie said, 'and I think we should try to pay him to do the job this time – don't you, Celly?'

She nodded. 'I do,' she said. 'We need to get the manor in the best state possible if we're going to put it on the market.'

'What?' Evie snapped. 'Back up a minute because I'm not sure I heard you properly.'

'What are you talking about, Celly?' Gertie asked.

'Oh, come on!' Celeste said. 'Don't tell me neither of you has thought about selling up before. You *must* have. I mean, it's the obvious solution.'

A look passed across Gertie's face which Celeste couldn't quite read. 'Well, I have, but not seriously.'

'What?' Evie cried again. 'I can't believe I'm hearing this. You can't be serious, Celeste.'

'I'm *dead* serious,' she said. 'In fact, I've never been more serious about anything in my life.'

Evie sank onto the bench. 'But that's crazy.'

'Why is it crazy?' Celeste said. 'Just think about it for a minute. Think about how much this place costs to keep going and how much it's going to take to keep it running in the future. There's just the three of us here now and I'm not planning on staying here, and it seems such a waste to maintain it all when we're not using it. If we sold the manor, we'd have the funds to buy a really great place and homes for us all too. Think about it, Evie. Selling Little Eleigh Manor would free us all up to do whatever we wanted!'

'But I don't want to do anything else but live and work here,' Evie said in protest.

'Really?' Celeste said.

'Yes, really! Why do you find that so hard to believe?'

'Listen!' Gertie said, raising her hands. 'I think we should hear Celeste out.'

'I can't believe you're siding with her over this,' Evie said.

'I'm not siding with anyone,' Gertie said, 'but there are definitely issues to consider here.'

'Like what?' Evie asked.

'Like what we all want out of life,' Gertie said. 'I mean, it's never been an option for us before, has it? We've all kind of been bound to this place because it was the family home and the business too. But that's changing now, isn't it?'

'Is it?' Evie said.

'It is if we want it to,' Celeste said.

'I can't believe you two are even thinking about this,' Evie said. 'Doesn't this place mean anything to you?'

'Of course it does,' Celeste said, 'but I really can't see how we can go on living here. It just isn't practical.'

'What about asking Dad for some help? He's got a bit of money tucked away in accounts, hasn't he?' Evie asked.

'Yes but can you imagine Simone letting him withdraw any of it to help us?' Celeste said. 'She hates us!'

'We could try Uncle Portland or Aunt Leda,' Gertie suggested. 'They always loved this place.'

'But they've got less money than us and they've always thought Mum was mad to even think about keeping the manor going,' Celeste said. 'They wouldn't be able to help us.'

Evie shook her head, her dark eyes wide and fearful. 'Can't we at least wait and see what happens with the paintings first?' she asked. 'Who knows – they might be worth millions and solve all our problems!'

'I doubt it,' Celeste said.

'But we can wait and see before we make any drastic decisions, can't we?'

Celeste looked across the table at Gertie, who nodded her consent, and then she got up from the table with a weary sigh.

'Where are you going?' Evie asked, panic rising in her voice.

'I'm going to ring a man about a painting.'

∽

Celeste should have gone straight to the study and made the phone call to Julian Faraday but she didn't. Instead, she walked across the hallway and into the drawing room where the painting hung. The drawing room was one of the loveliest rooms in the house, filled with two huge red sofas on which nestled heaps of tapestry cushions. It was also one of the few rooms in which one could keep warm in winter because, just before their parents had divorced, their father had insisted on a wood-burning stove being installed.

'I'm not going to spend another cold winter in this blasted house,' he'd told their mother. It looked tiny in the giant fireplace but the heat that it pumped out was quite remarkable and many a fine evening had been spent with the three girls curled up on the sofas drinking cocoa and watching films together. Their mother had rarely joined them. When she wasn't out socialising, which she did on most weekends, she virtually lived in the study, which had only a plug-in radiator to keep the room from freezing completely. There she would stay, wrapped up in her winter coat and scarf, until the early hours of the morning because there was always so much work to do and she simply refused to hire any help as she was a complete control freak.

'This is a family business,' she would tell anybody who challenged her on the matter, 'and I'm not paying through the nose for some outsider to meddle in our affairs.'

But Celeste wasn't there to reminisce – she was there to look at the painting. Hanging on the wall above a mahogany table filled with silver photo frames was the Henri Fantin-Latour. It wasn't a large painting and yet it grabbed the attention of everybody who entered the room. Celeste studied it now, realising that it was years since she had looked at it properly. In fact, she couldn't remember the last time she'd *really* looked at it. It had, she thought, been taken advantage of and had become so much a part of the fabric of the house that nobody really noticed it anymore, which was a great shame because it was very beautiful. But perhaps that was the true value of something – you did not need to sing its praises every day but, if it was suddenly lost, its absence would be enough to break the hardest of hearts.

Standing in front of the painting now, she took in the full beauty of it. It was a still life featuring a simple earthenware bowl full of roses; the background was dark and unobtrusive as if nothing should distract the viewer from the beauty of the flowers.

Celeste loved the way that the roses were all heaped together in voluptuous abundance, leaving little room for greenery and no room at all for any other species of flower. They were predominantly pale pink roses but there were also white roses, pale apricot ones and a single crimson rose that seemed to sing aloud in the pale palette. Each rose was at its most perfect with its full blooms unfurled and Celeste could imagine the heavenly scent of the flowers as the artist had painted them. She wished she knew the names of the individual roses but she guessed that they were Centifolias or Bourbons with their many-petalled blooms. Perhaps these were roses that no longer existed but had been lost to the world. Perhaps they now existed only in this painting.

Her grandfather had often speculated on this very question.

'You see that one?' he would say, pointing to one of the creamy-white roses in the foreground.

'Yes?' Celeste would say.

'Damask rose – *Madame Hardy*. I'd put money on it.'

'Are you sure?' Celeste would say, desperate to know the true identity of each of the roses.

'No,' he would say. 'Goddamn frustrating. Wish I could find out for sure.'

And so the Hamilton family had done nothing but speculate on the identity of each flower down the years.

'I think *that* one's *Souvenir de la Malmaison*,' someone would say, only to be shot down by somebody else.

'You need your eyes tested. The colour's not right at all!'

'What about *Charles de Mills* for the red rose?' someone would say.

'It doesn't open like that,' somebody else would point out. 'It's flatter. I thought you'd know that.'

Celeste smiled as she remembered the friendly disputes and then felt a deep sadness that those sorts of conversations would come to an end if they sold the painting. But what choice did they have? If one painting could keep the house from falling down around their ears, then they couldn't afford not to sell it.

It was common sense. Yet, as she looked at the painted roses, she couldn't help but think that she would sooner live in a tiny terrace with the painting than live in the big draughty manor house without it.

Leaving the living room, Celeste walked to the study and found the business card that she'd left on the desk. One simple call – that's all it would take. All she had to do was pick up the phone and dial the number on the card. That wasn't so difficult, was it?

She took a deep breath, willing herself to stop thinking about the beauty of the painting and think about the practicality of cold, hard cash. The manor didn't need the painting but it did need a new roof, rewiring and the damp situation resolved. The painting had to go, and so she picked up the phone and dialled.

'Faraday's,' a bright voice answered a moment later. 'How can I help you?'

'I'd like to speak to Julian Faraday,' Celeste said.

'I'll just see if he's available,' the bright voice chimed and Celeste was put on hold and her ear was blasted with Beethoven. She waited, drumming her fingers on the desk in time to the music, wondering if she should hang up. They obviously weren't interested in the painting. The whole being put on hold was a sign, wasn't it? She should take the opportunity to run away whilst she still had the chance.

'Hello. Julian Faraday speaking.'

Celeste blinked. 'Mr Faraday?'

'Yes. Can I help you?'

It was a pleasant voice – warm and patient, Celeste thought as she cleared her throat. 'I have a painting,' she began. 'A Fantin-Latour.'

'Right,' he said a moment later. 'And you'd like it valued?'

'Yes. Yes please,' Celeste said. 'And some other paintings too. Perhaps. I'm not sure yet.'

'Will you be able to bring the paintings into town?'

'You mean London?' Celeste said in horror. 'Oh, dear.'

'You can't come into London?'

'Well, I don't really like to if I can help it,' she admitted.

'Whereabouts are you?' the patient voice asked.

'Suffolk – in the Stour Valley. Do you know it?'

'Do I know it? I'm coming out that way this weekend,' Mr Faraday said.

'Really?' Celeste said. Perhaps he was just curious to see the paintings and wouldn't let a little thing like a trip into the country put him off.

'Why don't I swing by your place whilst I'm in the area? When would be convenient for you?'

Celeste swallowed hard. All of a sudden, this seemed far too real. Somebody was swinging by. Somebody who might take their paintings away forever.

'Hello?' he prompted. 'Are you still there?'

'Yes,' Celeste said, pulling herself together. 'Saturday morning would be okay,' she said, thinking that it was probably best to get things over and done with as quickly as possible.

'Okay,' Mr Faraday said. 'Would ten o'clock suit you?'

'Yes,' she said.

'And your address?'

'We're at Little Eleigh Manor. Just south of –'

'Sudbury – yes, I know it,' he said. 'A very fine house.'

'In need of many repairs,' Celeste said.

'I see,' he said. 'Well, maybe Faraday's can help you with that.'

'Yes,' Celeste said.

'Then, I'll see you on Saturday.'

'Ten o'clock,' she said and, as she replaced the phone, she realised that there were tears in her eyes.

6.

Evie Hamilton looked in the broken mirror that hung in the potting shed and grimaced. She wasn't sure she liked herself as a blonde. Perhaps she'd go back to being a redhead at the end of the month.

At least her hair was something she could control, she thought, unlike everything else that seemed to be going on around her. She paused in her work, her gaze blurring as she thought about the last few months and how so much had changed since their mother had been diagnosed with cancer. It had been swiftly cruel, only a few short weeks from her initial feeling that something wasn't quite right until the last goodbyes.

Evie blinked away the tears. She was still prone to crying at odd moments when her emotions would creep up on her unannounced. Her beautiful mother, who spoilt her and told her how wonderful she was each and every day. She missed her so much. Nobody would ever love her as much as her mother had, would they? From teaching her how to apply make-up to how to walk in high heels, Penelope Hamilton had been there for her daughter. A little smothering at times, it had to be said, but wasn't that a sign of her deep affection?

'You remind me *so* much of myself at your age,' she would constantly tell Evie. 'Only you're not *quite* as pretty as I was, of course.'

Evie had never thought that a strange thing for her mother to say because she'd known that it had been the truth. From the countless photographs her mother had shown her over the years, Evie knew that Penelope had been an extraordinary beauty and it had been hard for her to lose some of that beauty when she'd been ill. It had made her cruel, saying things that she didn't mean and behaving in an impossible way. Evie had never seen that side of her before but it was the illness that had done that to her, wasn't it? She knew Celeste would have said otherwise but she hadn't been there at the end so she couldn't possibly know.

Evie frowned. And now Celeste was back, thinking she could bulldoze her sisters into making decisions they didn't want to make. What right did she have to do that? Just because she was the eldest, it didn't mean that she was in charge. Yes, they needed her help, but Evie was quite determined that she wasn't going to be forced to do something she wasn't totally happy with. There was no way she was even going to consider selling the manor. The manor was her home – it was *all* of their homes and much more besides. It was the place her grandparents had fallen in love with, and she knew that Celeste had negative memories of it, so she was just going to have to make her sister fall in love with it again.

Evie wiped her hands down the front of her blue jeans and grabbed the keys to the van. She would have loved to have spent more time with her beloved plants but she had an appointment with Gloria Temple and she could not afford to be late. If she managed to secure this client, it would do the Hamilton coffers no harm at all and would prove to Celeste that selling the manor wasn't the only option available to them.

Following the path outside the walled garden, Evie made her way towards the front of the house. The white van could really have done with a wash but there wasn't time for that now. It was a terrible vehicle and Gertrude was always saying that they would have to replace it, but it just wasn't a priority. Evie looked at the faded paintwork that read 'Hamilton Roses' – although it looked more like 'Hamil ose' now. The back doors hadn't closed properly for years and there was rust everywhere. It really wasn't a good advertisement for their company and yet the reputation of their roses seemed to triumph over such small matters as the business vehicle. Just as well, really.

Getting into the driver's seat, Evie checked to make sure that their *Album of Roses* was on the seat next to her and she smiled when she saw it. It was the most precious of books, capturing the very best that their business had to offer. Sometimes, Evie would curl up on one of the sofas in living room and lose herself in the pages of the much-loved album. Each photograph brought back memories of a special occasion when Hamilton Roses had played an important role. There were christenings, weddings, birthday parties, retirement dinners – every kind of celebration one could imagine – and each one was made all the more beautiful by the presence of roses.

'And there are no more beautiful roses than ours,' Evie said to herself as she started the van and drove across the moat and down the lane onto the road that would take her to Lavenham.

It was always a little strange to leave the manor. Evie was so used to spending her days there that whole weeks could go by without her leaving home. But it was always wonderful to cross the moat and venture out into the Stour Valley and beyond, and she was particularly looking forward to today's little outing.

Gloria Temple was a bit of a local celebrity. She was in her late fifties and was about to be married for the fourth time. In her youth, she had been an actress on the London stage, wowing audiences with her beauty and her talent. But she had really hit the big time in the nineteen-eighties when she landed a starring role as the eccentric mother in a TV sitcom about a dysfunctional family living in a caravan. Evie was far too young to know anything about

Caravandals but she'd seen clips of it and was just a little bit dazzled by her client's illustrious past.

She was also just a little bit dazzled by her client's house. Although not as large as her own family home, Blacketts Hall was an impressive medieval manor house in the black and white timber framed style that tourists flocked to Suffolk to see. Standing in its own grounds just outside the pretty town of Lavenham, it had far-reaching views and yet remained a very private place, sheltered behind an enormous wall and gates that were opened only to visitors who were expected.

Driving up to them now, Evie wound down her window and pressed the intercom.

'Evelyn Hamilton to see Miss Temple,' she announced, and the gates swung open before her.

She drove down the driveway, which was lined with a tall yew hedge trimmed to perfection and opened up to a circle of gravel in front of the house.

Evie switched the engine off, picked up the *Album of Roses* and got out of the car, gasping as she realised that she hadn't got changed out of her jeans. She brushed them down quickly, for there were still the remnants of the potting compost down the front of them. At least she was wearing a pretty pink blouse – the one that always reminded her of one of her favourite roses, *Madame Pierre Oger*, a delightful shell-pink Bourbon rose.

She was just making her way towards the front door when it was opened and two tiny white Bichon Frise dogs tore out onto the driveway. They were halfway up Evie's legs before their owner came to stop them.

'Olivia! Viola!' Gloria shouted. 'Leave our poor visitor alone.'

'Good afternoon, Miss Temple,' Evie said with a smile, hoping that the little dogs weren't drawing attention to her casual jeans.

'Evelyn?' Miss Temple said. 'Is that you?'

'Yes, Miss Temple.'

'I didn't recognise you. You look different.'

'It's my hair.'

'Yes,' she said, 'it doesn't suit you.' Gloria Temple could always be counted upon to speak her mind. 'Come along inside.'

Evie self-consciously touched her hair and then followed her client inside. She couldn't help noticing that Gloria's own hair was Doris Day–blonde and kissed her shoulders with the sort of sexy exuberance suited to somebody less than half her age. She was a tall and imposing woman with the kind of shoulders that had probably inspired the shoulder pad revolution of the nineteen-eighties. She was wearing a scarlet dress that dazzled the eyes and a pair of red high heels that meant that she was forever ducking her head to avoid the low beams of the house.

'I'm sorry I couldn't make my mind up last time,' she said, ushering Evie into the drawing room. Blacketts Hall might have been medieval but its furnishings were modern. Where one would have expected antiques and ebony-dark furniture, there were, instead, chrome and glass tables and chairs, a blond wooden table, leather sofas and modern art in garish colours gazing down from the beamed walls. Evie had to admit that – in a strange sort of way – it worked, although why somebody with a love of all things modern would buy a fifteenth-century house was beyond her.

Sitting down on one of the leather sofas, Evie awaited instruction, watching as a young girl came in carrying a white tray on which sat a white teapot and two white mugs, a white jug full of milk and a white sugar bowl.

'I used to adore white,' Gloria said, motioning towards the tea things as she began pouring, 'and they were the only colour flowers I would ever have in the house. But I think white roses are a little too virginal for someone of my advanced years, don't you think?'

Evie swallowed. That was just the sort of question that one shouldn't answer directly. 'You can choose any colour you like,' she said diplomatically.

'And I shall. It's just deciding which colour. You see, for my last wedding, I went simply crazy with lilies. We hired a hotel room in London and I had it stuffed with lilies. I swear the whole of central London was asphyxiated. They were so overpowering. I don't want to make that mistake again. But roses . . .' Her thoughts seemed to drift for a moment and the dreamy expression came over her face. 'Roses are the very essence of romance.'

'We think so,' Evie said. 'You can't beat them.'

'But we're only halfway there. I might have settled on a key flower but what *colour* should I choose? Red is – well, too red, isn't it? And pink is very girly.'

'But very romantic,' Evie dared to interject.

'And I've never liked apricot much. Too wishy-washy.'

'There's orange and yellow,' Evie said, turning the pages of the *Album of Roses* to show Gloria some of their most successful displays in orange and yellow, watching in anticipation as Gloria's hand hovered over a page featuring a wondrous cascade of yellow and cream roses.

'Yeeees,' she said slowly, her eyes narrowing as she took in the images in yellow.

'Yellow is rather underestimated,' Evie said, 'and yet it's so charming and sophisticated.'

Gloria nodded. 'I'm beginning to come round to yellow.'

'It's such a happy colour, don't you think? And I know you'll love the roses we have in our collection,' Evie went on. 'We have a beautiful deep yellow rose called *Gainsborough*. Its scent is sheer perfection – like a good old-fashioned damask. Then there's *Suffolk Dawn* – it's one of our bestsellers and it's very popular at weddings. Its scent isn't as strong as the *Gainsborough* but it is a wonderful creamy yellow – like a primrose – and is perfect both as a bud and when fully open.'

'It sounds absolutely divine!'

'I've brought our latest catalogue,' Evie said. She plunged her hand into her voluminous handbag to retrieve it and then flipped through the pages to find the yellow roses in their collection. 'But nothing really beats meeting them in person,' she said, referring to the roses as if they were fellow human beings that one needed to be introduced to.

'I should like that very much. Shall we make an appointment?'

Evie nodded enthusiastically and pulled out her diary.

⁓

Ten minutes later and Evie was driving down the back roads to Little Eleigh. She wound her window down to inhale the sweet summer air. She couldn't wait to tell Celeste and Gertie the news about Gloria Temple's wedding. She hadn't told them about the first appointment she'd made with the actress but had kept the delicious secret until she was quite sure that Hamilton Roses was going to be hired. She wondered what Celeste would say when she found out and if it would go any way towards changing her mind about selling the manor.

Something else was preying on Evie's mind, however, as she splashed through the ford and climbed the hill the other side, and she wondered if she should confess her little secret to Celeste.

She shook her head. 'No, no,' she said to the empty car. Now wasn't the right time at all, was it? Anyway, she wasn't sure that she was ready to tell anyone her little piece of news. Not just yet.

7.

Gertrude had made spaghetti Bolognese for dinner and there was an end of a crusty white loaf shared between the three sisters.

'How did you get on in the office today?' Gertie dared to ask as she passed the salt down the dining table. It was the second night they'd eaten in the dining room and it didn't feel quite as formal as the night before.

'Well, I've made a start but it's going to take me more than a day to go right through everything,' Celeste said.

'Of course,' Gertie said. 'And did you think any more about the painting?'

Silence descended on the table and Gertie and Evie watched Celeste for her response. She pushed her spaghetti around her plate, making funny little circles and, finally, she looked up and nodded.

'He's coming tomorrow,' she said.

'Who's coming tomorrow?' Evie asked.

'Mr Faraday from the auction house.'

'Really?' Gertie said, her eyes wide with surprise.

'He'll be here at ten o'clock.'

Gertie almost swallowed her spaghetti the wrong way.

'What's the matter?' Celeste asked. 'You agreed that we should sell the painting.'

'I know. I just didn't expect you to move so fast.'

'Well, we can't afford to hang around with the house in the state it's in, and I suggest you make an appointment with whoever it is you've had visit us in the past for a quote on the work that needs doing.'

'Ludkin and Son,' Gertie said. 'I'll give him a call.'

'He'll probably faint when we tell him we actually want him to start work,' Evie said. 'But I've got some money coming in too. Hamilton Roses will be providing the floral arrangements for the upcoming wedding of Gloria Temple!' she announced with a huge smile.

'Oh, Evie! Well done!' Gertie said.

'I thought she was dead,' Celeste said.

'No, very much alive and well and eager to marry husband number four,' Evie said, 'amongst a profusion of yellow roses. So you see, Celly, I can provide for us all and keep this place going.'

Celeste looked at her sister. 'That's great news, Evie, but that sort of money isn't going to last long, is it? And even if our painting is worth something, and even if it sells for an enormous amount, we're not going to have the money straight away and it certainly won't last forever – not with the amount of work that needs doing to the house. We need to think about something else, some other way to bring some money in.'

'Okay,' Gertie said, 'but what?'

'I've been thinking about The Lodge,' Celeste said.

'You're not thinking of selling The Lodge now, are you?' Evie said aghast.

'Not selling it,' Celeste said. 'Not yet at least. Look, I don't know what state of repair it's in but can't we do it up and rent it out?'

Gertie frowned at her sister. 'Well, we could if there wasn't somebody already in it.'

'Who's in it?' Celeste frowned.

'Esther Martin,' Gertie said, saying the name slowly as if Celeste was missing a trick. 'Come on, Celeste! You've only been away three years. *You* might have changed, but things around here haven't changed at all.'

'She's *still* in there?' Celeste cried.

'Of course she is,' Gertie said. 'Where else would she be?'

Celeste rolled her eyes. The Lodge was the perfect solution to a good, steady income. It had two bedrooms and a private garden and would bring in a good rent from a paying tenant.

'And we can't just kick her out,' Gertie said.

'We could if there was somewhere else for her to go,' Celeste said.

Evie was still eating her spaghetti but Gertie had stopped. She was watching Celeste closely.

'It seems absolutely absurd that we have all these empty rooms in this house and Esther's inhabiting a place that could be earning us good money immediately,' Celeste said.

'What are you saying?' Gertie said.

'I'm saying that it would make better sense if Esther moved in here with us so that we could rent out The Lodge.'

'Oh, you've got to be kidding!' Evie said.

'Why would I be kidding? It makes perfect financial sense. After all, we don't really want random lodgers in our home, do we?'

'And what do you call Esther, then?' Gertie asked.

'A friend of the family,' Celeste said.

'Friend?' Evie said with a wild sort of laugh. 'She might have been a friend to our grandparents but don't forget she had that huge falling out with Mum.'

'Yes,' Gertie said. 'You must remember hearing the story, Celly? Esther's only daughter was in love with Dad and, when he married Mum, she became a missionary in South America and then died of a fever.'

Celeste nodded, remembering the fate of poor Sally Martin.

'But Esther doesn't hold a grudge against us, does she? I mean, all that stuff was years ago and it had nothing to do with *us*,' Celeste said. 'And, if she hated us all so much, why did she go on living in The Lodge?'

'She had nowhere else to go,' Gertie said. 'She put all her money into some dodgy pension, and Grandpa Arthur took pity on her and said she could stay in The Lodge as long as she liked.'

'And she took him at his word,' Celeste said.

'I don't see what we can do about it now,' Gertie said. 'It wouldn't be right to turn her out.'

'But we have all these rooms here,' Celeste said. 'There's the guest bedroom with its ensuite. It's absolutely huge. She'd be happy enough in there, surely?'

'But what about meals? She'd be using our kitchen, wouldn't she?' Evie said, her young face creased with anxiety.

'It's a big enough kitchen, Evie,' Celeste said, 'and I'm sure we wouldn't all be using it at once.'

'Oh, I don't like the sound of this at all,' Evie said.

Gertie turned to Celeste. 'She once gave Evie a scare when she was little. We were playing by The Lodge and Esther came charging down her path with a broom in hand to chase us away. Said we were making too much noise. Evie thought she was some mad old witch.'

'I did *not* think she was some mad old witch!' Evie said with a pout.

'No, of course not. That's why you just cried solidly for two hours afterwards!'

'Look,' Celeste said, interrupting quickly, 'nothing's been decided for sure yet –'

'*Really?*' Evie said sceptically.

'I have to go and speak with Esther and see how she feels about things but I really think it's the best way forward. The Lodge is a perfect little home and I think it could make us a really good income,' Celeste said. 'We're not a charity, and we're not Grandpa Arthur and shouldn't be expected to honour his promise.'

Gertie and Evie stared at Celeste.

'Don't look at me like that. I know what you're thinking – that I'm some hard-hearted harridan,' she said. 'But I'm not. I'm just trying to sort things out.'

'But there must be a better way to go about it – a *nicer* way?' Evie said.

'If you think of one, let me know,' Celeste said, pushing her chair out behind her and leaving the room, Frinton trotting lightly behind her.

∽

Celeste awoke in the middle of the night, her heart racing with a sort of nervous energy at the thought of what was going to happen the next day. She switched on her bedside lamp and, immediately, Frinton was awake, his head rising from the rug. She lay perfectly still for a moment, her eyes scanning the undulating ceiling of the old bedroom, but Frinton wanted to know what was going on and, with one light leap, he was up on the bed, pushing his cold wet nose into her face.

'Oh, Frinton!' she complained but she was secretly pleased to have the little long-faced companion. With a sigh, she swung her legs out of bed and reached for a jumper.

The manor was not the sort of house to walk around in the middle of the night if one was easily spooked. The dark furniture loomed up out of the shadows like malevolent presences but Celeste wasn't perturbed by such things.

A table lamp was always left on in the hallway and Celeste inched along the dark landing quietly so as not to disturb her sisters. Frinton's nails clicked across the wooden floorboards as they made their way towards the staircase and down into the hall. The comforting tick of the longcase clock greeted her, and she opened the door into the living room and switched on the lamp – the one that sat on the table next to the Fantin-Latour painting. At once, the colours leapt into life. As she stared deeply into its warm depths, once again she had the strange sensation that she could almost smell the flowers.

Could she really bear to part with this painting? Wouldn't it be a far better option to live in a house with half the ceiling on the floor?

She thought about how much her grandparents had adored the old house, choosing things like paintings to adorn the walls and bits of furniture picked up at antique shops and local vintage fairs to enhance the beauty of the rooms. They'd made it into the perfect family home even if they hadn't always had the funds to do every single little job that needed doing.

Penelope, on the other hand, had treated the manor as simply a place to run her business from. Any profits had either gone back into the business or were spent on frivolous things like clothes. The house had never been deemed important enough to invest in and the fallout from that was now left for Celeste and her sisters to sort out.

Celeste suddenly felt the friendly dampness of Frinton's nose on her bare leg and took pity on the poor dog.

'Let's go back to bed,' she said, and he shot into the hallway and galloped up the stairs. Celeste took one last look at the Fantin-Latour and, feeling like a traitor, switched the lamp off and plunged the painting into darkness once more.

8.

Evie was just burning some scrambled eggs when Frinton started barking upstairs.

'Is he here?' she shouted, removing the smoking pan from the stove and tearing out of the kitchen and up the stairs.

Celeste, who'd been in the study, now walked into the hall. Gertrude joined them and the three of them walked over to the window and looked out at their visitor.

'Look at his car!' Evie said, admiration in her voice.

'It's a vintage MG,' Gertie said as her eyes took in the wonder. It was hunter green and the pale roof had been rolled back. They all watched as the driver parked and got out.

He was tall and had dark red hair, which was lightly tousled from his airy drive through the Suffolk lanes, and he was wearing a dark navy suit with a white shirt which was unbuttoned at the throat. He looked to be somewhere in his mid-thirties.

'Isn't he a bit young?' Evie asked. 'I expected him to be older.'

'As long as he knows what he's doing,' Celeste said.

'I wish we didn't have to have him here,' Evie said.

Celeste turned to look at her sister. 'We've been through all this, Evie. It's the only option.'

'Don't you two start again,' Gertie said.

'I'm not starting,' Evie said. 'But you know how I feel about all this.'

'Yes,' Celeste said. 'I know how you feel.'

The three sisters watched as the man took a folder and a canvas bag out of the car and looked up at the house.

'Haven't you two got something to do?' Celeste said.

'No,' they both said in unison.

'Well, you're making me nervous,' she said.

'The painting is as much ours as it is yours,' Evie said.

Gertie sighed and took pity on her sister. 'Don't worry. We'll leave you to it. Come on, Evie.'

'But I think we should at least meet him,' Evie said.

'Okay, we'll say a very quick hello and then leave Celeste to get on with things.'

The knocker sounded, startling each of the sisters even though they'd been expecting it. Celeste took a deep breath and went to answer it.

'Miss Hamilton? Celeste Hamilton?'

'Yes,' Celeste said.

'My name's Julian Faraday. We spoke on the phone – about the Fantin-Latour painting.' A pair of bright blue eyes met her brown ones.

'Yes, of course,' she said at last. 'Come in.' She turned away from him just as he proffered a hand. 'These are my sisters, Gertrude and Evelyn.'

Mr Faraday smiled and nodded politely.

'What beautiful names you all have,' he said. 'Celeste is particularly unusual, isn't it?'

'Our mother named us all after roses,' Evie said. 'Celeste, Gertrude and Evelyn. Celeste is the oldest and was named after a pink Alba but we were named after modern roses that came out in the years we were born. Our grandparents started the rose naming and our mother was named after the rose *Penelope* – a really beautiful Hybrid Musk – and we have an aunt called Louise after *Louise Odier*, and there's Aunt Leda and Uncle Portland.'

'How marvellous,' Mr Faraday said with a smile that lit up his whole face. 'I didn't realise that roses had such pretty names.'

'Oh, not all of them do,' Evie continued, 'and we think ourselves lucky Mum didn't call us *Raubritter*, *Complicata* and *Bullata*!'

Mr Faraday gave a little laugh. 'How extraordinary!' he said.

Celeste held her hands up. 'Evie, I think Mr Faraday gets the idea.'

'Come on. I think I can smell your breakfast burning in the kitchen,' Gertie said.

'Why do you *always* assume that burning food has something to do with me?' Evie said.

'Just a stab in the dark,' Gertie said as she ushered Evie out of the hallway.

'Sorry about that,' Celeste said once they were out of earshot. 'Evie tends to talk too much when she's nervous.'

'I feel like I've had a little lesson,' he said good-naturedly. 'I have to say that I didn't realise you had a rose business here,' he said. 'I knew of the house, of course.'

'Why *of course*?' Celeste asked.

'I know the area quite well. I have a second home here – in Nayland.'

'Oh, I see,' Celeste said, and Mr Faraday cocked his head to one side.

'You sound disapproving.'

'Do I?' Celeste said. 'I suppose I am. There are so many beautiful villages where, I'm afraid, half the population spends most of its time in London. The villages seem half-dead and the house prices are pushed skywards, meaning that the locals find it impossible to get on the property ladder.'

Mr Faraday cleared his throat as if he were a little nervous. 'Well, if it's any consolation, I inherited my property from my grandmother. She lived in Nayland all her life so, although I'm not a local, I'm nearly as good as one,' he said calmly.

'But how much time do you spend there?' she asked, tucking her dark hair behind her ears as she was apt to do when she was rattled.

Mr Faraday looked surprised by her question. 'I try get down most weekends but it's not always possible, I'm afraid. I'd like to spend more time here because it's so beautiful and I'm rather addicted to the antique shops, but work sometimes keeps me in London.'

They stared at each other for a moment as if trying to work each other out.

'You look very young to be a fine art specialist,' Celeste continued, thinking that Evie was right. 'I was expecting somebody older.'

'You were probably expecting my father. He was a Julian too. I'm a junior. I took over the business when he retired but you can be assured of my professionalism, Miss Hamilton. I specialise in nineteenth-century European paintings and I believe that's what you have to show me today.'

Celeste nodded. 'Sorry if I sounded rude,' she said. 'We're in a strange situation at the moment and we're all finding things a little overwhelming.'

'Not at all,' he said. 'I perfectly understand.'

'Shall we get on with things, then?' She gave an uneasy smile and led him through to the living room.

She saw him clock the Fantin-Latour immediately and watched as he walked towards it.

'It's a good one,' he said.

'Is there such a thing as a bad one?' Celeste asked.

'Of course. Well, in terms of market value,' he said. 'It could be in bad condition or be too small to raise a good sum or even be just a sketch, but this is a full-size oil in very good condition. The subject matter is perennially popular and it's a good composition – a little looser than his normal style but very pleasing. Do you mind if I take it off the wall?'

Celeste assented with a brief gesture of her hand.

'The reverse can be just as revealing,' Mr Faraday explained.

'I've never looked at the back before,' Celeste said, inching forward to get a look.

'The secret life of paintings,' Mr Faraday said as he turned the painting around.

'And what does it tell us?' she asked, looking at the rather dull brown rectangle.

'Well, the canvas has still got its original lining so it hasn't been relined.'

'And that's good?'

'Most serious collectors prefer a painting to be in its original state, and relining can have a detrimental effect on valuing too,' he told her. 'And see the lovely dark patina? That tells us it's all original. The stretchers too,' he said, pointing to the wooden framework. He then reached into his canvas bag, which he'd placed on the floor, and brought out a strange flat black instrument.

'What's that?' Celeste asked.

'It's a UV light and it'll highlight any imperfections or areas that have been retouched,' he said, turning it on to reveal an eerie blue-green light.

'It won't damage the painting?'

'No, no,' he said. 'It's not in our interest to go around damaging great works of art.'

She blushed at her own naiveté and then watched as he floated the light over the canvas.

'Well, there's a tiny bit of retouching in the background here but nothing that would devalue the painting greatly. Are you sure you have to sell it?'

'Pretty sure.'

He nodded. 'Because it's a real investment. It will only increase in value over time.'

'Yes, well, time is something we don't have, Mr Faraday.'

'Please, call me Julian.'

She looked at him and gave a little nod. 'There are some other paintings too but I'm not sure they're worth very much. But I suppose I should let you be the judge of that.'

'You'd like me to look at them now?'

'Please,' she said. 'They're in the study.'

She led the way back out into the hallway and then down the corridor that led to the study.

'What a marvellous room,' he said as he entered. 'Look at the panelling.' He reached out to touch it. 'And that window is wonderful. When does the house date back to?'

'It's medieval in part. A bit of Tudor here and Jacobean there, and a touch of Georgian too.'

'Each generation adding its own bit of beauty,' Julian said.

'And our generation having to keep it all going,' she said, and then she saw his gaze settling on the desk. 'You'll have to excuse the mess. My mother died recently and – well – there's a lot to sort out.'

'Oh,' he said. 'I'm very sorry to hear that.'

She nodded and their eyes met briefly.

'Look, I could come back another time if you'd prefer,' he said.

'No, no!' Celeste said. 'It's fine.' She paused for a moment and then motioned towards the paintings in the room. 'Well, here they are. I really don't know if there's anything here worth selling. Our grandpa picked them up over the years and I don't think he paid much for them.'

It was a happy group of half a dozen paintings, each of them depicting roses. None was particularly large but each had its own warm charm and the colours sang out into the room.

Julian Faraday didn't say anything at first but looked at each painting in turn. Celeste couldn't help wondering what was going on in his mind. Was he trying to think of the right words to tell her that these were nothing more than pretty car boot purchases and that she might be lucky to get a tenner for each of them?

'What do you know about them?' he said at last, his eyes still fixed on them.

'Not a lot, really,' Celeste said. 'Grandpa used to buy one if the business was going well – usually after the launch of a successful new Hamilton Rose. It was his way of commemorating the moment with a rose that would last for generations. He used to present each one to Grandma and she liked to have them in her study here. Actually, we think one might be missing but we're not totally sure.'

'That's a lovely story,' Julian said, smiling. 'But you have no idea where any of them came from?'

'I think this one was bought from some major general who'd inherited it from his wife's family at Clevely House out on the coast.'

'That's just the sort of story a buyer would love to hear. Provenance is very important when buying a painting – especially an old one.'

'So, you think these might be worth something?' Celeste dared to ask.

Julian Faraday's eyebrows rose a fraction and he smiled his warm smile again. 'They're certainly worth something. This one – from the stately home – is a Frans Mortelmans,' he said. 'Late nineteenth – (Note: this should be nineteenth-century) century.'

Celeste looked again at the pale pink and crimson roses which seemed to explode out of the basket. It had been her grandmother's favourite painting. She said it reminded her of the abundance of summer.

'A rose basket painting – very similar to this one – went for over thirty thousand pounds a few years ago,' Julian said.

The colour drained from Celeste's already pale face. 'Thirty thousand?' she croaked. 'I don't think our grandpa paid that much for it.'

'And this is a rather good Ferdinand Georg Waldmüller. A little earlier than the Frans Mortelmans.'

Celeste looked at the bunch of cerise roses, so bright in their silver vase.

'I love the unashamed darkness of the background here and how it sets the flowers off,' Julian said, his face filled with boyish enthusiasm. 'So wonderful.'

Celeste nodded.

'And I'm pretty sure this one's a Pierre-Joseph Redouté. Early nineteenth-century. He was known as the "Raphael of Flowers" and was commissioned to paint Empress Josephine's roses, I believe.'

'Right,' Celeste said, feeling horribly uneducated.

'I think they're called cabbage roses, aren't they?'

'*Rosa Centifolia*,' Celeste said, glad that she knew something worthwhile at last.

'Just beautiful. And very collectible,' he added, his smile filling his face once more. 'These others are definitely nineteenth-century too. I'd have to check the artists, although I think this one is Jean-Louis Cassell. He fell out of favour and his sort of thing became really unfashionable – a bit like the Pre-Raphaelites did for a while. It's hard to believe, isn't it? How something beautiful can be publicly shunned for so long.'

Celeste nodded, looking at the exquisite painting of white roses. It was one of her personal favourites and she couldn't imagine it ever being out of favour.

'It should really be in the National Gallery where everyone can enjoy it,' he said.

'Is it really that good?'

'They're *all* really that good,' Julian said. 'This is quite a collection you have here. Your grandfather was obviously a man of great taste and judgement.'

'I think he just bought them because he loved them. I don't think he had investment in mind.'

'That's the best way,' Julian said. 'Buy something because you love it.' He turned his gaze from the paintings at last and looked at Celeste. 'It's all about falling in love with something and enjoying looking at it.'

Celeste couldn't help smiling at that, and he smiled back at her, which, for some reason, made her feel self-conscious. She looked away again.

'So, what are the paintings worth, do you think?' she asked, looking at them again, her eyes fixing on the white roses of the Jean-Louis Cassell.

'Well, I can give you an estimate right now, of course, but you have to bear in mind that the world of art is full of surprises and there's a good deal of luck involved on auction day as to what the final price may be. We'll also have to discuss a reserve price – that is the least amount of money you'd accept for it. If we don't get that on the day then the painting remains yours.'

'A reserve, yes,' Celeste said with a nod.

'Now, this collection here, we're looking at anything between ten and forty thousand pounds each, with the Frans Mortelmans probably being at the top end.'

Celeste eyes widened in surprise. 'Forty thousand?'

'At the top end.'

Celeste swallowed hard, doing the mental maths. There were six paintings and he was estimating anywhere between sixty and two hundred and forty thousand pounds.

'But the Fantin-Latour,' he continued, 'could go for two hundred thousand or more.'

Celeste's mouth dropped open. For a moment, she'd actually forgotten about the Fantin-Latour.

'Don't forget that there will be commissions involved, and tax, of course,' he said.

'Of course,' she repeated. 'I'll need to talk to my sisters.'

Julian nodded. 'Absolutely.' He paused. 'Is there anything else you'd like me to see whilst I'm here?'

Celeste shook her head, her mind still whirring with the thought of hundreds of thousands of pounds. That would mean they could do a substantial amount of work on the house and prepare it for market, which, in turn, meant that she could move on and start the life she had been promising herself since divorcing Liam.

Collecting herself, she led Julian out of the study and back towards the hallway.

'So, once you've spoken to your sisters and decided what you would like to sell, I can come by again to pick up the paintings.'

'You don't need me to bring them to London?'

'No, no. I can come out here when I'm next in Nayland.'

'Thank you,' Celeste said. 'Goodbye, Mr Faraday.'

'Julian,' he said. 'Here's my card,' he said, handing her one from his jacket pocket.

'I have one,' she said.

'This is the latest – with my home number on it.'

She took it from him and watched as he turned to leave.

'It was very nice meeting you – meeting you all.'

Celeste nodded. 'Thank you for coming.'

'I hope to see you again,' he said. 'Take care of yourself.'

'Right,' she said, surprised by how intimate his simple order had sounded.

She watched as he crossed the driveway and got into his vintage MG, giving her a little wave goodbye before starting the engine and driving across the moat towards the road.

9.

Celeste found Gertrude in the rose garden which wasn't surprising in June because the roses were beginning to open. It was the time of year that every rosarian looked forward to – the glorious awakening of their favourite flower. Early mornings would be spent walking up and down the rose beds, eyes eager to spot new buds and petals unfurling. There was no more glorious sight than a rosebud revealing its colour to the world for the first time. It was a pleasure that never diminished with the passing years and Gertrude obviously didn't want to miss a single moment

'Look!' Gertie cried as soon as she saw Celeste. 'The first *Gertrude Jekyll* is opening.'

Celeste smiled. It was the rose that Gertie had been named after and so held a very special place in her heart. She stepped off the path, her canvas shoes sinking in the soft, hoed earth as she bent to inhale her first *Gertrude Jekyll* of the summer. It was a deep, heady, old-rose scent to match its deep pink petals. Next to it were several tightly scrolled buds, withholding their delicious scent from the world until the time was right. Celeste knew the cycle. They would take their time and then open into the most perfect pink rosette one could imagine.

'Glorious,' she said.

'Better than our own *Queen of Summer*?' Gertie asked with a smile.

'Of course not!' Celeste said. 'David Austin's roses are good but they can't beat ours.'

They grinned at one another, eyes shining with pride.

'So, how did you get on with the art guy?' Gertie asked at last.

'Well, he's gone,' Celeste told her, returning from Planet Rose.

'And?' Gertie wended her way out of the rose bed and onto the brick path.

'They're worth a lot more than I thought. The Fantin-Latour could make us a quarter of a million on its own.'

Gertrude's mouth dropped open just as Celeste's had a few minutes before. 'Oh, my God!'

Celeste nodded. 'It means we'll have to sell them, of course.'

'I guess.'

'We've never had them insured properly and I doubt we could afford to now we know what they're worth. Plus all this work we have to do on the house, and the bills to pay . . .' Celeste's voice faded away.

'You don't want to sell them, do you?' Gertie said.

Celeste took a deep breath. 'It'll be like losing dear friends, but I can't see another way of getting out of this hole we're in.' She shook her head. 'It was strange but, as I was telling Mr Faraday about how Grandpa came to buy the paintings, I was remembering it all for the first time in years. And suddenly it felt as if I was doing the wrong thing and I know I'm now public enemy number one with Evie and she'll never forgive me for all this but what choice do we have?'

'There's nothing else we can sell?'

'Not of such value,' Celeste said.

'Mum left a couple of rings,' Gertie said.

'Keep them. They're not worth anything,' Celeste said, thinking of the semi-precious engagement ring set with a single garnet and the gold signet ring. Their mother had barely worn jewellery at all when she'd been working, preferring hands that could delve into the earth without the fear of damaging anything precious. But she'd had quite a collection of costume jewellery for when she went out. Celeste remembered the long sparkling necklaces and the oversized diamante earrings that looked like something from a Hollywood soap opera. They wouldn't be worth anything, however.

'I didn't think Evie would mind as much about selling the paintings as she does,' Celeste said.

'I know,' Gertie said. 'She was so young when our grandparents died, and I don't think she remembers how much they loved them and the stories they used to tell about them.'

'So why is she taking this so hard?'

'You really want to know?'

'Yes, of *course* I really want to know,' Celeste said. 'Why wouldn't I?'

She shrugged. 'Because you and she seem to be moving in different directions at the moment and I'm not sure you really care what Evie is feeling.'

'How can you say that? I care desperately about Evie!' Celeste's face took on a pained expression. 'Tell me, Gertie,' she said. 'Please!'

'Well, I don't think she wants anything to change at the moment. She's feeling really vulnerable since Mum died,' Gertie said.

Celeste nodded. 'She was so close to her, wasn't she? Well, as close as you could be to Mum.'

'And then you've come home like this huge whirlwind of change and I think she's on the defensive.' Gertie's mouth had set in a firm, hard line.

'Look,' Celeste said, 'there are going to be some difficult decisions to make over the coming days and weeks. Decisions we'd probably all rather not make but we've got to get through this, okay?'

'I know,' Gertie said. 'But you must stop treating us like children.'

'I'm not, am I?' Celeste said with a frown.

'You've always been a great leader, Celly, and we've always looked up to you but you can be really bossy too and, well, we're adults too, you know.'

'Sorry,' Celeste said after a pause and Gertie nodded.

The sisters were walking down the path now, stopping every so often to admire a new rose or to check leaves for black spot.

'I mean, you must have thought about it before, Gertie,' Celeste said after a moment.

'Thought about what?'

'About selling up.'

Gertie looked out across a stretch of lawn but she didn't seem to be looking at the scene before her.

'Gertie?' Celeste prodded. 'Have you?'

She took a deep breath. 'Evie would *kill* me if she knew this, but I have, actually.'

Celeste nodded. 'I thought you must have. Remember all those dreams you used to have about travelling around the great gardens of the world and seeing all the beautiful palaces and castles?'

Gertie gave a little smile. 'I still have those dreams.'

'But they don't need to remain dreams,' Celeste said. 'If we sold the manor, we'd all be free to do exactly what we wanted. I know, up until now, you've been tied up with the job and Mum, but that doesn't need to be the case anymore.'

'I can't just leave, though,' Gertie said. 'Even if we all agreed to sell the manor – and I'm not entirely convinced that's the right decision – we'd still have to keep the business going, wouldn't we? You're not suggesting we sell that too, are you?' Gertie's face had paled.

'No, of course not,' Celeste said. 'But it would be nice to have a few more options open to us, wouldn't it? If we sold, we could move to a much smaller premises and there'd be money left over to employ more staff so we wouldn't be so tied to the business. Just think about that for a moment.' Celeste could tell by the look on her sister's face that she was, indeed, thinking about it. Celeste had been thinking about it too. When she'd first arrived back at the manor, she'd been quite determined to do her job as quickly as possible and then leave it all behind her, but she'd slowly found herself becoming immersed in her old role again – a role that was evolving and that she was beginning to have second thoughts about. Could she really give it up again? She wasn't at all sure.

'Evie would never agree to it,' Gertie said, bringing Celeste back to the present.

'She'd have to if it was two against one,' Celeste said and she saw Gertie's eyes widen at the suggestion.

'*Please* don't put me in that position,' she said. 'I don't want to be the one with the casting vote. I really don't.'

Celeste tucked her hair behind her ears. 'I'm not going to make a decision today, okay? I just want you to think about things. Will you promise me you'll at least think about them?'

Gertie looked at her as if she didn't quite trust her. 'I know you, Celly. I know what you're like when you make a decision.'

'What's that supposed to mean?' Celeste said, immediately on the defensive.

'It means that you charge right ahead once you've got an idea in your head, just like when you left home to marry Liam.'

'Oh, come on,' Celeste said, her hands on her hips. 'That was a *long* time coming. Nobody can accuse me of running away from home at the first hurdle I met with.'

'I know you didn't,' Gertie said, 'and nobody blames you for what you did. All I'm saying is that you've got that same look about you now – that resolute look that I think is going to knock us all flat if we try and stand in your way.'

Celeste shook her head. 'You really think that of me? You honestly think I won't listen to you and Evie?'

'I don't know,' Gertie said honestly, 'but I know how you feel about this place. It doesn't have the same hold on you as it does Evie and me. It means something different to you, doesn't it? And I wish it didn't.'

Celeste closed her eyes for a moment as if that could make everything fade away into oblivion. And then an image surfaced and a tiny smile found its way onto her face.

'What is it?' Gertie asked.

'Remember the day Grandpa came home with the Jean-Louis Cassell painting?'

Gertie nodded. 'He'd wrapped it up in pink tissue paper. There were layers and layers of it, weren't there?'

'It was like Christmas, wasn't it?'

'And I used to love him telling us about that auction where he'd bought the Fantin-Latour,' Gertie said.

'With him bidding against some old eccentric who was sitting at the back under a huge hat?'

'Yes!' Gertie said with a laugh. 'And the bidding went on for hours, Grandpa said.'

'He used to tell us that they had to stop for lunch in the middle of the bidding just so that they could keep their strength up, and then they'd resume bidding afterwards,' Celeste said and she was laughing too.

'He was such a storyteller,' Gertie said, pausing to inspect a bloom on a rich pink *Madame Isaac Pereire*.

'You'll have to support those stems,' Celeste said and Gertie nodded.

They paused and gazed across the lawns towards the rose beds. There were tiny touches of colour everywhere, from the purest white to the deepest red, full of promise for the summer ahead.

'Do you think Grandpa would be hurt by us selling the paintings?' Gertie said.

It was a question that Celeste hadn't wanted to ask. 'He wouldn't want us to live in a house with no roof,' she said, skilfully avoiding the issue.

'I suppose not,' Gertie said.

'I'm sure he'd understand,' Celeste said.

'But he might not be quite so understanding about you wanting to sell the house.'

Celeste took a moment to lean forward and inspect the wonderfully striped bud of *Honorine de Brabant*. It was resplendent in fuchsia and shell-pink stripes – warm and cool all at once. It was one of her favourite roses, and she adored the name *Honorine de Brabant*. So beautiful. So romantic. She wondered if Grandma or Mum had been tempted to name one of their daughters Honorine. She could have been Honorine Hamilton, Celeste thought. But maybe she would save the name for a daughter of her own one day.

All thoughts of finances were forgotten as she gazed at the perfect bud. That was the effect roses had on you – they filled your head with beauty so that there was little room for anything else – but the dreamy concentration soon faded.

'Nothing's going to be easy,' Celeste said as they left the beautiful Bourbon rose and continued on down the path. 'I'm really going to need your support in all this, Gertie.'

'I know,' Gertie said, 'and I'll do everything I can to help, but don't put me in the middle of you and Evie, okay? You've got to be really careful how you handle all this.'

'I know,' Celeste said.

'Because I'm not sure how many losses Evie can cope with all at once,' Gertie said. 'So, are you going to see Esther Martin?'

'I'm going to do that this afternoon,' she said.' Might as well do all the awful things in one day and get them over and done with.'

'Do you want me to come with you?' Gertie asked.

Celeste shook her head. 'I think it's probably best if there's just one of us for her to contend with.'

'And you're sure you're the right one?'

'What you mean?' Celeste asked with a frown.

'Well, she always saw you as the child that her daughter never had.'

'Oh, that's ridiculous!' Celeste said. 'Our father wasn't interested in Sally. That's what Mum told us.'

'But Esther still holds a grudge all the same,' Gertie said. 'She still blames *all* of us for her daughter's death.'

'Then it's about time that we sorted things out once and for all,' Celeste said.

Gertie took a deep breath. 'Rather you than me,' she said.

෬

The Lodge was a sweet little building on the edge of the estate, almost perfectly round and made of brick and flint with tiny windows that winked in the afternoon light. To the front was a small garden stuffed with roses that had been given to Esther from the Hamilton collection, and Celeste recognised a few that were beginning to open. There were three well-established *Constable* bushes that would blaze fabulous crimson blooms in the next week or two, and several *Summer Blush* bushes lining the path to the front door, their pink buds about to unfurl. But Celeste tried not to let herself be distracted by roses. She had business here and had to get on with it, so she approached the black wooden door and knocked.

'Who is it?' a voice said a moment later.

'Esther? It's Celeste. Celeste Hamilton.'

'Who?' the old voice croaked on the other side of the door.

'Penelope's daughter.'

'Penelope died.'

79

'I know, but I'm her daughter and I'm very much alive and I'd really like to talk to you. Can I come in, please?'

Celeste heard a chain rattle and, finally, the door was open and the small slight figure of Esther Martin greeted her. She had white shoulder-length hair and her eyes were a pale blue, but she wasn't smiling. She did a half shuffle away from the door and Celeste assumed that that was her invitation to come inside.

The tiny hallway housed a large full-length mirror and an umbrella stand with three walking sticks inside and no umbrellas. Celeste followed Esther through to the living room at the front of the house. It was a charming room with a large fireplace and plenty of light streaming in through a bay window. A brass carriage clock sat on the mantelpiece surrounded by porcelain figurines of women in ball gowns but Celeste could see that each one was covered in a thick layer of dust.

'So, you're the eldest, are you?' Esther said as she sat down in a winged armchair by the fireplace.

'I'm Celeste,' she said, sitting down opposite her even though she hadn't been invited to do so.

'I haven't seen your sisters for years,' Esther said.

'Don't Gertrude or Evelyn visit?' Celeste asked in shock.

'Oh, they visit but I don't let them in.'

Celeste frowned. 'Why not?'

'What have they got to say that I could possibly want to listen to?'

Celeste bit her lip. This wasn't going well.

'Of course, I find the occasional Victoria sandwich on the doorstep,' Esther went on.

'That'll be from Gertie. She's a fabulous cook.'

'My Sally was a fabulous cook,' she said solemnly, her icy blue eyes seeming to pin Celeste to her chair.

'Esther,' she began, clearing her throat, 'don't you get lonely living here?'

She shook her head. 'No, I don't,' she said abruptly.

'Wouldn't you like somebody to keep an eye on you?'

She shook her head again.

There was no other way for it – Celeste just had to come out with it. 'If you lived up at the house with us, things would be a lot simpler. You wouldn't have to worry about looking after this place and you wouldn't have any bills to worry about either.'

'You've not come here to take care of me,' Esther said, her eyes fixed unnervingly on Celeste. 'You've come here because you want me out, haven't you?'

Celeste swallowed hard. 'We need to rent this place out, Esther. The manor needs a constant source of income and we just haven't got it.'

'That's not my problem,' Esther said, her mouth a thin straight line of defiance.

'It would be if we had to sell up,' Celeste told her.

There was a dreadful pause and then Esther said, 'Your grandfather promised me a home –'

'And you'll have a home,' Celeste said. 'Nobody's throwing you out. We just need to move you, that's all.'

The two women stared at one another as if willing the other to back down.

'I really wouldn't ask you this if there was any other way,' Celeste said calmly, thinking that she'd better not dare mention her idea of selling the manor at this stage. It seemed best to take things one small step at a time.

Esther gazed down at the swirling patterned carpet beneath her feet and then looked up at Celeste again.

'You want me to move into that big old house with you and your sisters?'

'Yes,' Celeste said.

'You've got some nerve, I'll give you that.'

'I'm afraid there's no way around it,' Celeste said. 'We really don't have much choice.'

Esther's eyes lowered to her lap where her tiny hands lay cupped in each other. The knuckles looked large and swollen and they were terribly pale. Celeste swallowed hard. She was asking this old woman to give up her comfortable cottage for a place in a draughty old manor house whose ceilings were collapsing.

'And where are you thinking of putting me exactly?' Esther asked.

'There's a lovely guest bedroom with an en suite on the ground floor. It overlooks the rose garden and gets full sunshine all morning,' Celeste told her.

'What about meals?'

'There's plenty of room in our kitchen and you'd be welcome to join us or make your own arrangements.'

Silence descended again and Celeste watched Esther's fingers twisting themselves around each other. She saw a large ruby ring on her left hand. She hadn't ever known much about Esther's husband, but he had died years ago and Esther had been a widow for a long time.

'I'm not making a decision now,' Esther suddenly said.

'Of course not,' Celeste said as she got up to leave. 'You need to think about this.'

Esther got up from her chair and followed Celeste into the hall.

'I'm so sorry to have sprung this on you, Esther. I really do wish there was some other way of working things out.'

'Like me dropping down dead?' Esther said, her pale blue eyes mercilessly fixed on Celeste again. 'That would be handy for you, wouldn't it?'

'Please don't say things like that,' Celeste said, opening the door and walking outside.

There was another pause and Celeste tried desperately to think of something kind and placating to say but Esther spoke first.

'You're just like your mother,' she said before slamming the front door.

It was, perhaps, the very worst thing anybody could say to Celeste.

10.

A full week after his first visit to Little Eleigh Manor, Julian Faraday returned. Celeste heard his MG pulling up outside the house and, putting down her paperwork, walked to the window of the study to watch him. He wasn't wearing a suit today. Instead, he was wearing a pair of blue jeans and a white shirt over which he sported a sky-blue waistcoat. Celeste did a double take. She'd never seen a man wearing a waistcoat outside of a clothes catalogue and couldn't help but smile at the sight.

She shook her head, feeling strangely disloyal towards the house for having thoughts about the man who was there to take away their beloved paintings. She might well have asked him to do just that but she couldn't help begrudging him all the same.

'Stay there, Frinton,' she told her dog as she left the study, tucking her hair behind her ears. She crossed the hallway and opened the front door to a smiling face.

'Thank you for coming, Mr Faraday,' she said.

'Please, call me Julian,' he replied, reaching out to shake the hand that Celeste hadn't yet offered him.

She gave an anxious smile and held her hand out, and he shook it.

'Not so cold today,' he said.

'I beg your pardon?'

'Your hand,' he said. 'It was cold last time.'

'Was it?' she asked in surprise.

He nodded. 'But not so cold today.'

'Oh, right,' she said, quickly removing her hand from his and leading him through to the living room.

As soon as he entered the room, Julian walked over to the Fantin-Latour. 'So, you've decided to sell all the paintings?'

'All of the rose paintings, yes,' she said. 'We just can't afford to keep them – not when they're worth so much and we have so little to keep the house going.'

He nodded. 'I'm sure it's been a difficult decision to make but perhaps it is the best one.'

Celeste took a deep breath. 'I think it is,' she said. 'I've cleared the desk for you in the study.'

'Thank you. I have a bit of paperwork and then we can take care of the paintings.'

She led him through to the study and, as soon as the doors opened, Frinton leapt up from his little wicker basket and tore headlong towards Julian, his bark shrill and full of enthusiasm.

'Whoa there, little buddy!' Julian said, bending down to stroke the soft chestnut and white head. 'Who's this, then?'

'That's Frinton,' Celeste said, 'who should be in his basket.' She pointed a finger in the direction of the basket and Frinton slunk back towards it.

'He's adorable,' Julian said. 'We used to have a Jack Russell when I was boy. I've never known a dog so full of mischief.'

'I think all terriers have some sort of mischief gene,' Celeste said.

Julian laughed. 'You could be right there.'

'Can I get you a cup of tea?'

'That would be most kind,' he said and she left the room, returning a few minutes later with a small tray. She watched as he added a splash of milk and took a sip and then got down to work.

'You said your grandfather bought a rose painting each time one of your family's roses did well,' he said as he examined the Jean-Louis Cassell.

'That's right,' Celeste said, looking at the painting fondly. 'I was just talking to Gertie about this one. Grandpa brought it home all wrapped up in pink tissue paper and Grandma was taking great care to unwrap it gently. She didn't want to make a mess of the paper and Grandpa was getting more and more frustrated with how long she was taking. "Just rip it, woman!" he shouted. We were all laughing so much and then we saw the painting and we were all stunned into silence. It was so beautiful.' Celeste paused, remembering the moment as if it was yesterday, her eyes moistening with tears so that the image of the white roses in the painting blurred.

'You okay?' Julian asked.

Celeste looked at him in surprise, almost as if she'd forgotten he was there. 'I haven't thought about that day in years,' she said, 'and now I've remembered it twice in one day.'

'Selling things like paintings can often stir up memories,' he said.

'Can it?'

'Of course,' he said. 'Paintings are usually an emotional purchase, you see. There are collectors who buy for investment but most people – people like your grandfather – buy out of love and they come to associate the painting with a particular time in their life.'

'And that makes it harder to part with them,' Celeste said, her voice barely above a whisper.

There was a moment's pause.

'If you want to change your mind at any time,' he said, 'you can. Just give me a call and we'll remove the painting from sale.'

'No,' Celeste said quickly. 'There's no need. We're selling.'

It took the best part of an hour to take down, inspect and wrap each of the paintings and fill out the corresponding paperwork. Celeste watched as Julian wrapped each painting carefully and then placed them into a large padded silver bag.

'Will they be all right in your car?' Celeste asked.

'I shall take very good care of them,' he said.

'But you don't even have your roof up,' Celeste pointed out. 'What if it rains?'

'Rain isn't forecast,' he said.

'But you might have an accident – the car might overturn – anything could happen.'

'I will put the roof up if it makes you feel better,' he said and she nodded. 'And,' he cleared his throat, 'I was wondering if, perhaps, you could give me a bit of a tour.'

'A tour? Of what?' she asked.

'The house – the garden –'

'Why?' Celeste asked, genuinely surprised. She wondered how a stranger could make such a request and how she could deflect him because she didn't like the idea of it at all. This was their private home, after all.

'Well, I just thought –'

'You're here to collect and sell our paintings, Mr Faraday, not our estate.'

'It's Julian,' he said. 'Please call me Julian, and it would help if I could put the paintings in a context – you know, "They belonged to the renowned Hamilton family who own the such and such manor house and garden". People *love* context.'

'But surely you can say all that without the need for a personal tour,' Celeste said with a frown.

'Well, I could, of course, but it would help if I could personalise things. I mean, I'm sure you wouldn't try to sell somebody a rose if you hadn't ever seen or smelt it yourself, would you?'

Celeste looked at him with suspicion in her eyes and didn't bother disguising a quick look at her watch.

'Look,' he said, suddenly appearing ruffled, 'I really don't want to impose. You've got more than enough to cope with without me putting pressure on you too. Perhaps I could come back another day –'

'No, no!' Celeste said, holding a hand up to stop his protest. 'I'll give you your tour.' Her voice was cool and official even to her own ears, and she couldn't help feeling a little bit guilty when he smiled at her.

'Thank you,' he said. 'It's really very kind of you.'

છ

Gertrude was forking a layer of mulch onto one of the rose beds and smiling idly at a particularly lovely pink *Baroness Rothschild* which had just revealed its many-petalled splendour to the world. She was trying her best not to think about the conversation she'd had with Celeste. Trying but failing miserably.

You must have thought about it before, Gertie.

Her sister's voice echoed around her mind. Of course she'd thought about selling the manor. During the last few weeks of their mother's life, Gertie had thought of little else. It had been her little escape, a wonderful *what if?* But she hadn't dared to talk to Evie about it. Everything had been so raw when their mother had died and they'd been buried under a mountain of paperwork and debts. There hadn't been an opportunity to talk about the future – their future – because they'd been so wrapped up in the present and sorting out the past.

But if they sold . . .

'That's an almighty *if*,' she told herself but she couldn't shake the thought from her mind. How many times had she dreamed of getting away, of leaving the confines of the manor, crossing the moat for the last time and seeking a new way of living? Since she'd met James, that dream had become even more enticing, with her imagining them running away from the claustrophobic Suffolk village and starting a new life together. It had been an escape for them both to talk about their dreams of the future, and they would spend hours talking about it. How perfect it would be, she thought, and selling the manor would go a long way to making that dream come true. But the time for dreaming, she felt, was coming to an end. It was now time to start building a real life for themselves.

It was just as she was picturing a gold-stoned villa in the lush Umbrian hills that she heard the strange hissing noise. She looked around her, half expecting to see a couple of boys from the village who liked to sneak into the gardens and play hide and seek, but it wasn't boys from the village. It was James.

She looked nervously around for signs of her sisters before she dared to approach the shrubbery where James was hiding very badly.

'What on *earth* are you doing here?' she whispered as he bent to kiss her.

'I had to see you!' he said, raking a hand through his hair like a bad actor.

'*Here?* You're not like a normal boyfriend, you know. You can't just call by on a whim!'

He nodded. 'It couldn't wait.'

'But what if you're seen?' Gertrude said.

'I was careful *not* to be seen.'

'Which way did you come?'

'Across the fields at the back. There was nobody about.'

'How can you be sure?'

'Gertie!' He protested, taking hold of her shoulders. 'We're wasting time. I've got to go away. I'm leaving this evening and I want you to come with me.'

'What?'

A smile broke out on his face. 'Come with me, Gertie!'

'But this is our busiest time of year. All the roses are out, we've got weddings and birthdays, hotel orders, private parties and the garden to maintain, and we're about to be invaded by workmen too. I can't just leave.'

He shook his head, his smile still firmly in place. 'Why don't you do just that – *just leave!* The roses can survive a couple of days without you. They're not going anywhere and your sisters will have to take over whatever needs doing.' He leaned in to kiss the tip of her nose.

'Where are you going?'

'There's a work's conference in Cambridge. Truth be told, I can get there and back easily in a day but I've told Samantha I'll be away for two nights. I've already booked a little hotel out in the Fens for the two of us, and we could have dinner in Cambridge first.'

A little hotel in the Fens, Gertie thought, and dinner in Cambridge together. She imagined walking hand in hand along the Backs with James – maybe they'd even have time to take a punt in one of those funny little boats. Then they'd go on to a beautiful restaurant where she wouldn't be scared of bumping into anyone from Little Eleigh. They could be a *real* couple, and then they would book into the hotel in some secluded part of the Fens. Two whole nights with James without him having to run back to Samantha. She'd have him all to herself for *two whole nights*. It was so incredibly tempting.

'Come with me,' James whispered, stroking her hair in that maddening way that he knew she adored. 'Your beloved roses will survive without you but *I won't.*'

She looked up into his face. His eyes were filled with desperate tenderness, and she relented.

'I'll come with you,' she said.

'You will?'

She nodded. 'I've no idea what I'll tell my sisters –'

'You'll think of something,' he said. 'Tell them you're going to a rose conference or an important meeting about mulch.'

She laughed at him and he kissed her. They were going away together and she could barely contain her excitement.

❦

It seemed that Frinton had a new best friend in Julian because the little dog was following him everywhere he and his mistress went, keeping close to his heels and looking up at him as if he was his new master. He followed them through all of the main rooms of the house, his little feet tap-tapping on the floorboards and flagstones as Julian took in the sights and delights of the manor, admiring everything from the ornate plasterwork of the ceilings to the exquisite metalwork of the window latches. Nothing, it seemed, went unnoticed.

'I've never seen a more beautiful house,' he said.

'Well, it's not all beautiful, I'm afraid,' Celeste said as she led him down the corridor to the troublesome north wing. Opening the door, she held her arm up, barring the way. 'It's not safe enough to enter but I thought you'd want to see it. This is the main reason for selling the paintings.'

'Ah,' Julian said, poking his head around the door. 'Now I understand.'

'It's needed attention for decades but we've never had the capital,' she said, 'and even if we had, I have the feeling that my mother would have spent the money on the business. Roofs come a poor second to roses here. The garden has always come before the house in our family, I'm afraid, and we seem to be paying the price for that now.' She closed the door and they retraced their steps to the hallway, Frinton following with his nose practically touching Julian's ankles.

'Frinton!' Celeste said in a warning tone but the dog took absolutely no notice of her. Julian looked down and smiled.

'I seem to have acquired a dog,' he said.

'I am sorry. He can be a real pain sometimes.'

'Maybe he can smell Picasso,' Julian said.

'Picasso?'

'Pixie – my cat.'

'Oh,' Celeste said.

'She's at the cottage in Nayland. She comes everywhere with me. I once tried to leave her in my flat in London and she hid under the bed and wouldn't come out. Didn't eat anything either. My neighbour was frantic so I've bought a little cat carrier for her and she comes away with me now.'

'I see,' Celeste said, surprised by this deluge of feline information that she hadn't asked for.

She opened the front door and they stepped outside.

'How wonderful it must have been to grow up in a moated manor house,' Julian said. 'I mean – a *moat!* That must have felt so safe.'

'Not if the threat comes from within,' Celeste said and then bit her lip. What on earth had made her say that?

Julian turned to look at her, a quizzical expression in his eyes.

'Forget I said that,' she said.

'Whenever somebody says, "Forget I said that," it's immediately flagged up as something vitally important which cannot be forgotten under any circumstances.'

'It's nothing,' she told him, glancing away quickly.

'And that usually means that it's something very important too.' His expression was kind and gentle.

They stopped walking and Celeste turned to look him. 'Whether it's important or not is irrelevant seeing as it's of no interest to the prospective buyers of our paintings – and that's the whole purpose of this little tour, isn't it?'

He held her gaze from moment. 'Of course,' he said. 'I'm sorry. I didn't mean to overstep the mark.'

'Let's get on with the tour, shall we?' she said, clearing her throat and marching across the driveway towards the rose garden.

Julian must have got the message because he quickly turned the conversation to a less emotive subject – roses.

'So, the rose business began with your grandparents?' he asked.

'Yes,' Celeste said. 'Arthur Hamilton was my grandfather and he and my grandmother, Esme, began breeding roses in the nineteen-sixties.'

'And they bought this place to do it?' Julian asked.

'My grandfather inherited a small fortune from his father's factory business in Yorkshire. He sold absolutely everything and ploughed it into this place.'

'Apart from the money he spent on the paintings,' Julian said.

'Oh, no,' Celeste said. 'He bought all the paintings with money made from Hamilton Roses.'

Julian smiled. 'I'm baffled as to why I've never heard of them before.'

'Not many people realise that there's a team of people behind a rose. A rose is just a rose. People don't really think of the person who has taken years to create it.'

He nodded. 'I was thinking, what would have happened if all you Hamilton girls had been boys?'

'What do you mean?' she asked.

'I mean, roses are a girls' thing, aren't they? I doubt you'd get three brothers running a rose business.'

Celeste looked at him as if he was quite mad. 'That's a common misconception,' she told him. 'All the great rose breeders were and are men – Alexandre Hardy, Wilhelm Kordes, Joseph Pemberton, Peter Beales, David Austin. There was Empress Josephine, of course, who grew hundreds of roses in the gardens of her chateau and took a passionate interest in rose breeding. She was even given the nickname "Godmother of modern rosomaniacs", which is rather wonderful.'

Julian laughed. 'And are you a rosomaniac?'

'Probably,' she said.

'You know, I had no idea that roses had such an interesting history,' he said.

'They're the most fascinating flower,' she said.

'But what if you didn't like roses?'

'Not like roses?' Celeste said with a frown. 'What do you mean?'

'I mean, what if you'd rebelled against your family? What if you'd wanted to do something else in life that didn't involve roses?'

'I don't think we could have,' she said. 'Roses are in our blood. We grew up surrounded by them, seeing them and smelling them, learning their names and breeding new ones. Some of our roses were like members of our family.' She looked wistful. 'I did try to rebel a few years ago. I got married and moved away. It was kind of a relief to leave the roses for a while. I loved them dearly but they were suffocating me and I felt I had to get away. So I took a job in my husband's company but, well, things didn't work out.'

For a moment, she thought about the Celeste she had briefly been, away from Hamilton Roses. It had been a whole new her and she couldn't help wondering if she could expect another change of job in the future. She still felt so uncertain about her role within the rose business.

Suddenly, she was aware of Julian's eyes upon her and she felt as if she'd said too much. She picked up speed and led him down the path towards a rose bed filled with glorious pink blooms.

'*The Queen of Summer*,' she said a moment later, and she couldn't hide her smile as she bent to inhale its sweet scent. 'She's our bestseller.'

'How lovely she is,' Julian said, bending down and sticking his nose in the centre of a bloom. 'Oh!' he exclaimed a moment later. 'The scent's so strong!'

Celeste couldn't help but laugh at his reaction. 'I should have warned you that you don't need to get *quite* so close to appreciate it.'

'I feel quite drunk!' he said, his eyes wide with surprise.

'Try this one,' Celeste said, moving him on towards another pink rose. This one was a deeper pink than the first and, when Julian bent to inhale, it didn't hit his senses quite as violently as the first rose.

'It's almost' – he paused, looking for the right word – 'sherbetty.'

Celeste smiled and nodded. '*Pink Promise*,' she said. 'One of my grandmother's creations.'

Julian stood back up to full height. Or rather, he tried, but the back of his waistcoat caught on a thorn. 'I – erm – seem to be stuck,' he said.

'Here,' Celeste said, taking a step forward, 'let me. That's the one negative with *Pink Promise*, I'm afraid. Its thorns are particularly vicious.'

'That's the price one pays with roses,' Julian said.

'Not *all* roses,' Celeste was quick to defend. 'There,' she said a moment later. '*Pink Promise* has released you.'

'Thank you,' he said.

'Well, I guess you don't want to spend your whole weekend caught in a rose bush,' Celeste said, giving a little shrug of her shoulders that clearly announced that the tour was over.

'Right,' Julian said, looking just a little lost. But, before he could say anything more, Celeste was on the move again, retracing their steps down the path towards the front of the house where his car was waiting.

'Thank you for coming,' Celeste said, daring to hold out her hand to be shaken.

Julian smiled. 'It's warm today,' he said.

Celeste cleared her throat and pulled her hand away from his. 'Come on, Frinton,' she said, and the little dog, who'd spent his entire time shadowing his new friend, reluctantly left Julian's side and returned to his mistress. 'Goodbye,' she said, turning to walk back into the house.

As she entered the hallway, she suddenly felt breathless. She stood in the middle of the floor, listening to the sound of the long-case clock ticking as she desperately tried to calm herself down. The strangest feeling had come over her in the garden as they'd turned back to walk towards the house. It was a view of the manor she was so familiar with but, being there with Julian, it had been as if she was seeing it for the first time: the old romantic house with its turrets and its casement windows, the beautiful moat and the serenity of the garden. She had seen it through the eyes of a stranger and a certainty had overcome her: she didn't hate the house at all. Yes, it held all manner of negative memories for her but there was room in her heart for another emotion too. An emotion she had been trying to ignore.

Love.

11.

Gertie sat in front of her dressing table mirror. She didn't often wear make-up but she'd applied the lightest of foundations and was now working some magic with a mascara brush. The lip gloss would have to wait because she didn't want to draw too much attention to herself before leaving the house. Also, she was grinning so much that she didn't trust herself to apply it properly.

She still couldn't believe it – two whole days and nights with James. They'd really get a chance to be together without looking at their watches or worrying that they might be spotted together, and goodness only knew that he needed some time away from Samantha. He'd been so stressed recently and she knew that some time out – some time out with her – would do him no end of good. It would also be a good time to talk about their future together, she thought, and make some serious plans about what they were going to do.

Gertie sighed with contentment and gave herself a little spray of the Penhaligon Gardenia which James had bought her, the summery fragrance making her smile as she awaited the warmth of the heart notes that included rose as well as gardenia.

As she brushed her hair, she thought of the time when she'd first met James. He and Samantha had moved to Little Eleigh two years ago. It had been after Samantha's riding accident and they'd bought the barn conversion on the edge of the village and had had it adapted to suit Samantha's needs. She'd seen him around when she'd driven by but it wasn't until the village show last summer that they'd actually spoken. Gertie had entered some of the home baking categories and he'd been standing by the table as she'd placed her Victoria sandwich down with consummate attention just before the doors were closed for the judges.

'You've done this before, haven't you?' he said.

'Once or twice,' she said.

'And won?'

'Once or twice,' she said. 'Are you entering?'

He laughed. 'Home baking? You must be joking. But I have a little something in the garden produce.'

'Oh?'

He nodded to the cucumbers. 'Second on the left.'

Gertie gasped. 'That's a pretty impressive cucumber!' she said. They caught one another's eyes and simultaneously burst into a fit of uncontrollable laughter. One of the judges had had to ask them to leave.

'I'm James,' he said as they left the hall together.

'Gertie.'

He'd shaken her hand and held it a moment longer than he really needed to, and their eyes had locked. Right then, Gertie had known that she was lost even though she knew he was a married man and even though she knew his wife was an invalid.

It sounded awful when you thought about it and she knew exactly how it would look to her sisters and the inhabitants of Little Eleigh if her affair ever became known. But nobody really knew the truth about James and Samantha. He'd told her bits and pieces about their past together and she knew how deeply unhappy he'd been before Samantha's accident.

'We were going to separate,' he'd told Gertie. 'We hadn't said as much in words but it was understood, and then that accident happened and neither of us broached the subject again. We've just been living this awful half-life where we can't stand each other's company but don't know how to escape. And then you came along and life was good again.'

Gertie smiled as she remembered his words and how much they'd meant to her during her mother's illness.

'I hadn't smiled or laughed in months, *years!*' he'd told her. 'But you made me remember that there was goodness and joy in the world and silly jokes about cucumbers.'

James had been such a comfort to Gertie whilst Penelope had been ill. He understood what it was like to be responsible for somebody who was sick and he made sure that Gertie never forgot how to smile even during the bleakest of times. He'd been so kind and sweet to her and she'd never forget that.

Gertie got up from her place at the dressing table. She'd packed a tiny overnight bag which she'd have to sneak out of the house without her sisters seeing. Her plan was to ring Evie later that evening and say that she'd met up with an old friend and was staying the night with her. How she'd explain the second night away was less straightforward.

She walked down the stairs and, sure enough, Evie was in the living room as if waiting to pounce on her.

'I'm off, then,' Gertie called through casually.

'Back late?' Evie called back.

'Very late, I imagine.'

'Have a nice time. I hope it all works out.'

'I hope so too,' Gertie said with a little smile before leaving on her secret assignation.

∽

After Gertrude had left, Evie walked through to the study where she guessed Celeste would be found. She wasn't looking forward to seeing her sister, she admitted to herself, because she knew that Celeste would have handed their family's beloved paintings over by now, and for that she could never forgive her.

She tapped politely on the door before letting herself in.

'You still working?' she asked, walking over to where Frinton was sitting and rubbing the soft spot behind his right ear.

'No, not really,' Celeste said. 'I can't concentrate.'

'I see he's taken the paintings,' Evie said, nodding towards the bare wall where the rose paintings used to hang and swallowing a hard lump in her throat. Six perfect rectangles of bright flock wallpaper, previously protected from the sun's fading rays, now drew the eye instead of the artworks.

'Yes,' Celeste said. 'He said we could change our minds whenever we wanted to.'

'Did he?'

'Yes.'

'But you won't, will you?' Evie said.

Celeste shook her head. 'We can't afford to. You know that, don't you?'

Evie looked down into Frinton's furry face.

'Evie?'

'*Yes!*' she blurted. 'I know that,' she added in a gentler voice.

Celeste sighed. 'You're not the only one who's going to miss those paintings, Evie. I am too, you know.'

'Are you?'

'Of course I am,' she said. 'Why do you keep making me out to be the bad guy here? I don't *want* to sell them. It wasn't on the top of my list of things I really want to do today but they could make us hundreds of thousands of pounds.'

Evie took this piece of news in her stride.

'Yes, well, the room looks horrible now,' she said, looking up from the floor.

'I know,' Celeste agreed. 'I feel like I've robbed it and that I should apologise or something.'

'And Mum would have hated selling them too,' Evie said.

'You don't know that, Evie.'

'Oh, and *you* do?'

'I just think –'

'After being away so long, you suddenly know what Mum would've thought, do you?'

'I'm not saying that,' Celeste said, trying desperately not to raise her voice and so escalate the argument. 'I actually think Mum would have been able to make the right decision for the house, just as we're going to do now.' She watched as Evie seemed to calm down a little.

'As long as all this saves the house,' Evie said, and she watched as Celeste bit her lip.

'It might not be enough to do that, I'm afraid,' Celeste said.

Evie stood back up to full height. 'Well, it had better be,' she said, 'because I'm not even going to discuss the alternative.' And she left the room before her sister could say any more.

12.

Gertie drove the little white van over the border in to Cambridgeshire. James had texted her the name of the village where she could park and he could pick her up, and his silver BMW was there waiting when she pulled up. She grabbed the little overnight bag she'd managed to sneak out of the house and locked the van.

'I feel like a spy or something,' she said a moment later as she opened the car door and got in beside James.

'As long as nobody spies *us*,' James said, giving her one of his heart-melting smiles and leaning forward to kiss her.

'We've crossed into a whole other county now,' Gertie said. 'We should be safe, shouldn't we? Or should I put a baseball cap and sunglasses on?' She was joking but something inside her couldn't help shrivelling up with shame because, no matter how many times she justified what she was doing, she was still having an affair with a married man.

'Don't cover yourself up,' James told her. 'You look so pretty.'

Gertie beamed with happiness.

'You know, I wasn't sure if you'd come,' he continued.

'Why would you think that?' she asked.

He shrugged. 'I thought you might not want to leave those roses of yours after all.'

She laughed. 'You're far more important to me than my roses!' she said. 'You're my *future*!'

He gave her a brief smile.

'And I have this really strong feeling that we're going to be together one day really soon – together *properly*. Don't you?'

He turned to look at her. 'Of course I do,' he said, and Gertie sighed with pleasure as they set off.

The landscape of the Fens stretched out for miles in every direction, flat and featureless. It was so very different from the gently rolling hills of the Stour Valley yet, in its way, it possessed a sort of bleak beauty, drawing the attention upwards to the enormous sky and the patterns of the clouds. The sky that evening was beautiful, with slashes of lavender and streaks of apricot as the sun slowly set.

They drove through a little village and then turned left along a tree-lined driveway. The hotel was a large Georgian manor house with enormous sash windows and topiary guarding what looked like an impressive garden.

'James, it's gorgeous!' Gertie said, finding it impossible to hide her excitement and play it cool as she'd told herself she would.

'I wanted to treat you,' he said, taking her hand and kissing it.

She flashed a smile at him.

After parking the car, James ushered Gertie across a lawn that led down to a beautiful stretch of river.

'This is really special,' Gertie said, looking across at the immaculate lawn and the impressive view back to the hotel. 'I feel thoroughly spoilt.'

'Good,' he said, enveloping her in a warm embrace. 'You smell so good.'

'It's the perfume you bought me.'

'No, it isn't,' he said.

'No?' She looked up at him.

'It's you! Essence of Gertrude. There's nothing quite like it in the world.'

She laughed. 'So what exactly makes up this "Essence of Gertrude"?'

James looked thoughtful for a moment. 'It's an indescribable blend.'

'Oh,' Gertie said, unable to hide her disappointment. 'I'd rather you'd been able to describe it to me.'

'Okay then,' he said. 'Let me see. It's like all the good things in the world, like sunshine and laughter.'

'You can't smell sunshine and laughter!' she cried, play-punching him in the ribs.

'Hey!' he said. 'This is *my* description, right?'

'All right,' she said. 'Go on.' She was absolutely loving being the sole centre of his attention.

'Well, we've covered the sunshine and laughter bit.'

'Yes. What else?'

'There's the gardenia perfume, obviously, and the roses. A little bit of the Suffolk countryside with willow trees and barley fields and moats and –'

'I do *not* want to smell like our moat!' Gertie protested.

'I'm not talking about the smell *exactly*,' he said, 'but more of a feeling. Do you know what I mean? These are the things I imagine when I'm thinking about you.'

She grinned up at him. 'What an old romantic you are.'

'Only around you,' he said and they kissed.

They walked back to the hotel and got their bags from the car. When they approached the reception desk, a young woman greeted them with a restrained smile.

'Mr Stanton,' James announced.

The receptionist's long nails tip-tapped on the computer keyboard and she nodded.

'Room eighteen – on the first floor,' she said.

Gertie breathed a sigh of relief that it was all so easy and unembarrassing and that James hadn't announced to the world that she was Mrs Stanton. Or that they were Mr and Mrs Smith.

James took hold of their bags and they walked up a grand staircase lined with fine portraits and studies of spaniels and pheasants.

'I've so been looking forward to this,' he said as soon as the bedroom door was closed. 'God, I've missed you.'

Gertie moved towards him and they embraced. 'I've missed you too,' she said.

'It's been a hell of a week,' he told her, kissing the tip of her nose.

'Samantha?'

He nodded. 'She's been so difficult.'

Gertie looked at him full of sympathy. She knew how awkward Samantha could be. She was like a particularly tenacious climbing rose that makes its mind up on one particular route and cannot be persuaded to take any other. She knew how difficult she made James's life and how helpless he was to do anything about it because who could possibly walk out on a woman in a wheelchair?

He sighed and Gertie saw how tense and tired he looked.

'Here,' she said, taking his jacket off. 'Let me ease some of that tension away.' She began to massage his shoulders.

'That's good,' he said.

'Yeah?'

'Oh, yeah,' he said, turning around a moment later. 'How wonderful you are.'

Gertie smiled and they gazed at one another.

'Have you spoken to Samantha?' Gertie dared to ask him at last.

James gave a weary sigh. 'Do we have to talk about that now? I just want to shut it all out and be here with you.'

Gertie swallowed hard as she looked at him. She was desperate to be with James and he had promised that they would be together one day, but it was impossible to know when that day would be because he never talked about it.

'Samantha has to let you go,' she told him, gently stroking his face. 'She can't keep you a prisoner when you're so unhappy. It isn't right. She can't expect that when she makes life so hard for you.'

'Shush,' he said, kissing the palm of her hand. 'I'm banishing her name from this room, okay? For the whole time we're together. I'm with *you* now and that's all that matters.'

He leaned forward and Gertie allowed herself to be kissed. It was wonderful, of course, but she couldn't help wishing that that was really all that mattered to her.

෬

It seemed quiet in the house without Gertie, Celeste thought. The longcase clock had just struck nine and Gertie had rung to explain that she'd met an old friend in Cambridge and that she wouldn't be coming home.

'Which just leaves me and Evie,' Celeste said to herself. She didn't relish the thought. Evie was being decidedly prickly around her. Celeste couldn't say a single thing to her without upsetting her in some way so she'd decided to give her little sister as wide a berth as possible. She carried a cup of tea into the living room, Frinton trotting at her heels.

It was as Frinton was settling down on a rug that Celeste noticed something on the coffee table and recognised it instantly. It was an old photograph album and Celeste was quite sure it hadn't been there that morning. Had Evie been looking through it, she wondered?

She picked it up and sat down on a sofa next to the enormous fireplace. A photograph album was a rare thing these days, she thought. A real physical one, at least, and not a virtual one you had to click on and which you wouldn't be able to access if there was a power cut or if your internet connection wasn't working. How lovely it was to sit and flip through the pages, staring at the images from the past.

The album was of black leather and was home to hundreds of black and white photographs which Celeste hadn't seen for years. There was Grandpa Arthur looking so young and handsome in the wilderness of the walled garden before he'd kicked things into shape. And there was Grandma Esme, her long dark hair, which all the Hamilton women had inherited, falling about her shoulders in glossy waves as she leaned against one of the towers, a huge smile on her face. They must just have moved in, Celeste thought, wondering what that must have been like after their modest terrace house in the north. Just imagine buying a medieval moated manor house. It had been such a crazy thing to do.

'A wonderful crazy thing,' Celeste said, causing Frinton to raise his head and look at her for a moment.

She'd forgotten how young her grandparents had been when they'd bought the manor. Esme looked to be no older than Celeste was now and they'd already got two children at that time: Celeste's Uncle Portland and Aunt Leda. What an adventure it must have been, but a real struggle too, making the old house liveable whilst restoring the garden, starting up the rose business and raising a young family too. It made Celeste realise that the battle they were facing now was nothing out of the ordinary in the history of the house. Each generation had to fight to keep everything together.

She continued flipping through the pages, delighting in seeing photos of her grandparents working in the garden, the young Portland and Leda dancing around their feet.

'They really loved this place,' a voice said from the door.

Celeste jumped and saw Evie standing there watching her.

'Did you leave this out for me?' Celeste asked.

Evie didn't answer the question but walked into the room and sat on the sofa next to Celeste. 'Look at these ones,' she said, taking the album from her and turning the pages. 'That's the first photo of Mum.'

Celeste looked at the picture, barely recognising the tiny infant sitting up in a big old-fashioned pram in the garden with the gate-house turrets towering behind her.

Evie pointed to another photo of the four Hamilton children, Portland, Leda, Louise and Penelope, all holding hands and looking into the moat, their little figures reflected in the water.

'Oh, that's lovely!' Celeste said. 'We should frame it.'

'I know,' Evie said. 'Three generations have lived here now. Isn't that amazing?'

'Yes,' Celeste said simply. 'It is.'

'And it could be four if we keep this place going long enough,' Evie said.

'Evie –' Celeste said in warning.

Evie raised her hands in the air. 'Don't say anything! Just think about it, okay?'

Celeste wasn't in the mood to fight with her sister that evening and so she nodded. 'Okay.'

They sat quietly together, turning the pages of the album over and looking at the photographs.

'That's the last one of Mum,' Evie said when they reached the end of the book. 'Gertie wanted it in the album. She took it just before Mum stopped her chemotherapy. We'd gone for a walk around the garden and the light was so beautiful. It was the last time Mum went outside. She looked really well, didn't she?'

'She did,' Celeste agreed, looking at her mother's pale but still astonishingly beautiful face.

'She went downhill pretty rapidly after that,' Evie said. 'We'd bring her flowers from the garden but nothing made her smile. She became moody – more so than usual – and would shout at us no matter what we did for her. She must have been in so much pain at the end.' Evie's eyes filled with tears.

'Oh, Evie,' Celeste said, putting an arm around her shoulder.

'You should have been here, Celeste,' she cried. 'I *hate* that you weren't here to help us!'

'I wish I could have been.'

'No, you don't!' Evie said. 'Don't lie to me.'

'Evie, listen to me –'

'We were so tired, Gertie and me. It wasn't fair of you not to help. Mum was' – she paused, her tears spilling down her cheeks, – 'difficult. Really difficult. We needed you here, Celeste. Where were you?'

Celeste bit her lip, not knowing what to say. Evie shrugged her arm away and got up from the sofa.

'I need some air,' she announced, whipping the tears away with an angry hand. 'Can I take Frinton out?'

'Sure,' Celeste said and watched as Evie motioned to Frinton and the two of them left the house together.

༄

Evie walked around the gardens until she felt quite sure Frinton's paws must be on the point of wearing out. He took some tiring, that dog, but it had been good to get out in the air after the scene with Celeste and to watch the garden slowly fading into dusk as her heart rate returned to normal. Rose gardens were often at their best in the evenings because the perfume from the flowers was so strong and scented the air with intoxicating power. Evie liked to test herself as she walked, trying to pick out the individual roses.

There was the deep, rich scent of *Madame Isaac Pereire* and the fruity muskiness of *Penelope* – the rose their mother was named after – and dancing softly through the air were the honeyed notes of their very own *Moonglow*.

The white roses were particularly glorious as night drew in, their luminous beauty still visible long after the sun had set, painting the garden in ghostlike swathes. There was the Hamilton rose, *Eden*, with its incurved petals; the classic climber, *Iceberg*, which tumbled over the pergola in a white waterfall; and the stunningly beautiful damask rose, *Madame Hardy*, with its double-bloom flowers and its bright, citrusy scent.

Evie stopped and admired each and every one of them, dipping her nose deep into the soft, cool petals. Moments like this weren't to be rushed even if there was a mad fox terrier barking his little head off for some attention on the other side of the border, and even if her heart was still racing after her latest conversation with Celeste.

Sometimes, inhaling the perfume of a rose was like losing yourself to another world. All the other senses seemed to switch off as scent took over, seemingly entering the bloodstream until the whole of your being was intoxicated – and that was just the very thing she needed at the moment.

'Hush, Frinton!' Evie said as her nose dived into a fully blown *Alba Maxima* – one of her favourite roses and one of the oldest. 'The Jacobite Rose,' she said to herself, knowing that the rose had existed in classical times.

Frinton's barking continued.

'Honestly,' Evie said, 'dogs have no souls! No passion for what is beautiful!' She shook her head in despair but couldn't help smiling as she saw that Frinton had found a stick and was shaking it from side to side as if it was his mortal enemy. 'Come on!' she said, and the two of them headed across the lawn at the back of the manor which sloped towards the river.

The fields beyond were slowly being enveloped by darkness and a startled pheasant ran out from its cover on the other side. Frinton dropped the stick and looked on after the bird, wondering if it would be worth leaping down the bank and swimming across the river in pursuit of it. He decided not and, instead, stuffed his square nose into a clump of grass that smelled decidedly rabbity.

'You love this place too, don't you, Frinton?' she said to the little dog. 'You don't want to leave here, do you? Well, we've got to persuade your mistress that she loves it too, haven't we?'

The little terrier went on sniffing amongst the grasses and Evie took a deep fortifying breath. After the long winter months and the cold East Anglian winds, it was wonderful to walk around the garden so late in the evening and to feel the warmth of the air on her skin. It was evenings like this that got her through the short, dark days of winter; this had been a particularly arduous one, reaching its icy fingers long into April. It was why rosarians worked long into the evenings in the summer, luxuriating in their special time of year – those precious few months when the roses were at their brightest and freshest.

Evie picked up Frinton's slobbery stick and threw it for him along the river bank, watching as he tore after it, a flash of white curly fur in the lengthening shadows. It was then that her phone beeped from the depths of her pocket. She gasped when she saw who it was from.

'Lukas,' she whispered.

He'd spent a month working with them during March when the pruning was done. He was an art student working his way around the UK and had wanted to see the county that had inspired Constable and Gainsborough – only he'd been far more interested in Evie's contours than those of the gently undulating Suffolk landscape. It had been hard to resist him, too, because he'd been so handsome with his butter-blond hair and piercingly green eyes but Evie hadn't wanted to get into any sort of relationship at the time. For one thing, her mother's health had been declining rapidly and she'd needed round-the-clock care. Evie had been constantly exhausted and a relationship was the very last thing on her mind. A fling had been good but she'd been happy and rather relieved to say her goodbyes to Lukas, vaguely promising him that she'd keep in touch.

'Oh, dear,' she sighed as she read his brief but passion-filled message. She'd hoped he'd forgotten all about her by now but it was quite clear that he hadn't.

13.

It was the next morning and Celeste was taking a rare break from working in the study with a walk around the garden. The early morning mist that had rolled across the fields of the Stour Valley had been vanquished by the sun and the rose garden looked perfect.

'I've *got* to spend more time out here,' she told herself, knowing that it wasn't possible, of course, and that she never would.

As she rounded the corner to where a bed of their famous *Queen of Summer* roses bloomed, she saw the spot by the moat, from the photograph in the album, where her mother had stood with her brother and sisters, all hand in hand. It had been such a sweet image and Celeste felt tears pricking her eyes as she remembered it. Then she remembered what Evie had said about a fourth generation living at Little Eleigh Manor and her sister's words stabbed her in the heart because she sincerely believed that that was never going to happen.

She was just about to return inside when she saw a man walking down the path towards her.

'Julian?' she said.

'Celeste!' he cried. 'I tried the house and Evie said she thought I'd find you out here.'

'Did you forget something?' she asked, surprised to see him there at all.

'In a way,' he said as he reached her. 'I meant to ask you something.'

'What?'

'How would you feel about a private sale? I'm thinking about the Fantin-Latour in particular. We have quite a few good clients on our books and we could put out a few feelers if you like.'

'That would be kind. Thank you,' she said. 'But you should have just rung us.'

He shrugged. 'It was no bother calling by,' he said. 'I don't head back to London until tonight and it's always a pleasure to come here. It's such a lovely spot.'

'Well, thank you,' Celeste said again, waiting for him to leave, but he didn't. Instead, she watched as he shielded his eyes from the sun and looked around the garden and then began to walk down the path alongside the moat.

'Isn't it a perfect day?' he said, rolling his sleeves up and revealing surprisingly tanned arms. 'It's on days like this that I wish I lived in the country all the time.'

'You want to leave the city?' she asked, the question out of her mouth before she had time to check it.

'God, yes!' he said with a sigh. 'I mean, don't get me wrong – I love my job. I can't think what else I would have done for all these years, but there's something in me that wants something more now. It's not *just* all about working anymore. I've got this great flat with a balcony but the thing is, I can only see other flats from it. There isn't even a single tree in sight. It's just all bricks and pavement.'

'I don't think I could live like that,' Celeste said.

'No,' Julian said, 'and I'm beginning to think that *I* can't for much longer.'

She took a sideways glance at him, seeing him as a human being for the first time rather than the man who was there to sell their paintings for them.

'So, you'd like a garden?' she asked as their feet crunched along the gravel pathway between a neat knot garden filled with deep red roses.

'Well, not one on this scale,' he said. 'In fact, the one at Myrtle Cottage would do me. It's quite small but there's a nice lawn, some flower beds and an area for a table and chairs. It's glorious at this time of year. I just wish I could live there permanently.' He stopped talking and smiled at the sight that greeted him as they rounded a corner. 'Wow,' he said. 'I've never seen *any*thing like this in my life. You didn't show this part of the garden to me last time, did you?'

'Er, no,' Celeste said, feeling slightly ashamed that he'd found her out. 'I was a bit busy.'

'It's extraordinary.' His face took on the stunned expression that Celeste was used to seeing in people who viewed the rose garden for the first time, and her heart leapt along with his own: it really was a glorious sight and it never failed to make her spirits soar.

There were roses everywhere. Roses creeping over banks, spilling out of containers, climbing up walls and scrambling up trees. There were arches, trellises, obelisks and tree stumps – anything and everything was designed with roses in mind. The whole garden was a playground for them, and they came in all colours, from the purest white through to the creamiest yellows, the most romantic of pinks and the deepest reds.

Julian's eyes were wide and full of wonder as he tried to take it all in. 'This one's just like one of the roses in the Fantin-Latour painting,' he said.

'Yes, we've always thought so too but we can't be sure,' Celeste said, softening towards this man a little; his enthusiasm for roses seemed so genuine, and there was something else about him too. His openness. Yes, she liked that.

She looked into the crowded petals of the rose frou-frouing into the air like an upside-down ball gown, and then she remembered something. 'Where are the paintings now?' she asked.

'Back at my cottage in Nayland,' he told her.

'And they're safe there?'

'Of course,' he said. 'Everything is insured. You don't need to worry.'

'I'm afraid I'm one of life's natural worriers,' she said, 'and the paintings are still ours until we sell them.'

'Yes,' he said, 'but they're perfectly safe. Please don't worry about them. You've got more than enough to take care of so please let me take care of the paintings for you. It's the very least I can do for you.'

They walked through an arch which was smothered in large salmon-pink roses.

'*Albertine*,' Celeste said.

'Pardon?'

'The rose,' she said, waving a hand towards the blooms.

'Of course,' he said. 'Lovely. They look like one of the roses at Myrtle Cottage.'

'You have an *Albertine*?'

'Well, I can't be sure,' he said. 'I'm not very good with identification.'

They walked on, passing a huge border stuffed with blooms.

'And these are?' Julian asked, bending down to take a fat purple flower in his hand.

'Geraniums,' Celeste said.

'Beautiful.'

'They make a good companion plant for roses.'

'Ah,' he said. 'So they're of no value in themselves? They're simply to set the roses off?'

'Pretty much,' Celeste said. 'It's all about the roses here.'

'So the other flowers are like a frame on a painting?'

She smiled. 'That's a very good way of looking at it. Roses are the most beautiful flower in the world, of course –'

'Of course,' he said, mirroring her smile.

'But it's possible to highlight their beauty by carefully planting around them with light, airy flowers in complementary colours – like deep purple geraniums and clematis mingling with rich pink roses. That's a favourite combination of mine. Lavender, too, and catmint and *verbena bonariensis.*'

Julian nodded as if he was beginning to understand.

'Now, let me show you some of our very old roses if you're really interested,' she said, charging ahead of him across the lawn towards another border, one of her favourite parts of the garden. It was a special place for Celeste because her grandfather had led her there by the hand on countless occasions and taught her about some of the world's oldest roses. How she had adored listening to him, hearing the romantic names and the stories associated with them.

'These roses date back to medieval times,' she told Julian now, the spirit of her grandfather deep within her. 'The red is *Rosa Gallica Officinalis*, also known as the *Apothecary's Rose*, and it's believed to be the red rose of the House of Lancaster.'

'Ah! The War of the Roses,' Julian said, at last recognising something.

'We like to plant it with the striped *Rosa Mundi* here,' she said. 'Another lovely old Gallica rose and a sport of the red one.'

'A sport?'

'A child if you like,' she explained. 'And these are the Victorian roses – the Bourbons are amongst the most beautiful. They have gorgeous double blooms and deep rich colours and the most heavenly of scents. No garden should be without at least half a dozen Bourbons.'

Julian bent down and sniffed. 'Delicious,' he said. 'I must buy some from you for Myrtle Cottage.'

'Gertie would be thrilled to help you choose.'

They walked down another path and under an arch, the scent of roses seeming to saturate the air.

Julian shook his head. 'I think I'm beginning to see the magic in roses now.'

'They do get a hold of you,' she said. 'There's a story about a rose grower called Joseph Pemberton who was obsessed with roses from a young age. He went to boarding school and took a bloom of *Souvenir de la Malmaison* with him in a barley sugar tin. It disintegrated, of course, but its scent would remain until the Christmas holidays.'

Julian smiled. 'And did you ever do anything like that?'

Celeste nodded. 'I've got a collection of pressed roses in an old book somewhere but it always seemed so sad to flatten them so I gave up and just tried to remember them instead. I suppose that's why Grandpa Arthur bought so many lovely rose paintings. The winters can seem so long and lonely without the company of roses and I really miss the long, light summer days of being in the garden too. Nothing gives me as much peace as roses.' She smiled lightly. 'I can be in the foulest of moods but a walk around the garden and a glance at a rose can dispel all sorts of horrors.' She looked wistful for a moment and then added, 'To sit in a walled garden on a sunny day is to be in heaven.'

They paused by a scarlet rose bush.

'What's this one?' Julian asked.

'That's a hybrid tea. They're the most popular roses now,' Celeste told him, 'but I prefer the old roses. They do have a lovely centre, though, don't they?'

They were walking back towards the house when Julian stopped and commented. 'The manor certainly is huge,' he said.

Celeste nodded. 'I often wonder what it would have been like to have grown up in a modern house – just an average little terrace somewhere with central heating and double-glazing. It would definitely have taken the pressure off everyone and we wouldn't constantly be stressed out and yelling at each other.'

'But – other than the money worries – you all get along?'

'Oh, yes,' Celeste said.

'I was best friends with my father,' Julian said. 'He was sweet and gentle but totally driven by his work. He always gave every-thing a hundred percent. He didn't know any other percentage.'

Celeste smiled at this.

'He was passionate about art and so we always had some common ground – always something to talk about. But he could never relax. He was always working. He never switched off. There was always some painting to chase or some way of improving business. Nobody was surprised when his second heart attack took him.' Julian sighed. 'I miss him. I miss hearing his voice. And I know I'm just a shadow of the man he was.' He stopped talking and looked momentarily baffled. 'Sorry,' he said.

'For what?'

'For rambling on so much.'

'But you're not,' she said. 'Anyway, it's all so interesting.'

'Really?' he said, a tiny smile on his face.

Celeste smiled back and he seemed to relax more. 'And you're happy in your work?' she said, encouraging him to continue.

'I am,' he said, 'but I do have this dream of opening up an antiques centre one day. You know – leaving London and setting up a business here in Suffolk.' His face took on a reflective quality.

'And giving up the auction house?'

'More like handing it over to somebody else. I'd still manage things but take more of a back seat,' he said.

'Well, Suffolk is full of antique centres,' Celeste said. 'Are you sure you'll make a living?'

He smiled. 'If I could do what I truly loved, I'd be happy just to get by.'

She nodded. 'I feel the same way about our roses. None of us have ambitions to become millionaires but we do want to be the very best that we can. Oh, and keep a roof over our heads.'

Julian held her gaze for a moment. 'Excuse me if this sounds rude, but have you ever thought of selling the manor and buying a smaller place?'

Celeste turned away from him for a moment. 'We've actually been discussing that,' she confided. 'But it's not going very well.

I know it seems that it's doing nothing but sucking all our money whilst falling down around us but my sisters really love it. It's hard to imagine Hamilton Roses being based anywhere else but we might have to rethink things – and soon, too, because I just can't see how we can go on living here.'

'It is a very special place,' he said.

Celeste nodded. 'Our grandparents poured their hearts and souls into it.'

'And your parents felt the same way?'

Celeste's took a deep breath. 'I don't think our dad ever really had that connection to the manor because it wasn't his family home. He sort of endured it for Mum and spent as much time away from it as he could. His work took him to London a lot and, when they divorced, he couldn't get away fast enough. I don't think he was ever really a part of this place or the rose business and, when he left, Mum made sure our names were changed to her family name, Hamilton. Dad never forgave her for that. She said it was just good business sense but I think there was more to it than that.'

'And he's in London now?'

Celeste smiled. 'Funnily enough, he isn't. He ended up buying the sweetest little cottage near Clare and lives there with his new wife, Simone.'

They continued walking along the bank of the moat towards the gatehouse.

'So,' he said, 'how are you coping with everything?'

Celeste gave a little shrug and Julian nodded knowingly.

'When my mother died,' he began, 'it was as if everything had been turned upside down. None of us seemed to know what to do for the longest time. It was the worst kind of pain. Nothing can prepare you for it and there's no right or wrong way to deal with it either. Everyone's different. So don't worry if it takes time to deal with everything. It's normal.'

'Thank you,' she said in a tiny voice. That was what people said if somebody expressed sympathy, wasn't it?

'You were close?' he asked and Celeste's eyes snapped wide open at the question. 'Sorry,' he added hurriedly. 'I didn't mean to pry.'

She took a deep breath. She'd spent a whole lifetime wondering how to answer that question. Whenever people asked her about her mother, she always felt completely lost. What was she meant to say? That her mother made her feel like she had no worth at all? That she belittled her, mocked her and called her names? Was that the normal behaviour of a mother? Celeste had had enough friends growing up to know that it wasn't. She'd visited their homes and seen that mothers could be kind and loving; they could be fun and open. They could be *real* people. And that was the problem for Celeste. Her mother had never felt real. There'd been nothing genuine about her, which was a puzzling and disturbing thing for a daughter to realise, but there it was. And how exactly was she meant to explain that to this man? It would be easier not to, she decided.

'It was very kind of you to call,' she said as they reached his car. 'Keep me updated about the paintings, won't you?'

'Yes, of course,' he said, pausing for a moment. 'Celeste?'

She'd turned to go but looked back at him. 'Yes?'

'If you want to talk about this – any of this – I'm a pretty good listener. It doesn't have to be just about the paintings. Anything you want to talk about.' He gave her a smile and a little wave before getting into his car and leaving her standing there feeling completely baffled.

14.

Gertie drove the company van through the lanes of the Stour Valley back towards Little Eleigh, passing the church with the leaning wall before descending the hill and crossing the river. She felt as if she'd been away for an age – certainly longer than two nights.

Turning down the tree-lined lane to the manor, she looked at her watch. It was a little after one o'clock on Monday. They'd left it as long as possible before saying goodbye but James had said he couldn't delay it any longer.

'Can't we have lunch together?' Gertie had asked him.

'I wish we could,' he'd said, kissing the tip of her nose, 'but I've really got to get back. Samantha –'

'I know,' Gertie had said with a sigh. 'She doesn't realise how lucky she is to have you all the time.'

James had laughed. 'She doesn't see that,' he'd said. 'I often think she resents me being there.'

'How can she resent you being there in your own home when you do so much for her?' Gertie had stroked her fingers through his fair hair.

'Because she's not as kind-hearted as you are,' he'd told her. 'I've never met anyone as sweet and caring as you are, Gertie.'

'Then be with me,' she'd said. '*All* the time.'

'I will,' he'd said, 'and soon.'

'You know, our little dream of moving abroad might be a lot closer than you think,' she'd told him.

'Really?' He'd sounded surprised. 'What makes you say that?'

'Oh, just something I've been working on,' she'd said. She hadn't wanted to divulge too much about the idea of selling the manor just yet in case it all fell through, but she'd needed to be able to feel as if things were moving forward with James. 'I can't stop thinking about it all. I get so excited when I imagine our future together!'

'Me too,' he'd said. 'Tell me about that little villa of yours again.'

She'd laughed. 'Well, it's set high up in the hills above a pretty village and it has blue shutters and vines clambering up around it. The soil in the garden is perfect for roses.'

'Of course!'

'Of course! And we'll grow all our own fruit and vegetables and eat outside on the terrace before going up to bed each night.'

'Just the two of us.'

'Yes.'

'That,' he'd said, kissing her sweetly, 'makes me so crazy for you!'

Driving through the gates now and crossing the moat, she tried to relive the moments she'd shared with James.

'I don't want to go home,' she'd told him that morning as they'd left the hotel with their overnight bags. 'Can't we stay here forever?'

'I wish we could,' he'd said. 'Maybe we can do this again sometime.'

'Sometime *soon*,' she'd said. But when? He hadn't committed to anything and she knew it would probably be next week before she could see him again.

She parked the van and got out. There was a part of her that felt mortified that she was seeing a married man. She was a romantic at heart and her idealised view of falling in love hadn't ever factored in a married man. But life was messy and unpredictable. It didn't conform to romantic notions and she had to accept that. James might be married but the marriage was over – he'd told her that a thousand times. She just had to be patient and wait for the right moment.

'And then we can be together,' she told herself, taking a deep breath before going inside, knowing that if she agreed to sell the manor then her dream would be closer than ever before.

It was lunch time. Gertie could hear her sisters' voices from the kitchen downstairs, and the welcoming barks of Frinton soon alerted them to her arrival.

'Gertie!' Evie said, rushing to greet her as she walked into the room a moment later. 'How was Cambridge?'

'Good,' Gertie said, bending down to pat Frinton's head as he bounced on the spot in an attempt to get closer to her.

'Yeah?' Evie said. 'So, did you do a deal?'

Gertie shook her head and walked across to one of the kitchen cupboards. 'Not yet,' she said, taking out a can of vegetable soup.

'No?'

'No,' Gertie said.

Evie looked at her, head cocked to one side and bright eyes narrowed as she watched her sister's movements. 'Cambridge wasn't about roses at all, was it?'

Gertie was busying herself with a pan and wooden spoon and didn't turn around. 'What do you mean?'

'I mean, you didn't go to Cambridge on business, did you? And you didn't stay with some old friend, either.'

'What makes you say that?' Gertie said, turning wounded eyes upon Evie.

'Because you're being all weird and vague,' Evie said.

'I am not.'

Celeste, who'd been quietly observing the scene whilst drinking a cup of tea at the table, spoke now.

'Evie – leave Gertie alone.'

'Oh, so you're in on this big secret, are you?'

'I just don't think you should go poking your nose in where it isn't wanted,' Celeste said.

'I bet it's some old Cambridge professor who wears tweed and reads poetry to you whilst punting you along The Backs and tells you that you're like a maid from Arthurian legend!' Evie continued with a giggle. 'Anyway, an old friend wouldn't have bought you such a pretty locket either,' Evie said.

Gertie's hand flew up to her neck. 'What nonsense you talk, Evie. I bought this myself ages ago.'

'Really?'

Gertie nodded.

'You're an appalling liar, Gertie,' Evie said with a laugh.

'Evie – stop it,' Celeste said. 'Haven't you got something to do in the garden?'

'Probably!' she said, pouting at being thus dismissed.

'Then I suggest you get on with it,' Celeste said.

Evie sighed. 'God, Celly, you're turning into Mum,' she said.

'Don't you *ever* say that,' Celeste retorted and the two of them glared at each other.

'Sorry,' Evie said. 'I was wrong. You're nothing like Mum. She was always *nice* to me! You're just mean.'

Evie left the room, muttering under her breath.

'Are you all right?' Gertie asked, bringing her soup to the table and sitting down opposite Celeste.

'I'm fine,' she said. Their eyes met and they smiled at one another. 'How about you?'

Gertie nodded and began to eat. Celeste watched her, wondering if she was going to volunteer any information.

'Did you have a good weekend?' Gertie asked.

'Yes,' Celeste said. 'I got through a whole heap of paperwork in the study.'

Gertie smiled. 'That's not what I meant,' she said. 'Evie texted me that Julian called this morning.'

'Oh, she did, did she?'

'And?'

'It was a business thing,' Celeste said.

'Then why didn't he just ring?' Gertie asked.

Celeste picked at a finger that she'd caught on a Hybrid Musk thorn earlier that morning. 'I expect it was easier to talk to me in person.'

Gertie finished her soup. 'I like him,' she declared. 'He's sweet.'

'He's not here to be sweet. He's here to get us the best price for our paintings.'

'Celly – you know he likes you.'

She shook her head. 'I know nothing of the sort.'

'Of *course* you do! You always know when a man fancies you,' Gertie said gently.

'Well, I'm not interested, okay? I have far too much to do and I haven't got time to think about men at the moment even if I was ready. Anyway,' she added, 'I don't think I'll ever fall in love again.'

Gertie looked as if she'd been slapped in the face with a trug. 'You can't really think that, can you?'

'I haven't had time to think about it,' Celeste said.

'But love isn't something that you pop in your diary. It just *happens*. You can't timetable it or hope it fits in with your busy routine because it never does. It never happens the way you think it will happen or plan for it to happen,' Gertie said. 'It's messy and wonderful and unpredictable.'

'And time-consuming,' Celeste said.

Gertie smiled. 'There's always time for love,' she said.

'Not for me,' Celeste said. 'Not anymore.'

Gertie sighed. 'You'll change your mind when the right man comes along.'

Celeste stared into the bottom of her teacup, hoping that the conversation was over.

'You know, Evie was right,' Gertie suddenly said in a voice barely above a whisper.

'What do you mean?' Celeste asked, looking up again.

Gertie chewed her lip before answering. 'I did go to Cambridge to see someone.'

Celeste frowned. 'Who?'

'I can't –' She paused.

'Remember?' Celeste said with a smile. 'You got drunk and can't remember who it was?'

Gertie reached across the table to hit her sister's hand. 'No!'

'Then what? You can't tell me?'

Gertie's eyes fixed on the table as her finger circled one of the dark knots in the woodwork. 'It's a bit complicated,' she said at last.

Celeste was just about to ask how it was complicated when her mobile rang. 'Rats. I've got to take this,' she said. 'I've been trying to speak to this guy all day.' She got up from the table and squeezed Gertie's shoulder before she left the room.

'No time for love, then,' Gertie said to the retreating back of her sister.

༄

That evening, after everybody had gone to bed, Celeste was awakened by a noise from the room next door, which was a little unnerving because that had been her mother's bedroom.

She switched the bedside lamp on and looked at her alarm clock. It was a little after two. Groaning, she got out of bed, grabbed a jumper to put over her nightdress and shoved her feet into her slippers. The last place she wanted to visit in the middle of the night was her mother's old room. It was pretty much the last place she wanted to visit at any time, but night time just made the prospect even more harrowing.

'Frinton,' she called softly, but the little dog didn't stir. 'Traitor!' she added, listening to his snores before leaving the room.

She walked along the sloping, creaking floorboards of the hallway and saw the light spilling out from her mother's room.

'Evie?' she said in surprise when she saw who was in there.

An ashen-faced Evelyn turned around as Celeste entered the room and it was instantly apparent that her sister had been crying.

'What are you doing in here?' Celeste asked. But it seemed obvious what Evie had been doing because the wardrobe door was wide open.

'I couldn't sleep,' she said in a tiny voice which reminded Celeste, once again, how very young her sister was.

'So you came in here?' Celeste asked, her head cocked to one side.

Evie didn't say anything for a moment, her hand reaching inside the wardrobe to stroke the clothes that were hanging so neatly there.

'I miss her,' she said at last. 'It doesn't seem real that she's gone, does it? The house doesn't feel right without her.'

Celeste watched as Evie pulled out a red velvet jacket with gold buttons. It was a typical Penelope item: bright, beautiful and very much a scene stealer. There was the little tartan skirt she had worn so much too. It was far too short on her, making her look like a school girl – which, Celeste suspected, Penelope had liked.

'Do you remember this?' Evie asked, pulling out a silk dress in emerald green. 'She looked so pretty in it. She wore it to your sixteenth birthday party, remember?'

'I remember,' Celeste said coldly. 'But I'm surprised you do. You were so young.'

'I remember it,' Evie said defensively but then she frowned. 'Or maybe I'm remembering the photos. I'm not sure now. Anyway, she looked so beautiful in it. Like a Hollywood star.'

Celeste watched as her sister ran the silky material through her fingers, her expression wistful and her eyes misty with tears.

'You should have it, Celly,' she said suddenly. 'You're the same height and size as Mum was and it would really suit you.'

'I don't want it,' Celeste said.

'But it's so beautiful,' she said, pulling it out of the wardrobe and holding it in front of her so that it shimmered in the light of the room, 'and it seems so sad that it won't be worn again.'

'I really don't want the dress, Evie.'

'But –'

'I would *never* wear it.'

Their eyes met and there was something in Celeste's tone that seemed to register with Evie. She put the dress back in the wardrobe.

'I think we should go to bed, don't you?' Celeste said and Evie nodded, closing the wardrobe door before crossing the room. Just before Celeste switched off the light, she noticed the gold-framed photo on the bedside table. It was a picture of Penelope.

'Of course,' Celeste said.

'What?' Evie said.

'Nothing.'

෴

It took Celeste hours to fall asleep once she'd said goodnight to Evie. Her mind kept spiralling into the past and back to the day when her mother had worn the emerald green dress.

'My dress,' Celeste whispered into the night. She hadn't wanted to tell Evie the full story because she wasn't sure her sister would believe it. She still idolised Penelope, and Celeste really didn't want to shatter the precious memories that she was still clinging onto so dearly.

If only *she* had some precious memories of her own, she thought. Most of hers were so painful, including the one about the emerald dress.

Her father had taken her shopping on the eve of her sixteenth birthday and Celeste had known exactly what she'd wanted: a brand new dress – something beautiful and sophisticated. The emerald green silk had been perfect, floating over her mature curves and making her feel truly beautiful for the first time in her life. But her mother had been appalled.

'It's *far* too stylish for you,' Penelope had told her. 'You won't be able to carry it off.' And Celeste had watched helplessly as her mother had taken the dress from her.

What she hadn't bargained for was that Penelope would wear it herself, floating down the stairs as Celeste's friends arrived for the party. Of course, everyone had thought that Penelope had looked fantastic.

'You're so lucky to have a mum like her,' one of her friends had told her. Celeste had simply smiled, holding her tongue and wishing she'd never bothered with the party at all.

Then there'd been the humiliation over the cake. Celeste had asked for a pink heart-shaped cake but, after tea, her mother had brought in a funny green one in the shape of a frog. As if that wasn't bad enough, one of its eyes was missing because it had been left out in the kitchen and one of the cats had jumped up onto the table and eaten it.

Celeste cringed as she remembered the inappropriateness of it all. It was so obviously a child's cake and, at sixteen, Celeste had definitely not been a child. She'd later found out that Penelope had forgotten to order a cake and, when she'd remembered, she'd gone into town and the frog cake had been the only one she'd been able to find.

Then there'd been her shouting to keep the noise down. It wasn't as if they'd been making a lot of noise either. They'd just been a few excitable girls trying to have a party but it had all been too much for Penelope, who'd soon announced that she had a headache and had made a big scene of swooning onto the sofa in front of everyone, yelling for Celeste to get her some tablets.

Celeste closed her eyes, remembering the scene as if it was happening again right in front of her. Of course, Penelope had managed to make a miraculous recovery in time to take over the dance floor they'd set up in the hallway. It hadn't been ordinary dancing either. Penelope Hamilton had been doing a strange sort of flirty dance and had zoned in on the one boy Celeste had invited to her party.

She could still see his bright red face now as her mother had taken his hands and made him dance with her, cheek to cheek. And Celeste had stood there in the shadows, wearing her tired old summer dress with the blackberry stain just above the right knee, watching her mother slow dance in the emerald green dress with her first boyfriend at her sixteenth birthday party.

15.

The days of summer slowly slipped by. Celeste was working her way steadily through the paperwork and accounts in the study, doing her best to restore some sort of order to the Hamilton Rose empire. Gertie was busy in the garden, keeping the borders immaculate for visitors and running the sales of container roses, and Evie was juggling Gloria Temple's wedding preparations alongside orders that were flooding in from hotels, restaurants and romantic members of the public.

The summer sky had remained a perfect eggshell blue for days now, with just hints of wispy white cloud and, although most rosarians adored such weather, Gertie couldn't help bemoaning the fact that the lawn had turned from green to amber and no amount of watering seemed to help. It was the price one paid for a good summer in the Stour Valley but at least it was better than grey clouds and endless rain which balled up the blooms on the roses so that they refused to open. No, the sunshine was most welcome.

What wasn't so welcome was the day that Celeste had been dreading, the day when Esther Martin was leaving The Lodge and moving into the manor.

'This is the last meal we'll have in private,' Evie said in the kitchen that morning.

'Don't be so melodramatic,' Celeste told her. 'We'll probably not even know she's there. I bet she gets up at the crack of dawn and will be in and out of the kitchen before we're even awake. Anyway, if you want to try and save the house, this is one of the ways to do it.'

'So, who's moving in to The Lodge?' Gertie asked.

'I've arranged for somebody to come and give it a bit of a make-over first,' Celeste said. 'Just freshen it up a bit. Esther's been in it such a long time, and the carpets and wallpaper were pretty tatty as far as I could see when I visited.'

'But you're putting it on the rental market through that agent?' Gertie asked.

Celeste nodded. 'They know all about contracts and checking up on people. I thought it would be safer.'

'I hope you're allowing pets,' Evie said. 'I can't imagine trying to find somewhere to rent which didn't allow animals. It would be horrible.'

'Pets are allowed,' Celeste said, bending to tickle Frinton behind his left ear. She smiled as he pushed his head towards her, as if to get as close as possible to the tickle.

'That's something at least,' Evie said.

'What do you mean by that?' Celeste asked.

Evie sighed. 'I just don't see the point of moving Esther into the manor if you're seriously thinking of selling it at some point. What would happen to Esther then?'

'I haven't thought that far ahead if you want the truth,' Celeste said, 'but renting out The Lodge is a good short-term answer to making some money to pay off some of the outstanding bills.'

'Well, I don't envy you the job of settling Esther in,' Evie said.

'Ah,' Celeste said in the kind of tone that instantly made Evie feel anxious. 'I meant to ask you earlier. Can you please take care of things?'

Evie's mouth fell open. 'You're kidding, right?'

Celeste shook her head. 'Esther Martin absolutely loathes me.'

'Well, she doesn't exactly adore *me*!' Evie pointed out.

'But you're going to have to do it. I've got some calls to make.'

'Celly! Don't be so mean!'

'I'm not being mean – I'm being practical.'

Evie huffed and pouted. 'This is *so* unfair. Why do I always get the really horrid jobs?'

'You don't,' Celeste told her. 'When was the last time you had to sort out an overdraft or ring a supplier who hasn't been paid for eight months and explain how sorry you are? And when did you last have a look in the septic tank and get that sorted? Or went up into the attics to make sure that the deathwatch beetles weren't back?'

'Yeah? And when was the last time *you* held a bowl all night whilst Mum was sick into it? Or had to carry her upstairs because she was too frail to walk?' Evie cried.

A dreadful silence fell between them.

'Evie –'

'I'm going,' Evie said. 'Don't worry. I'll do your dirty work for you. I'm used to it.'

❧

The small removal lorry pulled up outside the hall at eleven o'clock that morning and Esther's bits of furniture and boxes were unloaded and carried through to the room that she'd been allocated on the ground floor. It seemed a small collection for a lifetime but, then again, The Lodge was a small home and the room she was moving into was even smaller. But even though it was larger than many of the rooms in the manor and had its own en suite, there wouldn't be much room left over by the time everything had been put in place.

'Mrs Martin?' Evie said, holding her hand out to greet her as she walked across the driveway with a small handbag over her shoulder and a walking stick in her hand. Mrs Martin didn't smile. She didn't even raise her eyes to acknowledge Evie's presence.

'Follow me,' Evie said. 'It's not too far to walk.'

'I can walk for miles if I so choose,' Esther barked.

'Right,' Evie said, not for one moment believing her. She'd never once seen Esther Martin walking the footpaths surrounding the manor. She seemed to live permanently behind closed doors and it was hard to imagine her hopping over a stile with that walking stick.

They reached the room where the removal men had placed the furniture. Evie had to admit that it looked very homey with the pretty iron bed in the corner and the yellow sofa and winged chairs placed so that the occupant could enjoy an unrivalled view of the garden beyond.

'It's one of my favourite views from the manor,' Evie said, looking out across the moat towards the rose walk with its arches covered in pink and white climbers and ramblers. 'I think you'll be very comfortable here, don't you?'

Esther didn't reply. Instead, she sat down heavily in one of the winged chairs and let out a sigh as if all the air in her body was leaving her.

'Would you like me to help with anything?' Evie asked, looking around at the boxes on the floor.

'What?' Esther said abruptly.

'Would you like me to help you unpack?' Evie tried again.

'No,' she barked. 'I don't want a Hamilton poking their nose through my things.'

Evie sighed. She was finding this all very trying. 'Okay,' she said, doing her best to remain calm. 'Would you like me to make you a cup of tea, then?'

'I can make one myself,' she said. 'I'm not a complete invalid.'

'I didn't say you were. I merely asked –'

'I said no!'

'Okay!' Evie barked back and then bit her lip. She'd promised that she wasn't going to lose her cool but had failed miserable. She took a deep breath. 'I hope you like the way we've arranged your pieces of furniture. We can always move things if you don't.'

'Then move them back to The Lodge,' she said.

'I'm afraid we can't do that.'

'That's my home. Your grandfather promised me that house as long as I live.'

'I know,' Evie said, 'and I'm really sorry, but things are rather desperate here and we need the money.'

'That's a poor excuse for breaking a promise.'

'It's the only one we've got,' Evie said.

'Why can't you sell something?'

'We're doing that as well. We're having to part with some of our paintings.'

Esther looked appalled, her bright eyes seeming to spear Evie with their intensity. 'Not the rose paintings?'

Evie nodded. 'I'm afraid so.'

'But your grandfather adored those paintings.'

'I know,' Evie said. 'It's not been easy parting with them. I really wish we didn't have to but there's so much that needs doing to keep this place going.'

Esther still didn't look convinced. 'There's always something you can do.'

'I'll show you the north wing sometime,' Evie said. 'See if you can come up with any miracle solutions.'

It was then that an opened box caught Evie's eye. It was large and looked heavy, and Evie saw that it contained books. A lot of books. Instinctively, her hand moved forward and she cocked her head to one side, reading the titles as she lifted them up. There was Nancy Mitford's *The Pursuit of Love*, there was Stella Gibbons's

Cold Comfort Farm and a couple of novels by Barbara Pym. Evie frowned. She didn't know as much about literature as Gertie but she recognised that all these books were comedies. She smiled. She hadn't had Esther Martin down as a devourer of comedies.

'Put those down!' Esther suddenly barked from out of the depths of the winged chair. Evie sighed and returned the books to their box.

'I can help you unpack these if you like. Gertie always says that books furnish a room.'

'They furnished The Lodge up until yesterday,' Esther said.

Evie chose not to rise to this. 'Maybe I could borrow them sometime. I don't often get time to read but I should like to give them a go.'

Esther turned around and glared at her. 'If this is your crass way of trying to make amends for the indignation of moving me out of my home then it's not working. Now, leave me alone.'

Evie blanched at the rudeness of the woman and left the room, closing the door firmly behind her and resisting the urge to slam it. Esther Martin might be rude but Evie certainly wasn't.

She came back a few minutes later with a cup of tea on a tray alongside a pretty pink china jug of milk and a matching sugar bowl with silver spoon.

'I said I didn't want a cup of tea,' Esther said as soon as she saw it.

'No, you didn't,' Evie said. 'You said you didn't want me to make you one but I decided to ignore you and make you one anyway.' She placed the tray on a footstool in front on her. 'I'll let you add your own milk and sugar, okay?'

Esther gave a sort of disgruntled harrumph and Evie smiled. 'Gertie's going to include you for dinner tonight.'

'No, thank you.'

'Well, you'll have to speak to Gertie if you don't want any and she'll probably make you some all the same, so I wouldn't waste your breath.'

'Why can't you Hamilton girls just leave me alone?'

'Because that wouldn't be right,' Evie said matter-of-factly, 'and I have a suspicion that you don't want to be left alone. Not really.'

'Oh, you think you know me, do you? What are you? Seventeen? Think you know your way around a person's psyche? Bah!'

'I'm twenty-one, actually, and I think I'm a pretty good judge of character, thank you very much.'

'Is that right?'

'It is!' Evie said.

They locked eyes and seemed to be weighing each other up. Esther was the first to crack, lowering her gaze and rubbing the top of her walking stick, which was leaning up against her chair.

'Well,' Evie said at last. 'I've leave you to settle in.'

Esther gave a grunt and, shaking her head in despair, Evie left the room, determining to find a big patch of nettles in the garden and work out her anger with a fork.

❧

Celeste had just got off the phone, doing her best to apologise to the company who supplied the plastic pots for their roses. She had found their unpaid invoice under a heap of papers on her mother's desk and had made the call with her heart in her mouth, uttering apology after apology at what she called 'a horrible oversight' but which was really just another example of the hopeless administration of Hamilton Roses under her two sisters.

It had never happened when she'd been working in the office but, then again, she hadn't had to cope with running the house and business whilst coping with their mother whilst she was sick.

For a moment, she thought of the confrontation she'd had with Evie and how upset her little sister had been. Celeste felt so guilty about not being there for her more over the last few years, especially during the last weeks of their mother's life when Evie had needed her most. But how could Celeste ever explain how her mother had made her feel? Evie would never truly understand that.

Sitting on her side of the desk, Celeste gazed at the empty chair opposite her that had once been occupied by her mother. She could almost hear her mother's voice.

'You handle things all wrong,' Penelope Hamilton had once told her, and she could imagine her saying exactly the same thing to her now. 'You never really knew how to handle your sisters, did you? You never were confident like them or me. You were always the weak one, Celeste.'

Celeste shook her head. *Always* and *never*. They were the two words most frequently thrown at Celeste from her mother and they were always meant to wound.

'You've never dedicated yourself to this business,' she would say. 'You've always been self-centred,' had been another favourite. 'You've never been one to compliment me,' was another, for her mother had been the sort who needed constant praise. Everything had to be complimented and, if it wasn't, life could become hell.

'You're dead!' Celeste cried into the empty study now. 'You're *dead!* So leave me alone!'

She blinked the image and the voice away, her heart racing wildly. She had been right. Her mother still haunted this room, and no amount of ignoring the fact would change it. She leaned forward, pressing her head into her hands. This would never feel like home, would it? Even though it was the only home she had ever had. As long as she remembered the past, it would be all-encompassing, all-invasive.

She shook her head. She didn't have time to think about this now, and she was just about to make the next apologetic phone call when she heard a car pulling up in the drive outside. It was probably a delivery for Gertie or Evie and had nothing to with her but she couldn't resist looking out of the window. To her surprise, she saw Julian Faraday's green MG coming to a neat, sliding halt outside the front door. That was all she needed, she thought, making her way from the study to the hallway with Frinton barking loudly in front of her.

'Celeste!' Julian said with a big smile when she opened the door. 'How are you?'

'Surprised,' she said. 'Were we expecting you?'

'Well, I was passing by and thought you'd like an update on the progress with the paintings.'

'Oh, okay,' Celeste said.

'May I come in?'

She opened the door wide enough for him to enter and Frinton jumped up at his navy corduroy trousers.

'Hello, boy!' Julian said, ruffling Frinton's head and receiving a good licking in return.

Celeste led him through to the living room and they sat down on the two sofas which faced each other across a threadbare rug.

'This really is a charming room,' he said. 'I do love that little table and that clock.' He nodded towards the little French clock above the mantelpiece. 'And that's a very fine punch bowl,' he said, nodding towards a blue and white piece which sat on a table next to the fire.

'You said you had some news about the paintings,' Celeste prompted him, reluctant to be sat there all day talking about punch bowls.

'Ah, yes. You know I mentioned the possibility of selling to a private buyer? Well, we've got someone interested in the Fantin-Latour,' he said.

'Really?'

'If you'd be up for selling outside an auction. Our gallery has a list of clients whom we keep in touch with for when such pieces come onto the market. They're usually willing to pay top dollar.'

'And they've seen it?'

'Not yet,' Julian said. 'We've sent them images and information and they're going to fly in from the States in the next couple of weeks.'

'Wow,' Celeste said. 'Flying in for our little painting.'

'It's not just any little painting, though,' he said.

'I guess not,' Celeste said. 'Still, I can't quite imagine it hanging on any wall other than our own. Is that strange?'

'Not at all. It would be strange if you didn't feel like that.'

'But we've got to sell it,' Celeste said, thinking aloud. She couldn't do a U-turn now – not with somebody flying in from the States with their chequebook.

'Have you got a quote yet for the north wing?' he asked.

'Not yet,' she said. 'It's terrible but I've been putting it off until we actually have some money in the bank. I know it can't wait but I'm really dreading it. I just know the truth is going to be much worse than any of us can anticipate.'

They were silent for a moment and then Celeste cleared her throat.

'And that was it, was it?' she said.

'Excuse me?' Julian said.

'The news about the private buyer for the Fantin-Latour,' Celeste said. 'That was why you called?'

'Yes,' Julian said with a smile. 'Thought I'd better run it by you.'

Celeste nodded. 'Well, thank you for taking the time to call by,' she said, getting up from her chair.

Julian looked flustered. 'Right.'

'That *is* all, isn't it?' she said, seeing his face.

'Oh, yes,' he said. 'That's all.'

They walked through the hallway, where Julian stopped to examine the barometer.

'It's saying *Change*,' he said.

'It always says *Change*,' Celeste told him. 'No matter what the weather is doing.'

'I know a chap who could fix that for you,' he said.

'Oh, no!' Celeste said, 'I like it. It makes you feel optimistic if the weather's bad and makes you realise the importance of enjoying it if it's good.'

He smiled. 'That's a very lovely way of putting things,' he said, and they walked outside together. The sun was warm but there was a light breeze blowing and the scent of roses hit them almost immediately.

'*Gertrude Jekyll*,' Celeste said, 'and *Evelyn*.'

'Pardon?'

'The roses I can smell.'

'The roses your sisters are named after?'

'That's right. Two of Mother's favourite scents. We always make sure there are plenty near the house – look.' She pointed to a border nearby where the deep pink and apricot roses were growing in profusion.

'And where is yours?'

'*Celestial* is just around the corner but I'm afraid she's past her best now. She doesn't repeat flower like the David Austin roses. But she has a special beauty that's all her own.'

'What colour is she?' Julian asked.

'Shell-pink. Her petals are almost translucent,' Celeste said. 'She's a very healthy and robust rose.'

'Like you?' Julian said.

'I don't know about robust,' Celeste said.

'It sounds to me like you've weathered pretty well recently with everything you've had to cope with,' he said as their feet crunched lightly over the gravel path.

'What choice did I have?' she said with a shrug.

'Well, you could have gone under. A lot of people would have.'

'Gone under?' she said.

'Given in, given up, run away, gone mad,' he said.

'I don't think so,' she said.

'You see – you're robust!' he said with a smile.

She shrugged. 'I just try to get on. I've a job to do here. If only –' She stopped. Julian watched her for a moment before prompting her.

'If only?'

'Nothing,' she said, suddenly realising that they'd walked out into the garden.

She stopped and turned to look at the manor house, its castellations and mullioned windows perfectly reflected in the clear waters of the moat.

'It's an awful thing to say because I really love this place, but it doesn't feel like mine, you know? Growing up here, it was my grandparents' home and then it became my parents'. I was only ever passing through. When I left it to get married, I never thought I'd come back, and I can't help feeling that I'm no longer a part of life here.'

Julian frowned. 'I'm sure your sisters don't feel the same way. I bet they love having you back.'

'They love that I've come to help sort everything out,' she said and then bit her lip. What was it about this man that made her divulge so much? Was it that old adage about it being easier to talk to strangers than to friends?

'You sound so tense, Celeste. You find it impossible to relax, don't you?' Julian said, and they began walking back to the house, passing under an arch covered in creamy-white roses that smelled of heaven.

'That's not true,' she said.

'No? Well, you're doing a pretty good impression of somebody who can't relax.'

'It just might take me slightly longer than the average person to relax – that's all.' She took a deep breath. 'Smell that,' she said.

Julian inhaled deeply. 'That's lovely.'

Celeste nodded. 'That helps me relax. Sometimes, I come out into the garden and do nothing but breathe. Does that sound funny?'

'Not at all,' he said.

'I'll sit on a sun-warmed bench and close my eyes and inhale. Even when the roses aren't in bloom, there's always something wonderful to smell.'

'Like earth after rain,' Julian said.

'Yes,' Celeste said, looking at him. 'Exactly.'

'That's why I want to move out of the city,' he said as they reached the driveway and his car. 'I want to be able to smell more than the Chinese cooking coming through the vent from my neighbours' flat.'

Celeste laughed.

'That's the first time I've seen you laugh,' he said, which instantly made Celeste stop. The conversation suddenly felt far too intimate.

'I've got to go,' she said. 'Work to do.'

Julian nodded. 'Sure,' he said. 'I'll keep in touch about the Fantin-Latour.'

'Thank you,' she said, watching as he hopped into the MG and waved a hand before driving across the moat and out into the lane.

'What did Julian want?' Evie asked, walking out from under the gatehouse and joining Celeste.

'He had some news about the Fantin-Latour. Good news, I think,' Celeste said.

'About a possible sale?'

Celeste nodded.

'How can that *possibly* be good news?' Evie said, glaring at her sister before marching into the garden, no doubt to take her anger out on some poor rose bush.

16.

Gertie looked at her phone. James hadn't called her for a whole week and had sent only one text during that time too. She sat down on the wrought iron bench that was positioned against the outside of the walled garden. A few years ago, they had made a border filled with only white flowers in honour of the famous white garden at Sissinghurst in Kent which the sisters had visited many times and which was a great source of inspiration to them. As well as being filled with perfect white roses, it was planted with lilies, tulips, foxgloves, anemones, delphiniums, alliums and jasmine. Its real glory was at night when the flowers seemed almost luminous, holding within them a ghostly, glowing light.

Sitting there now, Gertie was little comforted by the white beauty that surrounded her. All she was interested in was her phone, willing it to ring or to beep. Any sign of life to tell her that she was important and merited thought from the man she was in love with.

She looked up, her eyes not quite focusing on the pure white petals of the roses before her. Instead, she was imagining a place far away. She and James had often talked about leaving Little Eleigh because they knew that their relationship would never be accepted in their village, where memories stretched back decades. Gertie would always be the woman who had stolen James from his wife – his *disabled* wife. She would be gossiped about even if she wasn't publicly shunned.

So, even though it would break her heart to leave her home, she was willing to make that sacrifice for him, and they had talked endlessly about moving abroad – to a hilltop town in the South of France or Italy, perhaps, somewhere they could lose themselves and start afresh. Gertie had always dreamed of a life abroad and it was a dream she clung to whenever she felt lonely and uncertain of the future and whenever the strains of their mother's illness had got to her. *If I get through this, I'm going*, she'd told herself. Only it hadn't been that simple. There had been so much to do after Penelope had died and Gertie simply hadn't been able to walk out on it all.

If only James would give her some indication of when it would happen. She felt as if she'd stopped breathing a long time ago and hadn't yet been given permission to inhale and exhale again.

If only I could tell Celeste, she thought, truly believing that the weight of secrecy she was carrying would be lightened considerably if she could talk about it to her dear sister. Celeste had always been the best listener in the world. Guarded in what she revealed to people herself, she was, nevertheless, the perfect confidante, for she never passed judgement.

Gertie had shared so many fears and doubts with her older sister over the years – fears about school and friends and the future, and doubts about boyfriends too. Celeste had always been there with her reassuring calmness and a sage nod of the head. But she had quite enough to cope with at the moment and Gertie didn't feel that she could unload all of her worries onto her. Not yet, anyway.

She looked at her watch and sighed. She'd spent enough time moping and had to get on. There was a lot to do before they left for dinner with their father.

Marcus Coombs was short and portly with small eyes and a nose that was far too big for his face, even though his face was a considerable size. But, despite the oddness of his appearance, he had an infectious laugh that filled rooms and made people feel instantly welcome. The same couldn't be said about his second wife, Simone.

'I *hate* her,' Evie said as they pulled into the driveway of their father's house.

'We know you do,' Gertie said. 'You tell us every time we visit.'

'I don't know why Dad can't just come over to ours,' Evie said.

'I don't think Simone would let him,' Celeste said.

'Why not?' Evie said.

'Well, he might decide he wants to stay with us rather than go back home to her,' Celeste said and Evie giggled.

'I wouldn't blame him,' she said.

'She must make his life a misery,' Gertie said.

'No worse than Mum did,' Celeste said, thinking of how life with their mother must have been a nightmare. Celeste often wondered how their father had put up with Penelope for so long, with her vicious mood swings and endless name-calling, but he'd seemed to have had the ability to shut off from her. Until the day he'd had enough, of course. Celeste remembered it well. It had been an unnervingly quiet departure, with their father packing a modest suitcase and walking down the staircase, whistling a tuneless whistle to himself.

'Where do you think *you're* going?' Penelope had cried after him.

'Away. I'm leaving you,' he'd said, as if it was only to be expected. Celeste, who had been fifteen at the time, had watched from the living room door as her father had taken one last look at the barometer, nodding sagely at the word *Change*, and then had opened the front door and calmly walked out.

The screaming hadn't started until later that evening when their mother had taken things out on Celeste.

'It's *your* fault,' Penelope had told her daughter. 'He can't bear to be around you anymore. You always ruin things for people.'

It wasn't until years later that their father had confided in Celeste. 'Your mother wasn't the easiest woman to love,' he'd told her, 'and I tried. I really tried.' And Celeste had known that he was telling the truth because she'd tried to love her mother too and had failed.

'*Why* do we have to do this?' Evie whined, bringing Celeste back into the present.

'Because we're grownups and we have to put ourselves through this sort of thing occasionally,' Celeste told her.

'But Simone hates us as much as we hate her.'

'Yes, but Dad loves her and we have to try and get along for his sake,' Celeste said.

'But she never makes an effort for us,' Evie said as the Morris Minor van pulled up outside Oak House, 'and every time Dad leaves the room, she says something nasty.'

'Well, not nasty, exactly,' Gertie said. 'More sly, isn't it?'

Celeste nodded. 'Like the time she said that you were looking well.'

Evie gave a mad sort of laugh. 'Yes!' she cried. 'She said I suited the extra weight I'd put on.'

'And the time she admired my dress,' Gertie said, 'and then went on to say that she wished they'd come in petite so that she could have one too.'

Celeste gave a knowing smile. 'I don't think it's natural to be as skinny as Simone,' she said.

'No,' Evie said. 'Didn't she once say that she hated chocolate? How can you trust anyone who doesn't like chocolate? It's not natural, is it?'

'It certainly isn't,' Celeste said, enjoying the jovial mood between them and wishing it could be like this more often.

'And if she says my fingernails look like a man's *one more time*, I swear I'm going to scream,' Gertie said.

The sisters laughed together before getting out of the car.

Oak House was on the edge of a pretty village in what was known as 'High Suffolk' – the area to the north-west of the county famous for its rolling countryside. The house itself wasn't attractive. Or at least it wasn't attractive to Celeste, who was suspicious of any architecture that came after the Arts and Crafts movement – which this one certainly had.

She still found it hard to understand how her father could have bought a mock-Tudor house when he had lived in a bona fide medieval home for so many years. She looked up at its black and white gable and couldn't help wincing at such modernity. It was the same inside, too, with neatly plastered walls and floors that neither sloped nor squeaked. But, then again, Oak House had never known damp or deathwatch beetle and there was never the slightest chance of being cold in the fully insulated rooms with their central heating.

'God, I'd rather spend an afternoon with Esther Martin,' Gertie said as they approached the front door, which sheltered in a neat little porch where Simone had placed a pot of begonias. Celeste didn't like begonias. Mainly because they weren't roses.

'I popped my head in to see if Esther was all right this morning and she nearly bit it off,' Celeste said.

'I've given up on her,' Gertie said. 'I've tried – I've *really* tried to be nice, but she is the rudest person I've ever met.'

Evie sighed. 'You can't blame her for feeling angry at having to leave her home.'

'But it wasn't really her home,' Celeste said.

'Well, Grandpa said it was hers for her lifetime,' Evie said.

'Yes, but it's easy to make that kind of rash promise when you don't know what the future holds,' Celeste said. 'He would have done the same thing, I'm sure.'

'Are you?' Evie said as she pressed the doorbell.

Celeste glared at her but she didn't get a chance to reply because the door was opened by their father.

'Girls!' he cried, opening his arms to embrace them all at once. 'Come in. Come in! Simone's been cooking for you all day. Go and give her a kiss.'

Evie grimaced but felt a hand shoving her in the small of her back, propelling her towards the kitchen.

The three sisters entered as one.

'Darlings!' Simone said, without actually turning around or moving to embrace them, which suited the girls just fine.

'Hello, Simone,' Celeste said in a neutral tone. Gertrude echoed her sister whilst Evie grunted something from behind.

'Something smells marvellous, doesn't it, girls?' their father said as he entered the kitchen. 'What is it, Simmy?'

'Mushroom risotto,' she said, taking her eye off the pan for a moment and giving him a tight smile. 'I did tell you, only you never listen.'

Celeste winced at her father being reprimanded in such a way. He didn't seem to notice the slight, however, and offered to get everyone a drink.

'Go and sit in the dining room, girls,' Simone cried.

'She *knows* I can't stand mushrooms!' Evie hissed to her sisters as they left the room. 'I made that perfectly clear last time when I left that big mountain of them on the side of my plate.'

'She's probably just forgotten,' Gertie said.

'Yeah, right!' Evie said. 'She just wants to test me. She knows how sweet and polite we are around Dad and she loves to prod us to see how much we can take.'

They walked down the hallway and Celeste clocked the radiator which was obscured by a lattice-work cover. The television in the living room was similarly hidden behind a fancy door. Nothing was allowed to be what it truly was in this home.

Five minutes later they were all seated in the dining room, a heap of mushroom risotto on everyone's plate.

'Are you not hungry, Evelyn?' Simone asked. 'Or perhaps you've eaten already. You growing girls have such a wonderful appetite, don't you?'

Their father laughed, obviously not registering the little snip.

'Will you excuse me?' Evie said, standing up from the table.

Celeste and Gertie threw her warning looks.

'I need to use the facilities,' she explained.

'Ah!' their father said, waving his fork in the air. 'Our cloakroom's out of action. Got a plumber coming round tomorrow. Use the upstairs bathroom. You know where it is?'

Evie nodded and left the room.

The upstairs bathroom was Simone's domain – as was the whole of Oak House, really. Evie could see very little of her father there. Everything was Simone's taste, from the frilly curtains and cushions to the patterned dinner service and embroidered napkins.

Her eyes scanned the shelves of the bathroom, each one crowded with bottles and potions and lotions. She probably needed every single one to stop her face from turning into the Wicked Witch of the East's, Evie thought with a naughty giggle. What on *earth* did their father see in her, she wondered for the hundredth time?

Evie sighed. She was feeling a little light-headed and it had nothing to do with the mushroom risotto. She splashed her face with cold water and stared at her reflection. Her eyes looked larger and darker than ever with her blonde hair and she wasn't sure she liked the look. She was very pale these days. Paler than she'd ever imagined, but maybe that would change.

It was then that her phone beeped. She took it out of her pocket and saw that it was a text from Lukas.

Missing you. Coming back to Suffolk. x

Evie groaned. That was the last thing she needed right now. What was it with him? She'd never given him any encouragement. Well, other than sleeping with him a few times. But she'd made it perfectly clear to him that she wasn't looking for a relationship; that was the very last thing she wanted.

For a moment, she thought about the way he used to walk around the garden. He had a funny, casual, shuffly way of walking as if he had all the time in the world, which used to aggravate Evie, and yet he'd always managed to get his jobs done. He just never looked as if he was working very hard. One of life's laid-back sorts of people, Evie thought, wishing she could take a leaf out of his book because she wasn't like that at all. She always seemed to be rushing and stressing which was a sign that the business was doing well, of course, but she sometimes wished that she could take some time out and just be – well – Evie.

But that's what you're going to do, she told her reflection now. *Just not today.*

Leaving the sanctuary of the bathroom, she walked along the landing and couldn't help noting that the door to her father's bedroom was ajar. Nosiness had always been a terrible fault of Evie's and had got her into trouble many times in the past, but she still couldn't resist peeping inside now.

The bedroom was a typical Simone production with its flowery bedspread and neat built-in wardrobes. There were none of the usual bedroom horrors like a friendly sock left on the floor or drawer that hadn't quite aligned itself properly. It was all so precise, and Evie knew that she would find it impossible to sleep in such a room.

She was just about to leave in disgust when something caught her eye. There on the far wall was a painting of roses that she instantly recognised. A gasp left her and she crossed the plush carpet towards it, taking in the simple spray of flowers depicted in careful oils. It was a classic composition of just the sort that her grandfather had favoured, and Evie instantly knew that it was, indeed, from her grandfather's collection. It was unmistakable. So what on earth was it doing here at Oak House, she wondered?

Taking her phone out again, she took a couple of quick photos of the painting before returning downstairs. Simone glared at her from her position at the head of the table when she entered the dining room, but her glare turned into a smile when her father looked up from his plate.

'Ah, there you are, Evelyn. We thought you'd fallen down the toilet.'

Evie grunted and sat down.

'Your risotto's gone cold,' her father pointed out.

'That's a shame,' Evie said, earning herself a reprimanding glance from Celeste.

'Well, I really don't know if you deserve dessert now,' Simone said as if Evie was a child.

Their father guffawed and then picked up a newspaper, which he was apt to do between courses so that he wouldn't actually have to engage in conversation. Evie took the opportunity to get her sisters' attention as soon as Simone had left the room, flapping her hands wildly at them both.

'What is it, Evie?' Celeste said, none too subtly.

Evie cleared her throat. 'I need to talk to you both,' she said, motioning to the hallway.

Celeste and Gertie got up from the table, apologising to their father, who didn't seem to notice what was going on.

'What on earth's the matter with you?' Celeste hissed once they were in the hallway.

'I've just seen that painting you were talking about,' Evie said.

'What painting?' Celeste asked.

'The missing rose painting?'

'What do you mean? Where?'

'Upstairs – in Dad and Simone's bedroom.'

Celeste frowned. 'Are you sure?'

'Yes! I'm positive!'

'Keep your voice down, Evie!' Celeste warned.

Evie groaned. 'You've *got* to go and look at it. It's ours! I'm sure of it,' she whispered urgently.

'Okay, okay,' Celeste said. 'I'll take a look. Just go and sit down and, whatever you do, don't say anything.'

Evie returned to the dining room with Gertie, and Celeste quietly walked up the stairs. The bedroom door was still ajar. Taking deep breath, she entered the room. Like her sister before her, Celeste couldn't help noting the decor of the room and the number of cushions that were heaped on the bed. Simone was one of those women who had more cushions than friends, but she wasn't here to look at cushions. She soon saw the painting Evie had told her about.

'Oh, no,' she said to herself, for it was, indeed, her grandfather's missing painting. This, she thought, was awkward. She knew her mother would never have given the painting to their father, and Celeste was pretty certain that her father had nothing to do with this anyway. He probably didn't even know it was in the room; he never noticed such things. So how had it got there? Celeste cast her mind back. Her father had had a key to the manor long after he had left and had made several trips to collect things, but had he been seeing Simone then? And had she come with him on such a trip and just stolen the painting?

With gentle hands, Celeste took the painting off the wall and examined it. She turned it around and noticed the tiny ink inscription on the top left-hand corner.

'To Esme, with love from Arthur.'

No, she thought, her mother would never have let his painting leave the house.

Placing the painting back on the wall, Celeste returned downstairs but there wasn't an opportunity to talk to her sisters because desserts had arrived.

'You been using the facilities too?' Simone asked Celeste. 'I must say, you girls have very weak bladders for your age.'

Evie rolled her eyes and they ate the apple strudel in silence.

It wasn't until half an hour later that the three of them got a chance to talk. Simone was making coffee in the kitchen and their father was snoozing in his favourite chair, his loud puffs signalling that he was sound asleep.

'Well?' Evie said. 'Did you see it?'

Celeste nodded. 'It's ours, all right.'

'I told you! You've got to go and get it.'

'I can't just pluck it off the wall and stick it under my jacket, can I?' Celeste said, looking outraged.

'I don't see why not,' Evie said. 'It belongs to us.'

'Celeste is right. We can't just take it,' Gertie said.

'Why not?' Evie cried.

'Keep your voice down!' Celeste warned as their father stirred with a frighteningly loud snort.

'If that painting is worth as much as the others, then surely we can't afford to leave it here. What if Simone goes and sells it herself? How would you feel then?' Evie asked.

Celeste shook her head. 'She wouldn't, would she? Not if she's had it this long already.'

'But she might get bored with it and decide to sell it then,' Gertie said. 'Didn't she go through that phase of collecting those dreadful figurines and then sell them all when she got bored of them?'

Celeste nodded. She'd forgotten about that.

'So what are we going to do?' Evie pressed.

'I don't know,' Celeste said honestly.

'Yes, well, don't think about it for too long,' Evie said, 'or I'll do something about it myself.'

17.

Evie had no idea how the job of looking after Esther Martin had fallen to her but, whenever anything needed doing, Celeste and Gertie just happened to be either at the far end of the walled garden or deeply engrossed in paperwork. Evie sighed as she took the vacuum cleaner into Esther's quarters whilst their new tenant was safely out of the way in the kitchen.

Honestly, she really had enough to do without turning into Esther's private housekeeper, she thought. For one thing, Gloria Temple was arriving to make the final choice of roses for her wedding. But, as Evie moved around the room, making sure everything was spick and span, her heart couldn't help going out to the woman who'd been thrown out of the home she'd been promised only to be forced to live with a family whom she detested. She must be feeling pretty insecure, Evie thought.

'A bit like me,' she whispered, wondering what it would be like if Celeste followed through on her threat to sell the manor. Where would they all go? Evie couldn't imagine a life outside its safe confines. She'd never known any other home and she knew her heart would break if she had to leave it. Was that how Esther was feeling now, she wondered?

Still, there was no need for the old woman to be so impossible all the time. There was never any excuse for rudeness, Evie decided.

She shook her head, trying – once again – to imagine what it was like to carry around so much hate in a human heart. It wasn't as if she and her sisters were to directly blame for the death of her daughter, was it? Goodness, she thought, even her father wasn't to blame. After all, you couldn't be held personally responsible for whoever fell in love with you and then be held accountable if they went off to Africa and contracted some terrible disease.

Evie paused by a little mahogany table where Esther had placed a few silver framed photographs. There she was on her wedding day – younger and prettier, but still with that disgruntled sort of expression that seemed permanently fixed on her face. Evie peered at her husband, who had a kind of resigned look about him as if he knew he'd never be a hundred percent happy with his choice of bride. But perhaps Evie was reading too much into things. They'd probably had the most marvellous life together and had been happier than any couple had a right to be, although Evie found that hard to imagine.

Another photograph caught her eye.

'Sally,' Evie said, picking up the oval frame and gazing into the pale face of the much-missed daughter. She was standing under an odd-shaped tree that was the most African thing that Evie had ever seen – tall and thin with a very flat canopy. Sally was holding a large straw hat in her hands and was wearing a loose dress in blue and white, her long hair hanging over her shoulders. She looked like a singer from some nineteen-seventies folk group, and her tiny smile elicited one from Evie that soon turned into a frown as she tried to imagine what it must be like to lose such a beloved daughter.

'I've left a book out for you.'

Evie almost left the ground with shock as Esther entered the room. Quickly replacing the photo frame, Evie turned around as the silver-haired harridan entered the room.

'What book?' Evie asked her.

'One of those books from the box you were eyeing up. It's on the coffee table,' Esther said with a nod, and Evie walked across to the table to pick it up.

'Jerome K Jerome,' she read. 'That's a funny name.'

'For a funny man. And a funny book.'

'It's funny?' Evie said, looking down at the unlikely title of *Three Men in a Boat*.

'Yes,' Esther said. 'If you have any sort of funny bone, you'll think so too. Look out for the dog. It might remind you of someone.'

Evie raised quizzical eyebrows and then watched as Esther slowly lowered herself into her winged chair.

'I'm not sure I'm in the mood to laugh at anything much at the moment,' Evie said.

'Give it a go,' Esther said. 'It's at times like this when books can save your life.'

Evie bit her lip, wondering if she was alluding to the death of her daughter again or maybe that of her husband, and she couldn't help feeling a little connection with the old woman.

'Thank you,' she said. 'I'll give it back to you as soon as I can.'

Esther waved a hand at her. 'There's no rush. My eyes won't allow me to read much these days. I find the print so maddeningly small and I don't get to the libraries much for those large print books.'

'Oh,' Evie said in alarm, not being able to imagine a world without reading. Like Gertie, she adored stories. Then something occurred to her. 'Have you tried a Kindle?'

'Pardon?'

'A Kindle,' Evie said. 'It's an electronic reading device and you can make the text as big as you want.'

'Never heard of it,' Esther said dismissively.

'That doesn't mean it's not a great thing,' Evie told her. 'I'll lend you mine,' she said, making a mental note to delete some of the racier titles she had already read.

When she left the room, closing the door quietly behind her, the copy of *Three Men in a Boat* in her hand, Evie couldn't help but smile.

Had she really just had a normal non-confrontational conversation with Esther Martin? Celeste and Gertie would never believe her.

∽

Celeste was surprisingly happy to have a reason to contact Julian Faraday again so soon. The painting discovered in her father and Simone's bedroom was nagging away at her so she decided to send the photographs she'd taken to Julian.

'*What do you think?*' she texted him, giving him the rough dimensions of the painting. She wasn't surprised when he rang her back just three minutes later.

'You found the missing painting!' he said in delight.

'Well, yes,' she said, not elaborating at this point. 'Have you any idea who it's by?'

'I do,' he said. 'It's by a little-known English artist called Paul Calman. He painted between the wars – mostly still life but the occasional East Anglian landscape.'

Celeste cleared her throat. 'And is it worth much?'

'It's not worth as much as the others,' Julian told her, 'but it's still a very nice painting. I'd have to see it, of course, to determine its value, but I'd estimate about five thousand.'

'Right,' Celeste said, acknowledging the fact that it wasn't going to swell the Little Eleigh Manor coffers greatly but also knowing that she'd want it back in their home even if it was only worth a fiver. It had been chosen by her grandfather for their grandmother and it belonged at the manor.

'Where is it?' Julian asked.

'Ah,' Celeste said, biting her lip. 'We don't actually have it in our possession at the moment.'

'Sounds intriguing,' Julian said. 'Well, perhaps I'll get to see it at some point and then I can give you a proper valuation.'

'Right,' Celeste said, secretly thinking that that was never going to happen.

'I'm popping through to Suffolk this weekend,' he said. 'I thought I might check out a few places to possibly rent. You know my crazy idea to open an antiques shop?'

'Oh, yes,' she said.

'I was wondering if you'd like to join me. If you're not too busy, that is.'

It was then that a horn sounded from outside and Celeste peered out of the window to see the scruffy white works van of Ludkin and Son.

'Julian, I've got to run. Somebody's just arrived. Goodbye,' she said, hanging up quickly before rushing to the front door.

'Mr Ludkin,' she said, extending a hand in welcome. 'Do come in.' His hand was rough with a whitish hue as if it had been dipped in plaster.

'It's been a long time,' he said, scratching his greying hair, which also looked full of plaster. 'You remember me boy?'

Celeste nodded. 'Tim, right?'

Tim shuffled a step forward and nodded shyly. He was a little taller than his father, or would have been if his head and shoulders weren't quite so slumped.

'Well, come on through,' Celeste said. 'I'm sure you know where we're heading.' She led the way to the infamous north wing, the sound of Tim Ludkin sniffing nervously behind her.

'Still holding up, then?' Mr Ludkin asked. 'Not tumbled into the moat yet?'

'I think some of it might have done,' she said.

'Oh dear, oh dear,' he said, shaking his head from side to side. 'I do love these old houses but sometimes they're more trouble than they're worth.'

'I know exactly what you mean but we've got to try and save it,' Celeste said.

'And we can actually go ahead with the work this time?' he asked. 'You're not just getting another quote to add to that the big pile I've already given you?'

'We're going ahead with the work this time,' Celeste vowed. 'I fear the whole of the north wing needs attention but there's one room that needs to be dealt with first.' She paused outside the Room of Doom and took a deep breath before opening the door. The two men walked inside.

'Right,' Mr Ludkin said ambiguously and Celeste watched in alarm as his son's mouth slackened and his eyes glazed over.

Suddenly, Celeste didn't want to be there at all. 'If you could take a look around here and the other rooms in this wing, that would be great,' she said. 'Of course, there are other jobs to tackle around the house but I think we should prioritise this wing for now. Can I make you both a cup of tea whilst I let you get on with it?'

'Thank you,' Mr Ludkin said. 'Never said no to a cup of tea.'

Celeste left them to it and retreated to the kitchen, where she found she was shaking.

'You can get through this,' she told herself as she grabbed a couple of robust mugs from the cupboard. 'You're doing the right thing.'

Still, she couldn't help hearing the voice of her mother deep in the recesses of her mind.

That money can be better spent. You should be putting it into the business – not wasting it on a building.

Penelope Hamilton had never really been in love with the manor. She'd only tolerated it as a base for the business, happy to be the beautiful host in a beautiful setting and using the romance of the building and its grounds to charm prospective clients, but she had never cared for it in the same way that her own parents had. It had never quite woven its magic spell upon her, and it had suffered the consequences. Consequences that now had to be dealt with.

Celeste made the tea, placing the mugs on a tray together with a little bowl of sugar and a jug of milk. She wished that she didn't have to return to the north wing at all; she wished that she could just hide herself away until the whole horrible business was finished. She hadn't even thought about what she was going to do with the north wing once it was renovated. It was an enormous space and it would just start to slowly decay once again if it wasn't used. She thought about all the possibilities. Perhaps they could let it out? Perhaps there would be another Esther Martin who would want to come and live at the manor or perhaps they could open the rooms for bed and breakfast, although that didn't really appeal to Celeste and might just get in the way once the property was put on the market.

Anyway, she thought, she didn't have to make up her mind there and then. There was an awful lot of work to be done before she started thinking about finishing the rooms and expecting people to want to stay in them.

Returning to the north wing with the tea things, she opened the door into the Room of Doom, where Mr Ludkin and his son were still examining the damage. She put the tray on one of the less rotten windowsills and stood silently watching them as they strode around, touching walls and gazing up at the ceiling and down at the floorboards. She dreaded, absolutely dreaded, what might be going through their minds.

'Mr Ludkin?' she prodded, unable to bear the suspense any longer.

He circled the pile of rubble that lay in the middle of the floor, tapping it with the foot of his steel-tipped work boot.

'Well,' he said a moment later, scratching his head again, 'I've seen worse.'

'I haven't,' Tim said.

'What I mean to say is, I've seen worse but not with somebody actually living in the house at the time.'

'Well, we're not living in this actual room,' Celeste pointed out.

'I'm glad to hear it,' he said with a chuckle.

'And you've taken a look at the other rooms and the damp in the corridor?'

'Seen it all before,' he said. 'I remember this place well. Been worrying myself about it for years but I'll give it a proper going-over before we leave and see how much more damage has been done since I was last here.'

Celeste winced. 'I'm just glad we can get to work on it now,' she said. 'If you're willing to take the job on, of course. We'd have to see your quote first.'

Mr Ludkin nodded, slurping his tea as he continued to move around the room, shaking his head here and sucking his teeth there.

He was at the manor for another hour, taking photographs and making notes and muttering all sorts of horrors to his son. Celeste tried not to listen. She really didn't want to know. Finally, they were ready to leave.

'I'll get that quote to you next week,' Mr Ludkin said. 'Brace yourself, now.'

'I will,' Celeste said, watching as the two men got into the van and drove away.

Gertie was walking across the lawn, a basket of eggs in her hand.

'Was that Ludkin and Son?' she asked.

Celeste nodded. 'Yes. I've just shown him the north wing.'

'What did he say?' Gertie asked.

'He shook his head a lot, sucked his teeth and told me to brace myself for his quote.'

'Well, as long as we've got enough in the pot from the sale of the paintings,' Gertie said.

Celeste sighed. 'Let's just hope we will have!'

18.

Celeste wasn't sure what exactly had woken her but she was only glad that it wasn't the sound of a ceiling collapsing somewhere within the depths of the house. She lay still, staring into the darkness of her room before switching her bedside lamp on. Warm light flooded the room and revealed Frinton at the bottom of the bed, softly snoring, his little furry body giving him the appearance of a soft toy. Moving carefully so as not to disturb him, Celeste got up and checked her clock. It was just after two.

She made her way downstairs with the intention of making a cup of herbal tea. It wasn't until she was in the hallway that she was quite sure she wasn't the only one up in the middle of the night. There was somebody in the kitchen.

Celeste sighed, immediately knowing who it was and realising that it meant trouble. Sure enough, the light was on and the sound of somebody moving about could be heard.

One of Gertie's great pleasures in life was baking but, when it happened in the middle of the night, it was a sure indication that she was stressed. The sight of her sister in her dressing gown, banging ceramic bowls around in the kitchen, instantly told Celeste that something was wrong.

'Gertie?' she said, hovering in the doorway as if testing to see if it was safe to enter the room. 'What are you doing?'

'Making scones,' her sister replied without turning around. Celeste saw that there were already two batches of fruit scones fresh from the Aga and, judging by the delicious smell, a third was well on its way.

'Can I come in?'

Gertie nodded and Celeste made her way towards the kettle.

'Would you like a cup of tea?'

'No thank you,' Gertie said. 'Would you like a scone?'

Celeste smiled. 'I have never been able to refuse one of your scones no matter what time of the day or night it is.'

Gertie took a plate out of the cupboard and Celeste watched as she cut open a warm scone and buttered it, bringing it to the table a moment later.

'Aren't you having one?' Celeste asked.

Gertie shook her head. 'I couldn't.'

'Want to talk?'

'No. I want to bake.' She walked back towards the Aga and lifted out the last batch of scones. There were few more pleasurable experiences than sitting in a kitchen filled with the cosy warmth of an Aga – especially an Aga that had just cooked over thirty fruit scones – but although it was a great treat to be eating one of Gertie's scones, Celeste knew in her heart that there was a problem to be addressed.

'Gertie,' she said, her voice low but firm. 'Sit down.'

Her sister stopped what she was doing and turned around. Celeste saw that her face was quite red and she didn't expect that it was just from the heat of the Aga.

'Come and talk to me,' she said a moment later when Gertie hadn't moved. Finally, her sister joined her at the table.

'Is the scone all right?'

'The scone is perfect,' Celeste said, 'but I don't want to talk about scones.'

Gertie looked down at her hands under the table, where Celeste knew that she was picking at her nails.

'It's a man, isn't it?' Celeste said and Gertie nodded. 'Is it a man I know?'

'Does it matter?'

'I don't know. You tell me.'

'I'd rather not.'

'What's going on? What's making you so unhappy?'

Gertie swallowed hard and her dark eyes misted with tears. 'I'm in love with him.'

'That shouldn't make you miserable,' Celeste said.

'I know.'

'Then what's happened?'

'He doesn't call me when he says he will and I hardly get to see him,' she said, her voice subdued.

'Was it him you were with in Cambridge?'

'How did you know?'

'A wild guess?' Celeste said, a wry eyebrow raised.

'It's the longest we've ever spent together,' she said, 'and it was wonderful.'

'So, why can't it be like at all the time? Is he a workaholic?'

Gertie gave a little snort but didn't answer the question.

'Gertie? What's stopping him from seeing you?'

The silence that filled the room was palpable and neither sister spoke.

'Gertie?' Celeste pressed, anxiety weighing her down. 'Tell me.'

Gertie looked across the table at her and Celeste feared that she knew what she was about to say, only she didn't get a chance.

'What on *earth* is going on?' Esther barked from the door, making both the sisters jump. 'I can't get to sleep for the racket you girls are making.'

Gertie leapt up from the table and Celeste knew that the moment was lost.

'I'm so sorry, Mrs Martin,' she said. 'We didn't mean to disturb you.'

'What you are both doing up at this time when good people are trying to sleep?'

'Nothing,' Celeste said. 'We're both going back to bed. Come on. I'll walk you back to your room.' She turned to try and catch Gertie's eye but her sister's back was to her. Their conversation would have to take place at another time.

❧

Gertie did a pretty good job of avoiding Celeste over the next few days, which wasn't hard in a house the size of Little Eleigh Manor with its accompanying acres of garden. It had always been the perfect place to lose yourself if you needed to, as Celeste had discovered growing up. Sometimes, when life and family became too much, she would find a little corner in a panelled room or a leafy arbour in the rose garden and tuck herself away until she felt strong enough to come out again. Perhaps that's what Gertie had been doing, Celeste thought, imagining her sister taking her work to some quiet corner of the estate where she wouldn't be subject to her big sister's questions.

Celeste couldn't help but worry about her. Had she been about to open up to her the other night in the kitchen before Esther Martin had barged in? Celeste had the feeling that she might well have been and it pained her that Gertie was carrying around this great hurt on her own. But she couldn't force her to tell her what was going on, could she? Gertie knew where to find her if she wanted to talk. As much as she wanted to, Celeste couldn't deny the fact that she hadn't been there for her sisters over the last few years. Evie was probably never going to forgive her for that, Celeste thought, and she was probably in the right. Celeste would never really understand what Gertie and Evie had gone through in the last months of their mother's life. She could only just begin to imagine what it must have been like.

'But I couldn't have been there,' she told herself. She'd been telling herself that over and over again since Penelope had died, but there was that tiny element of doubt sitting in her heart. *Could* she have made it good with her mother at the end? She sincerely doubted it but perhaps she should have at least tried.

Tears of frustration filled her eyes and she blinked them away, cursing the impossible situation she found herself in: she *should* have been there but she *couldn't possibly* have been there.

Would she ever be free of the overwhelming sense of guilt that she'd let her sisters down? They'd needed her – not just in her capacity as a good administrator to keep the office in check but as a fellow sister to talk to and to take comfort from when things got rough. Even if she hadn't been able to make things right with Penelope, she should have been there all the same – for Gertie and Evie.

'I failed them,' she said to herself. 'But I can put that right now. I'm here for them now.'

⟡

It was a long overdue bill and a spot of grocery shopping that took Celeste into Lavenham on Saturday morning. She'd found the outstanding invoice from the printing company they used for all their cards and stationery and thought that an apology in person was as overdue as the actual money. So she'd driven in, parked on the hill by the church and walked into town, passing the rows of timber-framed buildings that leaned forwards and sideways at the most alarming angles and attracted hordes of tourists in the summer months.

She was just passing a cafe when she saw him.

'Julian?' she said.

'Celeste!' he cried, a surprised smile on his face.

'What are you doing here?' she asked, looking at the vacant shop he'd just walked out of.

'I've been checking out a few properties, remember?'

'Of course,' she said. 'For your antiques?' She looked at the little shop with the bay window. 'Any good?'

'Too small,' he said. 'I wouldn't fit half what I wanted in there.'

'Really? You plan to have a lot of stock, then?'

'No point in doing things by halves, is there?' he said, his blue eyes bright with excitement.

'I suppose not,' she said.

'It's good to see you,' he said. 'Are you keeping well?'

'Yes, thank you,' she said.

'And your sisters?'

'Very well,' she said.

'Good,' he said. 'I often think about you all in that moated manor house of yours.'

'You do?'

He nodded. 'And I was going to give you a call about the Fantin-Latour,' he said. 'I might have some –'

'Julian?' a voice interrupted them from behind Celeste.

'Ah, there you are, Miles,' Julian said. 'I lost you.'

'Sorry,' the man said. 'I had to take a call.' He slipped his mobile into his jacket pocket.

'Celeste,' Julian said, 'this is my brother, Miles.'

'Well,' Miles said, taking hold of Celeste's hand and shaking it, a huge smile on his face. 'So you're the *real* reason why my little brother's been spending so much time in Suffolk, are you?'

Celeste felt her face heat up at the suggestion and saw that Julian's had coloured up too.

'Celeste is a client,' Julian told him.

'Is that what they're calling it these days?' He gave a laugh and winked at Celeste.

Celeste looked up at him. He was taller and broader than Julian but his features were similar and he had the same dark red hair. But there was something intrinsically different about him that Celeste couldn't quite put her finger on.

'Let me help you with those bags,' Miles said, nodding to the two carriers she was holding in her left hand.

'Oh, no,' she said. 'It's quite all right. I haven't got far to go.'

But Miles had already taken them off her. 'Where are you parked?'

'Up by the church,' she said, and the three of them walked up the hill together.

'I didn't realise Suffolk was so full of beautiful women,' Miles said, grinning at Celeste as they walked.

'Well, I don't know about that,' Celeste said, trying to catch Julian's eye, but he was looking resolutely ahead.

'You never thought of leaving Suffolk for life in the big city?' Miles asked her.

'No, never,' Celeste said honestly.

'I could show you all the best places London has to offer,' he said. 'I know them all. Restaurants, clubs, theatres – we could have a lot of fun.'

Celeste couldn't help but smile as Miles cocked his head to one side to gauge her response.

'Not tempted?' he asked.

'Not really,' she said as they reached her car.

'You don't know what you're missing,' he said in a sing-song voice.

Celeste shook her head in amusement. 'Thanks for carrying my bags,' she said.

'No problem,' he said. 'That's what these muscles are for.'

Celeste looked surprised by his declaration.

'You don't work out, do you, Julian?' Miles continued, turning to his brother after placing the shopping bags on the back seat of Celeste's Morris Minor.

'You know I don't,' Julian said. 'I much prefer walking to sweating at a gym.'

'Yes, but walking doesn't build your muscles up – and the ladies all love muscles!' Miles said. 'I work out four times a week – sometimes more.'

Celeste looked at Julian as if to ask him how the conversation had veered so strangely but he simply shook his head.

'We have a gym in our building with all the latest top-of-the-range equipment,' Miles went on, seemingly oblivious to the thoughts of his companions. 'It's superb. Of course, I'm the fittest man there. Even the youngsters can't keep up with the pace I set. Just feel these biceps, Celeste.'

Celeste did a double take. 'Pardon?'

'Go on! *Feel* them,' he said, taking his jacket off.

'She really doesn't want to feel your muscles, Miles,' Julian said.

'Nonsense! *Every* woman wants to feel my muscles.'

'I think I'll pass,' Celeste said, completely baffled by Miles's behaviour.

Miles frowned. 'You're missing a treat. The number of women who'd like to get their hands on my body!' He made an odd spluttering sound and Celeste caught Julian's eye again. Julian simply raised his to the sky.

'I think I'd better get going,' Celeste said, turning to leave.

'You see, Jules,' Miles said, 'you've always had a knack of chasing the women away.'

'We'd better get going too, eh, Miles?'

'You *always* take pleasure in embarrassing me, don't you?' Miles suddenly said.

'I don't do any such thing,' Julian said calmly.

'Yes! *Yes* you do,' Miles continued, his smile now replaced with a deeply engraved scowl.

'Look, I'd better get going,' Celeste said.

'No, wait a minute,' Julian said, and Celeste watched as he turned to face Miles. 'Would you mind giving us a minute?'

Miles glared at his brother. 'Take all the time you want,' he said. 'I'm off. I'm fed up of hanging around this backwater.'

They watched as Miles stalked back down the hill into town.

'What the hell was all that about?' Celeste asked once Miles was safely out of earshot.

'Don't pay any attention to him. He's an idiot.' Julian ran a hand through his hair. He looked flustered and it wasn't a look Celeste was used to seeing. 'Look, I wanted to give you a call. I've got some good news about the Fantin-Latour.'

'Okay,' Celeste said.

'So, is it okay if I call round?'

'Of course,' Celeste said.

'Are you about tomorrow?'

'I imagine so,' she said.

'Still chained to that desk of yours?' he asked.

'Something like that.'

'Okay, well, I'll pop over mid-morning, if that suits.'

'That would be fine.'

'Right,' he said, 'I'd better see if I can smooth things over with Miles.'

'I'll see you tomorrow,' she said, and he waved her a goodbye before heading back into town.

Celeste stood there watching him for a couple of minutes. For some reason, her heart was racing and it took her a moment to realise why. Miles Faraday had reminded her of somebody. Somebody who had made her feel confusion, anger and fear all at once. Somebody she'd had the good sense to walk away from and whose likeness she'd hoped never to meet again.

Her mother.

19.

Celeste took Frinton for a walk, ambling along the bank that edged the River Stour and then striding out into the fields towards Duke's Wood. It had rained in the night and both dog and mistress were delighted by the scents that the rain had released. Celeste took in great lungfuls of the woodland air, luxuriating in the early summer stillness of the place and the soft earth that supported her light tread.

Duke's Wood was a favourite haunt of Celeste's and had been since the first precious day when she'd discovered it for herself. Her mind spiralled back into the past as she remembered running through the stubble fields, her ankles scratched and bleeding as she fled towards the trees, not knowing where she was going.

The wood had welcomed her with a green embrace and had hidden her from the world as she'd sat at the base of a smooth beech tree, the wild beating of her heart slowly returning to normal as she'd watched a deer moving through the trees and listened to the song of a robin in a holly thicket.

She passed that very place now, remembering the comfort it had given her as she'd tried to banish the words of her mother from her mind.

'Get out of my sight – you *useless* girl!'

There had been other words too – cold, hurtful words as sharp as flints – too painful to remember, but they had left their mark in her heart. Celeste had sat in the wood until their sting had lessened, until the light had faded from the sky and the wood was shrouded in darkness.

She hadn't wanted to go home but where else did a thirteen-year-old girl have to go? So she'd walked home at twilight, the eerie shadows of the trees her only companions.

'Where have you been?' Evie had cried as soon as Celeste had opened the front door. 'You've missed your dinner! We had treacle tart for pudding.'

Gertie looked more anxious. 'Are you okay?' she asked and Celeste had nodded.

'I just lost track of time,' she lied.

'There you are, darling!' her mother chimed. 'We thought you'd left home for good this time. I was going to let your room out to a nice student.'

Celeste stared at her mother's smiling, bemused face. She seemed to have forgotten the whole incident and expected that Celeste would forget it too but she couldn't. How could she? But neither could she talk about it. Instead, she reeled with pain and confusion, unable to put her emotions into words even if she'd had the courage to confront her mother or confide in her sisters.

She remembered that evening now as she walked through the woods with Frinton. It was funny how places were tinged by the past. For her, Duke's Wood would always be connected with that lonely evening when she was a teenager.

She looked up into the brilliant green of the beech leaves and thought how long ago that night had been and yet she still carried that teenage girl inside her. She was still there, that young Celeste, hiding behind the memories that had been collected since. One had only to scratch the surface to discover her again.

Perhaps it was meeting Julian's brother that had made her think of that long-ago incident now, she thought. There'd been that same cold and callous quality about Miles Faraday that her mother had had. The same outspokenness, too, and lack of empathy with anybody else's feelings. It had shaken her to witness it in somebody else.

It was then that Frinton set up barking at the base of a great oak tree up which a squirrel had shot. Celeste watched as he jumped up on his back legs, his ears alert as if the poor creature might drop out of the tree into his jaws at any moment. She laughed. If only she'd had a fox terrier whilst growing up. They had a knack for vanquishing one's woes in an instant.

Celeste was glad to see Julian's MG pulling up in the driveway as she got back from her walk. She couldn't help but feel calmer somehow when he was around. He had an uncanny ability to chase the blues away and lift the spirit, and she really couldn't think of many people who did that. It would be a shame to lose his friendship when the business with the paintings was over, she thought. He really was a sweet man.

'Hello,' she called as she approached him.

'Good morning,' he said cheerfully, bending down to greet Frinton, who had torn across the driveway to reach him. 'Been for a walk?'

'To the woods.'

'Nice,' he said. 'Perfect day, isn't it?'

'I've been skilfully avoiding the study all morning.'

'Good for you,' he said.

'Cup of tea?' she asked.

'Thank you,' he said and the two of them fell into step together, entering the house a moment later.

Celeste served tea in the living room and that's when Julian began.

'So, I think I've got some good news for you.'

'Is it the buyer in America?'

Julian nodded. 'She's very keen to make us an offer on the Fantin-Latour.'

'So, you think it would be better to sell to her directly without going to auction?'

'Well, it depends how quickly you need the funds.'

'Pretty quickly.'

'I thought as much,' he said.

'Yes, we're about to get a quote for the work and I'm afraid it will be eye-wateringly high.'

'I can imagine,' Julian said. 'Well, she's told me that she wants that painting, and when Kammie Colton wants something, the amount she's willing to pay doesn't come into it. You can pretty much name your price.'

'Really?' Celeste said, still thinking of the quote. 'It certainly would be nice to have some money in the pot.'

'I've done a lot of research on Fantin-Latour and what his pieces have fetched in recent years, so you're not going to lose out by not going the route of the auction. Auctions can be so risky, too – so much of it is down to luck on the day – so you might actually be a lot better off settling things outside the auction room.'

Celeste nodded. 'I really appreciate your advice on all this.'

'All part of the job,' he said. 'It's a really special painting and I'd like to see it do well for you. I know how much it means to you.'

'Thank you,' she said.

'There's just one small matter to sort out.'

'Oh?'

'Mrs Colton is flying to the UK next week and will be coming to see the painting in London. It sounds like she's been doing her research about your family, too, and she's expressed an interest in meeting you all and seeing the manor and gardens.'

'Has she?' Celeste asked, feeling flustered.

'I think she just wants to know a bit more about the painting's background. A painting of roses belonging to a family who grow roses and live in a medieval moated manor house has really captured her imagination. She's an American. They don't have such places over there. She was very excited about the idea of seeing Little Eleigh Manor.'

'You've spoken to her about it?'

'Yes,' Julian said. 'I said I didn't think there'd be a problem but that I'd better speak to you first. So, what do you think?'

There was a pause before Celeste answered. 'I'm not at all sure about this, to be honest,' she said, suddenly feeling very anxious.

'No?' Julian said. 'It'll only take a couple of hours and it really would mean the world to her. She's flying all the way from America to do this deal and, from what I can gather, she's a real Anglophile. This trip will make her really happy. And I'll be with her, of course. You wouldn't have to deal with any of it on your own.'

Celeste nodded in understanding.

'But I can understand if you don't want a stranger in your home,' Julian went on. 'Just say the word and I'll let her know it's not really feasible.'

Celeste bit her lip. She felt mean now. 'Of course she can come,' she said at last, 'and we'll make cucumber sandwiches and a nice Victoria sponge if it would really make her happy.'

'Really?' Julian said. 'I'm sure she'd be thrilled.'

'And I'll just keep thinking about her chequebook,' Celeste said.

Julian laughed. 'I'll set up a day and time for her visit, then?'

Celeste nodded. 'So how did you get on in Lavenham?' she asked. 'Did you find the right shop in the end?'

'I'm afraid not,' he said. 'Nothing was quite right.'

'So, you're serious about opening an antiques shop?'

'Oh, yes,' Julian said. 'It's time, you know? And you helped inspire me.'

'*I* did?' she said in surprise.

'With your courage in deciding to sell your paintings and move forward.'

'But that wasn't courage – that was panic!'

Julian grinned. 'All the same, it made me think about my future and really start to plan ahead.'

'Well, I'm really pleased for you. I think it'll suit you.'

'Really?'

She nodded. 'You have the right personality.'

'I do?' Julian seemed taken aback.

'You like people. You get on with them. I'm sure they'll all flock to your shop.'

'Thank you,' he said, suddenly looking abashed. There was a pause before Celeste began.

'Julian?'

'Yes?'

'Your brother –'

'Yes, I must apologise if he offended you yesterday. He can be a bit' – Julian paused – 'insensitive.'

Celeste looked at Julian, wondering if she was brave enough to say what she wanted to say next. 'I was going to ask you about him,' she began tentatively. 'He reminded me of someone.'

'Really?'

She nodded.

'Who?' Julian prompted.

Celeste took a deep breath. 'My mother,' she said.

'Ah,' Julian said. 'She had a personality disorder?'

Celeste frowned. 'What do you mean?'

'Miles – my brother – he suffers from a personality disorder although he'd knock me into next week if I suggested such a thing to him. It's called Narcissistic Personality Disorder – to give it its full, grand title. It's a spectrum disorder which has all sorts of traits – some stronger than others. Basically, he's like the most self-absorbed person you can think of, only a hundred times worse. He finds it hard to empathise with other people and can turn on you at a moment's notice if you're not giving him what he wants.'

Celeste blinked. 'That's all sounding awfully familiar,' she said. 'You say this is a recognised disorder?'

Julian nodded. 'There's a ton of stuff about it on the internet, where you can run tests to see how people score on the spectrum. It's fascinating,' he said. 'Before I came across it, I thought I was going mad at times. I just couldn't understand why Miles would say the things he did and act in the most unforgivable ways and then – the next moment – act as if nothing had happened.'

Celeste laughed and then covered her mouth in shame.

'You know what I mean?'

'You could say that,' she said, staring down at the hearth, her mind whirling with thoughts. She then got up and closed the living room door, realising that she was intrigued by what Julian was confiding to her and desperate to know more and to share more with him.

'My mother,' she began as she sat down again, 'if I so much as dented her pride, she would threaten to disown me and would blank me for days – weeks sometimes. And then she'd start up again as if nothing had happened. It would make my brain somersault in confusion. I felt as if I was walking on eggshells the whole time with her – wondering when her next outburst would be. *When*, not if. Because that was the one thing you could be sure of: it would be coming.'

'Just like Miles, then,' Julian said.

'Then it's not just pride or vanity or selfishness?' she asked.

'No, no. It's something that goes much deeper and, I'm afraid, it's not something that can be dealt with easily. There's no magic pill or cure. This sort of disorder is so engrained that it's virtually impossible for a person to change. One of the reasons is that they think they're right. They're perfect, you see, and, if you dare to challenge them, they'll tell you that it's the rest of the world who has it wrong.

'Yes,' Celeste said, nodding. 'That's it exactly.'

'I've tried to point things out to Miles in the past, telling him his behaviour is unacceptable and that I simply won't put up with it any longer and, sometimes, I think he's understood me. But he hasn't. There'll be a calm period in our lives for a while when we are able to interact like normal people and I'll almost be fooled into thinking that he's changed, that he listened to me and really took on board what I said, but then the next eruption occurs and I realise that he hasn't changed at all – and that he never will.'

Celeste listened without interruption, watching Julian as he sat on the edge of the sofa, his hands clasped in his lap. He spoke so calmly about it all, but she couldn't help wondering if he was raging inside just as she was.

'Were you ever tempted to run away from it all?' she asked him.

'I've often thought it would be easier to end things between us,' he said, 'and to walk away, but I can't bear the thought of that. It just doesn't seem right, even though it might be the sanest thing to do, because it's an endless cycle of emotional abuse.' He paused. 'You okay?'

Celeste nodded, realising that there were tears in her eyes. She'd never spoken to anybody about this issue before – not really. Her sisters knew a little about what had gone on between her and Penelope but they'd always been too close to it all and unable to help her through it. So it came as something of a relief to realise that she wasn't the only one who had experienced such a thing.

'I never thought of it all as emotional abuse before,' she said.

'I'm afraid that's what it is,' he said and gave a tiny smile, 'and I'm sorry to hear you've experienced it as well. I sometimes wish Miles would just hit me and have done with it. I think it would be less painful in the long run and then at least people would understand what's going on. But this sort of abuse – well, people don't really understand it unless they've experienced it themselves.'

Celeste looked into the fireplace again, her vision blurring with tears. 'I've always thought it must have been a fault in me that made Mum act the way she did.'

Julian shook his head. 'It was never your fault, Celeste.'

'But all the things she said. Where did that all come from?'

Julian sighed. 'Miles says the most hurtful things sometimes and he stores things up, too – really trivial things, often from years ago. They seem to build up in his mind and then come rushing out in a vile torrent of abuse. It's like being bulldozed sometimes and it's a wonder I come out alive at the end of it.'

Celeste looked up at him. 'I never knew what to do or say when Mum was like that. There just seemed no words suitable and so I said nothing. I tried to put everything to the back my mind and tell myself that I'd imagined it and that she couldn't really have said such things. But then it would all happen again.'

They were both silent for a moment as if weighing up the words they had spoken and the memories they had shared.

'I wish I could but I can't ever forget the things she said to me,' Celeste said. 'I've tried. I've *really* tried but they're always there, ready to surface at any time and make me feel wretched again.'

'But you've got to keep trying,' Julian told her. 'You've got to let it all go. I find it's easier to cope with Miles now that we're grown up. We don't have to see each other if we don't want to. But it was different when we were kids.'

'He was like this as a youngster?'

Julian nodded. 'And there was no escaping from it then. Mum and Dad just thought he was a bit awkward and selfish, but these traits got worse the older he got. I knew there was something odd about it but it wasn't until I saw an article online about the condition that I twigged. Suddenly, everything made sense. I went through the tick list of traits for NPD and my brother virtually had them all. I couldn't believe what I was seeing. Now, I find myself examining him as if he's some case study and not a real human. It's really strange.'

'And you really never wanted to just end it with him?' Celeste said.

'Sometimes, yes, but it just doesn't seem right,' he said. 'There will be some days – some really brilliant days – when he seems so normal and so vivacious that it's impossible *not* to love him. But then the cracks will start to appear again and the real Miles will surface, and that other person who I glimpsed briefly just disappears.' Julian took a sip of his tea. 'I'm sure you had good days with your Mum, didn't you?'

Celeste gave a little laugh. 'It's all so mixed up in my mind now because the good stuff was somehow always linked to the bad.'

'Like how?' he asked.

Celeste took a moment as she remembered. 'Like the time she bought me this ragdoll. I must have been about eight. I remember seeing it in a shop in town and my eyes were glued to it for what seemed like hours. Well, Mum went straight into the shop and bought it for me. I loved that doll so much. She used to sit at the end of my bed and I'd make funny little clothes for her. But I'll never forget what my Mum said when she bought it for me. "Your father doesn't buy you gifts like this, does he?" It seemed the strangest thing to say and I really didn't understand it at the time but she did that sort of thing a lot. It was as if she wanted to be measured against other people.'

'Like she was the best?' Julian suggested.

'Exactly.'

'Miles is like that too. We were going to a party together to celebrate a friend's birthday. He was Miles's friend, really, but I'd met him a few times and liked the guy well enough. Anyway,

I asked Miles if he had any ideas what I could get him. I'd heard he liked whiskey and Miles said to me, "Any bottle will do. Don't go spending much, though." Well, I'd just put a deposit down on my London flat and I hardly had two beans to rub together but I found a pretty decent bottle. Anyway, I got to the party and watched in horror as Miles presented Anthony with the most expensive bottle of malt whiskey I've ever seen. You can imagine my embarrassment when I handed over my little bottle.'

'One-upmanship,' Celeste said. 'It used to drive me crazy. Mum was always comparing herself to other people. She'd say things like, "Your Aunt Louise couldn't do my job" or "Aunt Leda's hair is thinning. Have you noticed? It's not as thick and glossy as mine." As if I cared about such things.'

Julian smiled sympathetically.

'And she could be incredibly charming with people,' Celeste went on. 'I would often watch in amazement as she entertained them. She became this bright, dazzling creature and they would hang on her every word, and I would try to connect the person I was watching with the one I knew behind closed doors.'

Julian nodded as if he understood.

'She used that charm to make friends too. Over and over again I would see it. She would reel them in with such ease but she couldn't keep them. Something in her would flare up sooner or later. It always happened. The only friends she managed to keep were the ones she didn't see very often. They were lucky enough to escape the outbursts. That's why I knew I had to get away,' she said, 'and that's why I rushed into marriage. It was a mistake but, at the time, it seemed like a wonderful escape. I was trying to make something for myself – a new life – but I just made another muddle.' She closed her eyes.

'Listen,' Julian said, getting up from the sofa. 'I've tired you out with all this.'

Celeste jumped to her feet. 'No, no,' she said. 'Well, maybe just a bit. I can't seem to get my head round all this.'

'There's a lot to understand,' he said, 'but maybe it'll really help you to process what's been going on in the past. If anything, it'll help you realise that none of it was your fault. That's the thing that I couldn't get to grips with for ages – I'd drive myself crazy trying to understand what I could have done to change things. You mustn't do that to yourself, Celeste. You're a good person. A truly good person.' The expression in his eyes was soft and gentle and Celeste felt deeply touched by his concern for her.

'Thank you,' she said. 'This is all so – so incredible.' She gave a tiny smile. 'But it's been really good to talk about all this with you. I've never been able to do that with Gertie and Evie.'

Julian nodded in understanding. 'And if you ever want to talk about it some more – to talk about anything – you know how to reach me,' he said.

She nodded.

'Take care of yourself,' he said, and he reached a hand out towards her and squeezed her shoulder. It was so simple a gesture but it brought tears shimmering to Celeste's eyes.

20.

Gertie was staking a fabulous pink rose called *Summer Blush*. It was one of the Hamiltons' bestselling roses but it did need a little bit of support at this time of year when the plant was heavy with full blooms. Gertie took her time, supporting it gently and dipping her nose into a particularly perfect flower, its deep scent instantly making the world a better place.

She sighed, wishing roses had the power to banish all worries. James was being particularly elusive, texting excuse after excuse as to why they couldn't meet up and cutting their brief conversations short whenever Gertie tried to talk about their future.

Since the great scone baking session in the middle of the night, she had been doing her best to avoid conversation opportunities with Celeste, deciding that now wasn't the right time to confess to anything. She was desperate to talk to somebody about the situation she found herself in but she couldn't help worrying what her big sister would think. Celeste had never been one to judge a person but Gertie was still anxious as to how her sister would react to the news that she was seeing a married man. You couldn't really predict a person's reaction, though, could you? And Gertie harboured the great fear that Celeste would think less of her.

Not for the first time, Gertie cursed herself for the situation she'd got herself into. Why, oh why, couldn't she have met somebody else? *Anybody* else? But it was madness to rail against things she had no control over. Gertie was the sort of person who was led by her heart, and no amount of reasoning over her predicament would ever help. She was in love and that wasn't going to be vanquished by having a few stern words with herself over the morals of the thing.

She was just settling the *Summer Blush* rose into place when she spotted a young man walking over the bridge across the moat. He was tall with blond hair that fell over his face in a messy skein, and he was carrying a large rucksack.

'Lukas?' Gertie cried in delighted surprise.

He raised a hand in greeting and they shook hands as they met beside the round rose border in front of the house.

'How are you, Miss Hamilton?'

'Gertie! You must call me Gertie. And I'm very well. How are you? I didn't know we were expecting you back.'

'Well,' he said, looking down at his great big walking boots, 'I wasn't exactly sure what my plans were but' – he shrugged – 'I like it here. I really missed it.'

Gertie nodded, knowing exactly what he meant: he'd missed Evie.

'So, how is everybody?' he continued.

Gertie took a deep breath. 'I'm afraid I've some sad news.'

'Your mum?'

'Yes. She died in May.'

'God, I'm so sorry. How are you all coping? How's Evie taken it?'

'Badly,' Gertie said. 'Good days and bad days.'

Lukas nodded. 'I wish I'd been here for her.'

'It was probably best that you weren't,' Gertie told him. 'Anyway, listen; let's not talk about that now. Tell me, how was . . . *where* was it you went again?'

'Everywhere,' he said. 'I went down to Cornwall for a bit and painted at St Ives. Then it was up to the Lake District and then down to London to visit the galleries.'

'And now back to Suffolk?'

He grinned. 'It's a pretty good place for an artist.'

'Indeed it is,' she said, remembering earlier discussions they'd had about local boys Gainsborough and Constable.

'Is – erm – Evie around?' he asked shyly.

Gertie nodded. 'I think she's in the potting shed. Follow me.'

They walked around the garden towards the little row of sheds in which was kept every kind of tool and contraption with which to deal with roses.

'Evie?' Gertie called. 'You'll never guess who's here!'

Evie's blonde head popped out of the shed and her dark eyes widened and her mouth fell open. 'Lukas?'

'Hello, Evie,' he said, moving forwards and planting a kiss on her cheek before she could protest.

'What are you doing here?'

'Came to see you,' he said simply, pushing a hand through the fair hair that had flopped over his eyes.

There was an awkward silence with them both staring at one another, each waiting for the other to speak. It was Gertie who broke it.

'Well, aren't you going to invite him in for a cup of tea and a bite to eat?' she asked.

'I suppose so,' Evie said, sounding horribly put out that her work had been interrupted by an affable and very handsome young man.

21.

Evie was crashing pots around as Lukas was trying to talk to her.

'Let me help you,' he said.

'I don't need any help,' she told him.

'But I want to help.'

'We can't afford to hire you again,' she said, avoiding eye contact.

'You think I'm here for a job?'

'Aren't you?'

'No,' he said. 'I told you – I came to see you.'

'Well, it was nice seeing you again but I've really got to work now.' Evie brushed passed him and walked towards the flower beds, a pair of secateurs in her hand.

'I was thinking I might be able to stay here like last time,' he said, quick to follow her.

'What?' she cried.

'Stay here?'

'Impossible,' she said abruptly.

'Why?'

'Because we've got renovations being done to the house and we've already got somebody staying.'

'In my old room?' Lukas asked.

Evie didn't answer. She felt mean because there were several bedrooms which Lukas could easily make use of but she didn't know how she felt about him hanging around her twenty-four hours a day. She was still getting over her shock at him turning up again.

'I'll help with the chores,' he said.

'I'm not sure it's a good idea, okay?' The tone of her voice made him visibly flinch and he backed down.

'Okay,' he said.

She sighed. 'Look, Lukas, I don't know what you're doing back here but I think you might have had a wasted journey.'

'Isn't that for me to decide?'

She stopped what she was doing for a moment, much against her will.

'There's nothing between us,' she said in a low voice.

Lukas cocked his head to one side. 'But there was, wasn't there?' he said, looking genuinely confused now.

Evie was elbow deep in compost now, which was probably just as well because he wouldn't be able to see that she was shaking.

'I need some space, Lukas,' she said.

'Space? But I've been away for months,' he said.

'Please,' she said, her eyes two great wells of vulnerability.

'Listen,' he said, 'I'm really sorry to hear about your mother. I know how much you loved her, and it's a terrible thing to go through, but you don't have to go through it on your own because I'm not giving up on you, Evie,' he said. 'I don't know what's going on here but I know that we had something good. Something *really* good! Evie? Are you listening to me?'

Evie shook her head. 'No,' she said, 'and I think you'd better go.'

'Okay,' he said. 'I'll go. For now. But this isn't the end, you know? I'm not giving up that easily.'

He shoved his hands in his pockets and she watched as he turned to leave, his shoulders slumped and his gait one of a rejected suitor. Evie stood there, chewing her bottom lip in agitation and wondering if she had just made a big mistake.

❧

Later that afternoon, Evie was dusting Esther's room, the cloth flying over the surfaces as if possessed. When she reached the collection of figurines, Esther barked from her chair.

'I'd rather do those myself, thank you!'

'Do you want me to help or not?' Evie asked, an enormous scowl on her face.

'Not when you're in that mood.'

'What mood? I'm not in a mood!'

'Of course you're not!'

Evie paused, duster in hand. 'I'm just – just –'

'What?'

'Lukas is back,' she blurted before she could stop herself.

'Who's Lukas – a lost cat?' Esther asked.

'No. A lost man.'

'Oh,' Esther said.

Evie sighed. 'He was here earlier in the year doing some work for us in the garden whilst Mum was ill and I was taking care of her. He's an art student and he's been working his way around England looking at – whatever it is artists look at.'

'And he clapped eyes on you, is that it?'

'Something like that.'

'But you don't have eyes for him?'

Evie twisted the yellow duster in her hands as if she was wringing somebody's neck.

'I liked him,' she said, 'but I didn't think I'd see him again. I didn't ask him to come back.'

'Then tell him to go. If you're not interested, he'll have to listen,' Esther said.

Evie appeared not to have heard Esther.

'I didn't ask anything of him,' she said. 'I told him to go.'

'What do you mean?' Esther said, turning around in the winged chair and giving the girl her full attention. 'Evie? Why is this worrying you so much?'

But Evie didn't reply. She just shook her head and left the room with the duster in her hand.

22.

With a house as large as Little Eleigh Manor and only three other people living in it, one would have thought that it would be easy to slip out undetected, but Gertie's experience of such things proved otherwise.

She was just halfway across the hall when she heard Evie's voice coming from the living room. 'Where are you off to?'

'Why should I be off to anywhere?' Gertie said, stopping briefly.

'Because you've got that definite stride of yours that means you're going somewhere.'

'I'm only going for a walk if you must know.'

'Can I come with you?' Evie had got up and was now in the hall, looking at her sister.

Gertie's mind whirled around a number of excuses but her sister seemed to take pity on her.

'Go on, then,' she said. 'Be off with your volume of poetry or whatever it is you're going to read in the dappled shade of some ruin.'

Gertie could feel herself blushing. 'I'll see you later.'

She left the house, anxious that Evie might follow her because she was, indeed, going to some old ruin – the little chapel on the other side of the river. She was glad that Evie hadn't questioned her too much about her choice of dress because she was wearing her favourite, which was in the lightest of fabrics and was the exact colour of new bluebells.

The evening air was still wonderfully warm and the Stour Valley was bathed in golden light, turning the river into a sparkling wonder. The light breeze rustled the leaves of the willow trees and Gertie marvelled at the length of her shadow.

She should have been feeling more light-hearted than she was after the recent trip to Cambridge, but she'd only seen James a handful of times since then and each meeting had been horribly brief. Text after text had been sent explaining how very busy he was or how needy Samantha was being.

Forgive me, Gertie xxx

How many times had she forgiven him now? And could she really be expected to do anything else in her position? She had no right to expect anything from him, really, and yet she couldn't help feeling so horribly disappointed each time he let her down. Was it too much to ask to see him? All she wanted was to be in his company and to be held and kissed. How she missed those kisses. She lay in her lonely single bed each night imagining what it would be like to have James next to her. To be able to roll across a great double bed and kiss the man she loved whenever she wanted to. Especially when the woman he currently shared a bed with didn't really want him there next to her.

But at least she was seeing him now, she thought, as she wended her way through a field full of black and white cows. Large raised heads watched her progress but decided that she wasn't worth bothering about and continued with their evening meal. It was like a scene from a Thomas Hardy novel and Gertie couldn't help feeling like one of Hardy's doomed heroines, having fallen in love with the wrong man at the wrong time and wondering how the whole thing would end.

Keep hoping, she told herself. *He's on his way to you.*

She wasn't sure how and she wasn't sure when but, one day, James would be hers and they would be together in their little Italian villa, starting a family of their own. How Gertie had clung to that dream during the dark months of Penelope's illness. It had been the one thing that had kept her sane, the only little glimmer of light in a very dark world.

But reaching the ruined chapel, she saw that there was no James and no Clyde either. She checked her watch. Was she early? No. She walked through the tall blond grasses, admiring the patch of blue scabious, and found a low wall and sat on it, the knobbly flints uncomfortable under the thin fabric of her dress. She should have brought a jacket with her. The air was cooling rapidly now.

She looked out across the old grounds of the chapel. Beyond the tall pink spires of rose bay willow herb, there were two apple trees, their fruit as small and hard as golf balls. Gertie couldn't help wondering if she would still be meeting James here in secret when the fruit was ripe. It had been a year since they had first met. A whole year of secret meetings and promises that, one day, they would be a proper couple. But, as time went on, it was getting harder and harder to believe that that day would ever come.

As the light faded from the sky, Gertie came to the conclusion that he wasn't coming. She'd checked her phone a dozen times but there was no message, and then she remembered their secret hidey hole. Jumping down from the wall, she walked through the ancient arched doorway of the church and made her way towards what once would have been the altar. There, about six inches up from the ground, was a hole half-shrouded by gangly weeds. A large flint had been placed inside it and Gertie removed it now and found a piece of paper, which she unfolded.

Couldn't get a signal on my mobile so thought I'd leave a note in our secret place. I turned up early, hoping you'd be here too. S's not been feeling well today so I can't stay. Miss you loads. Love you. J xx

Disappointment coursed through Gertie. She wasn't going to see him and she'd waited so long for today. She closed her eyes and, when she opened them, she realised that it was getting dark and that she wouldn't have long to get home safely.

Leaving the ruins, she should have headed home straight away but something made her cut across a field towards the village, her feet unsteady on the hard ridges left by a tractor.

What do you think you're doing? a little voice inside her asked.

'I just want to see him,' she replied.

Don't be a fool. Go home!

But some mad need from deep inside her moved her towards the barn conversion at the end of the village. The lights were on and shone out of the huge windows as Gertie approached from the footpath. She could see quite clearly from the gap in the hedge at the back of the house and knew that she was well hidden in the shadows there. It was a ridiculous thing to do and yet she couldn't stop herself. She just wanted a little glimpse of him.

She gasped as he came into view holding a huge ceramic bowl filled with salad which he placed on the dining room table before wheeling Samantha's chair up to it. Gertie watched in envious wonder as James sat down. He was facing the window and Gertie wished with all her heart that he would sense her presence out in the darkening evening.

She watched as they ate. James was smiling. What did he have to smile about when he wasn't with her, she wondered? He was always professing to be so miserable at home.

Perhaps he's thinking about you, a little voice inside her said. She smiled, but she couldn't help feeling hurt that he was with Samantha and not her.

And then it happened – Gertie watched as if the moment was happening in slow motion as James leaned forward in his seat and reached out to take hold of his wife's hand, stroking it with his long fingers in a gesture so gentle and romantic that it brought tears to Gertie's eyes. Was that the action of a man no longer in love with his wife? A man who was planning to *leave* his wife?

Gertie turned away, her mind fogged with confusion and her eyes brimming with tears. What was going on? He loved *her*, didn't he? Not Samantha. He was always telling her that. Samantha was manipulative and cruel. She drained him of all energy. He'd told her that over and over again.

'It's you I love,' he'd say but, seeing him with Samantha in the privacy of their home, she wasn't at all sure she believed him anymore.

❧

Celeste had been hiding in the study with the door firmly closed and the radio on in an attempt to keep out the noise of banging coming from Mr Ludkin and his son, who had made a brutal start on the north wing. It was a bit risky starting work on the renovations before the actual sale of the paintings but Celeste didn't think they could wait any longer – not with a great gaping hole in the ceiling and the risk of rain damage, and Julian seemed quite sure that they were about to make a good sale with the Fantin-Latour, so there would be money in the bank before too long.

She was just thinking about looking up personality disorders on the internet when Evie charged into the room.

'So what are we going to do, then?' her sister asked without any sort of preamble. It was her usual way; she always expected people to be able to read her mind and keep up with her train of thought.

Celeste frowned. 'About what?'

'About the *painting!*'

'What painting?'

Evie sighed and placed her hands on her hips in frustration at Celeste's inability to understand what she was talking about.

'The painting that Simone stole from us!'

'Oh, that painting,' Celeste said.

'Don't say you'd forgotten about it,' Evie said, walking into the room and sitting down in their mother's old chair.

Celeste swallowed hard. She'd have never had the nerve to do that and yet Evie looked completely unperturbed by her movement.

'To be honest,' Celeste said, 'I hadn't given it much thought. Where's Lukas?'

'What's Lukas got to do with this?' Evie said, and Celeste noticed that her sister was blushing.

'Gertie mentioned he was back. I'd like to meet him.'

'Well, he's gone, okay?'

There was an awkward pause between them before Evie continued.

'So, you're going to let her get away with it, is that it?'

'With what?'

'The *painting*!'

'It's not a case of letting her get away with it,' Celeste said.

'No! I know what you're like. You'd do *any*thing to avoid confronting the old cow about this, and that's *so* wrong, Celly!'

'Then what do you suggest we do? We can't just take it and I don't think Dad would believe us if we told him. He'd probably deny knowing anything about it and the whole business would just leave a lot of bad feeling. You know what Simone is like – she'd twist this thing around and make *us* look like the guilty party.'

Evie shook her head. 'I can't believe you're just going to leave it.'

'I don't think we have a choice.'

'But that painting was our grandparents',' Evie said, knowing that that would hit her sister's weak spot.

Sure enough, Celeste gave a weary sigh.

'You want that painting back as much as I do,' Evie told her, 'and, if you don't do anything about it, then I will.'

❧

Evie was still fuming mad when she drove to Gloria Temple's for a meeting with her wedding planner. She knew Celeste had a lot on her plate at the moment but she would have thought that a stolen painting would be a pretty big priority, especially in light of what the other paintings had been valued at. She shook her head as she drove through the winding countryside, slowing down to overtake a horse before turning into the immaculate driveway of Blacketts Hall. She took a couple of minutes to calm herself down, pulling her fingers through her hair, which was still the frightful shade of blonde she had dyed it.

Opening the door of the van, she stepped out into the sunlight and it was then that she noticed a young man standing by the great yew hedge, his back to her. But Evie recognised him all the same.

'Lukas?' she said.

He turned around. 'Evie!' he said, obviously thrilled to see her, which was more than could be said for Evie.

'What on *earth* are you doing here?' she said, her eyes doing their best not to take in his strong tanned arms but failing miserably.

'I put an advert up in a few local shops and Miss Temple hired me,' he said with a big grin that was far too cute to be ignored.

'I thought you'd left Suffolk,' Evie said.

'What made you think that?'

But Evie didn't get a chance to answer because Gloria Temple appeared. 'Ah! Evie! Am I interrupting something?' Her eyes drifted from Evie to Lukas. 'Do you two know each other?'

'Yes,' Lukas said.

'No,' Evie said at the same time.

'Oh,' Gloria said. 'How confusing!' She clapped her bedia-
monded hands together. 'Well, let's make a start, shall we? Carolina
is here and wants to quiz you about your beautiful flowers.'

There then followed an intense hour with Gloria's wedding
planner in which Evie was made to feel like the very lowest of
minions as Carolina droned on and on about what she was planning
for Gloria's big day.

Evie was sitting on a black leather sofa that faced the window
overlooking the driveway, and she couldn't help but notice Lukas
halfway up the ladder as he trimmed back some foliage from the
front of the house. He seemed to be all too aware of her presence,
too, and caught her eye and waved. Evie rolled her eyes.

'Evelyn?' Gloria said.

'Sorry?' Evie said, her attention drawn back into the room.

'Don't you like Carolina's suggestion?'

'Oh, no!' she said. 'I mean – no – I don't not like it.'

'What?' Gloria cried.

'What?' Carolina echoed.

'I mean, I think a balloon arch is a wonderful idea!' Evie said,
seeing the two women's faces relax. Evie sighed. She wasn't a big fan
of balloons, it had to be said. She thought them cheap and nasty
and childish. At least, that's what her mother had said about them
but she wasn't going to confess to that and so she smiled. 'Balloons!'
she said. 'Let's have them everywhere!'

Once the meeting was finished, Gloria escorted Evie to the
front door.

'Isn't Carolina absolutely wonderful?' Gloria beamed.
'I wouldn't be able to operate without her!'

'I would,' Evie said under her breath, 'quite happily.'

'I'm so glad you two have met now. It makes me feel a lot easier
about things. Of course, she'll be here on the big day too, so make
sure you liaise with her.'

'I'm looking forward to it,' Evie said, hoping she wasn't about to be struck down for lying as she shook Gloria's hand. 'I'll see you on the big day.'

Gloria laughed. 'Can you believe I'm going to be a bride again?'

Evie smiled. She could believe it, all right. She wondered if Hamilton Roses would be called upon to supply the flowers for the wedding that would no doubt follow this one in two or three years' time, if the bookies were to be believed.

Lukas was still hanging around in that annoyingly persistent way of his as Evie made her exit.

'I like your hair like that,' he called from his perch halfway up the ladder.

'I don't,' Evie said. 'It was a mistake.'

'You look like Marilyn Monroe,' he told her, coming back down to earth. She smiled sarcastically at him. 'You do!'

'Well, I'm going to dye it a different colour soon so wave it goodbye.'

Lukas waved and Evie rolled her eyes at him. It was then that an idea crossed her mind.

'Could you get a ladder like that onto our van?'

'Why?' he asked.

'I'm just wondering.'

'I don't see why not,' he said. 'There's a rack.'

Evie nodded and pursed her lips together. 'Would you do something for me, Lukas?'

He took a step closer towards her. 'You know I'll do anything for you,' he said.

'Well, then,' she said. 'I might just have a job for you.'

23.

It was on a perfect English summer's day in mid-July when Kammie Colton visited Little Eleigh Manor. Julian had rung Celeste in plenty of time so that she was prepared and, after Celeste had made sure the house was looking as good as it possibly could with half the roof missing from the north wing and dust everywhere, she took a walk around the garden.

The roses were looking their very best, and Celeste stopped by a small round bed full of *Rosa Mundi* which was flowering for all it was worth, its stripy two-toned pink petals fully open to allow its golden stamens to drink in the glorious sunshine. Summer really was the most wonderful season and Kammie Colton couldn't have picked a better day to see the gardens, Celeste thought, as she nipped a dead rose head between her fingernail and thumb. It was a quick and simple movement that was done instinctively and almost without thought as she moved around the garden, but she cursed herself a moment later when she stepped off the path into a bed to nip off a shrivelled rosebud and caught her dress on an evil thorn of a Portland rose. She had put on a dusky pink linen dress that had been ironed the night before and hung in a room from which Frinton had been barred, and now she'd gone and snagged it.

She removed herself from the grasping thorns of the border and hoped that the little snag wouldn't be spotted. It was too late to change now, though, for as she walked back round to the front of the house, she saw Julian's little MG speeding along the lane. His roof was down and Celeste caught a brief glimpse of his passenger, who was wearing a pale blue headscarf and an enormous pair of sunglasses. Audrey Hepburn in the middle of the Suffolk countryside, Celeste couldn't help thinking, quickly diving into the house so she could greet her visitor properly and make sure that Frinton was safely behind closed doors.

A few minutes later, Julian knocked on the front door.

'How wonderful to meet you at last,' Kammie Colton said after Julian had introduced them to each other. They shook hands, and Celeste couldn't help but notice the absolutely enormous emerald ring Kammie was wearing. She was engulfed in a cloud of deeply sensuous perfume that had survived the open-top car experience.

'Come in,' Celeste said, leading them through to the living room, where she brought the afternoon tea through a moment later. Kammie had removed her headscarf to reveal perfectly coiffed hair in a shade of platinum blonde that Evie had been trying to master over the last few weeks. Celeste guessed her to be in her late forties and noted that she had the kind of ease and sophistication of somebody who was well travelled.

'This is charming,' Kammie said, leaning forward to take a china teacup covered in tiny rosebuds. 'What exquisite cups!'

'Everything is covered in roses here,' Julian said. 'It's one of the first things I noticed when I came here.' He caught Celeste's eye and smiled at her as Kammie chose a perfectly cut sandwich to put on a matching plate.

'And this *room*!' she enthused. 'How old is this place?'

'Parts of it date back to the fifteenth century,' Celeste told her. I'll show you around later.'

'I'd *love* that,' Kammie said.

True to her word, Celeste gave a guided tour around the house after tea, carefully avoiding the room in which she'd closed Frinton and the one in which Esther Martin now resided. It would be very unwise to disturb either of them.

There then followed a slow walk around the grounds, during which Kammie Colton gave a series of appreciative gasps.

'You know, in America, this is the kind of place we dream about when we think of England.'

'We're very lucky,' Celeste said.

'I love it. I love it *all*. Apart from that hideous north wing, of course,' Kammie said.

Celeste watched her, wondering whether to comment, and then Kammie laughed.

'It is a bit of a state,' Julian said, joining in the laughter.

'I guess your bad luck is my good fortune,' Kammie continued with the bluntness of a true American.

'I guess so,' Celeste said with a vague smile.

'Well, what can I say? I love everything. But I especially love the painting, don't I, Julian?'

'I certainly hope so,' Julian said.

'We've already discussed this and I'd really like to get things moving before I get back home.'

'That won't be a problem,' he assured her.

'Good,' she said, suddenly sounding very businesslike. 'I tell you what. I'll go outside and wait in the car and give you a chance to talk things over with Miss Hamilton, okay?'

'Of course.'

'Miss Hamilton? It's been a real honour to meet you and I can't thank you enough for showing me around your beautiful home.'

'It's been my pleasure,' Celeste said, shaking the hand offered to her and noticing the enormous emerald ring again.

Celeste and Julian watched as Kammie walked towards the car, fishing in her handbag for her enormous sunglasses.

'Shall we go to the study?' he suggested.

Celeste nodded, her heart thudding in anticipation of his news.

Once the study door was closed behind them, Julian began.

'Well, do you want to hear her offer?' Julian asked. 'Perhaps we should sit down first?' She watched as Julian sat himself down in her chair and, not wanting to sit in her mother's chair, Celeste perched on the side of the desk next to him.

'Well? I've been on tenterhooks for hours. Are you going to bowl me over?' Celeste asked.

'I certainly hope so. She's willing to pay half a million.'

'Dollars?'

'No! *Pounds*.'

'Half a million *pounds*?' Celeste said, her voice croaky with emotion.

Julian nodded and laughed. 'It's a good offer. Paintings of a similar size can go for as little as a couple of hundred thousand, but I think yours is definitely worth more and Kammie doesn't want to mess around. She's the sort of woman – well, you've seen – who knows what she wants and just wants to get the deal done, so she's happy to pay perhaps a little bit more than it would go for at auction. It's worth it to her. What can I say? She loves the painting. She told me she's been waiting for a good Fantin-Latour for years now and she loves the whole story about you girls and the rose business.'

'I don't know what to say,' Celeste said, shaking her head slowly.

'If I was you, I'd say yes before she goes shopping in Hatton Garden and spies some jewels she likes more than your painting!'

Celeste suddenly laughed. 'Yes! Of *course* I'm going to say yes!'

Julian grinned. 'I'm really thrilled for you, Celeste.'

'Thanks,' she said. 'Thank you for getting in touch with her.'

'All part of the service,' he said, opening his hands in a gesture that made her smile. 'I'll get the paperwork moving. We will, of course, have our commission from the quoted price.'

'Of course,' Celeste said, 'but at least I'll be able to pay Mr Ludkin something this month.'

'How's it going?'

'Slowly, noisily and expensively,' she said.

'Oh, dear,' he said.

'But at least things are moving forward now.'

'Will he be working on this room?' Julian asked, getting up from her chair and moving around.

'No, why?'

'It's a bit gloomy, isn't it?' Julian said.

'But it's in a pretty good state of repair compared to the north wing,' Celeste told him.

Julian nodded. 'Probably just needs a bit of a rethink. It's not really you, is it?' He turned to look at her and she could feel herself blushing under his scrutiny.

'It's my mother's study. She redecorated it after Grandpa retired and it's not been touched for years.'

'I thought as much. You really should make it your own,' he said.

Celeste looked thoroughly shocked by this assertion. 'But this is my mother's study,' she repeated.

'Not anymore,' he said. '*You're* the one working in here now. You're running the show, so why not do that in a room that says something about *you*?'

'I – erm –'

'I think that would really help you move forward,' he said. 'If you don't mind me saying.'

'I don't mind,' she said.

'So how have you been getting on since we last talked? You must have had a lot to process.'

'You mean about the personality disorder?'

Julian nodded. 'Have you looked into it at all?'

'I've read a bit about it online,' she admitted.

'And did it help?'

Celeste took a deep breath. 'I feel like my mind's a great big maze of memories at the moment and I'm trying to work my way through them. But, yes, some of the sites I found are helping me realise that there are other people who have gone through this too.'

They looked at each other, their eyes seeming to share something beyond words, and Celeste realised that this man truly understood what she was going through.

'Right,' Julian said at last, clapping his hands down onto his knees before standing up. 'I'd better get back out to Kammie. I've promised to take her to The Swan in Lavenham for dinner after a little jaunt to the coast.'

'She'll love that,' Celeste said, thinking of the beautiful fifteenth-century hotel.

'She'll properly try to buy it,' Julian quipped.

'Well, I don't mind if she does. Just make sure she buys our painting first.'

Julian nodded. 'I'll have to take you there sometime,' he said with a smile that made his eyes shine. There was a moment's pause between them. 'Listen, I hate to rush off like this. There's a hundred things I want to talk to you about. I'll give you a call, okay?'

'Okay,' she said, smiling, as she realised she was already looking forward to seeing him again. She followed as he left the study and walked down the hallway towards the front door.

'Is that your young man?' Esther Martin said as she traversed the hallway, a cup of tea in her pale hands.

'No,' Celeste said.

Esther looked unconvinced, but she didn't get a chance to say anything else because Celeste returned to the study and shut the door firmly behind her.

∾

Evie had arranged to meet Lukas at the end of the driveway to Little Eleigh Manor at ten o'clock that night because she didn't want her sisters knowing what she was up to. She also knew that that was the best time to put the plan into action.

'The ladder's over there,' she said as soon as he arrived, pointing to the wall where she had propped it up.

'And good evening to you, too,' Lukas said, his lopsided grin managing to wind her up within two seconds flat.

'There's no time to have a full-blown conversation,' Evie told him. 'Do you want to help me or don't you?'

'Of course I want to help you,' he said, and walked off to fetch the ladder. A moment later, Evie helped him to secure it on top of the van.

'What exactly are we going to do? You're not going to rob a house, are you?'

'You said you'd help me,' Evie said. 'You said you'd do anything for me.'

'I didn't say I wouldn't ask any questions.'

'Well, I'd rather you didn't.'

Lukas sighed. 'You can be very trying, Evelyn Hamilton,' he said.

'Just get in the car,' she said.

Evie drove through the dusky landscape. She put the radio on in the hope of avoiding conversation but Lukas just wouldn't shut up.

'I walked around the Lake District for a bit and visited Brantwood. Have you been there? It was the home of John Ruskin and they have loads of his paintings there. And you should see the views!' He whistled, startling Evie. 'You'd love it, Evie. We should go up there some time.'

She glared at him. 'I've not got any plans to leave Suffolk,' she said.

'But you should. Everyone should travel.'

'I went to Norwich once and didn't like that very much,' she said, totally po-faced. 'Sudbury on a market day is bad enough.'

Lukas laughed.

'I don't know why you find it so funny. I'm happy here,' she said. 'Suffolk's my home. It's where my family have been for three generations. Why should I go anywhere else?'

He nodded. 'That's wonderful, and I envy you that. I've never really had a home. My parents were always moving around with my dad's work and I never got a chance to settle anywhere. Whenever I arrange to visit them, I have to ask for their address.'

Evie didn't say anything but couldn't help thinking about her beloved bedroom at the manor, which she'd had since she was born. It must be strange and disorientating not to have a home – a real home – to come back to, she thought. Even when she'd gone to college, she'd always come back home each night. She couldn't imagine being away from it and that was one of the reasons she was so terrified now that Celeste had started talking about selling the manor.

Turning in to a village, Evie slowed the van down and turned into the driveway of Oak House.

'What are we doing here, then?' Lukas asked, as Evie switched the engine off and they sat in the darkness.

'My dad and his wife are out this evening,' she said.

'So I'm guessing you didn't want to see them?'

'Not exactly,' she said.

'Okay,' Lukas said, taking a deep breath. 'You're beginning to scare me.'

'There's nothing to be scared about,' Evie said as she got out of the car. 'It's a well-detached house.'

Lukas joined her at the back of the car. 'Evie – tell me what's going on.'

'Grab that ladder.'

'Not until you tell me what you're doing,' he said firmly, his face half-lit by the light from a street lamp.

Evie looked annoyed but realised that she'd have to tell him sooner or later. 'I need to get into one of the rooms upstairs,' she said, strapping a large rucksack onto her back.

'Why?'

'Because there's something in there that belongs to our house. Something my dad's wife stole from us.'

'Why can't you talk this through with your dad?'

'Because he won't believe me – he'll take Simone's side. You don't know her – she's sly. She manipulates people, and I'm going to get that painting back. Dad always leaves his bedroom window open. I'll be in and out in no time with the painting.'

'Are you crazy? You can't do that!'

'Why not? It's our painting.'

'But what if your dad rings the police or something when he finds it's gone?'

'He won't even know it's gone, and Simone wouldn't dare ring. She'll know what's happened and she won't make a scene.'

Lukas shook his head. 'This is just wrong, Evie. You can see that, can't you?'

'It's not wrong. I'm *undoing* a wrong, and if you don't want to help me, I'll do it alone,' she said, reaching for the ladder.

'Oh, for God's sake!' Lukas said, spurred into action. 'Let me do it.'

He undid the ladder and Evie marched across the driveway towards the back of the house where the bedroom window was. The garden wasn't overlooked by neighbours and was in total darkness apart from a tiny pool of light cast from a lamp that had been left on in one of the downstairs rooms.

'See – the window's open,' Evie said as Lukas leaned the ladder against the wall.

'It's too risky,' he said. 'I think you should forget this whole thing.'

'No way,' Evie said. 'That painting is going to be hanging in our living room before midnight.'

Lukas ran a hand over his jaw and then scanned the garden as if he expected a policeman to step out of the shadows.

'Well, let me do it if you really mean to go through with it.'

Evie shook her head. 'No, I want to. It's my idea. I should do it. Just keep this ladder steady.' She dug into her pocket and brought out a little black beanie hat. 'I'm too blonde to be a burglar,' she said as she squashed it over her hair. Her hand then returned to her pocket again and brought out a torch which she switched on and handed to Lukas.

'Are you all right with heights?' he asked.

'I'm fine with heights,' she told him, scurrying up the ladder like a pro.

Once she'd reached the window, she popped her hand through and pushed it open. She was lucky it was a large modern one, which made it easy to enter, but she hadn't remembered the dressing table next to it and crashed into it a moment later.

'Are you okay?' Lukas cried from outside.

'I'm fine!' Evie whispered back, her head out of the window. She turned back into the room and switched a lamp on, then crossed to where the painting hung. 'You are coming home with me,' she said, taking it off the wall and wrapping it in a hessian bag she'd brought with her, before placing it in her rucksack and returning to the window. She heaved the bag onto her back and switched the lamp off.

'Have you got it?' Lukas whispered from the ground.

'Yes – now hold this ladder still,' Evie said as she worked her way out of the window, careful not to knock the dressing table.

It was when she looked down the length of the ladder that the trouble began.

'Oh!' she cried.

'Evie?'

'I . . . feel . . . dizzy . . .'

'Hold on!' Lukas said as he dropped the torch, and she heard the sound of his feet on the steps as he climbed towards her.

'I don't feel great,' she said.

'It's okay. I've got you,' he said a moment later and she felt his arms around her. 'Can you move?'

'I'm not sure,' she said honestly.

'Let's just try things slowly. I've got you safe. Don't worry.'

They moved at the slowest pace imaginable, the sound of Evie's nervous breathing audible in the silent night.

'We're nearly there,' Lukas said a moment later as he felt the safety of the ground beneath his feet and helped Evie off the ladder. 'You okay?'

She nodded. 'I didn't know I had vertigo,' she said. 'I was fine on the way up.'

Lukas picked up the torch and switched it on, and she saw that he was smiling gently at her.

'You scared me to death,' he said, and that's when she fainted.

24.

Celeste was in the living room at Little Eleigh Manor when there was a series of loud bangs on the front door. Frinton, who'd been lying on his back by her feet, snoring sonorously, was up in an instant, charging across the hallway like a bullet leaving a gun. Celeste looked at the clock. It was after eleven. Perhaps it was Evie and she'd forgotten her key again, although it was a bit early for Evie after a night out.

She crossed the hallway to join Frinton at the door.

'Evie?' she called through the thick wood.

'Yes,' a male voice answered and Celeste opened the door.

'Who are you?' she cried a moment later as she saw her sister slumped against a young man's shoulder. She shushed Frinton, who was barking in excitement at the late-night visitor.

'I'm Lukas.'

'What's happened to Evie? Is she drunk?'

'She fainted,' Lukas said. 'She fainted!'

'Oh, my God, *Evie*!' Celeste was beside her in a moment, her arm around her sister's shoulders.

'She went to get the painting,' Lukas tried to explain as they brought Evie into the hallway.

'What?' Celeste said. 'QUIET, Frinton!'

'The painting at your father's house. I told her she was a fool to even think of pulling such a stunt but she insisted on going through with it.'

'But she told me she was going to Colchester to see a friend,' Celeste said.

'She wasn't going to Colchester,' Lukas said.

'Evie!' Celeste cursed. 'Let's get you up to bed, where you should have been in the first place at this time of night.'

'What's going on?' Gertie said, appearing in the hallway. She was wearing a long red cardigan over her nightdress and looked as if she'd been asleep. 'What's wrong with Evie?'

'She fainted!' Lukas said, and he told Gertrude what had happened that evening.

'Vertigo? I didn't know she had vertigo,' Gertie said.

'Neither did she until she was at the top of the ladder, on the way back down,' Lukas said. 'I've never been so scared in my life. When I think of what might have happened . . .' His voice petered out into nothing.

'Let's just get her upstairs,' Celeste said.

'I can do it myself,' Evie said. It was the first time she'd spoken since arriving home, but Celeste wasn't convinced.

'You're weak and in shock,' Celeste told her. 'Gertie – do you want to get her some hot milk? Maybe a splosh of brandy in it?'

Gertie nodded and left them.

When they finally made it to Evie's room, they helped her off with her shoes and eased her gently into bed.

'Better?' Celeste asked.

'I got the painting, Celly,' Evie said in a whisper, her bright eyes half-closing in the lamplight.

'We'll talk about that in the morning,' Celeste told her.

'Aren't you pleased?'

'I'm pleased you didn't break your neck,' Celeste said.

Evie closed her eyes and Celeste turned to Lukas. He was still looking pale and shaky, his fair hair sticking up at weird angles around his face as if he'd been electrocuted.

'Perhaps we should get you a splosh of brandy too,' Celeste said.

'I wouldn't say no,' he said, sitting down in an old armchair by the window. Like Celeste's bedroom, the room had sloping floorboards covered in an ancient and threadbare rug. Its walls were of oak panelling and the curtains, although of good quality, had long since had their heyday. Still, the room was very much Evie and you could see her touches everywhere, from the stuffed teddy bears and old ragdolls who sat in a happy jumble on top of a blanket box to the line of make-up bottles and hair dyes on her dressing table.

Gertie entered the room with a mug of warm milk.

'There's just a smidgeon of brandy in it,' she said, sitting on the edge of the bed and handing it to Evie, who sat up after Celeste had plumped her pillows behind her.

'Is Esther there?' Evie asked.

'Esther?' Celeste said in surprise.

'I want to see her.'

'Whatever for?' Celeste asked. 'She's probably in bed. It's very late.' Evie didn't answer as she sipped her hot milk so Celeste left the room. 'Keep an eye on her,' she said to Gertie. 'And I'll get you some of that brandy,' she told Lukas.

Celeste went downstairs, Frinton following close behind her.

'You can't come with me,' she told the dog, sending him into the living room, where he reluctantly curled up with a half-eaten toy for company.

'Esther?' Celeste called a minute later, knocking gently on their new house companion's door.

'Who is it?'

'It's Celeste. Evie's calling for you. She's not feeling very well.'

A moment later, the door opened and there stood Esther, her white hair loose around her shoulders and her face just as pale. She was wearing an enormous brown woolly cardigan that swamped her tiny frame and gave her a teddy bear-like appearance.

'I hope I didn't wake you,' Celeste said.

'Pah!' Esther said. 'I don't sleep until at least one o'clock. Let me see Evie.' She charged out of the doorway and headed for the stairs. She could move surprisingly quickly when she wanted to.

'Which room is it?' she barked when she'd reached the top of the stairs.

'On the left,' Celeste said. 'The open door.'

Celeste followed her in a moment later.

'Esther?' Evie said from the bed, her eyes opening and a small smile spreading across her face.

'I'm here,' Esther said, taking Gertie's place on the side of the bed. Gertie exchanged looks with Celeste. What was happening, they seemed to ask? Why had their sister asked for Esther, of all people? She didn't even like her, did she? She was scared of her.

'Lukas? Come and have that brandy,' Celeste said. 'I could probably do with one myself.'

He stood up. 'You all right now?' he asked Evie.

She nodded. 'Thank you,' she said and he smiled before leaving the room with her two sisters.

Evie and Esther were left alone.

The old woman leaned across the bed to pick up Evie's hand just as Evie had known she would. It was a simple but deeply comforting gesture and Evie immediately felt at peace.

'You've got yourself in a right state, haven't you?' she said. 'What happened?'

Evie took a deep breath and told her about the evening.

Esther shook her head. 'You risked your life for a painting?'

'I didn't risk my life,' Evie said with a tut.

'No? What do you think would have happened if you'd fallen from the top of that ladder?'

Evie shrugged. 'I might have been a bit bruised. But it wasn't me I was worried about.' She hesitated for a moment. 'It was the baby.'

'You're pregnant?' Esther said.

Evie nodded. '*Please* don't say anything!' she suddenly said, leaning forward and clasping Esther's right hand in both of hers. 'I haven't told anyone.'

'I wouldn't dream of it,' Esther said. 'It's his, isn't it? That boy out there?'

Evie nodded.

'Well, he looks a decent sort. He'll stand by you – do the right thing.'

'But I don't want him to do the right thing. This is *my* baby!' Evie said, her hands returning to her lap.

Esther looked confused. 'But it's his, too.'

Evie shook her head. 'He doesn't have to be involved.'

'Don't you think you should let him make that decision?'

'He won't be around for long,' she said.

The expression on Esther Martin's face changed and she suddenly looked like the stern old lady who had chased the young Evie from her garden with a broom. Startled, Evie wondered why she'd invited her into her bedroom and had her sitting on her bed.

'Now, listen here, Evelyn Hamilton! You *have* to tell that young man and let him make his own mind up. A baby isn't a toy that you can keep all to yourself – it's a living, thinking, feeling being and, one day, that baby is going to grow up and ask where its father is and why you took it upon yourself to hide him. What will you do then? What will be your excuse? Because, let me tell you, nothing you can come up with will be good enough if you've stopped a decent man from being involved with his own flesh and blood.'

Evie stared at Esther's serious and startlingly pale face. It was, perhaps, the first time in her life that an adult had given her such a selfless and honest piece of advice, and she wasn't quite sure how to respond. Her mother had never been one to offer any guidance on anything. Every conversation Evie had ever tried to open had always resulted in her mother turning the conversation around to herself, like the time when Evie had split up with her first boyfriend at high school. She'd been heartbroken and in tears, but when she'd told her mum about it, she'd reprimanded her and told her to forget him. That was all. *Forget about him.* That was the only thing she'd said about it and, of course, that was the very thing a heartbroken teenager was incapable of doing.

Evie couldn't remember a single time when her mother had offered her any useful advice at all, which was probably why Esther's tirade was so startling to her now.

'But I –'

'No buts!' Esther said, holding a stern finger up in the air. 'You have a responsibility to both father and child.'

They sat in silence for a moment, Evie absorbing Esther's words. Instinctively she knew that Esther had her best interests at heart and that she'd listen to her – *really* listen to her – if she had anything else to say.

'I just wanted something of my own,' she said at last.

Esther frowned. 'What do you mean?'

Evie sighed and her slim shoulders sank a little. 'I can't explain it,' she said.

'Try,' Esther said, and Evie looked into the pale blue eyes which were examining her so closely that it almost hurt. Growing up in a household full of women, it had been easy to be overlooked. Her mother had always been so obsessed about Hamilton Roses doing well, and Celeste had always had enough on her plate working alongside their mother and Gertie too. So Evie felt as if she'd more or less grown up alone.

'Don't get me wrong,' she said. 'I adore my sisters and I'm sure I only ever needed to ask if I wanted anything, but they were always so busy growing up. I felt like they never had time for me. I always felt so – so *young*. I was always in the way. "Go and play somewhere else, Evie," they'd say or, "I haven't got time right now – come back later." And Mum was always working during the day and going out to parties in the evenings. I never really had anyone to be with.' She paused.

'You mean you're having a baby in order to stop being lonely?' Esther asked.

'No,' Evie said. 'Well, maybe partly. It's more than that, though. I feel I've got all this love in me. Sometimes it scares me and I know that my sisters don't need it – not really. Celeste has always been such a loner. She's always taken care of herself in her own way, and Gertie would rather look for answers in a romantic novel than ever think to ask me for advice. But this baby – this baby –'

'Can't ever be a substitute for what's lacking in your own life,' Esther said gently.

'I know that,' Evie said. 'But I know I can be a good mother. I just *know* it! And I don't need anyone else to help me do that.'

Esther shook her head. 'We always need somebody else. Don't be going through life thinking you can cope on your own. Sure, you might be able to for a while, but it's a pretty lonely existence, I can tell you.'

Evie looked at Esther. 'How did you cope when your husband died?'

'I didn't. I fell apart. After losing Sally, it was almost too much to bear. I've never very much liked my own company, you see.'

Evie frowned. 'But you've lived alone for so many years.'

'I didn't have much choice, did I?'

'You could have moved in with us sooner,' Evie said.

'With your *mother*?'

Esther's horrified tone of voice made Evie smile. 'Ah, yes. That might have been tricky.' They lapsed into silence again and then Evie gave a little sigh. 'I've never talked to anyone like this.'

'Not even your mother?' Esther asked.

Evie laughed. 'You're kidding?'

Esther frowned. She did frowning very well. 'What would she have said about all this?'

Evie looked thoughtful but then shrugged. 'I don't think I would have told her. I would have had to leave home before she threw me out.

She always made it perfectly clear that none of us were to disgrace her because she wouldn't stand for it.' Evie shook her head at the memory. 'It seemed so strange to me at the time – she'd tell me these things when I was just fourteen and I hadn't even been kissed before. "Don't you bring shame on me!" she'd say. I suppose that was fair enough.'

Esther Martin stared at Evie. 'She would have thrown you out, and you think that would have been *fair enough*?'

'Of course,' Evie said. 'If I'd disgraced her.'

Esther shook her head in obvious disapproval.

'Anyway, I'd never have been able to talk to her like this,' Evie went on. 'She never really listened to me. Not that I ever opened up to her or anything. She was always so busy and I didn't like to bother her. That wouldn't have been fair. She used to spoil me with gifts and, when you're a kid, that's wonderful, isn't it? You think that's love. But you need somebody to listen to you too. You need someone who cares.' She gave another little laugh that had no joy in it whatsoever, as if she was just coming to terms with the true nature of her mother at last. 'I once tried to talk to her about a boy I'd fallen in love with, but she changed the conversation around to when *she'd* first fallen in love, so I just gave up.'

Esther picked up Evie's hands again.

'But *you're* a good listener,' Evie told her.

'There's not much else for me to do these days,' Esther said.

'Did you used to listen to your daughter?'

Esther looked confused. 'Of *course*,' she said. 'We used to talk for hours.'

'*Hours?*' Evie said incredulously.

'Oh, yes.' Esther's eyes misted over as she remembered. 'We used to go for really long walks along the river, chattering away about everything and nothing. Mostly nothing. I really wish I could remember what it was we talked about, but my memory isn't so good these days.'

'I can't even begin to imagine what that must be like,' Evie said. 'I mean, I can for you, but I can't imagine that with me and my mum.'

Esther didn't say anything but her face seemed to speak volumes and, all of a sudden, Evie was crying.

'Come here,' Esther said, putting her arms around Evie as she leaned towards her. 'I'm here and I'll listen to *any*thing you want to tell me.'

❦

Down in the kitchen, Lukas was pacing.

'It was my fault,' he said. 'I should never have let her go up that stupid ladder!'

'It wasn't your fault,' Celeste told him.

'No,' Gertie agreed. 'Once Evie sets her mind to something, nothing and nobody can stop her.'

'Well, at least she's okay,' Celeste said. 'This evening could have ended in a trip to hospital if she'd fallen. What's bothering me now is what Esther is doing up there. Why did Evie ask for her?'

Gertie shook her head. 'I have no idea.'

'She's not said anything to you about Esther, has she?'

'No. Not a word,' Gertie said. 'I just thought she was giving Esther's rooms the once over each week and then giving her a wide berth, but something's obviously going on.'

Celeste stopped pacing and took a sip of her brandy. Part of her wanted to march up the stairs and find out exactly what was going on between Evie and Esther, but she had to admit that she was still a little afraid of the old woman. But hadn't Evie been afraid of her too?

'What on *earth* is going on?' Celeste asked, but nobody had an answer for her.

25.

The sound coming from Ludkin and Son at work in the north wing was ear-splittingly loud. Celeste, who'd got up even earlier than normal after finding it impossible to sleep after the whole Evie and Esther thing, had tried to muffle the noise with earplugs and block it out with the radio before finally giving up and leaving the study. Frinton, who'd so far managed to snore his way through the whole morning, left the study, too, with high hopes that his mistress would be heading outside. There was a half-eaten rabbit down by the river which would probably smell even more interesting today, and he was desperate to get back to it.

They were just entering the hallway when Celeste saw Evie.

'Evie!' she called. 'Wait a minute.'

Evie stopped by the barometer which read 'Change.' Again. Perhaps it *was* stuck, Celeste thought, remembering Julian's offer to have it fixed. But she didn't have time to worry about the barometer right now.

'Hey! Are you feeling okay?' she asked her pale-faced sister.

'I'm fine,' Evie said.

'Are you sure?' Celeste didn't look convinced. She'd popped her head round the door of her sister's bedroom after Esther had finally left but Evie had been asleep. Or pretending to be asleep – she couldn't be sure. 'I was so worried about you,' she told her now. 'We all were.'

'There's nothing to worry about. I just got a bit of a fright, that's all.'

'Did you call Lukas this morning? He really wants to speak to you.'

'It'll have to wait,' Evie said.

'Well, don't forget, will you?'

Evie sighed. 'I won't forget.'

'So what did you want to see Esther for?' Celeste asked. She had meant to be more subtle in her line of questioning but it hadn't exactly worked out, because Evie's hand was on the doorknob and she was about to flee.

'What do you mean?'

'I mean, you asked for Esther last night and then spent an eternity talking to her.'

'So?'

Celeste frowned. 'I didn't know you two were friends.'

'Well, we are,' Evie said, her face impassive.

'Right,' Celeste said nonplussed. 'I didn't know.'

'There's a lot you don't know,' Evie said.

'What do you mean by that?'

'I mean, you don't know everything, do you?'

'How can I be expected to know everything, especially when people keep things from me?' Celeste said, not liking the direction their conversation was taking.

'Perhaps if you talked to me more, you might know a thing or two,' Evie said and Celeste could see that her eyes were filling with tears.

'Evie,' she said softly, reaching a hand out towards her sister and flinching when she backed away. 'I'm sorry if I haven't been there for you, but you know how mad and busy everything's been since I came back.'

'But everything is always mad and busy around here,' Evie pointed out. 'You've got to *make* time. Esther makes time for me.'

'Esther's retired. She has nothing else *but* time,' Celeste said, beginning to get annoyed now. 'Evie, what's the matter?'

'Nothing's the matter,' she said.

'Well, something's obviously bothering you. Come on – talk to me.'

Evie looked at her sister and, for a brief moment, Celeste thought she was about to say something, but suddenly there was a colossal sound of falling plaster or timbers or ceiling, or perhaps a combination of all three at once, from the north wing, followed by a torrent of expletives. Celeste's eyes widened and she was torn between running to see what had happened and staying right there with her sister. The north wing won.

'Wait right here,' she said, pointing a determined finger at the spot where her sister was standing, but, as Celeste turned to go, the front door opened and Evie disappeared into the garden, slamming the door behind her in reproach. Celeste's heart sank, and she couldn't help feeling that she had failed yet again.

◦~◦

It was so unfair that there was nobody around to take the phone call or fulfil the order. So unfair and so typical, Gertie thought as she heard the cut-glass voice on the other end of the phone.

'Hello? It's Samantha Stanton.'

Gertie knew exactly who it was, and her heart raced at the sound of James's wife.

'Hello, Mrs Stanton. It's Gertrude here. How can I help?' she asked, all politeness as she dug her short nails into the palm of her left hand.

'I'd like a few container roses delivered. Five, I think, would do the job. Would it be possible to have them today? My gardener is coming and I should like to get them planted. I'm not fussy what they are – just something that's flowering right now. Red if possible'

Red, yes, Gertie thought. Red for anger. Red for danger. Red for the blood Gertie would like to spill.

She shook her head, dispelling her negative thoughts.

'Of course,' she said. 'I'll get something to you as soon as I can.'

She was shaking when she put the phone down and stood in the cool dark hallway for a moment until her heart rate returned to something approaching normality.

'Okay,' she told herself, 'you can do this. Samantha Stanton is just another customer who wants some roses. You will choose them and you will deliver them and that will be an end of it.' Still, as she headed out into the garden, she couldn't help wishing the task hadn't fallen to her.

Gertie chose five fabulous red Hamilton roses called *Constable* – a plant named after the famous artist who had painted all along the Stour Valley. *Constable* was a large healthy plant with the voluptuous flowers of the Bourbon rose, which had been so popular in the nineteenth-century. It also yielded a perfect old rose scent and was a popular choice with florists because of its tall, straight stems. Indeed, they had vases full of them in the manor on special occasions.

Cursing the absence of her sisters when she needed them most, Gertie loaded the van with the five container roses and drove the short distance into the village to the Stantons' house, parking on the immaculate tarmac drive. She sat in the car as she gathered her thoughts. Did James know about this order, she wondered? Probably not; otherwise, he would have offered to collect it himself and contrived a meeting with her at the manor. Or would he have? After she'd witnessed the tender scene between him and his wife, Gertie really didn't know what to expect from him anymore. All she knew was that she wanted to speak to him and that he wasn't answering her texts, which was making her doubt their relationship for the first time. What was going on? She desperately needed to see him to find out. The thought that he might just have been using her for all this time, with no thought of their future at all, made her more anxious than she wanted to admit. She didn't want to acknowledge that at all. Not yet. Not when there was still hope that she might hear from him.

She took a deep breath, trying to quench the anger that was boiling inside her. She had to think of the job in hand and get the whole thing over and done with as quickly as possible.

The barn conversion was pretty impressive with its enormous windows and neat black timber. It wasn't the sort of property Gertie liked, but she could see its attraction all the same. James had told her that the place was nothing but lofty, draughty spaces and that he was looking forward to buying a teeny, tiny property with her one day – somewhere they could snuggle down together and keep warm and cosy – and it was that image Gertie held in her mind as she knocked on the front door and waited.

It took a while for Samantha to reach the front door, opening it from her wheelchair.

'Ah, Gertrude, isn't it?' she said, her voice clear and clipped and her brilliant green eyes looking up at her.

'Yes,' Gertie said, looking down at the figure in the wheelchair. There was no denying that she was a beautiful woman. With a mass of fair hair which reminded Gertie – unsurprisingly – of a horse. She had the kind of even features and flawless skin that most women can only dream about.

'Leave the roses over there by the wall and then come inside whilst I write you a cheque.'

Gertie returned to the car, took the roses out and went back to the house. The hallway was enormous and the tiled floor echoed as Gertie walked across it. Finding Samantha in the living room, she entered and, almost immediately, Clyde the greyhound left his basket and ambled across the room to greet her.

'He certainly seems to like you,' Samantha said with a gentle smile.

Gertie could feel herself blushing and hoped that she wasn't giving herself away. 'We have a dog at the manor,' she said. 'Perhaps Clyde can smell him.'

Samantha watched as Gertie looked around the room, noticing the enormous poster-sized photograph of Samantha on horseback racing across a beach, the horse's legs splashing in the surf.

'That's the brute who threw me,' she said matter-of-factly.

'Oh,' Gertie said. 'I'm sorry.'

'So am I,' she said with a sigh. 'You live and learn, don't you?'

'Yes,' Gertie said.

'You ever ridden?' Samantha asked.

'No. Never.'

'Good,' she said. 'James never took to it either.' She laughed. 'I did try with him but he wasn't at home on a horse.' There was a tender look in her eyes as she spoke about James and Gertie swallowed hard. 'Now, do I make this cheque out to Hamilton Roses?'

Gertie nodded, glad that they were getting back to business. 'Thank you.'

As Samantha wrote the cheque, Gertie glanced around the open-plan room again, taking in its enormous sofas and rugs in neutral colours. It was as bright and modern as Little Eleigh Manor was dark and old-fashioned. Gertie didn't like it. It wasn't a room she could ever feel comfortable in, she thought.

Her eyes then settled on a side table made of glass on which sat about a dozen photo frames. From where she was standing, she could see a photo of James and Samantha, their arms around each other, somewhere warm and sunny where Gertie could only dream of visiting. Another photograph showed them together on a boat in the middle of a turquoise ocean. It made Gertie think how little she had seen of the world. She'd barely been out of East Anglia, but how could she have gone off travelling when her mother had needed her help with everything?

'You won't leave me, will you, Gertie?' Penelope had pleaded so many times that Gertie had lost count. 'I need you here.'

'Of course I won't leave you,' Gertie had vowed, feeling the full weight of her guilt for ever having contemplated her own needs. But she wasn't going to stay in Little Eleigh forever because she and James were going to France or Italy or somewhere spectacularly beautiful, weren't they?

Gertie had the good grace to blush at having such thoughts about another woman's husband whilst in her very home. She looked at Samantha again and wondered what it must be like to be trapped in a wheelchair.

Suddenly, Samantha winced.

'Are you okay?' Gertie was beside her in an instant.

'Get me those pills, will you?' She nodded to a coffee table and Gertie retrieved a little bottle and handed it to her.

'Can I get you some water?'

Samantha nodded. 'Please.' She waved a hand in the direction of the kitchen and Gertie left the room. Like the rest of the house she had seen, the kitchen was bright and modern and filled with the very best that money could buy. Gertie found a glass and filled it with water before returning to Samantha, watching as she took two of the enormous tablets.

'I forgot to take them this morning,' she said. 'Well, that's not entirely true. I've been trying to give them up. I hate putting these things into my body but it's absolute agony if I don't.'

'Are you in constant pain?'

She nodded. 'Pretty much,' she said. 'Some days are worse than others. They're the days poor James gets it in the ear from me.' She briefly closed her eyes and sighed.

'Can I get you anything else?'

'No, thank you,' she said, her beautiful green eyes opening again. 'You're the middle sister, aren't you?'

'That's right,' Gertie said.

'I think it was you James mentioned the other day. Said he'd seen you about the village when he was walking Clyde. He certainly seems to know you.'

Gertie realised that the dog had sat himself down next to her feet and she smiled awkwardly.

They held each other's gaze for a moment and Gertie couldn't help wondering what was going through Samantha's mind. She certainly felt naked and vulnerable under that green stare. It was as if Samantha could see into her very soul and unearth all her secrets and all the plans that she was making to be with James.

'Right – here you go,' Samantha said at last, tearing the cheque from the book and handing it to Gertie. Gertie saw the slim gold wedding ring and the diamond solitaire, which seemed to taunt her with its smug beauty as if telling her that James would never give her such a gift.

'I hope you're happy with the roses,' Gertie said.

'I'm sure they will do the job perfectly,' Samantha said. 'Thank you for coming so quickly.'

Gertie nodded and Samantha gave her a smile that was warm and genuine and made her wonder if she was really such a difficult person to live with as James had made out.

She was just about to leave when her eyes focused on Samantha's neck.

'Are you all right?' Samantha asked. 'You've gone quite pale.'

'I'm f-fine,' Gertie said, her right hand flying to her neck to adjust her chiffon scarf. 'I'd better be going. I'll see myself out.'

'Goodbye,' Samantha said.

Gertie was shaking as she drove the short distance back to the manor, her fingers on the silver locket that James had bought her.

It was the exact same locket Samantha Stanton had been wearing.

༶

'It's all rotten, see?' Mr Ludkin said as he pointed to the timbers he'd unearthed in one of the rooms in the north wing. There were heaps of plaster on the floor and the air was full of dust.

'Yes, I see,' Celeste said, looking at the ancient wood before her.

'Good job we caught it now, otherwise this whole wall might have collapsed and the roof above, too.'

'I thought the roof had already collapsed,' Celeste said.

'No, no. Just the ceiling,' he said. 'You're lucky, mind.'

'Lucky, right.'

'Although this is going to add time onto the job. Going to have to get a specialist in.'

'Right,' Celeste said, visualising the money from the Fantin-Latour painting flowing away before it had even made it into her bank account. 'But you can rescue it?'

'Anything can be rescued if you've got the money to throw at it,' Mr Ludkin said.

Celeste took a deep breath. 'I was afraid you were going to say that,' she said.

26.

Gertie was furious. Furious and confused. Since leaving Samantha, she'd rung James several times and texted him at least a dozen before he finally got in touch with her and they agreed to meet at the chapel that evening.

As she crossed the fields with Frinton, under the perfectly good pretence of giving him a walk, Gertie couldn't help wondering if James would be there at all, after he'd let her down the last time. Was he trying to blow her off, she wondered? And what would he have to say about the necklace?

But, as soon as she saw him slouching against the ruined flint wall of the chapel in the last rays of the sun, her heart melted. It was impossible, absolutely impossible, to stay mad at a man as handsome as he was, and she cursed him for it.

'Darling!' he said, taking her face in his hands and kissing her fully on the mouth.

'I need to talk to you,' she said a minute later, determined to keep her head and have things out with him.

'I love *nothing* more than to talk to you,' he said. 'Well, there is *one* thing I like more.' He gave her bottom a little squeeze but she pushed him away from her.

'James!' she cried.

'What?' he cried back. 'What have I done?' He looked wounded and she instantly felt bad, but then she remembered how bad he'd made her feel – over and over again.

'I visited Samantha today,' she said.

'What?' he said, aghast.

'She ordered some roses,' she said, putting him out of his misery. 'What – did you think I'd gone and revealed myself as your mistress or something?'

James ran a hand through his fair hair. 'Well, I –'

'I wouldn't do that, James – you know I wouldn't.'

He breathed a sigh of relief. 'I know,' he said.

'But I should – I really should.'

He took a step towards her and caressed her cheek. 'I'm going to tell her myself. As soon as the time is right.'

'How long have I been hearing that?' Gertie cried. 'The time is never right, is it? Well, what about my time? *My* time is right! I don't have to stay here at the manor now that Mum's gone. I can leave whenever I want to! And I want to, James. I really *want* to!'

He tried to silence her with a kiss but she pushed him away.

'Gertie!'

'Listen to me,' she said.

'I'm listening.'

'I saw it. I saw what you'd done,' she told him.

'What are you talking about?'

'The necklace,' she said. 'The silver locket.'

He looked confused but Gertie's fingers pulled her own locket out from behind her scarf. 'I can't believe you bought me the same necklace as your wife!'

James seemed to pale a little. 'I can explain,' he said, like all men backed into a corner.

'*Can* you?' Gertie didn't look convinced.

James took a deep breath. 'Listen – I bought the locket for you but I left it in my jacket pocket and Samantha was trying to find the prescription I'd got for her and she opened the box and saw the necklace. I had to say it was for her, didn't I? But I didn't want to spoil the surprise for you. I know how much you wanted a locket and I wasn't going to let Samantha wreck that so I went back and bought another.'

Gertie frowned. Was he telling the truth? It was hard to tell when he smiled like that at her, and she so wanted to believe him.

'You do believe me, don't you?' he asked, moving closer to her, his long fingers scooping up the locket and gently brushing her neck.

Gertie stared at him, her brown eyes large and full of hurt, wondering if she should mention the night she saw him and Samantha together and if he'd have an explanation for that too. There probably would be one, she decided. She would simply have misunderstood the moment, he'd tell her. That would be it. So she didn't mention it now. 'You make me so mad sometimes,' she said instead.

'I don't mean to,' he said. 'I want to make you happy.'

'And I want you to make me happy too,' she said. 'I want us to be together.'

He nodded and leaned forward to kiss her forehead. 'You're so warm,' he told her in a whisper she felt dance over her skin. She was so lost in the moment that she didn't question that he was trying to change the subject or avoid it altogether. Instead, she let herself be kissed and, when his phone beeped a moment later and he told her he had to get back home, she let him go without another word.

❧

Celeste spent a good ten minutes pacing in the study before she rang Julian.

'Where are we with the auction?' she asked without preamble.

'Hello, Celeste! Are you okay?' he asked.

'I'm fine,' she said, 'but I need to know what's happening with the rest of the paintings.'

'Well, the catalogues are back from the printers now and are going to be posted out today, and I have to say that the paintings look great. The images are fantastic – they really do the paintings justice. I'll pop one round to you when I'm up this weekend, okay?'

'So the auction's in a fortnight?' Celeste asked.

'That's right,' he said. 'Will you be coming to London for it?'

Celeste twisted a lock of her dark hair. 'I'm not sure yet,' she said.

'I know you don't like London,' he said, 'but it can be fun. I could take you out to dinner afterwards to celebrate.'

'If we sell the paintings,' she said pragmatically.

'The paintings will sell,' Julian said. 'You don't need to worry on that score.'

But as Celeste hung up, she couldn't help admitting to being worried – not just about the paintings, but about everything else too.

❧

It was the middle of the night when Celeste woke up. She wasn't sure what had disturbed her this time but it was happening a lot lately and she'd learned to just give in to it.

She switched on her bedside lamp, stirring Frinton at the end of the bed. Looking across the room, she caught sight of her old copy of Dodie Smith's *I Capture the Castle* and gave a wry laugh. Cassandra Mortmain was one of her favourite heroines and had certainly known that living in an ancient building in the middle of Suffolk was far from romantic. When she'd first read the book, she'd felt an immediate connection with the resilient heroine, although she had frowned on her ability to fall in love so quickly and had shuddered at the thought of swimming in a moat. She and her sisters had never done anything quite so foolhardy.

'Only you have, haven't you?' she said to Frinton. One of his ears pricked up at the sound of her voice, but he gave a sigh and went back to sleep.

She got out of bed, stuffing her feet into her slippers and grabbing a cotton jumper. She didn't feel like reading tonight, no matter how comforting it might be to swap her own worries for those of Cassandra Mortmain. Instead, she headed downstairs, accompanied by Frinton, who thought that exchanging sleep for the possibility of a treat was a fair deal.

Leaving the sanctuary of her bedroom, she ventured down the corridor that linked all the bedrooms. A small lamp was always left on to light the dark passageway in case of night-time wanderings, but the wooden panelling meant that it was still spookily dark.

They were just passing Penelope's room when Celeste noticed that the door had been left ajar. Being a terrier, Frinton noticed it too.

'No!' Celeste cried as the little dog charged into the darkness. She groaned. She hadn't ventured into the room since the night she'd found Evie in there, and she certainly didn't fancy going in there again. 'Frinton!' she called softly. 'Come *out* of there.' But the little dog didn't respond, just as she knew he wouldn't. Shaking her head and silently cursing the day that the soft bundle of naughtiness had entered her life, she turned the main light on and walked into the room. Frinton was by the bed, eating what looked very much like a Jammie Dodger that he'd probably brought upstairs himself at some point.

Swallowing hard, she took a moment to look around the room. The mahogany king-size sleigh bed was still made up with its pink and white toile de jouy bedding, and there on the bedside table was the large silver-framed photograph she'd spotted when she'd been in the room with Evie. The photograph of Penelope. The room was filled with photographs of her, and her beautiful face stared out from each one of the frames now. Celeste felt tears brimming in her eyes.

Nobody would ever understand that such a beautiful woman could be so cruel, but those large brown eyes and the sensual lips hid so much meanness, and the looks she'd been capable of giving and the things that she'd been able to say still made Celeste shake with fear today and chased her from the room now.

'*Frinton!*' she called, her voice icy. 'Come on.' The little dog looked up from the carpet, licked up the remaining crumbs of the Jammie Dodger and followed her out of the room, knowing it was better not to push his luck when his mistress called his name like that.

Going downstairs, she heard the voices as soon as she entered the corridor to the kitchen.

'What are you both doing up?' she asked as she walked into the kitchen and saw Gertie and Evie there.

'Same as you, I imagine – couldn't sleep,' Evie said from the bench that ran the length of the old table. Gertie was stirring something lemony in a huge silver pan. 'She's making a cake and I get to lick all spoons and bowls, don't I? So don't even think of intercepting me because I was here first.'

Celeste took a seat opposite Evie.

'You look dreadful, Celly,' Gertie said as she turned around from the Aga.

'Thanks a lot!' Celeste said. 'It's the middle of the night. I don't suppose I'm meant to look like a supermodel.'

Gertie shook her head. 'It's more than that. Is something wrong?'

She sighed. 'Did you take a look at the north wing today?'

'I'm trying to avoid going in there,' Gertie said. 'Why? Is it bad?'

'You could say that.'

'But we knew that, right?' Gertie said, as she tipped the gloopy cake mixture from the pan into a loaf tin. 'We've known for years that it was pretty bad in there.'

'I know, but seeing it all so raw and exposed gave me a bit of a shock and I'm really worried what else is going to be unearthed around the house – and if we've got the budget for it.'

'We'll just have to do what we can,' Gertie said. 'Nobody expects you to do everything at once. You just have to tackle one bit of it at a time.'

Celeste rested her head in her hands and closed her eyes, listening to the movements of Gertie as she clattered cooking equipment around.

'Where've you put the missing painting, Celly?' Evie asked after a moment.

Celeste opened her eyes again and looked at her sister across the table. 'It's in the study for the time being.'

'You're not going to sell it, are you?' Evie's eyes were narrowed and accusatory.

'I'm not sure what to do,' Celeste said. 'I don't think we should do anything with it until things have quietened down.'

'What things? Dad or Simone haven't called, have they?'

'No,' Celeste said.

'Well, then. I think we should hang it up in the living room. Put it in that gap left by the Fantin-Latour. I hate that gap. It makes me feel all empty inside.'

Celeste knew exactly what Evie meant. Every time she walked into the room, the gap on the wall seemed to be staring her down and she wondered if she'd made the right decision in letting the painting go.

But you didn't let it go, a little voice inside her said. *You're going to make nearly half a million pounds for it.*

'Maybe we should hang it there,' she said at last.

'It'll look good,' Evie said. 'We should celebrate it being home.'

Celeste watched Evie as her face slowly sank into something that looked like melancholy, her beautiful eyes cast downwards.

'Evie?' Celeste began, remembering their aborted conversation in the hallway and that she hadn't had a chance to talk to her sister since. 'Are you okay?'

Evie sighed but didn't look up. 'Why does everybody keep asking me that?'

'Maybe because we know that something's wrong,' Celeste said.

'And how would you know that?' she said defiantly.

Celeste raised her hands in the air. 'Because of comments said in exactly that tone of voice,' she said.

Evie groaned.

'And groaning,' Celeste added, 'and moping around the house looking pale.'

'I'm not pale and I haven't been moping anywhere.'

'And talking in secret to Esther,' Celeste said.

'Ah!' Evie said. 'Now we're getting somewhere. You think there's something wrong with me because I've been having a perfectly normal conversation with Esther rather than talking to you. Is that it?'

'No, that's not it at all.'

'No? Because you seem to still be upset about that,' Evie said pointedly.

'I'm not upset. I just want to help.'

'There's nothing to help with,' Evie insisted.

'Then what were you talking to Esther about?'

'Does it matter?'

'It matters to me,' Celeste said. 'I'm your big sister.'

'Exactly,' Evie said.

'What does that mean?'

'It means that you're my sister. You're not my mother.'

'I'm not trying to be your mother,' Celeste said. 'Is that why you turned to Esther? As a substitute mother?'

Evie's eyes widened and suddenly seemed full of fear. 'What a thing to say!'

'Is it true?'

'I don't need to substitute mother. I'm twenty-one!' Evie said. 'Anyway, nobody could replace Mum.'

'Okay, okay!' Celeste said. 'I'm just trying to understand what's going on.'

'Why? You've never been interested before.'

'Evie!' Gertie said, turning around from the kitchen sink.

'What?' Evie snapped. 'You've said the same thing, too.'

Celeste's mouth dropped open. 'What have you said about me?'

'Nothing,' Gertie said. 'I've said nothing.'

'Really?' Celeste said, not sounding convinced. 'It doesn't sound like nothing. What have you two been talking about?'

'Just drop it, Celly,' Evie said. 'Just run back to your study.'

The kitchen filled with a terrible silence.

'Is that it, then?' Celeste asked after a moment. 'You think I lock myself away in there for *fun*? You think I shut you two out, don't you?'

'Well, don't you?' Evie said.

'If I do, I don't mean to,' Celeste said in a very little voice. 'But it was you two who asked me to come back – *begged* me to come back.'

'We wanted our sister back,' Evie said.

'And I am back, but you saw the state of the study. What am I supposed to do?'

'*Talk* to us?'

'That's what I'm trying to do *now!*' Celeste said hopelessly.

'You just don't get it, do you?'

'Get what? Tell me what it is I'm not getting because I really want to know.'

'You can't just come marching back here after three years and expect us to open up to you all of a sudden. Relationships don't work like that, Celeste!' Evie said. 'You managed to escape – you weren't around for the end and you've no idea what that was like. You were off with your fancy man in your new home, weren't you?'

'You think my marriage was an easy option?' Celeste said breathlessly. 'Well, it wasn't. It was the biggest mistake of my life and I did it just to get away from here. I thought it was the right thing to do at the time. I was desperate and I knew I couldn't go on living here.'

'We know that,' Gertie said, trying to calm things down between Celeste and Evie. 'We're not blaming you for leaving.'

'Aren't you?' Evie said. 'Don't speak for me because *I* blame Celeste.'

Celeste shook her head. 'Don't say that, Evie. You don't blame me – not really.'

'Why do you say that? Why are you two always putting thoughts into my head and words into my mouth? You don't *know* what I'm thinking or feeling.' Evie's face had gone from being as white as a *Boule de Neige* rose to as red as a *Munstead Wood* in a matter of seconds.

'I'm just trying to work out what's going on here,' Celeste said. 'With both of you. Neither of you talks to me about the things that really matter. I know something's been bothering you, Evie, but you just won't give me a chance, and Gertie's been hiding something too.'

'What do you mean?' Gertie said.

'You've been doing a lot of this midnight baking and you only ever do that when you're upset about something. I wish you'd tell me what it is.'

Gertie went very tight-lipped and refused to maintain eye contact with her sister.

'I *know* I don't spend enough time with you guys,' Celeste said, 'and it really hurts me that I've hurt you, but *please* talk to me about it. I really need you two.'

'No, you don't,' Evie said. 'You've never needed anyone. You just lock yourself away from everyone, don't you? You're so cold, Celeste. I've never known anyone as cold as you.'

'*Stop* it, Evie!' Gertie shouted. 'You always go too far.'

It was then that Esther walked in. 'What do you think you're doing shouting in the middle of the night?'

'Keep out of this, Esther,' Celeste said.

'Don't you *dare* talk to her like that,' Evie said.

'This has nothing to do with her, Evie,' Celeste said, a warning tone in her voice. 'This is between you and me.'

'You think that's for you to decide, do you?' Evie retorted. 'Well, I'm fed up with you thinking you can tell me what to do all the time. You can't do that to me anymore.'

Esther listened to the words flying between the two of them and then raised one of her small, bony hands. 'Girls!' she said. Her calm voice seemed to do the trick because they stopped fighting for a moment and turned to look at her. 'Now,' she said at last, 'I'm not sure what's caused this little scene tonight but I think I have an idea of what might be behind it.'

'Well, I'm glad somebody does,' Celeste said sarcastically.

Esther glared at Celeste and then turned her attention to Evie once again. 'I think you should tell them, Evie,' she said, 'don't you?'

27.

'Tell us what?' Celeste said. 'If there's anything to tell, then I think you should get it over and done with now.'

'Yes, what's going on?' Gertie said. She had joined them at the table and watched as Esther took a seat next to Evie and the two of them looked at each other for a long, silent moment.

'Go on, my girl,' Esther said, gently patting Evie's hand.

Celeste looked from Esther's face to Evie's and couldn't help envying them their obvious closeness. When had all this happened, she wondered? And how could she not have noticed their developing friendship?

Evie took a few slow breaths. 'I'm pregnant,' she said at last and gave a little shrug of her shoulders as if she had confessed to no more than forgetting to take the bins out.

'Pregnant?' Gertie said. 'Are you sure?'

'Of course I'm sure,' Evie said. 'I've been sure for some time now. It's due at Christmas.'

'A Christmas baby?' Gertie said and Evie nodded.

'Goodness!' Gertie said, a little smile breaking across her face, but Evie wasn't smiling because Celeste had yet to respond.

'Celeste?' It was Esther who spoke.

Celeste bit her tongue to stop herself from screaming. She wasn't going to scream. That would be too much like Penelope and she wasn't ever going to be like her, was she?

'Are you going to have it?' Celeste said at last.

Evie's mouth dropped open and her eyes filled with disbelief. 'Of *course* I'm going to have it. Why wouldn't I?'

'It's just –' Celeste paused. What was it she was trying to say exactly? 'I'm finding it hard to believe you'd want to bring a baby into this dysfunctional family.'

As soon as the words were out, Celeste realised that she shouldn't have said them. Three pairs of eyes stared at her from around the table, nobody daring to say a word.

'I can't believe you just said that,' Evie said a moment later, her voice a horrible whisper.

'I didn't mean it to come out like that,' Celeste said, shaking her head. She turned to Gertie as if expecting some words of support from her, but the wounded look in her eyes told Celeste that she would not be getting any backup from her.

'Then what *did* you mean?' Gertie asked her.

'I mean . . . I meant . . . are you sure this is the best thing for you – for the family?'

'For *you*, don't you mean? You're not worrying about me, are you?' Evie said. 'You're worrying about the possibility of more responsibility falling on *your* head.'

'I didn't say that,' Celeste said.

'You didn't have to,' Evie said. 'It's written all over your face!'

'Evie,' Esther said, her voice still calm and her hand still resting on Evie's. 'Hear Celeste out.'

Evie turned to look at Esther, her face full of betrayal.

'It's just – well – I guess I can't imagine anybody wanting to bring a child into this house. Not after what we all went through with Mum,' Celeste said. And there it was. Finally out. The sisters had never talked about it together before. It had just hung there between them with each of them thinking thoughts and feeling emotions that were never fully expressed.

242

'Why should that make a difference to me?' Evie said.

Celeste studied her sister's young face, wondering at her innocence. 'Aren't you scared?' she asked her.

'Of what? Giving birth?'

'No,' Celeste said. 'Of turning into Mum.'

Evie frowned. 'I loved Mum,' she said. 'I know she had her faults. Everyone does. And I know you had issues with her, but why should that affect me now? Anyway, if anybody's likely to turn into Mum, it'll be you, not me.'

'Don't say that,' Celeste said.

'But you're just like her – spending hours in that study and never really knowing what's going on with us.'

'Evie!' Gertie said in warning, but Evie wouldn't be stopped now.

'What?'

'I am *not* like Mum,' Celeste said, her dark eyes suddenly filling with tears and her voice wavering as something inside her suddenly cracked. 'Don't you ever say that to me again!'

'But you said –'

'You have *no* idea what I went through with her!' Celeste cried. 'What I'm *still* going through. No idea at all. She made me feel – so –'

'What?' Evie said, her voice still filled with fury.

'Useless,' Celeste said, the tears coursing down her face. 'I could never do anything right. I was always, *always* wrong and it hurts so much to hear you say I'm not doing a good enough job too.'

'But I didn't,' Evie said.

'You're so critical of me, Evie.'

'Celly, I'm not. I just – I don't like you shutting us all out. You've always done that and I hate it.'

'Because that's what Mum did to me,' Celeste said, wiping her eyes with a tissue that Gertie had passed to her. 'She never let me get close to her. She never wanted to know me.'

The room was silent for a moment. Evie was the first to speak.

'She never wanted to know me either,' Evie said.

Celeste frowned. 'But you two were so close,' she said.

Evie shrugged. 'No,' she said. 'Not really. I thought we were, but it wasn't closeness, exactly. It was something else.'

'What?' Gertie asked.

'Her vanity, I think,' Evie said. 'She loved to dress me up and parade me about. I was like a doll to her. A pretty little girl to spoil. But it was never love. I'm beginning to see that now.' She turned briefly to Esther, who gave her a little smile and patted her hand.

Celeste looked across at Evie and the two sisters exchanged a look, and a new understanding seemed to dawn between them.

'She made life pretty tough for all of us,' Gertie said.

Esther, who'd been watching the scene before her, cleared her throat and, squeezing Evie's hand, spoke.

'Your mother was a very difficult woman to get on with,' she told them. 'She was ambitious and stubborn and, yes, she could be cruel. I was a victim of that cruel tongue of hers on more than one occasion and I can only imagine what Celeste and you two have gone through, but I also believe that she did love you. In her own way.'

'Do you?' Celeste said, her eyes still shiny with tears.

Esther nodded. 'I do.'

'I'm not so sure,' Celeste said, her voice full of bleakness. 'I never felt it.'

Gertie reached her hands across the table and took Celeste's.

'I'm sorry,' Evie said. 'I didn't mean to make you cry.' There were tears in Evie's eyes too now.

'It's okay,' Celeste said.

'I guess we'll never really know what we all went through with Mum.'

'We will if we talk about it more,' Celeste said.

Evie gave a tiny smile. 'I'd like that.'

Celeste took a deep breath. 'I didn't mean to sound so disapproving of your plans for the baby. I'm thrilled for you. I really am. It's just –'

'What?' Evie asked, her voice gentle now.

'I just can't imagine having your optimism,' Celeste told her. 'Not after everything we've been through as a family.'

'Well, perhaps this baby will make things better,' Evie said simply. 'Maybe it's time to make things right.'

They all exchanged looks, softer this time. The fight seemed to have gone out of them.

'You mean play at happy families?' Celeste said.

'Why not? It would make a nice change, wouldn't it?' Evie said.

Celeste couldn't argue with that, but the enormity of the situation still hadn't really sunk in. A *baby*. Was Little Eleigh Manor really ready for a baby? A little child toddling around the crumbling rooms and tumbling into the moat? And babies were expensive, weren't they? As it was, the three of them barely had enough money to take care of themselves. But Celeste had the good sense not to voice these qualms.

'Do you know who the father is?' Gertie asked.

'Of *course* I know,' Evie said, frowning at her sister.

'It's Lukas, isn't it?' Gertie said. 'I've seen the way he looks at you.'

'Even *I've* seen the way he looks at you,' Esther said, and everyone laughed, instantly lightening the mood.

'Does he know?' Celeste asked.

'No,' Evie said, looking down at the kitchen table and drawing a little circle with her fingertip around a rough knot.

'So you've only told Esther?' Celeste asked.

'Don't start again,' Evie said.

'I wasn't starting,' Celeste said. 'I'm just trying to get things clear, that's all.'

'I think she should tell him,' Esther said, and everyone looked at her. 'I know I'm not family –'

'You're family to *me*,' Evie said and, once again, the two women exchanged a look that made Celeste feel like an outsider.

'But you should tell him,' Esther finished.

The four women around the table looked at each other in turn.

Gertie nodded. 'He's a sweet guy,' she said. 'He should know.' She then turned her gaze to Celeste, as did Evie and Esther.

Celeste cleared her throat. 'I agree,' she said. 'He should definitely know.'

Evie sighed. 'It's not what I wanted,' she said.

'What did you want?' Gertie asked, leaning forward slightly as if trying to get closer to the truth.

'I wanted something of my own. Something that nobody could take away from me.'

'You think he'll try and take the baby away from you?' Gertie said.

Evie shrugged.

'You're thinking of Betty, aren't you?' Celeste said.

'Who's Betty?' Esther asked, and Celeste couldn't help feeling just a little smug that she knew something about her sister that Esther didn't.

'Betty was Evie's kitten. It was a dear little thing. Totally white but with a tiny patch of black over her left eye,' Celeste said. 'She was given to Evie by one of our gardeners, I think. His cat had had a litter and he was desperately trying to find homes for the kittens. Well, Mum had always hated cats so we decided not to tell her about it and kept it hidden in the north wing.'

'We did a really good job too,' Gertie piped up. 'We fed it and let it out in the garden where we knew she wouldn't be seen.'

'But then I came back from school one day and she'd gone. We looked everywhere for her and finally had to ask Mum,' Evie said.

'I'll never forget the look of triumph on her face when she said she'd discovered our little secret and that she'd punished us for not telling her. I just couldn't understand it.'

'But that's crazy,' Gertie said. 'You can't not tell a father he has a child just because Mum got rid of your kitten years and years ago. Lukas isn't Mum, for a start.'

'But how will I know for sure that he won't try and take her away?'

'It's a her?' Celeste said.

Evie nodded. 'I think so,' she said. 'I don't know for sure but I think of it as a her,' she said, resting a hand on her belly. 'Anyway, it's not just the kitten. Mum used to come into my room all the time. She'd sometimes take things too.'

Esther frowned. 'Like what?'

'Like a little glass vase I once bought with my pocket money at the church fete. It wasn't very special, really, but it was this amazing green colour – almost luminous. I loved it so much. Well, Mum obviously did too, because one day I discovered it sitting on the hall table with a handful of roses in it. "It's selfish of you not to share it," she told me. "Now everyone can enjoy it." I never got it back,' Evie said. 'I never really felt like anything was mine with her around. I'd come home from school and wonder what would be missing or what she would have been snooping through.'

They both turned to Celeste. 'Did she ever take anything of yours?' Evie asked.

Celeste took a deep breath. 'My sanity? My will to live?' she said and they all exchanged sad smiles.

Gertie squeezed her hand.

'You know she had a condition? A personality disorder,' Celeste said.

Gertie looked thoughtful. 'I suspected something like that.'

'Julian told me about it and I've been reading about it on the internet. His brother has the same condition,' she said, turning to each of her sisters.

'You sure she wasn't just weird?' Gertie asked.

'Some forms of weird can be diagnosed, and the more I read up on it, the more I realise that there are so many people out there that we may never be able to get along with but that we can at least begin to understand,' Celeste said. 'I think that's important – to realise that the fault doesn't lie with us and that there was very little we could have done to change her.'

Evie's eyes were full of tears. 'I'm sorry for what I said about you, Celly.'

Celeste nodded. 'It's okay,' she said, getting up from the table. 'Look, it's late. We should be in bed – especially you, Evie. You're sleeping for two now.'

Evie gave a weak smile.

'Good night. I'm sorry we disturbed you, Esther.'

'Don't you worry,' Esther said. 'I wouldn't have missed this for the world.' And then she gave Celeste the first smile she had ever received from her. Celeste blinked in surprise. It was definitely time to go to bed.

'Celly,' Gertie said a moment later as she followed her sister and Frinton into the hallway.

'Yes?' Celeste turned to face her.

'What you said in there – about us turning into Mum. That really worries you, doesn't it?'

'More than anything in the world,' she confessed.

'Me too,' Gertie said.

'Really?'

'Of course,' she said. 'What daughter never fears turning into her mother? I can't think of any!'

Celeste smiled. 'When did you know?'

'What? That Mum wasn't quite right?' Gertie said. 'I'm not sure. It kind of sneaked up on me. I mean, it's hard to really gauge these things, isn't it? Because everything in a family seems normal when you're growing up. But I suppose it was when I was reading books – books about happy families. It made me wonder if our situation was normal after all. Then Dad left. At the time, I thought it was his fault but I slowly came to realise that he just couldn't cope with Mum anymore. Heaven only knows what he went through with her, and I know I didn't bear the brunt of it like you did with her. But there was one thing, one incident, that made me realise she wasn't quite right.'

'What was that?'

'It was that day you disappeared,' Gertie said.

'You remember that?'

'Of course I do,' she said. 'Where did you go?'

'To the woods,' Celeste said. 'I wanted to stay there all night but it was pretty cold and uncomfortable.'

Gertie shook her head. 'I wish I'd known. I would have come looking for you.'

'I really didn't want to be found,' she said.

'I remember what Mum said at the time,' Gertie said a moment later.

'What did she say?'

'That you were impossible to get along with,' Gertie said, 'and that you were spiteful and selfish.'

Celeste swallowed hard. She had heard those words from her mother's lips hundreds of times, but knowing that they'd been used against her in front of her sisters made her go suddenly cold.

'That's when I knew there was something wrong with Mum. It was like being hit by a truck to hear Mum lying like that. I couldn't believe it but the evidence was right before me. My Mum was telling me this big heap of lies and she expected me to join in with her too!'

Gertie gave a hollow laugh. 'She really thought I was going to side with her against you.'

'I'm very glad you didn't,' Celeste said.

'I know it was you who got the worst of Mum's condition,' Gertie said. 'Evie knows that too but she sometimes forgets. I think she's still really confused as to how she feels about Mum. There are so many mixed up emotions but I'm sure of one thing – she certainly didn't mean those things she said tonight.'

'Didn't she?'

'No, of *course* not.'

'But what if she's right? I know my faults, Gertie. I know I'm not open or warm and –'

'Stop it!' Gertie said, reaching out to hug her. 'You're the warmest person I know. Who else would have run home to bail us out of trouble?'

They gave each other a hug in the silent, shadowy hallway, the sound of the clock ticking the middle-of-the-night minutes away.

'Why didn't we all talk together like this years ago?' Gertie said at last.

'I don't know,' Celeste said. 'It might have helped us cope better with what we were all going through with Mum.'

Gertie nodded. 'I used to think her behaviour was my fault,' she said. 'It was hard not to when she was shouting me down.'

'Me too,' Celeste said.

They looked at each other for a long moment.

'Did you love her?' Gertie asked at last, and Celeste felt tears pricking her eyes.

'She made it very hard to love her,' she said, and Gertie nodded. 'I know.'

'I don't think I ever really knew how I felt about her,' Celeste said.

'Do you think she ever loved us?' Gertie asked, and her face was that of a child's again, soft and vulnerable. 'I mean *really* loved us?'

Celeste sighed. 'I don't know. I'm not sure she was really capable of it. There were flashes of pride sometimes – if we managed to achieve things that would reflect well on her – but that's not the same as love, is it? And she certainly didn't know about unconditional love. That's the true love of a parent, isn't it? To love their children no matter what they do or say or achieve?'

Gertie nodded. 'Or what they wear?'

Celeste groaned. 'Exactly. Let's go to bed,' she said. 'I'm exhausted.'

'Yes, family revelations like pregnant sisters always leave me exhausted too,' Gertie said and they both laughed.

'I can't believe Evie's going to be a mother,' Celeste said as they climbed the stairs together with Frinton sprinting ahead.

'I'm going to be an aunt!' Gertie said.

They walked along the corridor, passing their mother's bedroom.

'What do you think Mum would have said?' Gertie asked.

Celeste took a deep breath. 'I think she would have said something damaging and upsetting and shown Evie the door.'

Gertie nodded. 'I think you're right.'

28.

It was early the next morning when the phone went. Far too early for three sisters who had been up half the night arguing and then bonding. It was Gertie who got to the phone first, immediately regretting her alacrity as soon as she realised that it was their father's wife, Simone, and she wasn't in a good mood.

'Don't you think I don't know you did this!' she cried into poor Gertie's left ear.

'I don't know what you're talking about, Simone,' Gertie said innocently.

'The hell you don't! I don't know which one of you it was. It was probably all three of you. Thick as thieves you are, as well as thieves! Well, you're not going to get away –'

Gertie held the phone out to Celeste.

'I don't want it!' Celeste cried, but Gertie flung it towards her all the same.

'I've never known such sneaky, spiteful girls!' Simone was saying. 'Your father doesn't know the half of it. And after all I've done for you!'

Celeste guffawed, causing Frinton to bark loudly.

'Who is it?' Evie said, coming into the hallway.

'It's for you,' Celeste said, calmly handing the phone to her.

Evie took it from her sister and blanched as soon as she heard the irate voice at the other end of the line.

'Pardon?' she said. '*What* did you call me?'

Celeste and Gertie exchanged bemused looks.

'*You* ring the police?' Evie continued. 'It'll be *us* ringing the police and telling them about how you stole the painting from Little Eleigh Manor, along with a whole host of other things that are dotted around your house.'

'What other things?' Gertie asked, and Simone obviously asked the same question because Evie continued.

'Like the candlesticks in the dining room,' Evie said, 'and the little glass bowl that was in the hallway. Did you really think we wouldn't notice, you stupid old woman? Look – don't call here again, okay?' And, with that, Evie hung up the phone to a round of applause from her sisters and an excited round of barks from Frinton.

'Are you all right?' Gertie said when things had calmed down. 'I don't think you should really be getting yourself so excited when you're pregnant.'

'God, yes!' Celeste said. 'And when I think what might have happened if you'd fallen from that ladder!'

'I had to do it,' Evie said.

'I know you did,' Celeste said, 'but don't ever do anything like that again, okay? At least not when you've got a baby on the way.'

'Don't you two start treating me like an invalid, because I'm not,' she said, pushing her blonde hair out of her face and scowling. 'I feel fine and I absolutely insist on being *me* throughout this pregnancy.'

Celeste gave a resigned sort of look, knowing that no power on earth would get Evie to calm her ways unless she herself decided to take things easy. And that wasn't likely to happen any time soon.

She was just thinking about how wonderfully happy she felt that morning and how there seemed to be a certain ease between the three of them now when the phone rang again.

'Don't pick it up!' Celeste yelled. 'It'll be her again.'

'Then I'll give her *what for* again,' Evie said, picking up the receiver. 'Hello?' she said abruptly. 'Oh, *Julian!* Sorry! I thought you were someone else.' She laughed. 'No – everyone's fine. Yes, we're at home. Come on over.'

It was twenty minutes later when Julian arrived. Evie was there to greet him and hollered through the house for Celeste because she'd disappeared into the study again.

'Hello, Celeste,' he said, his face warmed by his smile as she entered the hallway. 'I've brought you the catalogue.'

'Oh, wonderful,' Celeste said, pleased to see him again. She led the way to the living room. 'Cup of tea?'

'I'll do the honours,' Evie said.

'Thank you,' he said as he sat down next to Celeste on one of the old sofas next to the fireplace. He put his neat briefcase on the coffee table and opened it up, reaching inside for the glossy Faraday's catalogue. 'Here we go,' he said, handing it to Celeste. 'Yours are from page four and on the cover too.'

'How lovely!' she said, gasping in delight as she saw the painting featured on the cover. It was the Ferdinand Georg Waldmüller painting of the silver vase tumbling over with deep pink roses that seemed to glow out of their dark background. It was luminous and so lovely that Celeste felt a lump in her throat at the thought that she would never see the painting again. Not at Little Eleigh Manor, at least.

'We've had a lot of interest in that one,' Julian told her. 'The painting we choose for the cover always gets a lot of attention.'

'Thank you for choosing one of ours,' Celeste said, and he smiled at her and nodded.

'I wouldn't have chosen any other,' he said.

Her fingers were trembling as she opened the catalogue. Page one showed an introduction underneath a photograph of Julian.

It made him look intensely handsome and Celeste almost did a double take. Was he really that attractive? She turned to look at him.

'Oh, that photograph!' he said. 'I look like a schoolboy!'

'No you don't!' Celeste said without thinking. 'Well, maybe that stripy tie is a bit schoolboyish.'

'I should get a new one done but I hate that sort of fuss,' he said, waving a hand in the air as if to bat all the attention away.

'It's nice. You should leave it.'

He looked surprised by the compliment and Celeste felt her face heating up. She turned her attention back to the catalogue. Pages two and three featured dark, bleak nineteenth-century landscapes, which made the rose paintings that followed absolutely sing, Celeste thought. She read the descriptions and saw the estimated prices, and her heart felt so heavy that she thought she was going to burst into tears again.

'It must be a bit odd seeing the paintings like that,' Julian said after she hadn't spoken for some time.

'I feel like the spirit of Grandpa Arthur is looking over my shoulder,' she said.

'I'm sure he'd tell you that you're doing the right thing,' Julian said.

'Would he?'

'He'd understand.'

'Here we are!' Evie chimed, entering the room with three cups of tea on a tray which she placed on the coffee table. She sat on the sofa next to Celeste, forcing her to move so close to Julian that their legs collided. 'Heavens! Are those our paintings?'

Celeste nodded as Evie took the catalogue from her. 'I'm afraid they are.'

Evie took a moment to look at them and then gave a little sniff. 'I wish we could keep them,' she said.

'So do I,' Celeste said. 'But it was either that or lose the north wing. You know that, don't you?'

'I know,' Evie said, 'but it still hurts.'

'I can let you have copies of the photographs we took of the paintings,' Julian said. 'They're very good.'

'It won't be the same, though, will it?' Evie said.

'Of course not,' Julian said.

They drank their tea in affable silence, and then Celeste stood up.

'Thanks for bringing the catalogue round,' she said. 'I'll walk you out. Frinton needs a run.'

Frinton, who'd been sitting on a rug by the fireplace, stood up, his stumpy tail wagging, and the three of them left the manor together, walking across the freshly mown lawn that sloped down to the river. Frinton ran ahead of them, eager to find something to sniff or roll in.

'This is such a special place,' Julian said.

'We like it,' Celeste said, 'and that's why we have to make sacrifices to keep it all going. Like selling the paintings.'

'I wish there was something I could do to help,' he said.

'But you are,' Celeste told him. 'I can't thank you enough for putting one of our paintings on the cover and for getting in touch with Kammie.'

He smiled. 'I feel like this place has become a part of me now. Does that sound too presumptuous?'

Celeste shook her head. 'This place has a habit of reeling people in.'

'I can understand why,' he said. 'I think if I lived here, I'd never want to leave.'

'Well, it's easy to say that,' Celeste said.

'Right,' he said. 'Sorry – that was insensitive of me.'

'It's okay,' she said. 'It hurt like hell to leave this place when I did, but it would have hurt even more if I'd stayed.'

'Are you glad to be back?'

Celeste looked out to the fields beyond the river and a light breeze blew through her dark hair. 'I love this place but there are so many strange emotions tangled up here that I sometimes hate it too. Does that make sense?'

Julian nodded. 'Yes,' he said, 'it does. But time will change that for you, won't it? When it becomes more your home – when you've put your stamp on it.'

'Ah, time!' Celeste said with a little laugh. 'I'm not sure there's enough time in the world to erase the past for me and I'm really not sure if I can stay here, although' – she paused – 'I'm beginning to feel a bit more settled here now, which is something I thought would never happen. Gertie and Evie want me to stay. I know that now. But I'm not sure what to do.'

Julian gave her a look that was so full of tenderness that Celeste had to turn away.

'You've got to let the past go, Celeste, and start making yourself a future, whether it's here or somewhere else.'

'I know,' she said. 'It's one of the reasons I feel it might be a good idea to sell this place.'

'Are you sure that's the only option?' he asked. 'It seems like a pretty final one to me.'

'I know,' she said, 'but we really need a lot more money coming than we have at present. The money raised by the paintings will be brilliant, of course, but it's all going to get eaten up by those long-overdue jobs, and Evie's doing amazing work with the business. She's even mentioned hosting weddings here, which could work if we all got behind it. But what we really need is a regular income from something in addition to the rose business.'

'Like rent or something?'

Celeste nodded. 'Evie would probably never speak to me again if we sold, but I think Gertie might be all right with the decision. She's always talking about going abroad anyway. I think selling the manor might be the catalyst she needs to actually do that.'

'But what about you? Where will you go?'

She shrugged. 'I'll get by,' she said. 'I usually do.'

Julian seemed to be watching her very intensely. 'You know you can talk to me about anything,' he said, 'and I think you should talk about this stuff. It might actually be easier with me than with your sisters.'

'Why do you think that?' she asked.

'Because it's often harder to talk to families because of all the emotions involved,' he said.

'You know, we talked about some stuff last night,' she confessed. 'My sisters and I.'

'You did?'

'I don't know why we haven't talked before,' she said. 'We've all been carrying around this great pain but unable to reach out to one another.'

'You see?'

'What?'

'Talk to *me*,' he said.

They looked at each other but the words just wouldn't come, and all that Celeste could say was, 'I can't.'

Julian swallowed hard. 'I wish you would,' he said. 'I'd really love to help you.'

'But you have already,' she said, genuinely baffled.

'But I want to help more,' he said. 'I care about you, Celeste. You must know that by now.'

She started walking again, moving away from the river and down into the rose garden.

'Celeste?' he called after her, running to catch up.

She stopped and turned back to look at him. 'What?'

He sighed and ran a hand through his dark red hair. 'I'm sorry if I am prodding too deeply. You obviously feel uncomfortable about all this.'

'No – I –' She paused.

'What? What is it?'

'I'm not sure I know *how* to talk.'

He cocked his head to one side at this strange confession. 'What do you mean?'

She looked down at the neat grass beneath her ever-so-practical lace-up shoes and shook her head. 'I'm not sure,' she said. 'Perhaps I'm not ready to talk.'

'Okay,' he said. 'Well, I'm here whenever you are. You know that, right?'

'I know you are,' she said, and she suddenly wanted to reach out to him, to let him know how much he meant to her, but something was holding her back and her hand remained resolutely by her side.

They both began walking again, reaching a path that led under several rose-smothered arches.

'I went to see another shop in Lavenham,' he said at last, stopping to smell a cluster of pale apricot roses.

'For your antiques business?' Celeste said, glad to turn the conversation back onto slightly safer ground at last.

He nodded. 'But it's fallen through, I'm afraid.'

'Oh, no!'

'Yep!' he said.

'So, what will you do?'

'Start again.'

'In Lavenham?'

'Not exactly,' he said and his eyes crinkled at the edges as he looked at her. 'Actually, you've given me a pretty good idea just now.'

'Oh?'

'Yes,' he said. They stopped walking. 'Celeste, I wanted to ask your opinion about something but I've been putting it off because I knew you were still thinking about selling the manor.'

'What is it?'

'Well, if you weren't going to sell, what would you think about opening an antiques centre here?'

'*Here?*'

'Why not?' he said. 'The manor would be the perfect venue, don't you think?'

'Are you serious?'

'I'm never anything but serious,' he said with a playful grin. 'Just think about it – it could bring in so many people. It could be Suffolk's new day out – browse a few antiques and buy yourself some roses!'

He turned to look at the huge expanse of the manor across the moat. It really was the most stunning scene – straight out of a fairytale book with its timber frame wing, its castellations and its soaring towers.

'But I'm still thinking of selling the manor,' Celeste told him. 'You know that.'

'I know,' he said, 'and I can't stop thinking about that.'

'Really?'

He nodded. 'What were your plans for the north wing?' he asked. 'Just out of interest.'

'Well, I – I hadn't really thought about it,' Celeste said. 'At least, not beyond keeping it from falling down again.'

'You know you can't leave those rooms empty – not after all the money you're spending on them.'

'I guess not,' she said. 'I've been worrying about that myself, actually.'

'Well, if you had somebody renting those rooms – keeping them heated, keeping them alive – I think they'd really benefit, don't you?

Just imagine them filled with wonderful old pieces – things that might once have graced such rooms.'

'You mean you'd want to use the *whole wing?*'

'Celeste, I could fill Wembley Stadium if I was given that much room,' he said with a chuckle. 'In fact, I'd have great pleasure filling it and imagining what it would look like!'

'I'm trying,' she said.

'And I could offer you a good rent, of course, and commission on the pieces sold.'

'Well – I –' She stopped and a little laugh escaped her. 'You're really serious about this, aren't you?'

'Absolutely,' he said. 'The north wing has its own entrance, doesn't it?'

'Yes, there's a door at the far end of the courtyard.'

'So you wouldn't be disturbed by customers,' he said.

'But you'd be in London, wouldn't you?'

He stroked his chin. 'I'd love to be based here but, to begin with, I think it's best if I hire somebody and come and go between the auction rooms in London until things are more sorted there.'

'Okay,' Celeste said, suddenly feeling rather excited about Julian's idea and wondering whether it could really work. If it could, it might mean a whole new future for Little Eleigh Manor. It really could be a viable option, she thought, turning the manor into a real place of business whilst allowing the sisters to live there together.

'With Evie's baby,' she whispered.

'Pardon?' Julian said.

She looked up at him. 'Do you want to take a look at the rooms now?' she asked.

'I'd absolutely love to,' he said.

'Mr Ludkin's at work so it's a bit noisy and dusty,' Celeste explained.

'I don't mind if he doesn't.'

They left the scented glory of the rose garden and walked through the courtyard, entering the north wing by the ancient wooden door.

'This is amazing,' Julian said. 'Imagine what customers would think. They'd already have their hands halfway to their wallets.'

Celeste grinned at the idea. 'You think so?'

'Once customers see this place, I think they'll want to take a little piece of it away with them, and that's when I'll be ready with the antiques.'

Celeste adored his confidence, and she led him down the long dark corridor which was filled with the sound of ferocious banging.

'Mr Ludkin?' she called. Turning to Julian, she added, 'I find it's best not to surprise him just in case he's about to knock a wall down.'

'Good point,' Julian said.

'Is it okay to come in?' Celeste asked, knocking on one of the doors.

'Aye – come on in!' Mr Ludkin called back.

'This is Julian Faraday,' she said. 'He's interested in renting these rooms out.'

'Is he?' Mr Ludkin said, his eyes narrowing. 'Not at the moment, though?'

'I think it would be wise to wait until you're finished work in here,' Julian said, reaching out to shake Mr Ludkin's dusty hand.

'Going okay, is it?' Celeste asked.

'No surprises today,' Mr Ludkin said.

'Good,' Celeste said.

'But you can never tell with these old houses,' he said. 'Just saying that to my boy, wasn't I?'

Mr Ludkin's son looked up from where he'd been scraping at some plaster and nodded.

'So, what do you think?' Celeste asked Julian as they crossed the room to the magnificent Elizabethan window which looked out over the moat.

'I think it's incredible,' he said. 'You could fit all sorts in here and it wouldn't look lost. Tapestries, four-poster beds –'

'Four-poster beds?'

'Just imagine!'

'I'm trying!' Celeste said.

'Listen,' Julian said, 'this is a pretty big thing to spring on you and I'm not expecting an answer right away but at least give it some thought, won't you? Just think about what it might be like to give this place a chance at a new life.'

Celeste nodded. 'I will,' she said.

'And maybe we could talk about it some more at dinner after the auction,' he said.

Celeste looked surprised. 'Oh, I'm not sure I'm coming,' she said.

'But you've *got* to come!' he said. 'You can't miss it. Come on in to London and I'll take you to my favourite restaurant afterwards to celebrate.'

Celeste took a deep breath, which still wasn't advisable in the north wing. 'I really don't know if I could bear to see our paintings going under the hammer,' she said, her eyes wide with hopelessness.

Julian nodded. 'I understand,' he said, reaching out and giving her shoulder a tiny squeeze.

It was then that a portion of wall came crashing to the floor behind them, showering them with ancient dust.

'Sorry!' Mr Ludkin cried, and the two of them left before any further damage could be done.

29.

Evie had been in the living room when Julian had left, and she waited a moment before leaving the house herself, finding a quiet corner of the rose garden. She sat down on a large white ornate bench under an arbour smothered in creamy white roses and took her phone out of her pocket.

'Lukas?' she said a moment later.

'Evie?'

'Where are you?'

'At Gloria Templeton's.'

'Can you come over?' she asked.

He was immediately on alert. 'Are you okay?'

'Yes, I'm fine,' she said with an exasperated sigh. Why did people keep asking her that?

'You're not planning on climbing up any ladders or anything, are you?'

'No, nothing like that.'

'And you're not stuck at the top of one now?'

'*No!*' she said with a groan. 'Look, if you're too busy –'

'I'm not too busy,' he cut in. 'I'll be right over.'

She ended the call and gazed up into the delicate white blooms above her head, drinking in the fragrance they exuded. Was she doing the right thing in telling Lukas? Her sisters seemed to think so. Esther seemed to think so.

She smiled as she remembered the long conversations she'd had with Esther over the last few weeks, thinking back to how scared she'd been around her at first and hating Celeste for appointing her house cleaner to the old woman. But, slowly, they'd begun to talk, sharing stories about their lives, asking questions that perhaps had never been asked before. They'd swapped books, read together and walked in the gardens. Evie had even shown Esther her beloved potting shed and Esther had soon been wielding a trowel.

It would be easy for somebody to look at their relationship and say that Esther was the mother that Evie had always longed for and never truly had, but it wasn't like that between them. They were friends, pure and simple. Evie didn't need a mother; she was soon to be a mother herself. But nobody could have too many friends, could they?

Leaving the arbour, Evie filled in some time in the potting shed before walking down the path to the front of the manor. She wasn't surprised to see Lukas's car at the top of the hill a moment later. She watched it as it got closer, feeling like her life was about to change forever and that she wasn't totally in control of it.

'But I am,' she told herself, 'and I don't have to tell him if I don't want to. I'll just see how I feel.'

She watched as Lukas drove across the moat and parked the old car he'd bought second-hand. It was a terrible car, with a dent in the rear passenger door and rust patches all over the bonnet, but both the mileage and the price had been low and Lukas had made the very best of it on his travels around the UK, even sleeping in it on a few occasions to save money.

'Hey!' he said as he got out of the car. He was wearing a faded pair of jeans that were covered in dirt and a T-shirt that was fraying at the neck and sleeves, but he still managed to look tremendously handsome.

Evie cleared her throat, trying not to stare at him or imagine what it would be like to kiss him again. This wasn't about how handsome and desirable her former lover was, she reminded herself. She had important issues to deal with and she was quite determined not to be sidetracked.

'Hi,' she said.

'Are we going inside?' he asked, pointing to the gatehouse.

'Can we walk?' she asked.

'Sure,' he said, falling into step beside her as she retraced her steps to the rose-covered arbour, where they sat down together. 'This is lovely,' he said a minute later. 'Romantic!' His bright eyes widened and he gave her a little grin that hinted at the day that she'd probably conceived the baby she was now carrying.

'Lukas,' she began, doing her best to put that day out of her mind now.

'Yes?'

'I have something important to tell you.'

'Okay,' he said.

But she couldn't. She just couldn't. So she told him something else instead.

'Gertie and I have been talking and we think we might be able to use you more around the garden.'

He looked surprised. 'You're offering me a job?'

'Yes,' she said.

'Part-time?'

She nodded. 'We'll see how things go after that. If you want to stay in Suffolk, that is.'

'You know I do,' he said with a light smile.

She nodded. 'Right.'

'Right,' he echoed.

'Aren't you pleased?' she asked. 'I thought you'd be pleased.'

'I am!' he said. 'It's just – is *this* what you called me for? Is this why we're sitting here surrounded by roses?'

'I like sitting here,' she said. 'It helps me to relax.'

'And you need to be relaxed to in order to offer me a part-time job?'

Evie nodded, but Lukas didn't look convinced.

'So, this *isn't* about us?' he asked, his eyes squinting at her in the sun.

Evie took a deep breath. 'No. Well, yes. Kind of.'

He laughed. 'What on earth are you trying to say?'

Her forehead crinkled and she looked as if she was about to cry. 'I have something else to tell you but you're not making it very easy.'

He looked crestfallen. 'Sorry, Evie. Go on – try now. I'm listening.'

She looked flustered and then stood up. 'Oh, this is hopeless! I knew it would be! This isn't my idea.' She was walking now, tearing along the path before heading out across the lawn towards the river.

'What isn't your idea?' Lukas shouted after her.

'Telling you,' she said.

'Telling me what?' He caught up with her and captured her hand in his. 'Evie! What's the matter? Has what's-her-name found out that you've stolen that painting? Are you going to be arrested or something? Do you need me to testify for you?' He was joking, but Evie obviously wasn't finding it amusing.

'This has got nothing to do with that painting. Anyway, I didn't steal it. It was ours in the first place. Simone stole it from *us!*

'Okay, okay! Then what is it?'

Evie threw her head back and gazed up into the big blue sky and wished that she was a little bird so that she could take off and fly far, far away. But she was an earthbound creature and she had to stay and face reality. So she looked at Lukas standing before her, taking in his fair hair and his bright eyes that were full of anxiety, and she knew that the time had come.

'I'm – I'm –'

'What?'

'Pregnant.'

From somewhere behind them, a startled blackbird cried its alarm and took off across the lawn. Evie hoped it wasn't a bad omen, but she wouldn't blame Lukas if he, too, took off. But he didn't.

Ever so slowly, he moved forward and swallowed hard. 'It's mine, isn't it?'

'Yes,' Evie said.

'How long have you known?'

'A while,' she said.

'Why didn't you tell me?'

'Because I didn't mean to get you involved in this.'

'But I *am* involved,' he said simply.

'Yes, but only biologically.'

'What the hell does that mean?'

'Lukas, you didn't come to England to be a father,' she said, 'and I don't expect anything from you.'

'Okay,' he said, 'but what if I *want* to be a father – a proper father?'

'But I never meant for any of this to get serious. You and me – *us* – it all happened without much thought about the future. You know my mum was dying and you were like a wonderful escape from all that. But I never thought beyond that. Then, when I found out, all I could think about was this new life growing inside me and it just seemed so right, even though it was unexpected.'

He looked at her gently. 'It is unexpected,' he said.

'I know, and that's why I was worried about telling you. You see, this is *my* decision. You don't have to worry about anything. I'll take care of our daughter.'

'A daughter?'

Evie nodded. 'I'm sure it's a girl. I've just got a feeling.'

Lukas took a deep breath and sighed it out. 'Wow!' he said.

'Please don't worry,' she told him.

'Evie – I'm not worried,' he said. 'I'm – I'm – really happy!'

'You are?'

He took a step towards her and, before she could register what was happening, his mouth came down hard on hers. She'd forgotten what it was like to be kissed by him but that one moment in the garden brought it all back to her, and she realised how foolish she had been in thinking she could live without him. She'd tried so hard to push him away and to build up the barriers between him and her heart, but it was no good. She loved him and she needed him.

Her breathing was thick and fast, and she felt as if she were about to faint when he finally let her go.

'Please don't tell me you didn't want me to do that,' he said.

She shook her head. 'I won't,' she said, 'because I *really* wanted you to do it.'

'God, Evie!' he said with an exasperated sigh. 'Why didn't you tell me about all this before?'

She sighed. 'I don't know,' she said. 'I guess I just want to try and do everything myself.'

'But you don't have to. *Why* would you want to anyway?' Lukas reached out a hand and stroked her cheek. 'I'm here for you. I always have been, ever since that time I crossed the moat and saw you in the middle of that huge heap of horse manure.'

She laughed. 'What a time you picked to say hello.'

He smiled and cupped her face in his hands. 'I've always been here for you, but you kept pushing me away.'

'I know,' she said. 'I'm really sorry. I wanted to be –' She paused.

'Whatever you do, don't say *independent*,' he told her.

'Why not? What's wrong with that?'

'It's pretty damned lonely, for a start.'

She gave a small smile. 'I guess.'

'I don't think people are meant to be on their own, do you?'

'But I'm *not* on my own.'

'Well, I know – not *now*. You've got your sisters and this place and that funny old woman.'

'*Esther!*'

'Yes, Esther,' he said. 'But what would happen if they moved away?'

She narrowed her eyes at him. 'They're not going anywhere.'

'Can you be sure of that?'

'We can't be sure of anything, I suppose,' she said. 'I'm not even sure if we'll all be living here much longer if Celeste gets her way. But I'll have this baby – whatever else happens. Anyway, you're one to talk – leaving your home and your family behind and travelling around the UK on your own.'

He laughed. 'I guess,' he said, 'but it's a lonely way to live and you know I didn't want to leave here once I'd met you.'

'I know,' she said.

'I thought about you every day. Every minute.'

She gave him a withering look. 'Right!'

'I did! You got my texts, didn't you?'

'You filled my entire phone!'

'I really missed you.'

Her face softened. 'I missed you too.'

He stroked the soft blondeness of her hair. 'So, this part-time job you're offering me – is it because you really want me here or just because you're going to be incapacitated for a while?'

'I am *not* going to be incapacitated!' Evie said. 'Gertie and I just think it might be a good idea to have an extra pair of hands whilst I'm busy with the baby.'

He grinned. 'I see.'

'Well? Are you going to accept the job or are you just going to stand here teasing me all day?'

He laughed. 'I'm going to accept the job, silly!' he said.

'Don't call me silly,' Evie said. 'I'm being serious.'

'I know you are,' he said, 'and I'm dead serious too – about you. I want to be with you forever.'

'But what about your studies? Your art? You can't just give all that up,' she said.

'I can still study,' he said, 'only I'll have you and this little one by my side.'

'I don't want you to regret anything,' she said.

'I won't.'

'You say that now, but you could quickly change your mind and I want you to know that I won't mind. You can walk away.'

'Evie – I'm not going to walk away.'

'But I'm just saying that you can. If you really want to.'

'I won't want to.'

Evie took a deep breath.

'You don't believe me, do you?' he said.

'I don't know what to believe,' she said. 'I believe I love you, and I've never ever said that to anyone before.'

'And you really think I'm going to walk away from that?' He moved an inch closer to her and she felt the warmth of his body against hers. 'From *this*?' He rested his large hand over her belly and she gasped, covering his hand with her own.

'I believe you,' she said, resting her head in the crook of shoulder. 'I really believe you.'

30.

The day of the auction came much too quickly for Celeste, which seemed strange for her to admit because she'd truly believed that she'd already done the hard part in agreeing to sell the paintings. But, as she caught the train into London, she couldn't quell the nervousness that was bubbling inside her at the thought of witnessing her beloved paintings being sold. How she would react was a mystery to her, but she sincerely hoped that she would not either bid for the paintings herself or land the winning bidder a fierce punch.

At Liverpool Street station, she caught the tube to the station closest to Faraday's auction rooms. Blinking in the bright city sunshine as she surfaced from the underground, she headed in the direction she hoped was right, passing a neat row of boutiques and a florist's selling the kind of roses she and her sisters despaired of: horribly gaudy hybrid teas with absolutely no scent whatsoever. Shaking her head in disapproval, she continued past the terrace of fine red-bricked mansions and then she stopped.

Reaching inside her handbag for her pocket *A to Z*, Celeste acknowledged that she was hopelessly lost. How many streets were there in London? How could it be so very complicated? What on earth had she been thinking of, coming here? She should have stayed at home in Suffolk where she knew her way around. She thought of the three rural roads that made up the village of Little Eleigh and how she could happily navigate her way around the myriad footpaths and fields that surrounded the manor.

Finding the correct page, she studied the tiny map, crossed the road, took the first right and was mightily relieved to see Faraday's before her. It was a large white Georgian building towering an impressive four storeys, with two enormous arched windows on the ground floor advertising today's event. It was all very impressive and it made it hard to believe that Julian really wanted to give up his position there and run an antiques shop in middle-of-nowhere Suffolk. But she had seen the passion in his eyes when he had talked about his plans for the future and she had no doubt that he would follow his heart, even if that meant leaving London behind.

Which brought her to the subject of the north wing. She had talked through the idea of Julian opening an antiques centre at the manor with Gertie and Evie, and they had been all for it.

'Does this mean we won't have to sell the manor?' Evie had asked.

'Well, let's not get ahead of ourselves,' Celeste had said, 'but it's a route that's definitely worth considering.'

'I think it's a brilliant idea,' Gertie had said. 'It'll be a good source of revenue and will bring more people here and help spread the word about Hamilton Roses.'

'And don't forget the rent from The Lodge,' Evie had said. 'We'll have tonnes of money coming in!'

Celeste couldn't disagree about that, but she did have some reservations. Having Julian working at the manor would be a strange experience and she wasn't yet sure how she felt about it.

Julian Faraday at Little Eleigh Manor.

There would be no getting away from him and no getting away from the fact that she was beginning to have feelings for him. Feelings she wasn't at all sure she was ready to have yet. At the moment, it was easy to avoid him if she needed to. She saw him when it suited her and could deflect his phone calls and ignore his emails if she wanted to. She couldn't do that so easily if he was in her home, could she? She couldn't hide from the knowledge that she liked him and that his feelings for her were growing stronger too.

Entering Faraday's now, she looked around the foyer at the crowds of people before making her way into the sale room, where she immediately saw Julian. He was wearing a crisp navy suit that made his dark red hair gleam, and Celeste had never seen him looking quite so businesslike. He was chatting to an elderly lady whose neck was encased in large pearls and whose fingers wore massive rings set with precious stones. Was she here for her family paintings, Celeste couldn't help wondering?

As soon as the lady walked away, a gentleman waylaid Julian and then a middle-aged couple stopped to chat. Celeste watched in amusement as he paid court to his customers, and then he saw her.

'Celeste!' he cried across the room, turning several heads. Celeste blushed as he approached her, kissing her on both cheeks, which caught her off guard. He'd never done that before, but perhaps she'd do well not to read too much into it. This was Julian Faraday in London, she reasoned. This was how he greeted people.

'Hello,' she said. 'It's certainly busy.'

He nodded. 'It's a good crowd. That's exciting. Where are you sitting? Come with me.'

He led the way down the aisle between the neat rows of chairs, his right hand in the small of her back.

'Oh, not the front!' Celeste said. 'I couldn't bear it.' She walked back a few paces, choosing herself an aisle seat in the middle of the room.

'Are you sure you'll be okay here?' he asked.

'I'll be fine,' she said with a tight smile. Her nerves were definitely getting the better of her. 'Go on, Mr Auctioneer – get those paintings sold.'

He gave her a grin and a funny little salute before making his way to the rostrum at the front of the room. An expectant silence followed and then the madness began.

The first few lots were rather dull landscapes in oil which went for staggering amounts of money. Celeste looked around the room in awe. Who were these people and how on earth did they make so much money? She noticed a row of tables along the side of the room which were manned by staff with telephones glued to their ears and computer screens in front of them. It seemed that the auction was not just confined to this little room in the centre of London but included the whole world.

Tens of thousands of pounds were exchanging hands at an alarming rate, the figures being shown in all the major currencies of the world on a large screen behind Julian. Celeste watched in wonder, her eyes wide and her heart racing wildly as the time approached for the rose paintings to be shown.

Celeste's mouth had gone quite dry when the first of her paintings was brought out into the room. Julian's eyes met hers across the crowds and then the torture began.

First was the Frans Mortelmans of the pink and crimson roses in the basket.

'Grandma's favourite,' Celeste whispered to herself, tears filling her eyes a few heart-stopping moments later as it sold. Even though it reached forty-five thousand pounds, it hurt so much to know that she would never see it again. She knew that Gertie and Evie would be watching the auction online at home and wondered if they would be cheering or crying.

The Frans Mortelmans was followed by the Ferdinand Georg Waldmüller and then the Jean-Louis Cassell painting of white roses that Celeste loved so much. Each of them made over thirty thousand pounds, but every time the gavel fell, its strike was like a bullet being fired into Celeste's heart.

The rose painting sale finished with the delicate Pierre-Joseph Redouté. 'The Raphael of flowers,' Celeste said to herself, remembering what Julian had told her about the painter. It reached a record price: sixty-five thousand pounds, receiving the first round of applause in the sales room that day.

All of the paintings had met and far exceeded their reserve price which, in a way, was a wonderful thing, but it meant that none of them was coming home with her. She knew then that she had secretly been wishing that at least one would. But at least they had the little painting that Evie had liberated from Simone, Celeste thought. That was some consolation.

She didn't stay for the rest of the auction but quietly left the room, feeling Julian's eyes on her as she exited. She couldn't bear to look at him; she needed to be alone and so left Faraday's and walked the streets until she found a little park. She sat on a bench in the London sunshine, taking deep breaths to calm herself.

They were gone. First the Fantin-Latour and now the other smaller paintings that had graced the walls of Little Eleigh Manor for so many years. Celeste closed her eyes, feeling the full weight of her guilt. She knew that most people would probably think she was a spoilt girl living in a medieval moated manor house full of antiques and that she had nothing to complain about, but she couldn't help mourning the loss of something so beautiful and something that had been so precious to her grandparents.

When her phone beeped, she took a look at the message, half-expecting it to be from Julian asking her where she had gone, but it was from Gertie.

You did the right thing. x

She blinked away the tears, taking comfort in the fact that her sister knew exactly how she was feeling at that moment.

As much as she wanted to leave London and slink back to her quiet corner of East Anglia, she knew how rude that would be after all of Julian's hard work and so, after a few more moments of relative solitude, she made her way back to the auction rooms. The sale was over and the foyer was full of people lining up to pay for their items. At first, she couldn't see Julian but then she spotted him in the corner of the room. He was laughing and smiling as only he could. She'd never seen such a warm and relentlessly happy person and she felt her sad mood lift just a little as she watched him talking to a customer. Then he caught her eye, excused himself and made his way across the foyer towards her.

'Celeste! Are you okay?' he asked, his hand firm on her shoulder.

'I think so.'

'You're shaking,' he said. 'Come with me.'

'Don't you have to be here?'

'No, no,' he said lightly, guiding her out of the room with his hand in the small of her back like before. They walked down a carpeted corridor and into a grand and spacious office overlooking a courtyard.

'Is this yours?' Celeste asked.

'Yes,' he said. 'Not a bad little pad, is it?'

'It's beautiful.'

'And fully equipped with a drinks cabinet,' he said. 'Can I get you anything?'

'No, thank you.'

'Are you sure?' he asked. 'You look as if you could use something.'

'A cup of tea, perhaps?'

'Of course,' he said, picking up the phone on his desk. 'Liza? Two cups of tea, if you wouldn't mind.'

'You sure it's not too much trouble?'

'Celeste – you were one of our big clients today. I think we can stand you a cup of tea.'

She gave a little smile.

'I got worried when I saw you leave,' he said. 'I hope you aren't too upset by this whole thing. I think we got you the very best prices we could.'

'Yes,' she said, 'I know you did and I can't thank you enough for everything you've done for us.'

'You know one of the paintings will be off to Brazil?' he said.

'Really?'

He nodded. 'The Jean-Louis Cassell. A businessman who is crazy about roses bought it,' he said. 'The others are staying in the UK.'

She smiled, strangely comforted by the thought that the rest of the paintings wouldn't be too far away.

'So,' he said, 'you're staying for dinner I hope?' He had an anxious look in his eyes, which seemed to suggest that he thought Celeste was about to up and run, and, much as she'd have liked to, she couldn't do that to him.

'Of course,' she said.

'Good!' he said, clapping his hands together just as Liza entered with the tea things.

❦

Back at Little Eleigh Manor, Gertie, Evie and Esther were sitting in the kitchen drinking cups of tea of their own.

'Did she respond to your text yet?' Evie asked Gertie.

Gertie looked down at her phone. 'She just sent a couple of kisses.'

Evie looked grim. 'She'll be feeling pretty miserable, won't she?'

'I'm guessing so,' Gertie said. 'I wish she was coming home right away.'

'I don't,' Evie said. 'Julian will cheer her up.'

'Maybe,' Gertie said. 'I just hope he doesn't push things with her. I think he's really falling for her.'

'Well, I think Celly needs a good big push and Julian seems just the right sort of man to do the pushing too.'

'Don't be insensitive,' Gertie said.

'I'm not,' Evie said, 'but she needs somebody to pull her out of this constant dark mood of hers.'

'She's just had a lot to deal with.'

'We've *all* had a lot to deal with,' Evie said.

Gertie gave Evie a look, the sort that was sure to wind her up.

'*What?*' Evie said. 'You don't think being pregnant whilst doing the work of three people is enough to be dealing with?'

'I thought you said Lukas had accepted the job?'

'He has,' Evie said.

'So, when's he starting?'

'Next week.'

'Then stop moaning!'

Evie shook her head and looked at Esther. 'Honestly, I get no sympathy around here.'

Esther gave a little chuckle at the sisterly banter.

'Right,' Gertie said. 'I'm off out to get some work done.'

Evie nodded. 'I'll join you in a bit,' she said.

'So?' Esther began as soon as Gertie had left, leaning a little closer to her young friend.

Evie grinned, knowing exactly what Esther was waiting to hear.

'I told him I was pregnant,' she said after a protracted pause. 'With his baby.'

Esther's eyes lit up with joy. 'You did?'

'Yes! And I told him something else too.'

'What's that?'

'That I love him.'

Esther nodded but, much to Evie's astonishment, she didn't look surprised. 'I thought as much,' she said.

'How could you *possibly* know that when I didn't even know?' she asked.

'Because I know the signs!' Esther said.

'Oh, really?'

'Really,' she said. 'Come with me. I've got something to show you.'

Evie followed Esther out of the kitchen and back to her room, where she walked across to a little chest of drawers, opening the top one and reaching inside for a small photo album.

'This is the last photo ever taken of Sally,' Esther said as she opened the album. Evie moved closer and looked at the photograph of the woman she had heard so much about. 'It was just before she got sick.'

Evie took in the long, straight hair and the smiling face.

'Who took the photo?'

'A man she'd met called Paolo. He was from Italy. He was training to be a doctor and she was madly in love with him. She never told me, of course, but I knew. Just look at that smile and her eyes. You can see it everywhere.'

Evie studied the photograph and nodded. 'But I haven't been going around smiling like that,' she said.

'Maybe not but I could still tell. You had that aura about you.'

Evie laughed. 'I don't believe in auras.'

'It doesn't matter if you believe in them or not. I saw it all the same.'

'I think you're being rather fanciful, Esther,' Evie said with a wry smile.

'But I'm right, aren't I? You've been in love with him this whole time.'

Evie stared out of the window, watching the swallows dancing in the sky high above the rose garden. 'Yes,' she said at last. 'I think I have.'

❧

When the meal was over and coffee was being served, Julian dared to ask the question that Celeste had guessed had been uppermost in his mind but hadn't dared to prompt.

'Have you had any time to consider my proposal?' he asked.

'About the antiques centre?' she said, as if he'd made any other sort of proposal.

He nodded. 'Yes.'

'Gertie and Evie are all for it. Even Esther got quite excited when I told her.'

'But what about you, Celeste? How do *you* feel about it?'

She ran her index finger around the rim of her coffee cup. 'How do I feel about it? I think it would be a very interesting business to have at the manor. It could be a really viable option for the future of the house.'

'Then you're for it?'

'Yes,' she said.

'But you sound hesitant,' he said, looking at her with great intensity.

She stared back at him, gazing into the kind eyes that she had grown so used to seeing over the last few weeks. It seemed odd to her that there had been a time in her life when she hadn't known him, when she hadn't had his gentle presence in her days, and she valued it – she truly did. Only it made her feel so uncertain of herself, and of the future, too, because she didn't feel that she had anything to give him.

'Celeste?' he said when she didn't answer him. 'What is it?'

'Julian – I –' She paused.

'Tell me. If something's worrying you, I want to know.'

She nodded. 'Yes,' she said. 'I – it's just that I feel that every-thing is moving so fast and that I'm not quite ready for it all.'

'Okay,' he said. 'I can understand that.'

'Can you?'

He nodded. 'Of course I can,' he said. 'You mean me in particular, don't you?'

They held each other's gaze. 'Yes,' she said. 'I think I do.'

He swallowed hard and reached his hand across the table to hold hers. 'You know how I feel about you, don't you? I'd be very surprised if you hadn't worked it out by now.'

'I know,' she said quietly.

He nodded. 'And I know that you haven't quite made your mind up about all this.'

She bit her lip. 'Julian,' she said, 'my head's a mess. I feel like I'm only just coping, you know?'

'I know.'

She took a deep breath. 'You've been so kind and patient with me,' she said, 'and I want you to know how much that means to me.'

He gave a little nod and smile and then cleared his throat. 'I've been so happy since I met you,' he told her, 'and I know you've got a lot going on.' He swallowed hard and his bright eyes were intense with emotion. 'But I can't wait forever, Celeste,' he said.

'I know,' she said. 'I know.'

When they left the restaurant, Julian hailed a taxi and accompanied her to the Liverpool Street station.

'I wish I was coming through to Suffolk with you but I'll be there this weekend,' he said as the taxi pulled up by the kerb. 'Perhaps we can have lunch or something?'

Celeste had been twisting and squeezing her fingers together since they'd left the restaurant, wrangling with her thoughts since Julian's declaration.

I can't wait forever.

She knew that. It had been a perfectly reasonable thing for him to say and yet the guilt it made her feel weighed heavily upon her. She turned to look at him.

'Julian,' she began, 'I don't want you to have any expectations of me because I can't promise you anything.'

'I know that,' he said, 'and I'm not asking anything from you.'

'But you are,' she said, her voice wavering slightly. 'You're waiting, and that's a great pressure. I *can't* take that responsibility – not now and maybe not ever.' She looked at him in the brief space between them on the backseat of the taxi and suddenly wanted to be anywhere but there.

'Okay,' he said at last. 'I understand.' His voice had changed; it had become colder and more controlled and his eyes had lost some of their warmth. Celeste had an awful premonition that she would never see that smiling, kind expression of his ever again.

'Goodbye, Celeste,' he said, unbuttoning his belt and leaning across the seat to open the door for her.

'Julian –'

'Goodbye.'

31.

It was a strange and lonely world without Julian's texts and phone calls, but Celeste could hardly expect to receive them now, could she? She closed her eyes as she remembered the expression on his face in the taxi. Those kind blue eyes of his had iced over in a matter of seconds, shutting off his warmth from her. Why had she done that? What had she been thinking of?

Herself. She had been thinking only of herself and how she felt about things. Not once had she thought about what Julian might be thinking and feeling. She hadn't asked him once. He'd been so attentive to her, so caring, and had done his best to try and understand what she was going through, but she hadn't returned that kindness to him. Instead, she had pushed him away from her, over and over again.

Sitting at the old desk in the study, she thought about calling him, but what would she say? She could feel tears brimming but quickly blinked them away when she heard a light tapping on the study door.

'Celly?' Gertie's voice called.

'Come in.'

Gertie entered the room. 'It's a bit dark in here, isn't it?' she said, walking across to the windows and drawing the curtains properly. Celeste remembered Julian's words about the room and how he thought she should change it, make it lighter, brighter.

'Did you want me?' Celeste prompted.

'Ah, yes – I've just had a call from Tom Parker. He wants to know if we'll be taking part in the show in September. He's not had the form back from you yet and needs to reserve our place if we want it.'

'Yes – tell him yes,' Celeste said, thinking of the local fair that Hamilton Roses took part in each year at the church to raise funds. It was a lovely event in which local craftsmen displayed their wares, filling the church with unique pieces and produce.

'I must have just mislaid the form,' Celeste said. 'Just when I thought I was finally getting on top of things.'

'You are,' Gertie said. 'You're doing the most amazing job.'

'Am I?'

'Yes!' Gertie said, observing Celeste closely. 'Are you all right?'

'I'm fine.'

'Really?' Gertie said. 'I don't believe you.'

Celeste looked at her sister and thought about spinning some lie about how she was probably just tired. She could get away with that but she knew it would be wrong and, anyway, there was a part of her that was desperate to confide in someone.

'I think I've messed up,' she said at last.

'What do you mean?' Gertie asked. 'The paperwork?'

'No, not the paperwork.' She took a deep breath. 'Julian.' Just saying his name brought a flood of emotions to the fore.

'How?' Gertie said, perching on the desk next to her sister.

'I told him that I thought we should take break,' she confided to Gertie.

'A break? But I didn't think you were really seeing him,' Gertie said.

'I know,' Celeste said. 'I told you – I messed up.'

'What did you say exactly?'

She closed her eyes, trying to recall her words. 'I told him that I felt pressured by him and that I didn't want him to have any expectations of me.'

'Oh, Celly! When did this happen?'

'After the auction.'

'But I thought you went out to dinner?' Gertie said.

'We did. And then he saw me to the station and I told him.'

'Why didn't you tell me what had happened?'

'I've been –'

'*Don't* say you've been too busy,' Gertie said, 'because you always say that.'

'But it's true.'

Gertie shook her head. 'You've been trying to bury it, haven't you? You were hoping you could hide it away and forget about it.' She leaned in closer to Celeste and watched as her sister slowly nodded.

'I'm so desperate not to feel anything but I can't stop this,' Celeste said, her dark eyes wide and wild-looking.

'And you shouldn't try to! It's not natural to try and stop your emotions,' Gertie said. 'Have you talked to him since?'

'No,' she said, the one word filled with more anguish than any word had a right to be.

'Celly, he *adores* you! You've only got to pick up the phone for him to come running back to you.'

Celeste shook her head. 'You didn't see the way he looked at me. It was awful, Gertie, and I've only got myself to blame. *I* made him look at me like that!'

Gertie got up from the desk and hugged her sister. 'You really like him, don't you?'

'I didn't know how much until I said those stupid things.'

'Well, tell him that! Tell him what a silly idiot you've been. He'll understand!'

Celeste gave a funny laughing cry as Gertie continued to hug her.

'I'm too scared to call him. I've blown it. He was so patient with me but I just went too far. I can't ask anything else from him.'

'I think you're wrong,' Gertie said. 'I think if he knew how you really felt, he'd be by your side in a minute.'

Celeste shook her head. 'I can't do that to him. He probably hates me now.'

'He won't hate you.'

'He'll have made a voodoo doll of me and have it full of pins, which is probably why I'm in so much pain!'

Gertie squeezed her shoulder. 'You're in love and that can be the worst pain in the world when it isn't going right.'

Celeste looked up. 'You said that like you know what it means.'

'Did I?' Gertie said.

It was Celeste's turn to scrutinise her sister. 'Is there anything you want to tell me?'

Gertie smiled. 'No,' she said. 'The only thing I want to tell you is that you're wrong – completely wrong – if you think Julian won't want to hear from you. I think you should ring him. Just talk to him.'

Celeste shook her head again. 'I can't,' she said.

Gertie hopped down from her perch on the desk. 'Okay!'

'And don't *you* dare ring him, Gertie!'

Gertie stopped when she'd reached the door. 'I won't,' she said.

'Promise?'

'Promise,' Gertie said.

But it was a promise destined to be broken.

                              ∾

Celeste wasn't the only one obsessing over not hearing from a man. Gertie had spent more time checking her phone for messages from James than she had looking at roses, which – for a rosarian in summer – was downright irresponsible.

She had lost count of the number of times she had cried herself to sleep. It was just so hard for her to keep the faith when she had nothing tangible to hold on to. She still hadn't told anyone either, although Celeste had been on to her a couple of times, knowing something was going on.

Poor Celeste, she thought. Like Evie, Gertie adored Julian and knew that he and Celeste would make a really great couple, but Gertie feared that it was never going to happen now. At least Evie had got things right in the man department, she thought as she walked into the relative darkness of the manor after having spent the day in the garden. She was carrying a little basket filled with fresh eggs from her hens. Her bare limbs were a rich brown and she felt the wonderful fatigue of a hard-working gardener.

The grandfather clock was striking seven as she crossed the hall and saw Celeste.

'I've come in search of tea,' Gertie said.

'Me too,' Celeste said. 'I didn't realise what the time was.'

'You should really forget about that study once in a while and get yourself outside. It's been a beautiful day.'

Celeste rubbed her eyes. 'Perhaps you're right,' she said.

'You know I am,' she said. 'The summer won't last forever, you know.'

The sound of laughter could be heard from the kitchen and Gertie and Celeste soon saw that Evie and Esther were cooking something on the Aga.

'There you both are!' Evie said. 'We were about to send out a search party!'

'What are you cooking?' Gertie asked, worrying about the state of her beloved Aga.

'What is it again, Esther?' Evie asked.

'Half-the-garden soup,' Esther said. 'Basically, it's whatever you can find that's in season.'

'Sounds ominous,' Celeste said.

'Well, there are plenty of eggs here if it all goes horribly wrong,' Gertie said, placing her basket on the table.

'It won't go wrong,' Evie said. 'Esther is the most amazing cook!'

'Oh, is she?' Gertie said, feeling that her position in the kitchen was being usurped.

'Hey! Have you guys heard the latest?' Evie said.

'No, what?' Celeste asked.

'James and Samantha have sold their house,' she said lightly.

'Really?' Celeste said. 'I didn't even know it was for sale.'

Evie nodded. 'They're leaving Little Eleigh.'

The colour drained from Gertie's face. 'No, you've heard that wrong,' she said. 'You're always getting things wrong, Evie.'

'I haven't got it wrong. Not this time. I saw James in the post office. He told me.'

'You talked to James?'

'Yes,' Evie said. 'He told me to tell you both. He's trying to let everyone know before he flies out next week.'

'Flies out where?' Gertie said.

'To France,' Evie said. 'They're selling up here and buying some ramshackle gite over there. It sounds amazing – like the sort of place you're always talking about with shutters that open out onto the hills. Hey! Maybe he'll invite us out there. What do you think?'

Celeste had been watching Gertie's face during this exchange, noticing its pallor and stunned expression.

'I don't think we should fish for an invite, Evie,' Celeste warned. 'Didn't you sell her some container roses the other week?'

Gertie nodded.

'Probably to make the garden look good for buyers,' Evie said.

Gertie, who'd only just sat down at the table, stood up.

'Where are you going?' Evie said.

'I'm not hungry,' she said.

'But we've got absolutely gallons of this soup!' Evie said, but her sister had already left the room. 'What's the matter with her?'

Celeste sighed. 'I'm not sure but I think I'd better try and find out.'

Celeste did her best to track Gertie down but she'd obviously left the confines of the manor. She didn't get a chance to talk to her until later that evening when she heard a series of loud, angry thumps coming from the kitchen once everybody was safely out of the way.

Taking a deep breath and not quite knowing what she was going to discover, Celeste entered the kitchen.

'Hey,' she said softly.

'Hey,' Gertie replied without looking up.

'What are you doing?' Celeste asked.

'Making bread,' Gertie said. 'What does it look like?'

Celeste flinched at the tone of her voice. Bread. That was probably the worst-case scenario. It was far worse than scones or lemon cake, that was for sure. Gertie obviously had a lot of anger inside if she'd felt compelled to knead dough last thing at night.

'I've been trying to find you,' she said.

'Yeah? Well, I've been trying not to be found.'

'I guessed,' Celeste said, sitting down on the bench on the other side of the table and feeling the top vibrate under Gertie's vigorous ministrations. She watched as her sister threw and kneaded the bread dough with great force, Gertie's face flushed to its very limit with her efforts.

'Are you going to talk to me?' Celeste asked after a while.

'What would you like to talk about?' Gertie said, her tone cold and closed.

'How about James Stanton?'

Gertie stopped what she was doing and wiped a floury wrist across her forehead. 'Why do you want to talk about him?'

'You know why.'

The sisters stared at each other for a long time before the tears rose into Gertie's eyes.

'Oh, sweetheart!' Celeste was on her feet in a second and had rounded the table to take her sister in her arms, embracing her as huge sobs wracked her body.

'He told me he loved me!' she cried. 'He said we were going to be together and I believed him.'

She continued to cry and Celeste continued to hold her, waiting until she was ready to say more.

'I wish you'd told me,' Celeste said eventually.

Gertie gave a big sniff before wiping her eyes with a tissue from out of her apron pocket and looking at her sister. 'You didn't tell me about what happened with Julian,' she said.

Celeste nodded. 'Ah, yes,' she said, 'and Evie didn't tell us about the baby.'

They looked at each other with sadness in their eyes but tiny smiles on their faces.

'We seem to be very good at keeping secrets from each other,' Gertie said, giving her nose a fierce blow.

'I wonder why,' Celeste said with a touch of irony.

'Because Mum never let us talk about our feelings?' Gertie said.

Celeste nodded. 'Whenever I tried to tell her anything important to me, she'd just brush me off. It was impossible to get close to her and open up.'

'But we mustn't become like that,' Gertie said. 'Not ever.'

'I know,' Celeste said. 'So are you going to tell me what's been going on with James?'

Gertie took a deep breath and the two of them sat down at the kitchen table, and Celeste listened to her sister open up about the man she'd fallen in love with.

'I finally managed to talk to him this afternoon,' she said, bringing the story up to date. 'He's been offered a job in France. I said I'd go with him. Can you believe that? I was going to give all this up here just so I could be with him, but he said he owes it to Samantha to make things work. He said the climate will do her the world of good and they want to make a fresh start of things.'

'Oh, Gertie. I'm so sorry.' Celeste reached across the table to hold her sister's hand.

'He'd said he was unhappy. He'd told me he couldn't live without me and that Samantha made him miserable. Was he lying all that time? Was he just using me?'

Celeste bit her lip. 'I think maybe he was exaggerating the truth,' she said.

'I thought he loved me, Celly. I thought we had a future together.' Tears welled up in her dark eyes again but she managed to hold them back this time. 'I've been so stupid! I should never have got involved with someone who was married! Why did I do that to myself? *Why?*'

'Because you're a romantic,' Celeste told her. 'You're led by the heart rather than the head – you always have been.'

'Well, he's broken my heart so I guess I won't be making that mistake again.'

Celeste watched as she got up and began to scrape all the bread dough from the table into one big messy heap.

'What are you doing?' she asked.

'Binning it,' Gertie said. 'It wouldn't be very good anyway. I forgot to add the yeast.'

32.

It was the next morning when Evie came charging into the study without so much as knocking on the door.

'Why are Tennyson's *Love Poems* floating in the moat?' she said.

Celeste looked up from an invoice she was trying to decipher. 'They must belong to Gertie. Did you rescue them?'

'No. They're kind of half-stuck on a lily pad, though, if she wants to try and reach it.'

'I'm not sure she'll want to. The moat might be the best place for it.'

'Did you find out what's bugging her?' Evie asked.

'It's a who rather than a what, and his name's James Stanton,' Celeste said.

'You mean –'

'Yep,' Celeste said.

'Then he *was* having an affair all this time!' Evie said, a light in her eyes. 'Jeepers! I'd never have guessed it would be with *our* Gertie!'

Celeste shook her head. 'Look – don't make a big scene about it, okay? She had real feelings for him.'

'Well, he's a good-looking guy,' Evie said, flopping down into their mother's chair. 'A complete sod, obviously, but pretty handsome. Poor Gertie! It's a good job he's left Little Eleigh already or I'd punch him in the nose.'

Celeste sighed. 'That wouldn't solve anything.'

'Maybe not, but it would be the right thing to do,' Evie said.

'Evelyn, you've really got to put a stop to this whole *doing the right thing* business. It always gets you into trouble.'

Evie sighed and her hand rested on her belly.

'You okay?' Celeste asked.

'Yes, Aunt Celly, I'm fine,' Evie said, raising a smile from her sister. 'Well, I was a bit sick this morning but I'm okay now.'

'Can you feel anything yet?'

'Just indigestion,' Evie said. 'Gertie's going to make me a big vat of peppermint tea and she's expecting me to drink it all. Disgusting.'

Celeste smiled. 'She's put me on a strict rotation of lemon balm and camomile to counter stress.'

'Holy herbal!' Evie said.

'But listen,' Celeste said, 'you mustn't tell anybody about Gertie and James, okay?'

'*Don't* say it would have brought disgrace to our family,' Evie said, suddenly serious.

Celeste looked shocked as she remembered the frequent reprimand of their mother. 'I'd never say that,' she said. '*Never!*'

'Okay,' Evie said, placated by her sister's look of total horror.

'But we live in a small village and you know what it can be like, don't you? Gertie's such a private person and it would be awful if she became the victim of malicious gossip. I think it would break her.'

Evie had the good sense to nod. 'Poor Gertie,' she said again. 'Shall I go and talk to her?'

'If you can find her,' Celeste said.

It was late in the afternoon when the three sisters all found themselves in the living room. Earlier, Evie had found Gertie in a corner of the walled garden cuddling one of her hens and crying into its feathers, and the sisters had a good heart to heart before working companionably together and then heading into the house.

'It's too hot to do any more work,' Evie complained, flopping on to a sofa, her blonde hair flattened against her head where she'd been wearing a sun hat. 'At least I've dealt with the order from Mrs Peters. Her husband's coming to collect it all tomorrow.'

'And I've attacked the greenfly problem. Poor *Madame Pierre Oger* was smothered!' Gertie said.

'And I've cleared yet more paperwork,' Celeste said. 'I can finally see some of the desk now.'

Her sisters smiled.

'Well, as soon as you're done, you can help us out in the garden,' Gertie said.

'Yes, there's that troublesome border with the bindweed you can help us with,' Evie said.

'Wow, thanks!' Celeste said and they all laughed.

Celeste's eyes roamed the room, resting on the auction catalogue which Julian had brought. She leaned forward and picked it up, acknowledging the fact that Julian had held it, too, not so long ago. Her mind spiralled over the time they'd spent together – brief snips of days snatched from busy working schedules. Would they have fared better if they'd spent more time together, Celeste wondered? But she'd been convinced she hadn't wanted that. Why, oh *why* had she been such a fool? Why hadn't she seen what a special man he was? And why hadn't she realised just how deep her feelings were for him until it was too late?

'You really should call him,' Gertie said.

Celeste put the catalogue down. 'No,' she said.

'I really miss him,' Evie said. 'I would have liked him as a brother-in-law.'

'Evie!' Celeste cried, rolling her eyes.

'What?' Evie said. 'I thought you said you wanted us all to be more open and honest with each other?'

'Yes, but not like that.'

Evie frowned and fiddled with her earring. 'Oh, no!' she said a moment later as she dived onto the floor. 'I've lost its back.' She looked around on the carpet, finally finding the gold fastening, and it was then that something caught her eye from under the sofa. It was a book, and she pulled out. 'Is it yours, Gertie?' she asked.

Gertie took the proffered book, a modern novel, and looked at it. 'No,' she said. 'I think it was Mum's.' She flipped through the pages. 'Hey! Look at this.'

Evie leaned forward on the sofa as Gertie pulled something out from between the pages.

'It's Mum!' Evie said, looking at the old photograph. 'When was it taken? I don't recognise it.'

Celeste joined her sisters on the sofa. They handed her the photograph and she looked down into the smiling face of her mother. She was wearing a pretty dress the colour of primroses and her long, dark hair was loose and glossy. It had been taken over fifteen years before and Celeste instantly recognised it.

'Mum looks pretty,' Evie said.

'Always,' Celeste said. 'That was one thing she could never do wrong, wasn't it? And it was the most important thing to her too.'

'I wonder where it was taken,' Gertie said.

'Don't you remember it?' Celeste said.

Evie and Gertie looked clueless.

'Tell us,' Gertie said.

'It was at Aunt Leda's party that summer we drove through to Oxfordshire. She had a little marquee up in the garden and that funny little band was playing jazz, and Mum was saying how awful it all was and how she would have done things properly but that Leda always had to have her own way – which was only fair, really, as it was *her* birthday. But you know what Mum was like – if she wasn't involved with something or hadn't even been consulted then it was always a complete disaster in her eyes.'

'But she seems to be having a good time,' Evie said.

'Oh, yes,' Celeste said. 'She met a man there. He was plying her with drinks and they were flirting like mad. He was the one who took the photo. That's why she's smiling: she's flirting.'

The sisters looked at the photograph again.

'You really don't remember?' Celeste asked.

'No,' Gertie said.

'Nope,' Evie said.

'Well, you should, because we were all standing right there with her.'

'No we're not,' Evie said.

'Well, not anymore, because she's cut us all out.' A strange look had entered Celeste's eyes and she stood up, the photograph still in her hand as she left the room.

'Celly?' Gertie called after her but she didn't respond.

৶৩

Two hours later, Gertie started to get worried.

'Celly?' she called, knocking on the study door. 'Please come out and talk to us.'

Evie appeared in the corridor. 'She's still in there?' she whispered.

Gertie nodded and knocked again. 'Just talk to us! We're really worried about you.'

Evie stepped forward. 'Let me give it a go,' she said to Gertie before hammering on the door like an angry woodpecker.

'Evie!' Gertie hissed.

'Celly?' Evie called. 'Are you in there?' She tried the handle but the door had obviously been locked. 'You need to talk to us. You've wheedled out all of *our* secrets. We need to listen to you now!'

'That's good,' Gertie said, nodding in approval.

'Yes, but she still isn't responding. You don't think she's done anything silly, do you?'

'Like what? What could she possibly do to herself in the study?' Gertie asked.

'Slash her wrists with an unpaid invoice?'

'That isn't funny, Evie. What are we going to *do?*'

'I think we should ring Julian,' Evie said. 'I think Celly was really beginning to open up to him about all this stuff with Mum. Maybe he'll be able to help her now.'

Gertie nodded. 'Good idea!'

They went through to the hall.

'You do it,' Evie said.

Gertie picked up the phone. 'Damn! What's his number?'

'I've got it,' Evie said, taking her mobile out. 'I made a point of getting it from him because I knew Celly wouldn't let me have it.'

Gertie dialled the number and waited.

'Julian? You're in Suffolk? Oh, good! I'm worried about Celeste. She's locked herself in the study and won't talk to us,' Gertie said. 'I'm not really sure what's happened. She's been in there for hours.' There was a pause. 'Okay. Bye.' She put the phone down. 'He's coming right over.'

33.

Julian was pale-faced and tight-lipped when he arrived at the manor. 'Is she still in there?'

'Yes,' Gertie said. 'She's never done anything like this before. I'm not really sure what happened. We found this old photo of Mum and Celeste just went all weird and then bolted.'

'I'll go and talk to her,' Julian said, leaving Gertie and Evie standing in the hallway as he sprinted down the corridor.

◦↺

'Celeste?' Julian's voice called through the closed door, breaking her out of her thoughts. 'It's me, Julian.'

She had been standing by the window, looking out into the garden, but now she turned back into the room and cursed her sisters, who must have called him.

'Are you in there?' Julian called. 'Can you open the door for me? I want to talk to you.'

'Go away, please,' she said, her voice croaky.

'I'm not going anywhere,' he said. 'I'm staying right here until you open this door.'

She didn't move.

'Celeste?' Julian called again. 'There are people on this side of the door who care about you.' There was a pause – a long pause – and Celeste wondered if he was going to either give up or try to break the door down, but he did neither. Instead, she heard him clear his throat. 'And there's one who might even be a little in love with you.'

Celeste blinked hard. Had she heard him right? Had he just said he was in love with her? She stared at the solid door that stood between them.

'So, are you going to let me in or am I going to talk to this door all evening?' Julian's voice said.

Celeste swallowed hard, quite sure that Julian was both willing and able to do just that, so she walked slowly across the room and unlocked the door.

'Hey,' he said as he saw her.

'Hello,' she said. 'Gertie rang you, didn't she?'

'Yes,' he said. 'She's really worried about you.' Celeste stood to one side and Julian entered the room. 'Do you want to tell me what this is all about?' he asked, closing the door behind him but not locking it. 'Celeste?'

She took a deep breath. 'I found a photograph,' she said.

'Gertie mentioned that. Do you want to show me?' he asked.

She walked across to the desk, picked up the photograph and handed it to him.

'Is this your mother?' he asked and Celeste nodded.

'Go on – say it,' she said. 'Everybody else does.'

'Say what?' Julian asked.

'That she's beautiful.'

Julian's eyes widened. 'Well, I suppose she is,' he said, squinting at the picture. 'It isn't the first word I'd use to describe her, though.'

'No? What word would you use?' Celeste asked.

'Proud,' Julian said. 'Proud and vain. Look at the way she's holding her head.'

'She's trying to appear taller than she is,' Celeste said. 'She often did that in photos. Gertie and I were taller than her, you see. We took after Dad and Mum hated that. She was always complaining that we were taller than her.'

Julian gave a wry grin. 'That seems like a strange thing to worry about.'

Celeste nodded in agreement. 'It was always about looks. She was forever fiddling with her hair or adjusting her clothes or looking into reflective surfaces. She could never truly live in the moment because she was always worried about other people's perceptions of her.'

'So why has this photo caused you to lock yourself in here?'

Celeste didn't know what to say. How could she explain just how the picture had made her feel?

'It's only half the photograph,' she said at last, deciding to start from the beginning. 'See where she's cut it?'

Julian looked again. 'Ah, yes,' he said.

'Gertie, Evie and I were standing next to her.'

Julian looked up at Celeste. 'She cut you all out?'

Celeste nodded.

'Why did she do that?'

She shrugged. 'I can only attempt to understand,' she said, 'but I remember that day. Gertie and Evie don't, and perhaps it's just as well. Mum had been drinking a lot of champagne and had been flirting with this man. He's the one who took the photo.'

'Wasn't your dad there?'

'Oh, yes, but he was . . . I'm not really sure where he was. Trying to find a quiet corner of the garden away from Mum, I suppose. Anyway, this guy kept telling Mum how beautiful she was and how it was impossible that she had three children, and Mum was just lapping it all up, saying how she'd sacrificed so much to have us and that she sometimes wondered if it was all worth it.'

'Oh, Celeste,' Julian said. 'That's awful.'

She nodded. 'But you know what bothers me most? What did she do with us when she cut us out of the picture? Did she cut us up into tiny little pieces or did she burn us? Maybe she shredded us!'

'Celeste –' Julian reached out and held her shoulders in his hands.

'We didn't really matter to her, did we?' she cried. 'Why couldn't she love us? *Why?*'

'Because that wasn't possible for her,' Julian said. 'You know that, don't you? You do understand that now? It wasn't your fault. It wasn't anything that you or Gertie or Evie did or said. You couldn't have changed her.'

'I know,' Celeste whispered. 'I know these things now but it doesn't make the pain go away.'

Julian shook his head. 'That will take time and there will be days like this when it all comes tumbling back into your head – just when you think you've got a handle on things. But I know you can get through this and I want to help you. I want you to know I'm here for you.'

She looked up at him. 'Even though I pushed you away?'

'Celeste – you could push me into the moat and I'd still come back to you.'

She gave a little laugh and a big sniff. 'I'm so sorry, Julian.'

'It's okay. Just promise to talk to me next time. I want to know what's going on in here,' he said, tapping her forehead gently. 'You've got to open up about these things. You've got to let them out.'

Suddenly, a strange light came into his eyes and he turned to look at the desk and the chair on the other side of it.

'What do you want to say to her?' he asked.

Celeste frowned. 'What do you mean?'

'If she was here now – what would you say to her?'

'I wouldn't say anything,' Celeste said, looking puzzled.

Julian moved round to the other side of the great Victorian desk and pulled Penelope's chair out from behind it.

'What are you doing?' Celeste asked, instantly on her guard.

'Talk to her,' he said. 'She's sitting here *right now*, ready to listen to you.'

'No, Julian – don't!' Celeste said. 'I can't!'

'Yes you can! *Talk* to her! Tell her how you feel!'

Celeste's heart was racing as she looked into Julian's face. He was completely and utterly serious about this.

'Go *on*, Celly! Tell her how you feel!'

Celeste's breathing was wild and ragged and her mouth had gone quite dry but something was stirring deep inside her.

'I want to know,' she began slowly, 'I *really* want to know why you had us when you didn't want to get to know us – when you didn't *love* us? Why, Mum? *Why?* And how could you say all those things to us? Couldn't you see the damage you were doing? Couldn't you see how much pain you were causing? Or did that not matter to you? Didn't you care about anyone other than yourself? Was that it?' she cried. 'God! I wish I could understand this and I'm trying – I'm *really* trying – but I just feel so helpless. I'm mad too. I'm *so* mad with you for still making me feel like this even when you're dead!'

Suddenly, the energy that had been driving her seemed to ebb away and she broke down, the tears flowing from her eyes in uncontrolled torrents.

'It's okay,' Julian said, moving towards her so he could hold her in his arms and stroke her dark hair. 'It's okay. You've been locking all this pain away for so many years.'

'I'm sorry,' she said between sobs. 'I didn't mean to –'

'To what?' he said. 'Don't apologise, for heaven's sake! You needed to release all that, and I know how awful you must be feeling right now but it'll have done you the world of good. I'm sure of it.'

'But I should have been able to cope better with all this,' she said, drying her eyes on the sleeve of her blouse.

'But that's what you *have* been doing. Don't you see? You've been trying to cope on your own for so long and that's not good for anybody. You've got to share all this stuff otherwise you'll go out of your mind.'

'I know,' she said, her head resting on his shoulder, 'and I will. I promise.'

'Good,' he said, his hand firm yet gentle as it continued to stroke her hair.

They stood like that in the middle of the study for some time before Celeste spoke again.

'Everything's changing so fast,' she said. You know Evie's going to have a baby?'

'Is she?'

'And Lukas – that's the father – is moving in to be with her. We've got Esther living here now and then there'll be your antiques business too.'

'You mean you're still up for that?' Julian asked, leaning back so that he could look at her face.

She nodded. 'Of course,' she said, and Julian grinned. 'But it's going to be chaos here with all these people coming and going and a baby too and –'

'But that's good, isn't it?' Julian interrupted. 'That's just what this old house needs – a bit of chaos and noise. It's *life!*'

'It makes me anxious,' Celeste said.

'But it shouldn't,' Julian told her. 'It just means there'll be more people around to help you with everything.' He grinned. 'I'm so glad you're not going to sell this place. I know it holds a lot of bad memories for you but I also know that it holds a lot of good ones too. I've seen the look on your face when you remember them. You love this place.'

'I know,' she said. 'You've helped me to realise that.'

'And you can make it work too. I know you can.'

Celeste gave a wry smile. 'Why can't I see things like you do? You always see the positive and I always focus on the problems!'

'I'll teach you,' he said, 'and I think we should start with this room.'

'What do you mean?'

'I mean, just look at it! It's so dark and gloomy in here,' he said, leaving her side as he paced around the study. 'Don't you think so?'

'I – er –'

'It needs some changes,' he said, running his fingers along the dusty old bookshelves. 'Some drastic changes. Starting with these curtains, right?'

'Well, I –'

Before she could finish her sentence properly, Julian had ripped the ancient curtains down, pulling on the great weight of them until they landed in a heavy, dusty heap on the floor of the study, with the curtain pole and a good deal of plaster clattering down in its wake.

Celeste looked at him in bewildered astonishment.

'Ooops,' he said, a shy smile brightening his face.

'*Julian!*' Celeste cried, her hands flying to her mouth.

He crossed the room towards her. 'Listen to me,' he said, suddenly serious. 'You're not doing yourself any favours locking yourself away in this room. It's oppressing you. You're not allowing yourself to be *you* in here. You'll always be a daughter in this room and that's not good enough. You've got to be your own person, Celeste. You're worth that. You've got to let yourself *live.*'

She stood staring at him, her eyes wide and frightened. 'But I –'

'Get rid of the curtains. Get rid of all these dusty old books –'

'But the books are important for business.'

'But you don't *need* them in here, do you?' Julian said. 'I'm not suggesting that you get rid of them – just put them somewhere else where they're not reminding you of the past all the time. Don't you want to do that? Don't you want to make this room *yours*?'

She stared at him for what seemed like an eternity and then she nodded as a huge bubble of excitement built up inside her.

'Listen,' he said, 'I got you a little something. Wait *right* there!' He left the room and she heard him running down the corridor into the hallway. 'Yes,' she heard him say. 'She's okay. No – not yet. Give me a moment with her, okay?' She imagined Gertie and Evie waiting in the hallway to make sure that she was all right and, as much as she wanted to see them and to apologise to them, hug them and tell them that she loved them and that everything was going to be all right because they weren't going to sell the manor, she stood fixed to the spot because Julian had told her to stay right where she was.

When he returned, he was holding something large wrapped in brown paper.

'I wanted to get you this,' he said. 'Now, don't go getting excited because it's not the original – as much as I'd have loved buying that for you. But I think it's a pretty good copy,' he said as he handed it to her.

Celeste unwrapped the brown paper, which had been tied with a great big bow the colour of a summer sky.

'Julian!' she said a moment later as she gazed at the painting. 'The Fantin-Latour.'

'It's just a reproduction,' he said, 'but it's by a great artist friend and –'

'It's *wonderful!*' Celeste said. 'I love it!'

'You do?'

'What a lovely gift,' she said, tears of joy sparkling in her eyes. They gazed at one another and Celeste swore that she could see tears swimming in Julian's eyes too, making them even brighter than usual, and she could wait no longer.

It was hard to tell who was the more surprised by the kiss – Celeste for giving it or Julian for receiving it – but it was a moment that changed everything, sealed everything, made everything perfect, and Celeste had never felt happier in her life.

When they stepped apart, the painting still held between them, they laughed.

'I really wasn't expecting that,' Julian said.

'You should have been,' Celeste said, 'and I should have done it a long time ago.'

The smile that graced his face – the one that she had thought she'd never see again – made her heart soar with joy and love.

'Come on,' Julian said. 'Let's share all this with those sisters of yours.'

They left the study hand in hand and walked into the hallway, where Celeste's eyes caught sight of the barometer. As always, it was reading 'Change' and she couldn't help smiling because, for once, it was right.

ONE YEAR LATER

Celeste opened a window in the study. The room had been stripped of its old furnishings and was now a bright and beautiful work-space. The Victorian partners' desk had been moved into another room because Celeste hadn't been able to part with it, no matter how it made her feel. In its place stood a modest table which Celeste had made her own by placing photographs and vases of flowers around it.

Julian had been right to push her to make the changes in the room. It had been a painful process but a necessary one.

There had been so many changes at Little Eleigh Manor, Celeste thought. Lukas had moved in and he and Evie were now officially engaged.

'I don't *need* to get married,' Evie kept protesting.

'We know!' her sisters kept telling her.

'But I think it's nice for Alba, don't you?' Evie said.

Celeste smiled now as she thought about her beautiful niece, Alba Rose. Lukas had been with Evie during the entire length of the nine-hour labour and she had a feeling that he was very much a part of their family now.

It was wonderful having a baby at the manor. Celeste had been absolutely terrified of the thought of her youngest sister being pregnant but Evie, who was now a redhead, was a brilliant mother.

Things seemed to be moving forward for Gertie too. After James and his wife had left for France, Gertie had given all of her poetry books to a charity shop and had taken up kickboxing instead, enrolling in an evening class where she had met a man called Aled who was very cute and who, crucially, wasn't married. Since then, the two had gone travelling around Italy, Switzerland and Spain, carefully avoiding France, which no longer held an appeal for Gertie.

Meanwhile, Mr Ludkin had finished his work in the north wing and Julian had been converting it into his antiques centre, much to the fascination of Esther Martin, who had actually offered to help out once it was up and running.

'Do you know how many years I've spent sitting in a chair by myself? Let me be *useful*, for pity's sake!' she told Julian and Celeste when they asked if it would be too much for her.

The reproduction Fantin-Latour – or the *Phantom*-Latour as it was affectionately known, because it was but a ghost of the real thing, had been hanging with pride in Celeste's study. And it really was *her* study too these days, with its freshly painted walls the colour of a *New Dawn* rose, its light, bright furniture and the beautifully delicate curtains which swayed in the gentlest of breezes, making the room a heavenly place to work in.

Celeste smiled. And what about her, she thought? Well, she'd been spending more time with Julian – a *lot* more time. They'd walked and talked and laughed and kissed, and she felt happier than she'd ever felt in her life.

Leaning out of the window now, her bare arms on the sun-warmed stone windowsill, Celeste looked out across the moat to the garden and sighed with deep satisfaction as the scent of roses drifted towards her. Julian was out walking Frinton down by the river and Gertie, Esther, Evie and Lukas were in the walled garden with baby Alba. Celeste had promised to join them as soon as her desk was clear.

'Which it is,' she said to herself as she turned back into the room. There had been a time when she would have spent an extra hour in the study, tidying, planning and organising, but not anymore: she was finally learning how to let go, enjoy herself and relax, and there was no better way of doing that than by joining her sisters and the rest of her family in the rose garden.

ACKNOWLEDGEMENTS

To Emilie, Sophie and Jennifer at Amazon Publishing for believing in this story and for helping me make it the very best it could be. To fellow rosarians Richard Stubbs, Jo Skehan and Nattaporn Vichitrananda. To Adele Geras for her wonderful novel, *Watching the Roses*. To Alison for her story *Teddy Bananas*, which inspired my 'ceiling on the floor' scene. To Judy for listening to my ideas for this book over the last two years. And to Roy, who taxied me around a fair few rose gardens and who has dug endless holes in our own garden in which to plant my own ever-expanding rose collection!

ABOUT THE AUTHOR

Victoria Connelly studied English literature at Worcester University, got married in a medieval castle in North Yorkshire, and now lives in rural Suffolk with her artist husband and family of rescued animals.

She has had ten romantic comedies published around the world as well as books across many genres including novels, novellas, short story collections, children's adventures and autobiography. Her first published novel, *Flights of Angels*, was made into a movie in 2008 by Ziegler Films in Germany. *The Runaway Actress* was shortlisted for the RNA's Romantic Comedy award.

Ms Connelly loves books, films, gardening, walking, historic buildings, and animals – especially ex-battery hens. She is also passionate about roses, and her home is surrounded by more than 30 different varieties of rose bush.

Her website is www.victoriaconnelly.com, and readers can follow her on Twitter @VictoriaDarcy.